My
Cleveland
Story

Rick —

You have a great sister-in-law. . .

She has been of great help in this project

Best Wishes

[signature]

My
Cleveland
Story

by Greg Cielec

Pink Flamingo Press
Cleveland, Ohio
1998

My Cleveland Story

First Edition
Copyrighted 1998 by Greg Cielec
Copyrighted 1998 by Pink Flamingo Press

Library of Congress Catalog Number 98-96292

ISBN 0-9665724-0-8

Cover artwork and design by Chris K.

Interior design by Greg Cielec and Dave Hostetler

Printed in the United States of America
Pink Flamingo Press
Post Office Box 93912
Cleveland, Ohio 44101-5912
pinkflamingopres@hotmail.com

For my family and friends

Introduction

But love is many things, none of them logical.
    from The Princess Bride *by William Goldman*

You can take your wars and your starvation and your
fires and your floods, but there's no heartbreak in life
like losing the big game in high school.
    from Semi Tough *by Dan Jenkins*

Although my book is intended mainly for the enter-
tainment of boys and girls, I hope it will not be
shunned by men and women on that account, for part
of the plan has been to try pleasantly to remind adults
of what they once were themselves, and how they felt
and thought and talked, and what queer enterprises
they sometimes engaged in.
    from the preface of The Adventures
    of Tom Sawyer *by Mark Twain*

The best part of having friends is you are allowed to
be fools with them.
    Ralph Waldo Emerson

I first got into writing some time in the late Eighties. I sent a
couple of letters to the Plain Dealer that turned into essays published
on the Opinion Page. I then sent a couple of record reviews to some
regional magazines and that really took off. I started to get disks and

tapes in the mail to review, and it has turned into a fun and slightly profitable hobby.

After school during the spring, and often during the summer, you can find me on the front porch with my note pad in hand working on a project, good tunes playing in the background, maybe a cold one nearby. Often Uncle Gus or Mrs. Mate strolls across the street and sits and talks for awhile.

One day last summer Mrs. Mate walked across the street and came and sat quietly on the glider. I finished the paragraph that I was writing, and looked up and greeted her with a smile. She smiled back at me, and I noticed she had a slightly more serious demeanor than usual.

"You enjoy your writing, don't you," she said with those eyes that still sparkle now deep into her late seventies.

"Yeah, I guess I do," I responded.

"I want you to write something for me," she said.

"Anything, Helen. You know I'd do anything for you," expecting a letter to a faraway relative or something for church.

She got up and did something I never saw her do before. She grabbed the front rail of the porch with both hands and looked down both ends of the street. She turned and looked into every nook and cranny of the porch and then turned and looked at me. "I want you to write about what happened. I want you to write about everything."

We looked at each other through several moments of silence, both knowing what she was talking about. "I want my grandchildren to know about what happened. Someday you'll want your children and your grandchildren to know. I want them to know about everything. Everybody will never forget the bad stuff, but I want them to know about everything else. There were so many good things that happened. I want them to know about all the good stuff."

I saw a tear starting to crawl down her cheek, and I got up and we hugged and I held her tight. "Barb's kids were so little when my husband died. He was such a good man, and all they got to remember him are some old pictures and a few stories that get told over and over again. I want them to know what he was like. And what happened to you guys, I would just hate..." as her voice trailed off and I kept hugging her.

2

Part One
Sometime in the Early Seventies
The High School Years

I can't help remembering all of the times
when love was new, and love was you
When we were dancing in the dark, a couple of fools
Holding you close, breaking all the rules
Doesn't everything get colored
by those first love blues?
*   from "Dancing in the Dark"*
*   by the Michael Stanley Band*

They say just once in life
You find someone that's right
*   from "If He's Ever Near" by Karla Bonoff*

Back when we were in high school we had the greatest job, working CYO. We hung out at school on Saturdays and Sundays, and helped our coaches run the basketball league for the seventh and eighth graders from all the local parishes. It was a great job because once you learned the ropes and gained a little seniority, all you really did was sit around and eat junk food and flirt with all the little girls who were cheerleaders for all the teams.

If there was a varsity game on a Friday or Saturday night, we would often stay to work the concession stand. That wasn't bad either because we would get into the game for free and make a few extra bucks.

We were working the concession stand on a Saturday night during our sophomore year. We were playing them in basketball. We had always considered them our archrivals, but until then it really wasn't much of a rivalry because they usually beat us, especially in football and basketball. They were always bigger and stronger and gave off the impression that they were just playing with us.

I was trying not to burn some pizza that we used to make in this little Dutch oven we had when one of their cheerleaders asked me for a popcorn and coke. Busy as I was I leaned over and asked Mate to get it for her. Without looking at her, he filled up a coke and reached into the popcorn machine for a full bag of corn. He and I both turned at the same time and I saw the expression on his face when he first saw her.

It was like the scene in *The Godfather* when Michael meets the village girl in Italy, like a thunderbolt. For the first time in my life I saw him speechless. He momentarily wavered, then regained his composure, reached out and handed her the popcorn and coke. He paused for a loooong moment, looking right into her eyes.

"Here, it's on me."

Awkward silence and stares.

"On you?...Why?"

"Because every basketball game me and my buddy Greg give the best looking girl in the whole place a free popcorn and coke," he said very straight faced and sincere.

Another long pause. They stared each other down and then both burst into loud and sincere laughter.

"Thanks," she said with one final lingering stare, and turned back toward one of her girlfriends to tell her what happened. For a quick moment, I thought I caught the same look that was in Mate's eyes in hers.

While we cleaned up and closed the refreshment stand after half time of the varsity game, I kept noticing Mate trying to peer through the lobby and into the gym, trying to get a peek at her. He didn't have much luck, but he was so eager to get in the gym that he did more than his share of the work. The quicker

4

we got everything done, the quicker we got into the gym.

When we finally made our way into the bleachers, he couldn't keep his eyes off her. For a moment, I even thought I caught her staring back but I quickly thought not. Being an interested third party, I remember I made several mental notes about the situation:

1) She was cute in her own way. Dark blonde hair turning to brown, nice breasts (two, the perfect amount), slightly big in the behind. Very healthy looking. Big, brown eyes. 2) I could tell by the number on her sweater that she was a junior, an older woman, and I knew that eliminated Mate from any serious romantic involvement. Being the good friend that I was, I immediately told Mate she probably had some hot and heavy romance with Kowalchy or Haggerty or one of the other studs on their football team, or some big and burly college guy that could rip any high school sophomore's arm out of its socket. 3) Since she was a cheerleader for them, that meant that she probably went to one of those girl schools on the far west side, and that meant she lived miles away. 4) Although Mate was obviously fascinated with her, he was, at the time, too much of a chickenshit to ask a girl out anyway. It was quite obvious to me that nothing would ever come of it.

Our major time-consuming activity through the rest of that winter and into spring and summer was preparing for the upcoming football season. Playing football at a school like ours (and there was only maybe a dozen like us in the state) took much time and effort. The all boys Catholic high schools played great football, but to make the team, to make the team and really play, took an awful amount of hard work and perseverance. At schools like Benedictine, Ignatius, Moehler, Elder, Joe's, Latin, and ours, you worked year round if you wanted to see the field in the fall.

Although each school had its share of studs, each also had many average kids with limited size and/or ability who worked hard to earn a spot on the team. This hard work came in the weight room, where you made yourself bigger and stronger (this was the old-fashioned way before steroids invaded high schools). If you didn't feel like spending the winter making yourself bigger and stronger, there was someone else to play your position who did. You could be damn sure the coaches knew who was working and who wasn't.

Nothing beat Ohio High School football. The names of those teams, the Catholic schools as well as the traditional powers, were the poetry of my youth. The Cathedral Latin Lions. The Saint Joseph Vikings. The Lincoln High Presidents playing the John Marshall Lawyers. The West Tech Warriors. The East Technical High School Scarabs. The Massillon Tigers verses the Canton McKinley Bulldogs. The Parma Redmen against the Valley Forge Patriots. The Great Holy Wars in the old Crown Conference. I could go on and on. Before I ever played it, I loved high school football. Even today, well into what you call middle age, I still can't live without it.

Sometime that summer, we were at the old Cleveland Agora, over by Cleveland State, for college I.D. night. Of course, none of us were in college or old enough to get legally into the Agora. And, of course, that was no problem because we all had fake college I.D.s and borrowed driver's licenses.

In this current era of political correctness and the twenty-one drinking age for everyone, it is hard to imagine what those Thursday nights at the old Agora were like. It was sixteen hundred kids dancing to real rock and roll while drinking as many twenty cent beers as humanly possible. The place just jumped, and from the time I was a junior in high school to a senior in college, if I was in town, we never missed a college I.D. night at the Agora (we also did not miss a drink and drown night at the Mad Hatter, but that's a whole other story).

It was at one of those Agora college nights that we saw her, the cheerleader from the basketball game that Mate gave the popcorn to. After we had spent the night power drinking 3.2 beer and ogling the real college girls out on the dance floor, we saw her as we were leaving. We followed her and her girl-friends to their car, keeping a big enough space behind them so they didn't see us. The whole time I was quite supportive of my buddy and was saying things like, "You big pussy. Chickenshit

6

mother fucker. When are you going to talk to her?" But every time it seemed he was going to run ahead and say something to them, he couldn't. I had never seen him act that way before. The girl had him confused and scared, and helplessly and distantly in love.

Finally she climbed into a red Camaro with her girlfriends and they hopped on the inner belt heading toward the west suburbs.

We ran to our car and followed them onto the highway. I just assumed when the freeway split that we would get on the Denison Avenue exit and head back to Mate's house. I was surprised when we followed the red Camaro onto I-90, heading out to the western suburbs.

"Holy shit, where the hell are you going?" I said as Mate floored the woody to get all that it had, just to get it up to speed onto the next freeway.

"We're following them!!!" He said with a smile, and that made it sound like a good idea as we jockeyed in and out of cars and trucks trying to get caught up with the red Camaro.

They got off at one of the Rocky River exits and we ended up in a residential neighborhood somewhere in Fairview Park or Rocky River.

The red Camaro pulled into a driveway, and we could see her getting out of the car. She spoke to the girls still inside the car, waved good-bye, and walked into the back yard where we assumed she went into the house. I was ready to go home; Mate had other plans.

"Let's check it out," he said as he parked and got out of the car.

"What are you, fuckin' nuts?" I replied.

"Follow me."

Mate and I walked around the block and trudged through back yards, peeking into windows looking for who knows what. We left our other buddies, Pete and Mike, passed out in the back seat of the car.

Finally we were in what we assumed was her back yard. It was a traditional two-story suburban spread, with a five foot above ground circular swimming pool in the middle of a cramped back yard.

We saw a light go on and off in one of the upstairs bedrooms and we assumed it was hers.

"What light in yonder window breaks?" Mate said aloud.

"Shut the fuck up before someone hears us," I responded.

Mate didn't know his next move. He was so close yet far, far away.

"I know," he said, "Let's go for a swim." Before I could do anything, he whipped off his shirt, stepped out of his cut offs and high tops, and slid quietly over the side of the pool. What the hell, I said to myself, and did the same thing.

We made sure we weren't making too much noise as we huddled in the water, contemplating our next move. We were like a couple of Marines in an old WWII flick, hiding in a river from the Japs. Again I gave him some verbal support. "What are you going to do now you chicken shit fuckhead?" I whispered.

Then he had his next great idea. "I know, I'll wake her up. Figure we got this far, might as well finish the job."

He slid back over the side of the pool, and walked over and started to shimmy his way up the vine covered trellis at the corner of the house. His goal was the little ledge along the second floor windows. It wasn't until he was halfway up the wall before he realized that he forgot to put his clothes on.

Are we in trouble now, I said to myself. Here I was naked in the backyard pool of people I didn't even know, at three in the morning, and I had to get up in three hours for work. My buddy was scaling someone's house, whose house we weren't even sure. To top it off he was naked, had about twenty beers in him, and unsure of what he was going to do when he finally got up on the ledge.

Mate finally found himself outside the window we assumed was hers. He started lightly tapping the window, but did not get a response. He started banging the window louder, loud enough that I got scared that he was going to wake the whole neighborhood.

Finally, after what seemed like forever, he gave up. He turned away from the window and looked down at me in the pool and said in a loud whisper, "She must be sound asleep.

8

Let's get..."

At that moment, when he turned and faced me, I saw an image of a woman in the window behind him. Suddenly, a light went on and the window quickly opened. The timing could not be any more perfect, for what the woman saw in the window was not Mate's smiling face but his fat hairy ass. And boy did she scream!!!

As soon as the scream started, I was over the side of the pool, gathered my clothes and shoes, and bolted back through the back yards toward where our car was parked.

Mate heard the scream behind him and immediately jumped off the ledge, doing a belly flop in to the pool below him. He too then jumped over the side of the pool, gathered his clothes and sneakers, and followed me racing through the backyards.

Suddenly the neighborhood was coming to life, and a variety of noises and lights filled the air. The sounds of us panting and ouching in pain as our bare feet stepped on gravel and rocks and tomato plants, and our bare thighs and pride and joys encountering more than one rose bush. The once silent and dark backyards were now lit by back porch lights being turned on and dogs barking frantically.

As we cut, slashed, and dodged our way back to our car we were scared shitless, but filled with a great adrenaline rush.

When we finally found ourselves back on the street, Pete and Mike were waiting for us in the woody. But as luck would have it, they were a hundred yards up the street facing in the other direction.

They had fallen asleep in the car while we had investigated the backyards but were awakened by the sounds of dogs barking. When we emerged on the street, Pete immediately put the car in reverse and barreled backwards toward us as we ran toward them. The car made a loud screech as he hit the brakes, and we dove through the open windows into the back seat. We made a beeline to get out of the neighborhood and we never looked back until we were safely on I-90 heading home.

Fall came and we won our first few games, and things started just the way we had planned. Mate and I were the only juniors starting on an all-senior offense and we both were playing well.

Starting before your senior year might be a common thing on many high school football teams, but when your high school had a thousand boys in it, and over two hundred in the football program, most times you were a company man, paying your dues by working hard and earning your job your senior year. It didn't always work out that way, like if you just didn't have "it," but most times it did.

Mate and I were both lucky enough to fall in the cracks. Neither one of us was exceptionally talented (exceptionally? Man, we weren't slightly talented). We were hard nosed and naive enough to think we could go toe to toe with anyone.

We weren't exceptionally big either. Mate had just quit growing, that's all. When we came in as freshmen, he was one of the biggest guys on the frosh team but he never got any taller. By the time we were on the varsity, he ended up being the smallest lineman who started. He was quick enough and strong enough to go against almost anyone, even with his lack of real size.

We all knew that our season would come down to one game, us versus them. Even though we had ten games on the schedule, one meant more than others. Although we didn't play them until the sixth game and we started out on a roll, it was as if we were going through the motions waiting for the big one.

We had, on paper, the best team the school had ever had. The varsity had gone 7-3 the year before and on the junior varsity we had gone 8-2. Of course, both teams had lost to them. We had Eldridge coming back as quarterback, and Becka and Wilson at the running backs. Wozniak, who later would play at Michigan State, at linebacker. We had a bunch of tough little kids rotating in at the corners. Our one true stud was our free safety, Thunder Bailes. Best pure hitter I, to this date, have ever seen in high school. Six feet two, one hundred ninety pounds. Quick, strong, aggressive. He would go on to be All Big Ten, and then float around the USFL for a couple of years.

The heart and soul of the team was the offensive line. Even though I was the tight end, I always considered myself part of the line. You have to remember this was before Ozzie Newsome and Kellen Winslow changed how tight ends played. It was still during the time when midwest football on the high school and college levels was still dictated by a screaming maniac in Columbus and his three yards and a cloud of dust offense. Man, we had a tough line. Mate was center. He just came in and took the job from two seniors by kicking ass. He came into doubles that year with one thing on his mind, not to sit on the bench. He hustled and played so well in practice and scrimmages that they had to give him the job. He beat out one senior who thought he was going to be given the job, so he worked after school in the spring and blew off weight training. He never caught up to Mate when summer practices rolled around.

The rest of the line was all seniors. Mike Schley at one guard, a tough Irish Mick. Took no shit from anyone, and when he trapped, there was no one better. The other guard was Vasilick, the meanest guy on the team. In the Latin game the year before, the guy over him kept on sticking his fingers in Vas's nose and eyes. First chance he got, Vas bit him. Everyone in the whole stadium heard the kid scream. Vas came to the side lines with blood dripping down his chin out of his mouth, and a shit eating grin on his face. The tackles were a couple of big Polish kids, Jablonski and Krasowski. They were big and slow, yet smart and aggressive. I don't think either one of them got outplayed the whole season.

Not many of the Catholic schools in Ohio have their own stadiums so most of them play on Saturday night. We never minded that because there were fewer games to compete with, and we always got big crowds and received much attention. They were the only Catholic team in Cleveland that had their own stadium and played every Friday night, so we got to see them play almost every week. We would go see them on Friday, and then play on Saturday. I remember seeing them against Latin two weeks before we played them, and they were awesome. They had only lost three games over the last five years, and were calling that year's team the best ever. They had at least a dozen guys who would go Division I and with another hundred guys on the sidelines they looked unstoppable.

They had those Green Bay Packer green uniforms with their names on the back, ran that flashy double slot bullshit, and the game was over by half-time. Their two inside linebackers would both go big time, and one would later play eight years in the NFL. One end would play for Ohio State, the other for Michigan. Their quarterback would end up pitching in the Indians organization, spending five years in AAA. Both their tackles would play at Miami, O., and their guards, center, plus a couple of kids on the bench would all play Division II or III.

Mate was the one who always wanted to go see them play. He would round six or seven guys up, throw them in his parents' old station wagon, and drive us out to the far west side to see them play. His first objective was always to watch them and pick up something, anything that would help us beat them. Secondary to that, I always noticed that he spent much time peering through an old pair of Boy Scout field glasses at a certain brown haired cheerleader.

We screwed up the week before the big game. We beat Tech. We beat Parma. We beat South. We beat Latin. But we lost to St. Joe's. We should have won, but we didn't. We dicked around and dicked around, blowing one touchdown chance after another. I dropped two passes that I shouldn't have, costing us at least one score. It was a night of bad snaps, blocked punts, and stupid penalties like having twelve guys on the field. I still thought throughout the whole game we were going to win, and we had a chance right up to the last play. It was fourth and goal on the one yard line with time running out. We ran a 627 (over tackle lead out of the power I). I remember doubling down on the tackle and just burying him, and waiting for the cheer of the crowd to tell me we scored. The cheer never came and we lost 12-7.

The coaches were afraid that the loss would hurt our self-confidence going into the big game against them. We had lost to a team with a little better talent than us, a common situation where we would still usually come out on top, and had to play a team that had a lot better talent. We had to play in overdrive and catch a few breaks if we wanted to come away with a "W."

The coaches came into practice on Monday not talking

about the loss, directing all of our energies toward the game on Friday. The acknowledgment to the Joe's game was watching the film, and we only watched the first half instead of the whole game, an unprecedented event. That was great because all of our coaches had read *Instant Replay* too many times, and subscribed to the Vince Lombardi school of film watching. Lights out, everyone quiet except for the coaches who were only screaming "for your own good," and each mistake shown over and over so it was re-enforced into you so many times that you would never make any mistake again.

It had been twelve years of playing them, and it had been twelve years of getting our asses kicked. 51-0. 37-3. 26-0. 49-9. The year before they crushed us at our Homecoming Game, 37-6, breaking our backs and our spirits with three first quarter touchdowns. It was one of those games that seemed to be over before it got started. They kept it on us until the end, keeping their starters in until there were three minutes left in the game. They humiliated us, and there was no apparent reason why they wouldn't do it again.

Our whole school, as well as a nearby all girls school, revolved around our football team in the fall. Everyone from the frosh to the seniors, from the city kids to the ones from the suburbs, from the druggies to the jocks, was into it. Although everyone was behind us and gave us great support, even the staunchest supporters deep down in their hearts didn't give us much of a chance of beating them. They had gone through too many years of getting their hopes up and having them crush 'em. Not only crushing us, but rubbing it in by running up the score and keeping their studs in to pad their stats.

Our school had much success in every other sport but in places like Cleveland, as well as the rest of Ohio, Pennsylvania, and Texas, your athletic program, as well as the quality of your whole school, is judged by what you do on the football field. It doesn't matter how many cross country or swimming champions or National Merit Scholars you had, it was what you did on Friday and Saturday nights in the fall that matters. Dan Jenkins in his great novel *Semi-Tough* tells an old Texas saying, 'there is nothing worse in life than losing the big one in high school football,' and we had lost the big one to them too many times. Years before I had ever gotten to Franciscan, someone hung a poster in our locker room, handwritten on cheap poster board in black magic marker, that said WE WILL ALWAYS BE MICKEY MOUSE UNTIL WE BEAT THEM IN FOOTBALL. Every year the score was scribbled across the bottom. My locker was right underneath it, and every day I had to look up at it. Mate and I decided that before we graduated, we were going to bring that sign down.

The game was the only thing that was on our minds. I remember I couldn't sleep the night before. All that I had ever worked for up to that point in my life was going to happen. I was going to play against them in a varsity football game, at their place on a Friday night, in front of a packed house. How often do dreams come true?

When you become older and you have experienced a few of life's disappointments, and you become weighed down with your job and your responsibilities, you just don't have any big games anymore, unless you coach. The Browns will have a big game, your son or nephew might have a big game, but all you ever become is a spectator. You have bigger and more important things, but you just don't have us versus them, and nothing else matters. It was a moment when your dreams become reality, something that doesn't happen when the dreams of childhood turn into the realities of adulthood.

As I get older, there are less and less things I remember about high school and playing high school sports. Bars and saloons everywhere are filled with sad people whose lives peaked and then went downhill at the age of eighteen. They can retell games play by play, can tell you who took whom to this dance and that party. I don't remember much, just too much has happened since then. I set the school record my senior year for catches in a game against Benedictine; my name is still on the boards, and I don't remember any of it. I have had people describe to me what happened, but it is just too far buried somewhere in the stack of floppy disks inside my head.

What I do remember about high school and high school football...what are the only events from that time in my life that

I really do remember as if I was there...was the weekend we played them in football my junior year.

I walked into study hall late that morning because I had stopped to talk with one of the coaches in the hall. When I entered the room, I received a standing ovation from the guys. Nobody could get settled down. Study hall was in the cafeteria, a large hall beneath the gym (and just as large), with long rows of tables with one or two students at each one. Just as it seemed everyone was going to finally settle down to do some work, the soft, rhythmic pounding started to build as seventy guys started chanting, kick ass, boom-boom, kick ass, boom-boom, kick ass, boom-boom, until it got louder and louder, so loud the kids on the third floor in chem. lab would say it caused their beakers and test tubes to rattle. KICK ASS, BOOM-BOOM, KICK ASS, BOOM-BOOM.

I just sat there, taking it all in. I remember doing the same thing when I was a freshman, and now it was my turn and I was ready.

Our rallies were unbelievable. We have good spirit at the school I teach at now. Most of the kids, most of the teachers, and most of the parents support the athletic programs, and a couple of times a year, at the start of each season and before big games, we have a rally. The cheerleaders put on a good show, the captains get up to talk, and the students respond with a good deal of enthusiasm. But I'm never there, unless I'm scheduled to talk, because I always volunteer for parking lot duty, watching for the kids sneaking out for a smoke instead of going to the rally. Frank Willis, a guy who went to Latin in the Sixties when they had Clint Jones and the boys, and I sit outside, just knowing what is going on inside the gym just doesn't even come close to the standards that we grew up with. Our adolescent visions of rallies from years ago floating through our minds can only be understood by someone who had gone through similar experiences. Frank or I will occasionally try to explain to someone what it was once like, what it was like to be inside a packed gym with a thousand screaming maniacs.

The rally on the day of the game was totally out of hand. It was always the best rally every year, even better than the homecoming rally with the girls in the gowns parading through the gym. The day of the big game it was a thousand horny teenage males with all their energies directed into a common goal, to finally beat them. Although amongst the crowd there weren't too many total believers, too many broken dreams from past years, there was no doubt that everyone was into it.

The football team waited out in the lobby while everyone else filtered into the gym. The spirit band, heavy with horns, blasted "Tequila, da dat da da dat da da dat da." The cheerleaders, with skirts rolled up as high as possible, danced along with the band. The guys in the stands were uncontrollable. We walked into the gym in pairs lead by the captains. The place erupted. Nothing but a standing "O," and rolls of toilet paper unfurled in the air. Classmates called out your name. The floor shook.

I walked in next to Mate, and I noticed his eyes were watering, and I guess mine were too. We sat down in chairs on the floor. We sat there for a good ten minutes as the gym filled with spontaneous cheering. Everyone but the team was on his feet. First it was WE ARE clap clap THE BEARS clap clap WE ARE clap clap THE BEARS...over and over until it faded into KICK ASS clap clap KICK ASS clap clap, and so on and so on. Everyone was so psyched by then, clapping their hands and stomping their feet.

Finally it quieted down enough so that the skits could start. A bunch of guys dressed in green and gold cheerleading outfits came out and did a drag version of their fight song. The next skit questioned the academic capabilities of several of their studs. Every time a line put them down the gym filled with laughter.

Everything in the rally was, as always, leading up to the high point, the Old Man speaking. He was the best. If I could relive anything over from high school, it would not be trying again for a certain girl or replaying a certain game, it would be just to hear him speak at a rally in front of a packed house.

He was introduced, and stepped slowly but deliberately to the podium. The applause was loud and sincere, but ended when he reached and adjusted the mike. Dead silence.

"Distinguished guests," and then he paused. "Faculty, staff"... another long pause ... "Parents, relatives, friends"...

another long pause, not a sound in the gym. He had introduced everyone but his people, and they were waiting. "And MEN OF FRANCISCAN" and the whole place went bullshit. The gym was filled with yelling and screaming, with everyone standing and pounding on the bleachers. The team stayed nailed in our seats, with our egos floating somewhere near the ceiling and our hearts pounding. He just stood up at the podium, looking over his domain. Rolls of toilet paper flew across the room like bottle rockets. And the chants began again...GO NUTS...BEAR HAIRS ARE EVERYWHERE...THEY ARE MICKEY MOUSE...THEY ARE CYO...WE DON'T MESS AROUND, HEY...on and on for ten then fifteen minutes. When it finally quieted down, and he tried to say something about the game, it would erupt again and start all over.

Finally the crowd quieted down, and he told them what they wanted to hear. He told them that this was the team that finally was going to do the impossible. "These men sitting behind me," he said, "are going to bring our school tonight our finest moment." More applause, more cheering. He waited until they quieted down again. "But we can't do it alone. We need everyone in this room to be there. We need you people to take things over in the stands, and we'll take care of business on the field." By this time, the crowd was really worked up. He was making believers out of everyone once again. He waited for it to be stone quiet again, looking around at the crowd on all sides of the gym. "I'll be the first to admit, on paper, they might have more talent than we do. But there are two things we can count on, and those two things are going to lead this team and this school to victory tonight. The first one is, that absolutely, without any doubt, we have the best fans and student body in the city." When he said that, the place went crazy. We all sat there on the floor still taking in each glorious moment. Then it got quiet again and he continued. "And the other thing is the pride that runs deep through the hearts of each of these men sitting today in front of you. These are the men that tonight, when they step on that field, are going to refuse to lose. Defeat will not be accepted." He turned around and signaled for us to stand up, and we walked out of the gym behind him two by two, as our classmates stood and cheered and screamed at the top of their lungs.

We showed up at their place excited, scared, awed. We walked into the hallway leading to the visitors' locker room. They passed us going to their locker room, as Mate stopped and let them all cross before we continued. Jesus, they were big. They all towered over him. When Haggerty walked by, with no shirt on and carrying the biggest pair of shoulder pads I had ever seen, Mate's eyes showed his surprise and concern. I had never seen a bigger or better built high school athlete, with muscle upon muscle, a small tight waist, and ripples up and down his back as he disappeared down the corridor.

When we got to our locker room, that was all everyone was talking about. "Did you see him?" "Holy fuck is he built!!!" Mate and I dressed in a corner surrounded by mostly juniors, guys who would only play on special teams, if that. They were really good on the encouragement. We heard comments like, "Greg, if I were you, I'd watch my ass over the middle," and, "Christ, Mate, what the hell are you going to hit him with?"

For as much as I hated them, I loved their stadium, and was jealous we didn't have one like it for our own. It's not there anymore, ripped down when they expanded the school. It was squeezed in between the school, the railroad tracks, and the houses. Games were sometimes halted because of passing trains. Steep stands on both sides and in the end zones painted, of course, ugly green. The stands were exceptionally tight to the field, and gave the impression the fans were right upon you. The place smelled of football; mud, grass, and sweat, along with popcorn and booze on the breaths of the guys working the chains.

They were always able to squeeze more than the eight thousand capacity into the place. By game time, the stands would be jammed, and people would be lined three deep on the fence around the field.

It was a clear, warm October night, perfect for high school football. We went out and warmed up. Stretching, cals, group work, and then team up. They again looked huge, going through the same routine at the other end of the field. I caught a glimpse of their cheerleaders crossing the field during unit work, noticed one looked familiar, and then remembered it was Mate's "babe," the girl who had caught his fancy at the basketball game. I tried to get his attention but couldn't. He seemed totally involved in what was going on around him in the huddle.

As we jogged off the field, Mate came up next to me and with a slight smile on his face said to me, "Did you see her? Nice, huh?" Then the smile disappeared and his game face reappeared.

The Old Man in his pep talk stressed long range goals, talked about history, and appealed to our emotions. "It is an emotional game that must be played with emotion," he said looking around the room, using his rare talent of looking each person in the eye, even if only for a moment. He told us about "when they kept Roginski and the first line in so he could rush for 250 yards while we had already cleared the benches." He told us that when he recruited us, that he had promised a night like tonight, "An opportunity to be the best, by playing the best, for a conference championship." How everyone in the room was a "product of sacrifice by parents, classmates, but most importantly, by yourselves." He told us "this is your chance to go out and prove that everything we have done has been for a good cause." He told us to win it for "everyone who had ever gone to Franciscan, especially for everyone who had worn the brown and orange against them only to come up unfulfilled...Win it for your parents who have always made sacrifices for you...picking you up after practice...paying your tuition...But most importantly win it for yourselves...For all those hours in the weight room...for all the hours on a hot and dusty practice field during the summer...for all those times in every sport, when we have walked off the field rejected, after they had beaten us and rubbed it in our faces."

We were introduced first, and then had to stand on our sideline as they went through their routine. They had their band split, lined up on the hash marks. They introduced each starter as if each one was all pro. Height, weight, year, parish, any all-star recognition. Each player ran through the goal post, through the band, and then to the bench. They looked so fudging big. Each one looked bigger and stronger. By the time they got to Haggerty, it was out of hand. "SIX FOOT THREE...TWO HUNDRED AND FORTY POUNDS...OUT OF OUR LADY OF THE ANGELS...FIRST TEAM ALL STATE AS A SOPHOMORE AND A JUNIOR...PARADE MAGAZINE HIGH SCHOOL ALL AMERICAN...STARTING AT LINEBACKER FOR THE BIG GREEN MACHINE, CO-CAPTAIN NUMBER FIFTY FOUR TOM HAGGERTY!!!" And he came running out, wearing those huge shoulder pads, with the sleeves ripped to make them fit, followed by their fifteen plus coaches and the hundred plus other players on their squad, all in green and bright gold uniforms.

It was crunch time, time to shit or get off the pot. They kicked off, and I was on our front line with Mate in the middle. Decent kick, I dropped back and got a good hit on someone, and much of the nervousness inside me disappeared. Our ball, our own 38. Silence in the huddle...Jesus, did they look big!

Our game plan was a little confusing when first presented to us, but seemed to make more sense the more the coaches hammered it into us. Run right at Haggerty. He played five yards off the ball and pursued so well to the outside. We wanted to run right at him, maybe use a little counter action and short passes, trying to get quick, safe yardage. With his lateral speed and their two stud defensive ends, the outside belonged to them. Our game plan worked immediately on the first drive. We ran an inside trap, inside counter, a dump to me, the trap again, a few quick dives, and the next thing you knew we were inside their ten.

They went to their short yardage defense, a straight six-one with Haggerty head up over Mate. Until then I had assumed Mate was having a good game because of all the inside yardage we had gained.

On first and goal, we ran power off tackle away from me. We were running two tight ends and Miller came in to play the other side. Mate tried to cut Haggerty, but ended up clipping him, even though he didn't get caught. Haggerty must have seen his OSU scholarship slip momentarily away with a bad knee, because he grabbed Mate's face mask and spit into his face saying, "If you do that again, I'll kill you!!!"

Mate looked him in the eyes for a moment, wrestled his head free, and walked back to our huddle.

We got a couple of yards off tackle and then came back to my side and got a couple of more. Fourth and goal on the three.

The Old Man was on the sidelines, clipboard in hand and headset on, and said to no one and everyone in particular, "We didn't come this far for just a field goal," and he sent in another play.

We came up again to the line with double tights. They were yelling, "Watch the dive!!! Watch the dive!!!" Mate snapped the ball, and then became the vertex of a wedge block aimed at the heart of their defense.

Eldridge opened to his right. Campano sprung out of his stance at fullback and started his leap over Mate before he ever got the ball. Our line fired out as one. Haggerty was waiting, poised. He leaped and met Campano with full force, both of them suspended in mid-air, high above the linemen fighting below.

While all that was going on, Eldridge was carrying out his fake, except it wasn't fake. With the ball hidden on his hip, he ran naked around the end into the end zone. Unbelievable!!! For the first time in history, we were leading them in a varsity football game!

After the extra point and kick off, I found myself sitting next to Mate on the bench.

"Look at the time," he said, and I glanced at the scoreboard and it said 2:08 left in the first quarter. We did what we had to do, eat up a lot of time and score when we got the chance.

I don't remember the rest of the first half except that our defense was on the field most of the time yet held them score-less, and we lead 7-0 at the half.

Our locker room was filled with the feeling of quiet confidence. I remember guys huddled in small groups saying to each other, "Hey, we can really beat these guys!"

Mate and I just sat on the floor, backs against the wall, listening to the coaches go over the second half adjustments. I was totally wiped out and we still had a half to play, but nobody looked in worse shape than Mate. He and I were the only guys on either side of the line under two hundred pounds and Mate was showing the beating he was taking. He had a nose bleed; his uniform was covered with stains from grass, mud, sweat and blood; and his face was imprinted with marks showing the shapes of the pads inside his helmet.

Just before it was time to get up and go back onto the field, the Old Man was making his rounds around the room, whispering comments to individual players, usually about something to look out for in the second half. When he got over to where Mate and I were sitting, he just bent down on one knee and said in a voice that only we could hear, "Right now I'm very proud of you boys...But just remember we have another half to play and that..."-slight pause-"... no matter what it takes..."-slight pause-"...that it is at times like this that pride runs deep."

I saw the emotion swell in Mate's eyes as we got up to go back onto the field.

10-10, less than four minutes left in the game. We're driving, very similar to our first series. Both teams beating the shit out of each other. It was past the point of no return across the line of scrimmage. Mate had a broken face mask and a stream of blood flowing down his face. I was hurting from head to toe but trying not to show it. We had tried to get fancy for a while and it hurt us, so we were back to our original game plan. Trap, counter, dive, sprint, draw. A good ground game eating up yardage and time.

Finally inside the ten again, first and goal on the seven. Both sidelines going nuts. Everyone in the stands on their feet. Time slipping away. For a moment I thought I saw their confidence flicker, when the ref signaled that we had gotten another first down. They were bitching at each other, losing composure. They weren't used to us giving them a game, let alone having to play for what looked like a tie. On first down we ran up the middle and got nothing. Haggerty went right over the top of Mate and jammed the line. On second down we quick pitched into the sideline and they just ran it out of bounds. Third and six.

The play came into the huddle. "Pro tight 426 pass, backside drag." Before he repeated the play, and without looking at me, Eldridge said, "Make sure you're in the end zone before you make your cut," and then he repeated the numbers.

I was so surprised to hear the play because Haggerty was so great at taking away any route across the middle. All the times I had seen him play, and in all the film we had watched, he would either intercept the pass using his great leaping ability and great hands, or would lay the receiver out with a forearm to the chin. The ball would always come free as an incomplete pass or fumble.

The game films would show that Haggerty for a moment took the fake and then stopped, turned and made his drop. He looked directly at me when I was making my cut. We were heading to a collision point somewhere about a yard deep in the end zone.

Without looking, I sensed the ball in the air. I ran a squared route, not making my cut until I was sure I was in the end zone. When I did look up, it was all instinct. I took one more step, then with both hands reached as high as I could, extending my whole body to the ball. I didn't think about Haggerty until we met a fraction of a second after I felt the ball on my fingers. He hit me with a force I had never felt before or since. Forearm up and through my chin, his shoulder pads going through my chest. My mind went blank, then I saw stars and felt a sharp pain in my chest.

I lay on my back and the only thought that went through my mind was a vision of Jim Brown standing over me saying, "Hop right up, Don't let them know you're hurting!" But it wasn't Jim Brown, it was my buddy Mate. When I got up, the pain in my chest was unbelievable. It was then, however, that I got a big surprise. I was still hanging onto the ball!!! I tossed it to the nearest ref who couldn't catch it, because his hands were raised signaling a touchdown. I saw Haggerty, his head down and shaking in disbelief. I was mobbed by teammates. When I finally got to the sidelines, I collapsed on the bench.

When they got the ball back for the last time we were

leading 17-10 with less than two minutes to play. Within thirty seconds they picked up some big yardage and found themselves inside our 30. Suddenly there was a crack in our confidence, and a sense of impending doom was slowly filling our sideline. Our defense had been on the field for almost the whole game, except for the first and last drives, and they were beat. Could they hang on?

Then we got a break. They tried for the first time their wrap around draw, where the quarterback drops and hands the ball around from behind to the fullback, who acts as if he is blocking. All our linebackers read pass and our linemen thought the quarterback still had the ball. It was wide open, and with a couple of down field blocks maybe a touchdown. But the fullback, Ristagnato, left a moment early and he never got the hand off, and the ball was bouncing on the ground. A big pile up, then the ball went shooting backwards into their zone. Another big pile up and then another. Finally bodies buried six deep and the referees trying to unstack it. All of a sudden Thunder Bailes jumping up and down with the ball in one hand above his head. The referee pointing first down for us. Everyone on our sideline going berserk.

Mate ran down the sidelines looking for me and grabbed me off the bench, just as Doc Schnell was taking off my uniform to look at my ribs.

"C'mon, our ball!" He screamed at me and grabbed my arm like a little kid looking for someone to play with.

"He is not going anywhere," Doc said with a serious look on his face.

I looked at Mate, realized what was about to happen, grabbed my helmet and said to the Doc, "I wouldn't miss this for anything in the world."

That was the finest moment of our lives, killing the last 1:36 of that game. They kept going for the ball and had to use all of their time outs. We moved the ball with simple stuff up the middle, and even broke one for a big gain.

We were back on their seven yard line, and looked up and saw that there was only six seconds left in the game. I turned toward our sidelines and saw it jammed with all of our fans and the Old Man up on someone's shoulders. I turned toward the clock again and saw it start ticking away. I looked and saw Mate run up to the line of scrimmage and grab the game ball and wave it over his head, and the refs running off the field before time was up because pandemonium was about to erupt. Mate and I ran towards each other and tackled each other and rolled around in the mud in the end zone. "We did it!!! We did it!!!" We screamed into each other's ears.

We were mobbed by everyone who was on our side of the field. Friends, classmates, everyone's younger brothers and sisters. I had never seen so much emotion.

Mate and I were the heroes of the junior class. Pazzelli, Archer and Zinski, a group of non jocks who went to every Franciscan sporting event, tried to lift us on their shoulders. They then threw us down and joined a mob of our school mates who were in the north end zone ripping down the goal post. Mate and I walked off the field with our arms around each other and tears running down our cheeks.

At the gate, behind all of our fans, stood their cheerleaders in complete shock. It was the first time they had lost in three years, and the first time they had lost at home in seven. They also were taken in by the emotion of our team and fans over the outcome of the game.

As we turned to go into the locker room, Mate stopped for a moment and said to me, "Watch this."

He walked towards their cheerleaders and found her with her back facing us, talking to another girl. Mate walked very confidently up to her, put down his helmet, and gently but firmly turned her around. He looked her in the eyes, wrapped both arms around her, picked her up off the ground, and laid the first kiss I had ever seen him give a girl smack dab on her lips for what seemed like at least ten seconds. He then dropped her and they both stared at each other for another loooong moment. She seemed surprised and it showed in her big brown eyes. He paused, then let out a big laugh, picked up his helmet and ran back to join me. I saw the look of complete happiness and contentment on his face as I gave him a high five and we ran into the locker room.

The locker room was a zoo, everyone crying tears of joy. It was the first time I had ever seen grown men cry as the coaches were as happy as we were. Just as the Old Man finally got everyone quieted down for a prayer, Father Steven came tumbling into the room. He was our principal, had been for twelve years, and tears were also flowing down his face. He interrupted the Old Man in the middle of the Hail Mary and he said, "God damn it, we finally did it!!! Didn't we boys!?!" The whole place went berserk once again. Our locker room was a circus. It would be a good half hour before we rounded up our gear and headed back to Franciscan.

As we walked to the bus, one of their cheerleaders approached Mate, however, it wasn't the one he had kissed.

"She had to catch a ride so she left, but she wanted me to give you this," and she handed Mate a note and he shoved it into his traveling bag.

The ride back to Parma was wild as everyone on the team bus was yelling, screaming, and hugging each other. About half way home Mate remembered the note and dug it out of his bag and read it. A big smile filled his face as he passed it to me.

> *Dear Mate (I think that's what they call you)*
> *Thanks for the kiss. It was even better than the popcorn and coke you gave me last time. Call me!!! Please?*
> > *Hugs and Kisses,*
> > *Mary Beth 333-5432*

Mate just beamed, "She remembered! She remembered!" He screamed over the excitement on the bus.

By the time we got back to Franciscan the parking lot was jammed. There must have been five thousand people there, passing parts of the goal post above them as they waited for us to arrive. I guess people at the game just had to call someone and tell them and told them to go up to the school. When we stopped outside of one of the bars on State Road, it emptied out with people coming out to the bus to congratulate us.

When the bus got up the hill, but before it pulled into the

lot, the Old Man had the driver pull over and stop. He got up out of his seat in the first row and faced the team. For the first time, the bus became quiet as we looked up and saw his eyes swollen and red from the emotions of the game.

"Men," he said. "You are going to go on and fight bigger and more important battles in your life...There will be bigger challenges to meet...Bigger mountains to climb. But I want you to remember anytime you don't think you can do it. Anytime you think you're out of your league. Whether it's in school or in business or even when you finally meet the woman you'll want to marry...Anytime you need that little extra something to give you that surge to get the job done, I want you to think of the men on this bus and the night we went over to their place...And when no one except us knew we could do it...And we kicked their ass!!!" The bus again was filled with cheers, but he raised his hand to signal that he had one more thing to say. "I want to thank you...Except for the births of my children, this is the happiest moment of my life."

We had to make our way through a mob scene to get from the bus to the locker room. It was unbelievable. When we finally got inside, the locker room was filled with guys I recognized from when I was in grade school, guys who had played for Franciscan in the Sixties and early Seventies. They seemed as happy as we were.

I was standing in front of my locker completely engulfed in the emotions of the moment when Mate grabbed me and said, "The sign!!!"

We both turned and looked up and saw it still on the wall, unnoticed by the frenzy below.

"Let me get on your shoulders," he said.

"Why not me get on yours?"

"Why? It was my idea."

He had me for a moment. "But wait...You got the note from the girl. If I got to rip down the poster we'd be about even on the night. What do you think? Huh?"

He paused for a moment, saw the logic (or illogic) in my statement, and stooped over and let me hop on his shoulders.

No one remembered the poster, but just as I pulled it off the wall it seemed that everyone in the place noticed me. The locker room got momentarily silent as I pulled it off the wall and held it over my head. I held it so everyone could read it. Every fucking eye was on me. WE WILL ALWAYS BE MICKEY MOUSE UNTIL WE BEAT THEM IN FOOTBALL. I paused, Mate swayed underneath me, and I ripped it into two big pieces. The place went berserk one more time, and I kept ripping until Mate finally fell backwards and we toppled to the floor.

The next morning we gathered to watch the game films, and our emotions were still running high as we saw on the screen how we had outplayed the best high school football team in the state. Each touchdown was cheered, every player got complemented on every big play. We were stunned into silence when the game ended and we saw ourselves getting mobbed on the field. I think we were all blown away by the fact that it really was us up on that screen. It really was us jumping up and down and hugging each other. In the middle of the post game celebration the film suddenly ended. The last thing on the film was the goal post swaying back and forth, about to come down. The room was dead silent for a moment as all we heard for several seconds was the end of the film flapping around on the projector's spool. You heard someone fighting back tears. Then, it seemed all at once, we burst into a tremendous cheer. We knew our school, and our football team, had come of age with our big win.

We left school after films and watching the JV game and went over to Mate's house to raid the fridge and plan our course of action for the rest of the weekend. As we lay around his living room, he was trying to get up the nerve to give Beth a call. Since it was he who got the note the night before and not one of us, we were jealous as hell but weren't showing it. In fact, we were busy edging him on about calling her.

"You pussy, it's only a girl," Big Pete said.

"She probably forgot already that she gave it to you," Kaz chipped in.

I was rather excited. I saw it as a chance to meet new women. Because of my then lack of social skills around girls,

Greg Cielec

and my fondness for beer, I had burned every bridge with the limited amount of girls that we knew at the time.

Suddenly, Mate looked up from the sports page he had been reading and said, "I have an idea. I'll be right back," and took off running down the street in search of his dad, whom he knew would be at one of the neighborhood joints watching college football.

He returned fifteen minutes later with a big smile on his face. "I got it. We're going to the Browns game tomorrow."

"Who is?" I said.

"Us and Beth and three of her friends."

"Do they know that?" Big Pete asked.

"No. But a mere technicality. I mean, how could any women say no to four studs like ourselves?" He again disappeared, this time to the kitchen, away from us to make the call. As he finally dialed her number he said to himself, it's now or never.

"Hello, may I please speak to Beth?"

"Speaking."

"Is this Beth the cheerleader of that high school football team that got their asses kicked last night?"

The line was quiet for a moment. "Maybe. Who wants to know? One of the ass kickers?"

"Yes. The good looking one."

She responded with a healthy laugh.

"You are probably wondering about the purpose of this call. Well, some buddies of mine were wondering if by chance, tomorrow you and several of your girl friends..."

I don't know why sometimes I remember such stupid things like the car we took to pick up our dates for that Browns/ Bengals game that Sunday. Out of the four of us, none of us had a real car. We were all lucky that our parents would let us use one of theirs if we asked. My parents, as long as I did my stuff around the house and worked at school on the weekends, would let me have a car usually one night a week. But none of us could ask our parents to take a car downtown. To the mall, yes. To downtown, never. So we had the woody.

The woody was a late '66 Ford Country Squire station

29

wagon, an ugly green thing complete with fake wood sidings stretching the length on both sides. It had once been the Majowski's family car, then sat in their garage, and then was only used when we were desperate to go some place and really needed a ride. It was a piece of shit, but we considered it our piece of shit, and it almost seemed appropriate that it would be our mode of transportation for that Sunday afternoon. Many good times in that car, to the Stadium, to high school dances, to the old Agora. Mate would never drive it to school, since it had only so many more trips left in it, and those were to be left for the good times.

The girls had all gathered at Beth's house, and that's where we picked them up early Sunday morning. Mate and I went in and met her parents, and I remember her mom giving us one of those 'where have I seen these guys before?' looks. The girls all laughed when they saw our ride. A couple of us climbed in the back to make room for them, and we turned the machine towards downtown as we headed to the game.

Behind the old Stadium there used to be a huge parking lot, where the inner harbor and the museums are now. Mate's parents had been tailgating in that parking lot on Browns Sundays since the early Fifties. They had the scam down and that is where we headed with our dates.

Mate's parents and their friends really knew how to put out a spread. They usually had about thirty people, the usual cast of characters. The had two grills going as well as several long tables filled with cold cuts, all sorts of salads, and, of course, a bar and coolers of beer. They had polka music blasting from the eight track in Uncle Gus's Cadillac. Many of them brought lawn furniture and the women sat in clusters to gossip, while the men drank whiskey and beer and played horse shoes.

Everyone was really nice to us, as we brought the girls over. Mate's mom and the other ladies forced everyone to grab some food to eat, and Uncle Gus poured each of us a tall glass of coke. I sipped mine and almost choked. I turned to him and he was just grinning.

"Thought you might need a little anti freeze in case it doesn't warm up."

Mate and Beth tried their hardest to keep the conversation going amongst us eight young people, and with a few more glasses of Uncle Gus's cokes we all had loose tongues and started to get to know each other.

When we finally made it into the Stadium, we were all surprised that it was the bleachers that we had tickets for. "My dad got them from some of the black dudes at the mill," Mate said. "We all got to remember that you can't beat the price!!!" Which meant the Mate's dad got them in return for some forgotten favor.

This was the Browns' bleachers ten years before Hanford Dixon would coin the term Dawg Pound. At that time, it resembled more of a third world country. This was back when you could take almost anything into a game as long as it was in a brown paper bag. When the bleachers were pretty much for the minority fans, and the smell of dope was constantly in the air. It was still relatively cheap, rowdy, and everyone had a buzz on. The game was often secondary to the party in the stands. It was a great place.

We grabbed our seats in the lower part of right field and everyone was finally relaxed and having a good time. At half time, Mate took Beth up to the top of the bleachers next to the scoreboard. They looked out over the back parking lot out at the lake, at a couple of tankers making their last runs of the season out of Cleveland.

She watched him as he looked out at the lake, and then turned and scanned the massive insides of the huge stadium. He looked up into the upper deck behind the Browns bench where he knew his parents were sitting. With the Browns getting drilled at the half, he knew his mom was bitching up a storm. "What the hell did they do all week, 'cause they sure as hell didn't practice," she would be shouting to his dad.

Beth and Mate took in the sounds and sights of half time. The high school band playing show tunes on the field. Many fans laughing, joking, and passing bottles wrapped in paper bags and funny looking cigarettes.

He broke into a huge smile and she just kept looking at him. "You know," he said, "this is my favorite place in the whole world."

"Really?"

"Yep."

"Why?"

"I've had so many good times here. Do you ever come here with your family?"

"Once a summer for an Indians game, but never to see the Browns play."

"How about with your friends?"

"Our parents would never let us come here alone. In fact, most of them told their parents we were going somewhere else today."

"I've seen every Browns home game since the year before I was in Kindergarten."

"You're kidding."

"And probably about forty Indians games."

"That's about thirty more than I've seen in my life."

"That's a year. We come all the time."

"What are you, gluttons for punishment?"

"No, my parents just love it here. They came here a lot as kids when the Browns and Indians were both good, and they just never stopped."

"Do your parents and their friends party like that before every game?"

"As long as I can remember."

She paused for a moment. "I saw them have more fun at that tail gate party today than my parents have had in the last five years."

"Really?"

"Yeah."

He saw her frown for a slight moment so he changed the subject quickly. "You got to come to a Sunday baseball game with us next summer and sit out here with us. It's a blast."

"With you and your parents?"

"No, on Sundays with our friends from school. It only costs fifty cents, you can just hang out, and we even have our own beer man."

"Your own beer man?"

"Yeah, Chris. Chris the beer man. And the best part about it is he always remembers that we're eighteen."

"No trouble remembering you're eighteen, huh?" She said with a smile that he returned.

He turned and looked down on the field as he saw the Browns returning to the field through the dugout along first base. He then turned back to her and said, "There's one more reason why this will always be my favorite place in the whole world."

"What's that?"

He, with the right amount of touch, intertwined his fingers with hers in each of their hands. "It will always be the place that I took you on our first date," and he leaned into her, and for the second time in their young lives, laid a long, sensual, electrically charged kiss across her beautiful young mouth.

They stood their lip locked onto each other until they were interrupted by the cat calls of the people sitting up there who wanted to watch the kick off to start the second half.

"Hey you, take that shit someplace else, it's time for foot-ball!!!"

We left the game early as the Bengals were pounding the Browns, and headed back to where we parked the woody. Even though we all had eaten a lot at the tail gate party before the game, everyone was hungry.

This was over twenty years ago, back when there was no downtown life to speak of, especially on Sundays. The girls all started to suggest places that were open out around where they lived on the west side, while all the guys looked at Mate. We were all running a little short on money, but we also knew that there was only one place to munch out on a Sunday evening after a Browns home game, the Majowski household.

"Mate," Pete asked, "What did she leave in the fridge this morning that she plans on popping in the oven?"

"A huge pork roast."

"Pork roast?"

"Yeah, with those chunky mashed potatoes she makes with that gravy with the whole mushrooms in."

The guys started to get excited.

"And I'm pretty sure there is a roaster full of stuffed cabbage too."

The guys started to get really excited.

"And I know she spent a couple of days baking this week. You know, poppyseed rolls and nut rolls and bread."

The thought of Mrs. Majowski's homemade bakery smothered in whipped honey butter clinched it for us. The girls protested. "We can't go to Mate's house."

"Why not?"

"I'm sure Mrs. Majowski has enough food to feed eight people showing up unannounced," Colleen said.

All the guys burst into laughter.

"Ladies," I said, "You are always expected for dinner at the Majowski house, as well as breakfast and lunch."

The guys kept laughing, the girls looked slightly confused. Mate suddenly stopped and looked at us as if he was hurt. "You guys mean to tell me, for the last three years, the only reason you've hung around me is because of my mom's cooking? I thought you guys really liked me."

"We like you Mate," Kaz said. "We love your Mom's cooking."

As always after a Browns home game, the Majowski house was rocking. It was most of their crowd from the game, a few new faces, plus Mate's sister Barb had brought some girlfriends from work to the game and home for a real meal. There was the usual kitchen table of food, a thousand conversations going on at one time, and Old Mate and Gus already had their accordions out.

Mate led us into the living room, and by that time we were old friends to everyone we had met at the tailgate party before the game.

Kaz, Pete and I already knew the routine, as we went straight to the kitchen table to make huge plates of food. The girls sorta paused once in the front door to take everything in. Mate turned around, smiled and said, "Ladies, make yourselves at home. Can I get you anything to drink?" Immediately Barb and some of her girlfriends came over and introduced themselves and led everyone over to the buffet table in the kitchen.

Even though everyone was bummed the Browns had lost, everyone was still riding high on our big win on Friday night. The crowd before the game and at Mate's house afterward really made us feel like kings. A lot of them had been at our game, and I know amongst the men in the crowd more than a few bucks were won on the game with the bookies down in the mills. But everyone was especially nice to Beth and her girl-friends, and everyone made sure that they had a good time. They were good heartedly teased about being cheerleaders for the wrong team, and Uncle Gus wanted to know if they were coming over to our side for good. "To the victors go the spoils," he proclaimed, and everyone laughed along.

By the time we left to drive the girls home after eight, we had eaten, drank, and laughed to our hearts' delight. We dropped Kaz and Pete off first over in the old part of Parma, before we took the girls back to the west side. When we dropped them off at Beth's house, Mate and I were spinning. He spent another five minutes playing kissy face with Beth in her drive-way, and each of the other girls gave me a big hug and a peck on the cheek, and told me what a great time they had. I don't know if it was the autumn chill in the air or what, but when each of them kissed me, all I felt was their lips on my cheek and their breasts touching my chest. Colleen was the last to hug me good-bye, and before she turned around to run into Beth's house, she gave me a long lingering stare with her deep blue eyes that told me that we would soon see each other again.

As Mate got on the freeway to take me out to my house, there could not have been two happier guys anywhere.

"Do you believe all the shit that has happened to us this weekend? The game on Friday, and then taking them out today. This is just like you dream it, you know. Is this been the best weekend ever or what?"

I just sat there smiling, with the scent of perfume still in the air and a smudge of lipstick still on my cheek.

Thinking back to that time makes my senses fill with the sights and sounds of long ago. The feel of the wind blowing in off the lake in late autumn chilling everyone to the bone, and the taste of the whiskey in the coke that warmed us back up. The smells of the stadium bleachers; popcorn, beer, dope, mud and hot dogs, and how that weird combination intoxicated me. And, of course, the aroma of the Majowski house when any sort of party was going on, the smell of a house where food was always being prepared, with the warmth of the kitchen spread through each room.

Mate's father was a real piece of work. He was a person who, like his son, enjoyed life very much. He was also a lot more intelligent and observant than people give him credit for, because most people never got past his appearance that made him look like what he felt he really was, just another guy from the mills.

Old Mate was a supervisor for Republic Steel down in the Flats off Jennings Road. He usually worked third shift from 11:00 p.m. to 7:00 a.m. He worked hard during the week, and on the weekends he loved to do nothing more than to spend time with his family, drink shots and beers with his buddies and Mate's uncles at the VFW or several of the local taverns that dotted their neighborhood, and go down to the Stadium to see the Indians or the Browns play.

His love of life stemmed from the fact that he knew things could always be worse than they were, and that life was too short to worry about too many things. His parents, Mate's grandparents, came over on the boat from Poland and settled in one of the many Polish Catholic neighborhoods that filled up Cleveland's south side before World War II. Although he grew up a child of the Great Depression, he also grew up hearing stories about starving people in eastern Europe and learned to appreciate what you had. After high school, he enlisted in the Navy, and was in on the end of the fighting in the Pacific Theater. Although he came out unharmed, he knew more than one schoolmate that never made it back. He came back from the war still a relatively young man and got a job in the mills and pretty much goofed off for a time, enjoying life as a young man in his twenties with very few cares. He drifted along in life until the conflict in Korea, when he re-enlisted and did another tour of duty aboard an aircraft carrier in the northern Pacific.

It was during that time between tours of duty that Mate's father, uncles, and their pals from the old neighborhood thrived as young men. It was such a great time to be young, footloose and fancy free and the streetcars could take you anywhere to see a game or a fight, or to a dance or a social. It was such a prosperous time and there was no reason it was ever going to end.

When Old Mate wasn't working or running off with his buddies to some game or saloon, he spent some time with the young girl he had met at a church dance. Introduced by his boyhood friend Gus, they immediately became an item.

They would later like to tell their children and their children's friends that they were attracted to each other because they made each other laugh, and they went through what was considered at the time a rather lengthy courtship of almost seven years. Much of that courtship was spent taking the street car to games, the fights, Euclid Beach, or to one of the many dance halls that Cleveland had at the time. The Aragon on West 25th, the Marcane on Euclid, or if they could borrow a car, the Springvale out in the country. They would drink beer, laugh, tell jokes, and dance the night away to polka or big band music.

When we were still in high school and college there was nothing I loved doing more than listening to Mate's dad and mom, uncles and aunts, and the other assorted characters that hung around their house, talk about the Cleveland of their youth. It seemed such a romantic, honest and fun time, and it seemed to set the standard for what Mate (as well as his best friend) would want out of life as they got older.

Mate's mom, Helen or Matilda to her friends, was a good old broad. Her life paralleled somewhat with that of her husband. She was the daughter of Polish immigrants living on the south side of town, and she always gave off the impression to me that she was completely in love with her husband. She let him make the major decisions and let him bring home the paycheck, and she would always laugh along and tell people she was just along for the ride. Mate's old man had a great sense of humor, and no one enjoyed it more than his wife.

Old Mate decided to marry Mrs. Mate when he was half-way around the world on the deck of an aircraft carrier, off the coast of Korea right smack dab on the thirty-eighth parallel. With bombs dropping and the sky lit red, and after what he had seen earlier in the South Pacific, he said to himself, "If I make it through this one, I'll marry that girl."

Mate's old man was always his own man. There were many examples why. He never joined the white flight of the Sixties and moved out to the suburbs, to Parma, Garfield Heights or Maple Heights. He always said he bought one house and one house was enough. It was a big old colonial on a quiet tree lined street with the church at one end and a saloon at the other. He would say that as long as you rooted for the Cleveland Browns or the Cleveland Indians, you might as well live in Cleveland. That was the type of logic he had.

He also felt that when it was time to work, you worked your ass off. And when you weren't working, you should be having a good time. He hated the guys on the street that would spend all day Saturday during the summer working in the yard, doing things like weeding the garden or raking leaves. Old Mate always thought Saturday afternoons should be spent sitting on the front porch, drinking beer, and listening to the ball game on the radio. Mate and I showed up at his house after a Saturday morning baseball game of our own, Old Mate and Mate's Uncle Gus were kicking back with a cold beverage or two and listening to Herb Score broadcast an Indians game, and they were totally disgusted with the guy across the street pruning his bushes.

"Look at that asshole," Old Mate said. "Doesn't he know that work like that could lead to a coronary?"

"Coronary?" Uncle Gus added, "A guy that stupid to work that hard on a day off work is not smart enough to know anything about any coronary."

Needless to say, Mate's house was never on the cover of *Better Homes and Gardens*. What that house lacked in beauty, it made up with laughter. There was always something going on at the Majowski household, and it always seemed to be filled with friends and relatives. Things usually got started during what came to be known as "Fridays." Old Mate usually snuck out of work early on Fridays, to give him time to go down to the food terminal down on East 40th and buy enough provisions to cook his family and whoever else showed up for breakfast. His last shift of the week was over, and it was his way of getting the weekend started.

He would cook a feast, and do most of it by himself. He'd fry Canadian bacon and Polish sausage in big heavy black skillets. He would make scrambled eggs loaded with diced onions and ham, and layered with cheddar cheese. As people showed up, he would flip them blueberry pancakes hot off the griddle.

The crowd at the Majowski home on a Friday morning was substantial. There would be a few of the guys off Old Mate's shift at the mill, and neighbors coming by before they had to head into work. There was Uncle Gus and a few other of Mate's uncles who never seemed to work a lot, and always seemed to show up at anything that involved free food or booze. Mate's older sister and her girlfriends would be there, stopping by before they went to school or work. I would usually try to sleep over on Thursday nights and wake up there to simply watch all this happening. During the times that they went out, Beth would show up on her way to school.

When one entered the kitchen on those Friday mornings, he or she would see Old Mate at his best. He presided over the grill, can of beer in his hand and a stinky cigar sticking out of his mouth, pinching his wife's ass as she circulated the room with the coffee pot. Every time he grabbed her she'd laugh, and he would whisper something dirty in her ear and she'd giggle. All this would be going on as polka music played on the stereo in the living room. To this day, when I hear polka music, I think of those Friday mornings.

Old Mate was the most content adult I knew when I was growing up, and consequently the most happy. He never got caught up with the 'keeping up with the Jones's bullshit that was prevalent in the Sixties and Seventies. He lived life one day at a time and just tried to make sure he put in five honest days of work and a hearty weekend of fun. He passed that philosophy onto his children, especially to his son.

I don't want to slam my own parents, they are both still alive and our relationship has never been better, but if my parents would have been more like Mate's parents, I think they would have been a lot happier. My dad and mom sometimes worried a little too much about what other people thought of them, as if someone was keeping score. We first lived in Parma, and then as our family got bigger, we needed a bigger house. We moved out to Brecksville, to a quarter acre lot with a four bedroom split level. And with a mortgage payment, which I didn't know at the time, that had to really put a strain on my dad. The family vacations disappeared, and so did the family going out to dinner one night a week. All my mother worried about for years was the fucking house, and how it looked whenever any of our relatives came over to see it. I don't know. It was just so frustrating when I would spill something on the carpeting in my own home and my mother would just ream me for it. "The new carpeting! The new carpeting!" She would scream, and it would be a major hassle for weeks. At Mate's house if you spilled something on the floor they threw you a rag and told you to wipe it up, and asked you if you needed another beer in the same breath. I'm not knocking my parents you understand, it's just for a while there I think they rather lost a little vision about what it's all about.

At the Majowski house there was never any bitching about why there wasn't any money. There wasn't any bitching about cutting the lawn before the neighbors said anything. There were no fights over credit cards or when Mate's dad came home a little late with booze on his breath. No worries about all the bullshit that was so typical of white suburban living at the time. The Majowskis were a content and happy family that just didn't give a shit about many things.

The Majowski house was one that was suspended in time, one that just didn't quite seem to keep pace with the rest of the world. It was a place filled with laughter and good cheer, and they always made everyone feel at home.

Mate's old man's theme song was "Waltzing Matilda," the

Australian drinking song. There are many different versions of the song, and the one that the soldiers of World War II sang was about a soldier far away from home who loses both his leg in battle and his girlfriend back home, and spends many sad nights drinking and drowning his sorrows because he couldn't go waltzing with his Matilda any more. Although written as a sad song, the Australians, with their love of drink, use that song as an unofficial national anthem, and it is often sung during happy times as well as sad.

When Old Mate was a young eighteen year old navy seaman being trained on some island in the middle of nowhere in what historians call the Battle of Guatacanal, he was scared, lonely and afraid. He had never ventured outside northern Ohio at any time in his young life, and now he was halfway around the world.

Luck would have it that he would be assigned to a combined American/Australian outfit that got a weekend furlough just before the big battle. It was during a weekend of drinking in a small island bar on a South Pacific island no longer there that Mate first heard Matilda. His Australian 'mates,' who loved the fact that their American friend's nickname was 'Mate,' loved their new American friend who shared with them the popular American songs of the day. Mate taught them "Stardust" and "Stars Fell on Alabama," and they taught him "Waltzing Matilda."

From the South Pacific to the south side of Cleveland and his sweetheart still in high school, Mate wrote long romantic letters as he tried to hide the fact that he was scared out of his mind. In one such letter, he told her of his new favorite song. He told her that he was looking forward to the day that he would be back home, and he could sing his new favorite song while playing the accordion in his family's parlor.

Old Mate returned from the war in time for Christmas of 1945, and the neighborhood was filled with joy as young men returned from the fighting overseas. On Christmas night after Mass, the opening of gifts, and several huge meals, friends and family did indeed gather in the front room, and Mate's dad pulled out the accordion and he played for the first time on

American soil "Waltzing Matilda." The song became his and remained with him for the rest of his life.

> *Waltzing Matilda, waltzing Matilda*
> *You'll come a waltzing Matilda with me*
> *And he sang as he watched and waited till his billy*
>   *boiled,*
> *You'll come a waltzing Matilda with me.*

It was "Waltzing Matilda" that Mate's father would play, with a slight gaze in his eyes and a big smile across his face, on any special occasion at the Majowski household. He and Gus would play the melody, Old Mate would sing the first verse, and everyone would join in the chorus. By the end of the song, (usually after five or six verses that were never quite the same each time it was sung), Mate's mom would be sitting next to him, with her arms wrapped around his shoulders and planting big kisses on his cheeks.

Mate and I never did figure out what a billabong was, although years later during our college years we both certainly found out what a bong was.

The best night of the year at the Majowski household, as far as Mate was concerned, was the night that they put up the Christmas tree. Mate would say, "It's the only time I ever really see my parents misty eyed." This was back before the days of VCRs, cable TV, and hundreds of channels, when it now seems like every Christmas movie is broadcast daily at all hours of the day and night. When we were still in school, when a classic movie was on TV, it was an event. And when Channel 43 would show *White Christmas* at the Majowski household it was more than an event, it was a happening. Because it was on the night that Channel 43 showed *White Christmas* that the Christmas tree would be put up.

Of course, everyone was there. All of Mate's family, including assorted aunts, uncles and cousins, as well as neighbors and many of his parents' friends from lodges and posts and church.

Old Mate, Gus and their pals would sit around the kitchen

table eating perogies, drinking whiskey, smoking cheap cigars, and telling stories about Christmas during their war years. Old Mate would talk about Christmas Mass on the deck of a cargo ship in the South Pacific. Uncle Gus would tell about Christmas Mass in a foxhole in a mine field in Northern Italy. All this, along with Bing Crosby and Danny Kaye in the background.

The accordions would come out, everyone would sing Christmas carols, and the story telling would continue. Mate's great Uncle Kas would talk about Christmas in Poland when he was a boy before World War I, and walking ten miles in the snow to go to Midnight Mass. Old Mate would then start telling stories about his parents, both long dead, and how much he missed them when he was halfway around the world fighting in the war. All the men would start talking about "those who didn't come back" from the war, and with each name mentioned or toasted at least one of the women would dab a kerchief to a misty eye. While all this was going on they would be going through Kessler's as if it were Kool Aid.

By this time the movie was finished, the tree would be up, and Mate would be manning the stereo as the stories continued. Hearing stories that he had heard over and over again his whole life, but enjoying them more each time, he knew which song to put on the turn table at what time. Mostly World War II big band tunes and ballads, the songs would get the adults more and more melancholy, and the stories would keep on coming.

I remember Mate and I falling asleep on the couch, with the sounds of stories still being told in the kitchen, and Mate's dad and Uncle Gus singing along with Jo Stafford...

> *Who knows, if we shall meet again?*
> *But when the morning chimes ring sweet again*
> *I'll be seeing you, in all the old familiar places*
> *That this old heart of mine embraces all day through*
> *I'll be seeing you in every lovely summer's day*
> *In everything that's light and gay*
> *I'll always think of you that way*

I got my chance to pursue a relationship with Colleen soon

after we all went to the Browns game. She called me out of the blue, and asked if I would like to double date with Beth and Mate at their school's Christmas Dance.

Their school was out on the west side and out of our territory. Most of those girls hung out with guys from Ed's and Iggy, and Beth and her crowd were the first girls we had ever known from out that way.

Little did I know why Mate was so excited about going. I heard mixed reviews about those types of dances. The band that played at this one the year before, and was going to be the band this year also, was made up of guys from our school. "It was a real drag last year," one of them told me in study hall. "All the douche bags from Ed's on one side of the hall, and all the douche bags from Iggy's on the other side, trying to macho each other out, singing stupid drinking songs. You know those fuckers couldn't hang with us if they ever tried." I just shrugged, but I noticed Mate's face light up when he heard of the scenario.

The night of the dance found Mate and I rather buzzed on beer trying to fit in with Beth and Colleen's friends at a big round table in the front near the dance floor. I was feeling very uncomfortable with my date, Colleen, trying to say or not say the right and/or wrong thing.

For the first hour or so, Mate sat there with a stupid look of anticipation on his face. Whenever I asked him what he was so hyper about, he'd just reply, "Just wait. Just wait."

The band was good, made up mostly of guys from Franciscan. The guys in the band, Mate and I and were the only guys from our school at the dance, surrounded by huge fucking guys from other schools acting like we were nobodies. The guys from Ignatius hung out at one end and started singing some frat beer drinking songs. The guys from Ed's were answering from the other end of the room. We were stuck in the middle, not knowing what to do. They were all there, Haggerty, Kowalsky, O'Boyle. They looked fucking huge. How the hell did we beat them?

I was getting annoyed because we weren't getting our due respect. Just because we were outnumbered we had still beaten both of them that season, and protocol called for us to receive our just due respect. Whoever had the best football team owned the city until the next season started, and certain privileges and moments of respect came with it. Instead the guys from the other schools were both acting as if they owned the place and that we weren't even there, and I was getting pissed about it. Little did I know what Mate had up his sleeve.

The band had the place jumping, playing boogie woogie and party tunes. They really were good, and we were bragging to everyone at our table that they were from our school. They paused for a short break and that was when Mate said to everyone at our table, "Please excuse us for a moment. We'll be back shortly."

Mate led me backstage where the band was taking a break. When we walked in Johnny Miller, the lead singer, looked up and said, "Are you ready?"

I turned to Mate and said, "Ready for what?"

He just smiled, "You're going to love this..."

The crowd was getting restless, waiting for the band to start again. All the jocks from the other schools were still trying to act tough and impress the girls. The stage lights dimmed and everyone's attention was directed towards the stage.

"Ladies and gentlemen...A special treat for you tonight...Direct from Parma and Franciscan High School, home of Cleveland's Number One High School Football Team...It's the world famous Ethnic T-Shirt Band..."

Entering from stage left came Mate, Johnny and I, dressed in white tank top T-shirts and tacky plaid Bermuda shorts. We had on black socks stretched to our knees as well as cheap sunglasses. The kids in the crowd laughed, seeing the joke but not expecting what came next.

The band behind us broke into the opening riff of "Brown Eyed Girl" and we just took it from there. All the kids started dancing, Mate knew all the words, and everyone knew the chorus.

It was quite a rush. I was up there on stage with a tambourine singing background, and it was my first and only brush with 'stardom' and I loved it. Colleen, my date, was standing in front of the stage, with her eyes on me, and moving to the rhythm of the song.

In the middle of the song during the bass solo, Mate and I just looked at each other, jumped off the stage, grabbed our dates, and started a Congo line that within moments included everyone in the room and snaked through the gym. It was too cool. Mate was in front and led the line out of the gym, through the lobby, and out the front door, where he led everyone around the huge fir tree filled with Christmas lights that stood in front of the school. It was quite the sight seeing all the kids outside, their breaths showing in the cold and everyone kicking through the foot of snow that covered the night.

When we made our way back into the gym and towards the stage, we jumped on and hopped back into the song. We soon had everyone singing the chorus again. When we finished, the crowd went nuts, especially the girls, and every guy in the place was jealous, wishing they were one of us. Every girl in the place for that moment said to themselves, *I wish I had a guy like one of those*.

"Thank you, Rocky River...We love you," Mate yelled to the audience as we exited the stage.

A picture of us leading the Congo line was on the cover of Beth's school's yearbook that spring. When we came back to school after Christmas break, everyone in our school heard about the dance, how we were outnumbered, yet showed everyone up and did our school proud. It really was great when guys we didn't know, and even some teachers, came up to us in the halls and said, "Good Job."

After football ended, Mate and I dedicated ourselves to find out what all this sex business was about. The problem, however, as far as I was concerned, was Mate had Beth and I had my left hand. Advantage Mate. Although I had a great time with Colleen at the dance, and I think she did too, any further interaction with her eluded me. She wouldn't return my calls, and when I did see her, she always seemed to be in the company of some college guy.

Mate had no such problems with Beth. And, what made it worse, I had to listen to him talk about it. It was like I was doing it with them but without any of the gratification.

Every Sunday Beth's parents played bridge at her aunt and uncle's house. Mate would hide up the street until they pulled out, then he'd sneak over and stay until they came home. Often they would be pulling the car into the garage in the backyard and Mate would be sneaking out the front door.

He really liked the sneakiness of it. They would wait until the car pulled in the driveway and into the backyard. When they heard her mom opening the backdoor, they would unlock themselves from each other, and he'd go out the front door and run up the street.

We had a morning study hall together that year and sat at the same table. Every Monday I'd get the play-by-play on the previous Sunday's action.

They started out like most teenage couples did, necking and giving each other sucker bites. He'd walk into study hall with his shirt collar a little loose so all the fellas could see his battle scars. He'd nonchalant the comments he heard, sit down, and tell me how he got them.

For someone who was starting to fall halfway in love with the same girl, I started to really hate his Monday morning comments, especially when they got more graphic. He had to tell me, because being a guy, the second best part about having sex with a girl is telling one of your buddies about it.

Every Monday I heard the previous night's play-by-play. At first nothing big, except if you were a lonely horny high school junior who never had a girlfriend before.

The closer it got to Christmas, the more interesting it got. I remember when he encountered her breasts.

'Hey, guess what happened last night," he whispered across the table to me as I pretended to be totally engulfed in my math homework.

"What?" I casually responded without looking up.

"Tits."

My eyes darted to his. "Tits?"

"Tits."

My mind wandered for a moment. That lucky fucker I said to myself.

"How were they?" I said slightly disinterested, acting like I was working on a problem.

"Unbelievable. Better than I thought." Of course, this just got him started. He then went into a five minute monologue that included an analysis of the shape, texture and color. I got a chubby just hearing about them. (But, to be perfectly honest, at that time in my life, anything gave me a chubby).

"And there was one really neat thing about them that I was kind of worried about. They weren't no pancakes. I mean, when they were standing by themselves they both pointed up slightly. For a sorta large set, I was worried that they would just lay there. You know?"

So every Monday morning until Christmas break I heard about Beth's breasts during second period study hall.

The first Monday we were back after Christmas break, he was uncharacteristically quiet when he sat down in study hall. I knew he had resumed his Sunday night rendezvous the night before, and I was expecting the usual play-by-play.

About half way through the period, as we both worked on assignments, I casually whispered over to him, "Hey, did you go to Beth's last night?"

He looked up from his work and said real seriously, "Yes."

A five second pause.

"How did it go?"

He kept writing with his right hand, took his left hand, stuck his middle finger under my nose, and said, "How does this smell?"

"You got in her pants?" I squealed loud enough to solicit a dirty look from our study hall teacher across the cafeteria. Boy, was I jealous now.

That's were it stood for a month or two until the time he walked in, put his books down, looked at me and said, "Last night it got out of hand."

"What happened?"

"You can't tell a soul this. O.K.?"

"O.K."

"She..." he paused slightly embarrassed, looking around making sure no one was listening. "She touched the big fella last

48

night."

"Hand job!!!" I squealed.

"Hand job," he responded seriously.

"How was it?"

"Unbelievable. I got to tell you this, it feels an awful lot better when someone else does it than when you do it to yourself."

Was I bummed. In my own frustrating sexual non experiences, I felt as if I was being left behind by Mate and some of the other guys we hung around with.

A few weeks later Beth and Mate started to discover oral sex. When he now told of his adventures he made them sound like some drugstore romance novel. "The streetlight's glare was coming through the window while she groped for the buttons to my jeans," he would start out. Then he would go in great detail as she "unzipped my Levi's and played with the elastic of my jockey shorts." By this time, the table was rising in front of me and he continued, "My large erection protruded out..." and on and on he would go describing every part of each action.

One Monday his soliloquies stopped, and it was then that I knew that they had done it. Gone all the way. Hit the home run. Closed the deal. That first Monday we sat in silence doing our homework as we did the next. It just wasn't on Mondays that his behavior changed, I also noticed it as a full time thing. He seemed to be in a funk for a while. When a group of us went to a basketball game together, I noticed Beth and Mate to be in their own little world, hugging and holding onto one another and ignoring the conversations going on around them, talking and paying attention to only each other.

I went a couple of weekends without doing something with him, then we went hanging out one Friday and I ended up staying at his house. As we lay in bed trying to fall asleep, I was startled when he said, "Beth wants to break up."

"Why?" I responded with much surprise.

Pause. "Because all we ever do any more is fuck. If we go out on a date, we do it in the car on the way to and from the movie. If she's over my house, we wait until my parents go to bed, so we can do it on the couch in the living room. And on

Sunday nights, Oh man, I limp out of there when her parents come home."

He went on to explain that she was worried, and he was a little too, that either they were going to get caught by her parents one day, or she might get pregnant. He was confused. He absolutely loved this sex stuff. He absolutely loved Beth. But he knew he was too young to be a daddy, and he knew if something like that happened it would deeply hurt his parents. He never wanted to do that.

A week later he was back to being Mister Happy. "You're in a good mood, what happened?" I said in study hall on a Monday morning. "A great night over Beth's last night or what?"

"Modern science. I owe my new outlook on life to modern science." I was confused for a moment and then remembered freshmen health. "Birth control. Beth got on the pill. Right?"

A shit eating grin crossed his face. "I owe my life to modern medicine."

By now I was really jealous and/or pissed at him, and I would not have been heartbroken if Beth and he ended it. If I wasn't going to have a sex life, neither should he. You might think this was selfish of me, but I know that he would have thought the same way if our roles were reversed. There would be times when the roles would be reversed, and he would have the same attitude towards me. Call it honor amongst thieves.

Mate ended the winter on top of the world, and a big part of that was his relationship with Beth. He had no big cares or plans for the future, and thought things would go on forever the way they were. He had no idea that they would soon suddenly change.

During this whole time my relationship with Beth took all different forms. When we first really got to know her and her crowd, I really liked her. I fell halfway in love with her in a jealous best friend's way, and sometimes wished Mate and she would break up, and then I could go out with her. When I started to date some of her friends, I got upset with her because they were not as affectionate towards me as she was towards Mate, and I had a chronic case of blue balls. She and Mate doing who knew what each Sunday night when her parents went to play bridge, and I was getting nowhere with several of her best friends. I mean, at least she could clue one of them in, huh?

We would double date on those Sunday nights for awhile. She'd have a friend over to study, and her parents would leave for bridge. We'd sneak in after they left. Mate and Beth would go in her room and shut the door. I would be out in the family room with my arm around some dead fish watching some stupid movie on TV. Over the sound of the television, I'd hear giggles and strange noises coming out of the bedroom that would only make me more horny. I'd try to kiss arms, shoulders, necks, and nothing would ever happen.

Some of you readers are saying to yourself, why didn't I get to know the girl first? At that time, I was just another dumb horny sixteen year old kid looking for his first roll in the hay, and I was quite focused on that goal. I wasn't looking for a girlfriend, all I wanted was the mother lode. My routine definitely needed to be refined.

I never saw their breakup coming; neither did Mate, and it floored him. There he was playing the part to the hilt, high school football stud with a beautiful girlfriend, and another year of high school in front of him. He was on a roll, and didn't have a care in the world.

I did think he took her for granted, and one day might screw up. "Nah," he said. "We were made for each other. Nothing will come between us." But I was around them a lot, and sometimes it seemed to me Beth's mind would wander someplace else.

Although it wasn't obvious to Mate, Beth had some personal stuff that was soon to come to a boil. For the first time, their difference in age, although only a year, caused their relationship to have some friction. When someone is thirty-eight and she is dating someone who is forty, nothing is said of it. But the difference between a senior in high school concerned about having to make decisions about the future, and a junior whose only concerns were lifting weights and buying high-powered beer, can be monumental.

Beth was affected by several incidents early in the spring. As guys at all the boys' schools started to be concerned with having to find someone to take to their proms, she was, for the first time, being asked out by several different guys. She would at first say, "Thanks, but, no thanks," but several guys just kept asking her. I would have asked her out, if I didn't know Mate. She was one of these girls whom you weren't afraid to talk to, and who wasn't afraid to talk to guys. She had a great smile, a hearty laugh, didn't smoke, and drank enough to get buzzed, but never enough to get stupid.

She and Mate were still having their Sunday night rendezvous, so she had the disposition of someone who was having regular and satisfying sex once a week. She wasn't out trying to impress other people, she was just being herself.

Beth was at the time when she had to make some important decisions about the future. Do I go away to college, or stay at home? Do I want to go to nursing school, or get a four year degree? Throw in the usual senior year bullshit: proms, pictures, parties, graduations, etc., and her pressures suddenly became quite different from Mate's. Two incidents, both happening within a week of each other, caused a huge riff between her and Mate.

Beth's best friend was her cousin and classmate Monica, the daughter of Beth's mother's brother. The girls had gone through grade school and high school together. They became close during the time Beth and Mate dated because Monica had a similar relationship with a guy named Mike. Mike was a year out of school, lived at home, worked at UPS, and attended Cleveland State.

Both girls shared similar dreams about the future. Both planned on going to school, possibly for nursing. Both planned to enjoy life for the next few years. Marriage was definitely in their futures, but only after a degree was finished, and a few wild oats had been sown.

Both girls also liked to share secrets about what they did with their boyfriends when no one else was around. The kind of things good Catholic girls weren't supposed to talk about. Although everyone at school talked about sex, no one actually talked about what they actually did. Monica and Beth became each other's confidants on such matters.

Mate, as a typical male jock high school junior, did not worry about a thing. Nothing was bothering him; everything was going too good. He was playing the role of the high school football player, going out with the coolest girl we knew, and all this sex stuff he was discovering was better than previously imagined. Plus, he was the only high school kid in America who wasn't having some kind of parental conflict. He had it too good.

The day Monica told Beth she was pregnant was one of those days Beth never forgot. The earth stood still for a moment and everyone directly involved took a big step in the coming-of-age department. Beth went with Monica to the doctor, who only confirmed what she had known for four weeks since her period never showed up. Tears, hugs, eyes staring off into space. No talk of the A word. These were Catholic high school girls of the mid Seventies, and they just didn't do that sort of thing.

Monica and Mike did what had to be done. They told his parents, then hers. Plans were made to do the right thing, and a wedding right after graduation was planned. Mike would keep doing what he was doing, full time at UPS and full time at CSU. They would move into the basement at her house, and preparations were made for the child expected around the holidays.

After the initial shock, it appeared that Monica took it better than Beth. Monica's getting pregnant was just one more thing that made her rethink her relationship with Mate. How she loved him in a high school romance type of way, but she did feel as if she were outgrowing him. She had been ready for what came after high school for quite some time; he was still right in the middle of it. As much as she liked her Sunday night rendezvous with him, and all the other times they fooled around, this Monica thing cast too much stress on the situation. She took her birth control pills religiously, but she knew they weren't 100% safe. Stupid Mike and Monica, they were bound to screw up sooner or later. And what about her plans for the future? Did she want to surrender that to an unplanned baby? Was she ready to handle that if it happened? She realized no way was Mate ready for the responsibility of fatherhood, plus he had one more year of high school left.

Every time she tried to talk about Monica's situation with him, he'd end up changing the subject. On what was going to be the last Sunday that he would go over to her house, she tried her hardest to finally discuss it with him. "At least once can we talk about this?" She said to him as he tried to kiss her neck.

"Oh honey, we don't have to worry about that. We have the protection of modern medicine."

"Yeah, well, just suppose something goes wrong. What would we do then?"

"I guess I'd get my old man to get me a full time job down at his plant and we'd go from there," he said as he made another attack on her breasts.

That would be great, she said to herself, to be a teenage wife of a ten dollar an hour steel worker. Why didn't he take anything seriously? Everything is still fun and games with him. Doesn't he take anything seriously? Maybe it is time to end this, she thought for a moment, until she did what she always did, and responded to Mate's advances as pieces of clothing started to hit the floor.

When she walked into her house the next day from school and her mother said, "Elizabeth come here," she knew she was in trouble.

Her mother was sitting at the kitchen table. An overflowing ash tray told Beth she had been sitting there for awhile. Beth sat herself in the chair opposite her, afraid to look up and make eye contact with her. Is this about Monica or is it something I did? She rarely saw her mom in this mood, mostly when she was mad at her dad for something. But Beth knew she meant business.

"I found these under your bed today," she said as she pulled out a pair of Mate's undershorts and laid them upon the table. Beth filled with complete panic. She started to tremble with fear of what her mother was going to do or say next. Her eyes fixed on the shorts, afraid to make eye contact.

Her mother had planned what she was going to say. If her daughter was sexually involved with her boyfriend, then things had gone too far. She had not raised her daughter to start a family while still a child, and the relationship must end. She also was smart enough to know that if she started to yell, Beth would take things the wrong way and rebel or lie about the situation.

Her calmness surprised Beth. She didn't yell or scream. She kept her voice low and steady, but with the right amount of restrained anger and disappointment to let Beth know she meant business.

"I only want what's best for you. Just see what your cousin Monica put your Aunt Anna and Uncle Paul through. I don't want anything like that to happen to us, especially to happen to you."

"This fall you are going to enter a big exciting world, with new friends and challenges and a whole new social world. You don't want to miss out on all you've planned for because something unplanned happened. Look how you have been lately. You've slacked off in your school work, all this senioritis talk, plus you still haven't decided on which school yet, have you? Did you finish filling out all those scholarship forms yet?"

Beth knew that her mom knew that she hadn't.

"It's time for you to make some adult decisions about a lot of things, including your love life. Your future is too bright. You're too young and have too much in front of you to let anything unplanned bring you down."

Beth knew her mom was right. She knew she was juggling too many things at one time. Her mom was right about a lot of things, especially when she said that Mate was so much younger than she was right now. All he was worried about was football next fall, drinking beer with his buddies, and borrowing his dad's car to come over on Sunday nights. All this stress about school the next year, applying for scholarships, and Monica having a baby was just too much.

She called Mate and told him that she couldn't see him that Friday, and not to come over on Sunday. He just assumed it had something to do with 'this Monica problem,' and that he and

Beth had to lie low for a couple of weeks. A couple of weeks went by, and when they finally did go out he knew something was bothering her. In the parking lot of a McDonald's they had the talk. She was open, honest, and blurted out what was on her mind, relieved to get it out and in the open. "We can't, I can't, go on like this any more. There's just too much shit going on right now and I can't do everything, including having a boyfriend." She told him there was no one else, that he was her first and only love, but it was time to separate, at least for a time.

He was bummed. He did not see it coming. He begged for her to reconsider. She stuck to her guns.

"You think this is easy for me? Do you think things are the same for us? You know where you're going to be in six months, I don't. I have to figure out really soon what exactly I'm going to be doing."

More pleas. He tried his serious eye look, and she turned away. "That's it with you. Every time we start to talk about something serious, you want to fool around."

He tried plan B. He talked about all the good times. Their first date to the Browns game. Her Christmas Dance, his Junior Ring Dance. The notes with the song lyrics they wrote to each other. The Sunday nights at her house when her parents were off playing bridge.

She was swaying, but the look on the face of her mother whom she would encounter when she got home kept dancing across Beth's mind. I must end it now, she said to herself.

She looked him straight in the eye. "Mate, we aren't going to see each other until the summer. Maybe by then all this Monica stuff and school stuff will blow over. I just can't deal with all of this right now, and I would really appreciate you seeing things my way. At least for awhile. Please?" She pleaded with tears rolling down her face.

Beth missed Mate tremendously, but she had a better spring than she thought. The constant worry about waiting for her period disappeared, and when word got out she was a free woman more than one guy asked her out. She went to three proms with three different guys, hers, Ed's, and Iggy's. Because of her grades, she got a full ride to nursing school at Charity

Greg Cielec

Hospital. She played the role of best friend to Monica, helping plan her wedding/baby shower, being maid of honor at the late June wedding, and helping her settle in the small basement apartment that she and Mike moved in to.

Every time Beth would think of Mate that summer, she would think of Monica and Mike living in the basement at Monica's house, with her parents and her four brothers and sisters living upstairs with Monica's stomach getting bigger and bigger, and she would say to herself, *I don't want that.*

She didn't give into her temptations to call or see Mate. That was the way it was going to be. And when the summer came it was wait until the fall. And when fall came, she never gave him her number at school and he was afraid to ask her mother for it. As far as I know, they would go almost two years before they saw each other again.

Mate was bummed out all summer. Everything ended so quickly, he was constantly horny, and no girl he met compared to her.

Years later when I discussed this with Beth, one thing she emphasized was that her mom was right. "I've been angry with her for a lot of things she forced upon me, but when she told me to break it off with Mate the first time, she was right. We really were just a couple of stupid high school kids, and the way we were going, we could've very easily ended up like Mike and Monica."

In his own way, Mate repaid me that spring for the mental anguish he put me through that winter with his Monday morning quarterback sessions of his Sunday night fun and games with Beth.

By the time prom season came around, he was a pretty depressed young man. The fact that Beth would need a prom date always stuck in the back of his mind as the reason they would get back together. But as proms started to come and go he started to realize that she wasn't coming back.

I, on the other hand, finally hit the mother lode.

My main man Thunder Bailes searched me out at school one day.

"Hey, Greg, my man," he said as he approached my locker

57

at the end of a school day. "You are going to do me a big favor and have a good time to boot."

I always loved Thunder Bailes. He and I had been a year apart since grade school, and I had always been smart enough to know that much success on the teams that I had played on through the years was because he was usually on the same team. He was the main man in our school, a three-sport starter highlighted by being an all state free safety in football. He would go on to be a two-time All Big Ten selection in college, and would play for the Philadelphia Stars in the USFL. But back then he was my friend, and someone I admired a lot and was willing to help in his time of need.

He went on and explained the situation. His girlfriend's best friend had just gotten dumped by her boyfriend and was without a date for their prom. She thought I was cute and asked Thunder if I was an available young man. At first I was immediately going to say no, until Thunder explained how little time and effort it was going to be.

"She just wants a date for the dance. She knows you're a busy dude, so you don't have to do any of the other shit. No Cedar Point the next day. No staying out all night if you don't want to. Plus, she's footing the bill, including your tux. Watcha think? If I don't find her a date, I'm going to have a bad time. Debbie and she have been planning this weekend for a year, and if Molly isn't a part of it I'm never going to hear the end of it." He showed me her picture and she looked good, and went over it again and it started to sound O.K. He gave me her number and told me to call her that night.

I went home and would have probably chickened out if I didn't talk it over with Mate.

"What do you got to lose? I know who she is and she doesn't look bad. Plus, who knows, you'll probably have a good time. You'll be hanging out with Thunder, and there will be some other guys there that you probably know. You ain't exactly been knocking them dead by yourself."

I called her on the phone and she seemed nice. "I hate to bother you with this. Did Thunder tell you how I picked you? He showed me the picture of your football team and I thought you were the cutest one of the bunch."

She explained that she and her boyfriend had just split, the prom was already paid for, including her dress and my tux. She didn't want to miss out on her senior prom with her friends. She had been on the prom committee all year, and it would be so disappointing to miss it.

I had the usual high school thoughts in my mind. She was probably a dog in real life. It was going to be a lousy time. I wasn't going to know anybody. Thunder and Mate assured me things would work out, and I said yes.

Even without all that happened, I was glad I did. Thunder's girlfriend went to one of the west side Cleveland schools and I really wasn't expecting that nice of a dance, but it really was. They had it at one of the party centers out by the airport, the food was good and the band was great. We started the day with cocktails at Thunder's girlfriend Debbie's house. Picking up my date was awkward because I didn't know her or her parents, but they seemed fine and she looked nicer than I imagined all dolled up in her prom dress. I had a few beverages to calm my nerves at Debbie's house, and by the time we got to the dance I was feeling no pain.

Molly turned out to be a good time and a great date. The first time we were alone to talk at the dance she turned to me and said, "I can't tell you how happy I am that you decided to do this for me. I was really panicking and in a terrible state of mind for the last several weeks. I just want you to know that I'm going to make sure you have a good time and that you'll never regret coming with me. Plus, you're even cuter than you are in your picture!"

I really did have a good time. Thunder knew most of the people who sat at our table and he kept the conversation and stories going. You can't forget that we were from the number one high school football team in Cleveland and so we could do whatever we really wanted to do and protocol allowed us to do it. A couple of their studs came over and introduced themselves to us, (they had a shitty football year, 2-8, last in their league), and gave us our due respect.

We danced the hokey pokey and the chicken dance, snuck

outside for beers several times, and posed for pictures.

Molly filled me in on her boyfriend who had showed up with some sleazy looking blonde, and made a hard ass look at me most of the night. "He's such an asshole, I don't know what the hell I ever saw in him besides the back seat of his car," she said surprisingly carefree to me. "After next week I hope I never see him again." She explained to me that she was leaving the next week to go live with her father in Arizona. She got a job for the summer working in an office and started at Arizona State in the fall.

By the end of the night we had gotten a little tipsy. Thunder had snuck into the dance some of that fine MD 20/20 that we used to love so much, and I had a nice little buzz going. Molly and I had such a fun time together that I ended up going to the after-prom with her. Since neither of us had planned to go originally, we didn't think we'd get along so well, we had to zip back to her house so she could change. Thunder was going to run by his house and grab some stuff for me.

When we got to her house, she led me downstairs. Everyone seemed to be asleep. The basement had a family room with posters on the walls and ceiling. She pointed towards the stereo and said, "Pick out an album while I go upstairs to change."

I looked at the record on the turntable and it was *Led Zeppelin IV*, which was fine, so I put it on.

I sat on an old couch and looked at the surroundings. She must have some brothers and sisters, I said to myself, as the room looked as if it got a lot of use with records, sports gear, and what have you spread about.

She came back downstairs in a T-shirt and a pair of cut-offs. She sat down next to me on the couch and turned to me and said, "Thanks again for the great time. This has turned out far better than I ever could imagine. Plus, you didn't have to stay to take me to the after prom. That's really nice of you." I just smiled, happy to be there. The night had also gone better than expected for me, and I was ready to go to the after prom and bowl, dance some more, and stay out until the sun came out.

"Listen. You have to do me one more favor. You've done a lot for me already, but I don't think you'll mind this."

And then it happened. I wasn't expecting it. The mother lode. I closed the deal. I hit an inside the park home run off the top of the fence in right center.

It wasn't the best sexual experience I would ever have. It wasn't the most romantic. I was more than a little scared, confused and fucked up to enjoy it completely, but it was the real thing. I was finally on the scoreboard. As it was going on, I kept on thinking 'wait until the guys hear about this one.'

Actually, when we got over a rather shaky start, it went rather well. I was so excited as I tried to put on the rubber that materialized out of who knows where, I shot my load early and sent it three quarters unrolled across the room. By the time we both got out of our clothes and situated on the couch for our second go round, it went as good as expected. We didn't move the earth, but I had at last done the nasty and, boy, was that a load off my mind.

By the time we got back to the after prom, I don't know if anyone had a bigger smile on his face or had a better time than me.

The next day I had to tell Mate about it, and giving him a good play-by-play of the details brought a smile to his face for the first time since Beth had put him on waivers. He then, being a good buddy and paying me back for listening to his adventures all winter, spread the story around our school that I had done the prom queen at John Marshall's prom on prom night. What a guy. Mate made sure amongst the eleven hundred fine young men of Franciscan High School that I was 'Stud for the Day.'

I took Molly out one more time before she left for Arizona. We had another go at it that went a little better, and had one of those mushy conversations of 'if I only would have met you sooner/I'll write you when I get settled in/and call you the next time I'm in town.' Of course, like a lot of good plans at that time, nothing ever happened between us and I never saw her again.

There was one more important moment from that time in our lives that needs mentioning. It was sometime that same school year when Mate started to get really excited about an upcoming concert. From the time I had first become friends with him in ninth grade, he was always dragging me to concerts and dances. He just loved live music, and through these early experiences with him I did, and to this day, still do.

Until that point, he had dragged me to some great shows. When we were freshmen we went with his sister Barb and her friends to see the Beach Boys, Deep Purple and Led Zeppelin. That next summer we went to Blossom and saw James Taylor, America and Sha Na Na. Our sophomore year we got a little exotic and saw David Bowie on his Ziggy Stardust tour, and Bryan Ferry and Roxy Music. I still remember him singing John Lennon's "Jealous Guy." All of these just led up to the concert we would see our junior year at the old Allen Theater on Euclid Avenue.

He came up to me in school one Monday morning and said, "Tell your parents you're staying at my house Thursday. My sister got us tickets to see Bruce at the Allen."

Bruce who? I said to myself. Being easily led as I was at the time, I just shrugged my shoulders.

All week that's all I heard. Bruce this, Bruce that. By the middle of the week I had some idea about whom he was talking about. Mate had his second album, the only person besides Chuck Sudetic at our school who had it at the time, and I did think the song about *skipping school, act real cool, stay up all night*, was pretty catchy. I had heard several times the song that WMMS had started to play on Friday afternoons, with the hoarse vocals, the great sax solo, and with that great line *some day girl I don't know when we'll get to that place we really want to go.* That's all I knew, and that did not prepare me for what happened that night at the Allen Theater.

Up until then we had seen some pretty good rockers. Besides the afore mentioned, this was at the time when it seemed as if Bob Seger played in town every other week and, of course, we thought he was great. This was also during the early days of the Michael Stanley Band, and we had seen them play in high school gyms and open up at big shows for national acts, and they were great. They had not prepared us for what happened that night at the Allen Theater.

Our seats were about halfway down on the floor, and we were surrounded by kids who were just as excited as Mate was to see the show. I got caught up in the enthusiasm, and when he finally took the stage, I stood up and screamed like everyone else. He stood on the stage in a black leather jacket, T shirt, and faded jeans. He reached into his pocket, pulled out a harmonica, and he played the opening to "Thunder Road" and the crowd went nuts. It was still months before the album that it was on would come out, but for the people at the concert who had been chasing him around the East and the Midwest the song was already known and appreciated.

We sat down and settled in our seats as he opened the ballad about being twenty-three and out of luck. The song picked up in tempo, and when he got to the line about *I got me this guitar and learned how to make it talk* he did a little dueling guitar riff with the other guitarist, and we stood up and applauded and never sat down again. Everyone in the whole place stood, clapped, cheered and danced in the aisles for the whole show. He would not sing another ballad until "Sandy" as one of the encores, just rocker after rocker that drove the crowd crazy. As soon as the opening song was over, Mate grabbed my arm and said, "Let's go!" We ran down and got lost in the mess of people standing in the front rows. The ushers tried to stop us, but it was to no avail.

I was mesmerized by what I saw on that stage that night. During "Spirits in the Night" Bruce dove into the crowd and we held him up, passing him above the audience from hand to hand. He then jumped on top of the piano as the opening chords of "Hard to be a Saint in the City" rolled out of the piano. After that he told some story about getting kicked out of a Catholic grade school for pissing in his desk and sang "Growing Up." Then another story about a girl who was so pretty that he and his buddies were afraid to talk to her, that lead into the Manfred Mann classic "Pretty Flamingo." When he finally got to "Rosalita," he introduced it by asking the audience if they were ready for a love song, and he ripped into it when he had us expecting a slow one.

The first encore featured the big black guy on saxophone in

a tune that just brought the house down. Years later I would find out that the song was "Paradise by the C," and the sax player was Clarence Clemons. He stood stage center that night and literally whipped us into a frenzy. I felt my heart pounding and about to burst through my shirt. For the rest of the encores, Bruce took back over and ripped through some rock and roll standards including "Twist and Shout," "The Detroit Medley," and "Route 66." The whole time his band was right with him, including the huge black dude on sax. He had the place going crazy during each of his solos. When it was all over, I remember standing in the crowd outside the theater and everyone being on another emotional level, staring at each other as if we were asking each other, Do you believe that? Mate just stumbled back to where we parked mumbling, "Oh my God, Oh my God..." I was freaking out because someone told us that it was past midnight, πnd that they were on stage for three and a half hours straight.

Since that night I have seen hundreds of shows and the only ones that equalled that one were ones we saw him do up until *The River* album. I've seen everyone. The Who, The Stones, Tom Petty, Zeppelin, and they've all been great. But nothing, absolutely nothing, ever beat those Springsteen shows. Seeing that first show, to know what all this rock and roll thing could do to you, was just as an important coming of age moment to me as my roll in the hay with Molly Henderson or Mate's Sunday nights at Beth's were to him. It was just as emotional as what we did in the fall under those Friday and Saturday night lights, and would stay with us forever.

So, as far as this story goes, that just about ends the high school years.

We didn't have a great season of football our senior year, We went 8-2 and lost to them in a war 31-25. Mate and I had good years, being the only two-way players on our team. We were quite proud of the fact that we did it as non DI talents. None of the big schools were interested in short, one hundred ninety pound white linemen with little athletic ability but lots of heart.

But, boy, did we hear from the small schools. We heard from every school from Whitman College in Walla Walla, Washington, to Utica College in Schenectedny, New York.

I had resigned myself to the fact my athletic career was over, and that I was going to go to Ohio State. I had been in love with the place since we had gone down to watch the state wrestling tournament, and it fit into my financial picture.

My desire to become a teacher and coach did not sit well with my parents, who expected more out of their son than a "lousy job that paid ten grand." I enrolled that fall as an accounting major, but that didn't last too long.

Mate, on the other hand, wanted to go to a small school, something several hours away, play football and be an education major. We spent that winter visiting most of the schools in Ohio. We knew someone at each one, going to frat and dorm parties and drinking much keg beer.

I don't think Mate saw Beth at all that school year. She buried herself in her school work at nursing school and hung around with a slightly older crowd, kids already out of high school a few years, hanging around places out on the far west side.

I got stuck taking my little sisters and their girlfriends to Parmatown Mall for Christmas shopping and I bumped into her and her mom. She looked so much older. I was dressed in my usual high school rags, T-shirt, sweats, varsity jacket, and she gave off a slightly adult-like aire about her.

I told her about what our plans looked like for the future and she smiled and nodded, "Getting away from Franciscan would be good for you guys. You'll like college." When I suggested that we round up some of the crowd from the previous year and go out she just smiled. "We're pressed for time with school and everything," she said, "maybe something next summer."

Mate spent our last year in high school missing Beth a lot, confused and hurt about how things ended between them the preceding spring. Neither of us lacked female companionship. Getting let go by Beth made Mate unafraid to talk to women. He said he was conducting his own field studies. He would say, what else could happen? I, of course, was along for the ride. Since we both swore we were going to go off to college the next fall, we promised not to take any of them seriously. It was a year full of grab ass high school stuff in the back of cars, down hallways at school dances, or in basements during parties.

When Mate finally picked a college, he surprised all of us by picking Ohio Wesleyan. It was the most "eastern" of the schools we had visited, but I think that was what won Mate over. Big stately frat houses, old Gothic classroom buildings, a big, old ivy covered football stadium. Throw in a brand new phys. ed. building, and Mate was hooked. Plus, I was going to be thirty minutes away down old Route 23.

We spent the summer working the jobs his Dad got for us down in the mills, and there seemed to be a graduation party almost every weekend where we ate ham sandwiches and potato salad, and drank massive amounts of keg beer. We both looked anxiously to the fall, and going off to college and the adventures it would bring.

Part Two
Sometime in the Mid to Late Seventies
The College Years

It's the Weekend, yeah
It's another Saturday Night
I could waste my life away but that don't seem right
> *from "Strike Up the Band"*
> *by the Michael Stanley Band*

Gonna take a freight train
Down at the station
I don't care where it goes
Gonna climb a mountain
The highest mountain
Jump off ain't no one gonna know
Can't you see
Can't you see
What that woman, Lord, been doin' to me...
> *from "Can't You See"*
> *by the Marshall Tucker Band*

Great underachievement in the classroom, experimentation with drugs, abuse of alcohol, casual sex at every opportunity, foolish times with irresponsible friends. Needless to say, the years away at college were the best times of our lives.

When Mate came down to visit me after we had both been in school for six weeks, we had the time to analyze our lives and talk about how much fun we were having.

"You got to do me one favor," he said.

"What?"

"Under any circumstances, you can't let my parents know how much fun we're having. I mean, they kind of think it, but they can't know half of it."

"I don't get it."

"I'm telling you the truth. We can't let them know how much fun this really is."

"Why?"

"They think college is really hard, and I'm the first one in my family ever to go away to school. They think it's nothing but study, study, study. My mom asked me on the phone how I'm handling the pressure. Pressure? The only pressure I have is getting to bed before I have to get up to go to class."

And it was true. Whenever we would come home for a break, Mate's mom would always give me a big hug, and she was a big woman and it really was a big hug, and she would say, "My poor boys off at school, studying so hard. I worry so much about you."

For Mate at Wesleyan, every day was a picnic and every meal was a banquet. He was a happy and content young man who spent his time in college working on what he always called his "liberal arts education."

Ohio Wesleyan University is one of the many small liberal arts colleges that dots Ohio. It wraps in and around the town of Delaware, just north of Columbus. Mate spent his first year living in an old ivy covered dormitory on top of a hill. The dorm was co-ed and had no curfew. This was quite a pleasant surprise to someone from an all-boys high school. Mate was able to make the adjustment.

OWU's curriculum called for Mate to take just three classes a quarter, usually each being an hour long and meeting four times a week. You were left on your own the rest of the time to study and do research. Mate, being of above average intelligence and trying to keep up the practice of making every class and keeping good notes, never had a hard time with his studies. He found them enjoyable, and never felt any real pressure to work very hard at them.

At the same time Mate was at Wesleyan, I was down the road in Columbus at Ohio State leading a similar life, and like him, having the time of my life. After four years at a Catholic high school with eleven hundred boys and one good looking typing teacher, I found myself on a campus with over twenty thousand girls, and every one, every damn single one, was pretty to me in her own way.

Mate's life changed forever the fourth week of college his freshman year, when he went through midterm exams for the first time. Coming up through the Catholic schools, Mate had fallen entrapped to the educational philosophy started by the nuns in kindergarten and kept up by the priests through your senior year in high school. Kindergarten, if you can remember back then, was much fun and fairly easy for the most part. Once you get down the alphabet, numbers to one hundred, and how to tie your shoes, you pretty much cruise. But when you and your classmates started to have a little too much fun., Sister Mary Whatever would remind you that it wasn't going to be like this the next year in the first grade. You and your buddies would settle down and be good for a couple of days, making sure the necessary skills needed for the first grade were being attained.

This shit keeps up year after year, and especially starts to get heavy around seventh and eighth grade, and the threat of not making it into high school is enforced. Seventh and eighth grade are a wild time, with the sexes starting to look good to each other and school getting more and more boring. So in all the Catholic grade schools across America, every student heard how tough it is going to be in high school, and how everyone had better straighten their act out. You started getting scared because, God forbid, you didn't want to end up in a public school.

When you finally made it to high school, they separated you by sex to keep you out of each other's pants. After you learned the ropes a little, you found it isn't as hard as promised, and it can be a good time. Make some new friends, play some sports, chase girls on the weekend. But now there were some new twists to motivation by Catholic guilt. First, they told you that you had to have the grades to go to college. Then you had to have the grades to go to not any college, but a good college. The colleges were in cahoots a little bit here. There wasn't a college anywhere that didn't recommend extra classes, filling up everyone's schedules with extra science, math and writing classes.

The teachers in high school had another tool in enforcing guilt to develop study habits and keep your grades up, the names of those distinguished alumni who flunked out of college. That was before you knew that over indulgence in alcohol and pharmaceuticals were the cause of most academic demises, not the ability to handle the schoolwork.

This Catholic guilt method to academic discipline for Mate ended the fourth week of his freshman year at college. He had been good until then, but several instances burst his bubble. First, he did real well on his midterms. He went back to his dorm every night for a week, turned off the stereo, and went over and over his notes until he knew everything expected. Even after all this preparation, he was still scared. After all, this was college. The place where the little man in the back of his head was telling him that it was finally going to catch up to him. All the cheating and conniving through grade school and Franciscan was finally going to nail him to the wall. It never happened.

First English exam:B+. First Spanish exam:A-. First history exam:A-. Mate couldn't believe his grades were so high, that things had gone so well. In a letter to me he told me that he was pissed at himself for the stupid mistakes he had made. He was beginning to realize that if you just keep a little disciplined, this college gig wasn't going to be that hard.

That wasn't the only bit of Catholic guilt that disappeared that fourth week of college his freshman year. Mate was completely enthralled by the girls at school, yet was afraid to really talk to any of them. Mate came from an all boys school and most of his classmates came from co-ed schools. Many of them had gone to prep school, meaning they had been going away to school since grade school. All of them seemed a little more schooled at the fine art of intermingling.

Mate had found it fascinating that the older guys on the football team would talk of having sex with a co-ed so freely over dinner in the dorm. Mate had only gone the distance with Beth at this point, and remembered how hard he had to work for any little piece of sexual satisfaction with other high school dates. Because of his relationship with Beth, Mate had this quasi-idea that fornication was tied into true love. This would all change the fourth week of his freshman year.

Girls were always attracted to Mate. In high school, he was always one of the guys always asked to dances, proms, and Christmas formals. In his freshmen Spanish class, Mate knew the attractive, tall brunette who sat next to him had a thing for him. He would make small talk, and give her an occasional smile. He was interested, but was not sure of what to do. She seemed so exotic to Mate. After all, she was from Long Island and spoke with an accent that Mate found threatening and mysterious.

The Friday night of his fourth week of his freshman year was a night of celebration. Mate had made it through his first serious academic challenge, and the fraternities were heavy into their fall rush. Parties were plenty, and kegs were aflowing. The football team had an away game and most of the freshmen, including Mate, had not made the traveling squad. It would be their first day off since the beginning of summer practice.

It was in the smoky basement of the SAE house, with music blasting and Mate filled with twenty beers and several gin and tonics, that he caught the eye of the girl from his Spanish class. The guys he was with saw the look they gave each other, and immediately razzed him into going over and talking to her. The next thing he knew he was out on the dance floor with her, sweating through a medley of Beatles tunes.

After a couple of dances, sweat was pouring down both of their faces. She suggested that they go outside, and Mate went to the bar to grab a couple of beers and met her at the door.

He handed her a beer thinking to himself, should I try

anything? Will I get anything? God, she's good looking.

As they came outside, she grabbed his hand and said, "Over here," and took Mate onto the other side of a small hill underneath some trees. They were out of sight of the party, yet its sounds were almost as loud as if they were still inside.

Mate found himself with his back to a tree and his eyes locked into hers. Nothing was said, as Mate moved his head forward and planted a kiss on her lips. He was self-conscious. What should I try? I don't want to try too much, she's probably a good girl.

He wrapped his arms around her. She wrapped hers around him. She lifted her knee slightly and tenderly rubbed her leg into his groin. He felt her nipples through her shirt, as hard as rockets and begging to be touched.

The next thing Mate knew was that clothes were flying through the air, hands were groping and grabbing everywhere, and he found himself pinned on the ground with the girl straddled on top of him, her breasts bobbing in his face, totally oblivious to the party less than twenty feet away. Mate was in a state of complete shock and enjoyment.

After 'twice on the bottom and once on the top' she whispered in his ear, "Let's get dressed and go get a beer," and they gathered up their clothes and started dressing. "I'll meet you at the bar, let me tidy up a bit," she said as she headed to the girls' room, as Mate went to get some beers.

She never reappeared, and Mate spent the rest of the evening searching the frat parties trying to find her.

The next morning Mate found himself confused about all that had happened to him and he shared his feelings with Blair Russell, an upperclassman who took a liking to Mate and helped him learn the ropes.

After Mate had finished the part about the night before, Blair looked at him and said, "So, what has you so confused?"

"You mean stuff like that happens all the time?"

"Not all the time, but it does happen."

"You mean I don't have to call her? I don't have to take her out or anything?"

"Not if you don't want to," Blair said as he leaned back in

his chair and laughed. "No, you idiot, don't you see? She just wanted to get laid, just like you. She had a great time. You had a great time. And that's it."

Mate was still perplexed, but ideas and thoughts were coming together in his head.

Mate and Blair were having this conversation over breakfast in one of the dorm cafeterias. They were eating French toast and Mate was staring at a piece on the end of his fork, watching the butter and syrup drip off, when he said, "Let me get this straight. There are girls at this school, good looking attractive girls, who like to go out on Friday evenings, drink lots of beer, and then go out and find someone to have sex with?"

Blair nodded his head and talked through a mouth of food. "Yeah, for the most part. They all do it sooner or later. It's a natural biological function."

"Let me finish," Mate interrupted. "And college is never really going to be that hard. I mean, for the next four years all I really have to do is show up for class two or three times a day, and take some notes and keep up with the reading, and I can go out at night and do things like I did last night." He was still staring at his French toast.

"Yeah, that's about it. It's the best years of your life, and you might as well enjoy them. Everybody who graduates will tell you how they just fly by."

Mate sat there staring at the piece of French toast on the end of his fork, as a slight grin filled his face and visions of twelve years of "Wait until you're in..." disappeared from his mind forever.

We soon found out that college is the closest you ever come to complete freedom, and when your studies got in the way it could really fuck things up. Mate used to always say that it was a vacation that you paid for in advance. You send them a check at the beginning of the year and they feed you, furnish a great place to live, and give you all the opportunities you need to have too much fun.

At Thanksgiving break, I needed a ride home from Ohio State for the holiday weekend. I was given several phone numbers of kids who would be driving back to Cleveland for the weekend from the RA in my dorm.

I gave the first one a call and he said no problem. I told him where I lived, and he told me to be waiting outside my dorm at a specific time. Imagine my surprise when I hopped into the nondescript beater that pulled up, and looked across and saw Tom Haggerty behind the wheel.

"Hi, Greg's the name," I said, trying to act nonchalant toward the best college linebacker in the country.

"Tom. Get in," and we were off, heading up I-71 to the bosom of our families for the holiday weekend.

For the first half hour there was an eerie silence in the car. Traffic out of Columbus and on the way north was brutal, with people heading everywhere for the holiday. Tom had gotten cut off twice, and had mumbled some profanities under his breath.

I was tempted to bring up the fact we had crossed paths in a previous life, but then I thought that would be unimpressive to him. The fact that I had held onto that pass two years earlier in the only defeat that he had experienced in four years of high school football would not be a topic that he would want to talk about. Besides, that high school stuff was old news to him. The weekend before he had just helped the Buckeyes dough pop the Michigan Wolverines on national television to help send us to the Rose Bowl. A stupid high school game was nothing to him anymore.

I thought I saw him staring at me out of the corner of his eye, eyeing me up as if he might have seen me somewhere before. I thought no way. I tried to fall asleep, and when I couldn't, I just pretended that I was.

Glancing over at him out of the corner of my eye, he looked physically imposing even in his street clothes. Although it was cold and wet outside, all he wore was a pair of cut-off shorts and a battered OSU hooded sweatshirt. His legs had muscles upon muscles, rips stretching down the lengths of his calves. He had long, shaggy, brown curly hair, hanging down upon the most muscular neck and upper body I had ever seen.

I started to feel him eyeing me up more and started to get scared. Why's he doing it? What about me didn't he like? Was he going to kick me out of the car?

We pulled into a rest area, parked the car and he muttered, "Piss break." I got out, feeling cramped in the car, and walked around and hit the head.

I got back in the car, closed the door and looked at him. He was giving me the most evil look. I was scared and it showed. Instead of starting the car and getting on our way, he kept staring at me and then he finally spoke.

"Just tell me one fucking thing, will you?" Then a long pause, me shaking in my boots. "Tell me one fucking thing. How the hell did you hold onto that pass? I mean, I have hit kids that hard who have decided to quit the game. Last year in the Michigan game I caused Rick Leach to fumble on an option play, and I didn't hit him half as hard as I hit you. How the hell did you hold onto the ball?" Another long pause, then he shifted personalities completely, broke into a big smile, and said, "I must say, though I hate to admit it, you guys really did kick our asses that day. You really did."

That is how I first met Tom Haggerty. After the smoke had cleared, we found ourselves talking about almost everything. We got into some small talk and it struck me immediately how much the talk was about what average college kids talk about. I mean, here I was really talking to the big man on campus, a big man on a big campus, about where to get pizza, what classes I took, and what I planned to do over the weekend.

We talked about mutual friends we knew from high school, and I brought up Beth.

"What a great chick. How well do you know her?"

I filled him in on Mate and Beth's relationship, and how she had broken his heart last year when we were still in high school and she was in nursing school.

"That sounds like something she'd do. She's great, but her mom is kinda domineering and I think Beth sometimes lives a little too much of her mom's life instead of her own. Her mom always loved my ass because I was Tom All-American Haggerty in everything. But she isn't so nice to Beth's friends that aren't that."

He drove me all the way to my house and dropped me off

at the front door. He surprised me when he refused the ten bucks that I wanted to give him for gas. "Don't worry about it. Just take me out for some beers some night and we'll call it even."

Then he surprised me again and said, "What time Sunday? I have a football meeting at four and need to get back for it. What about sometime around noon? Would that be good?" I mumbled, "Sure," and thanked him again, hopped out and walked towards the front door.

My family never believed me that I rode home from school with Tom Haggerty.

"Yeah, sure, and at Christmas Archie Griffin will drive you personally," my dad said.

They never believed me until Tom called Sunday morning to tell me he was running late and my mom answered.

"Mrs. Stanley, this is Tom Haggerty. Can you please tell Greg I'm running a little late, but not to panic, I should be there by 1:00. I'd sure appreciate it, Ma'am."

She was dumbfounded. *Why would the biggest man on the biggest campus in the country drive me back and forth from school?*, she wondered.

Why did he? And why did he almost every holiday and break after that? I often wonder, even to this day, why Tom Haggerty became our friend. Whenever he did show up in our lives, it was always just to hang out, and meet people, and be the type of guy his regular celebrity life status usually didn't let him.

It was college I.D. Night that Thanksgiving night down at the old Agora. Although we had been going to college I.D. Night since we were sophomores in high school, we felt honored that we were attending as 'legal' for the first time. We were with a whole gang of guys who went to high school with us, most home from different colleges. The place was packed, the rock and roll loud, the beer cold and abundant.

We both immediately turned when we heard her voice.

"Look at you guys. Shirts with collars. Clean jeans. Is that styled hair I see? What a couple of lady killers."

She looked great. Hair slightly on the big side. Breasts slightly on the big side. Great smile. It was great to see her, and I could tell by the look on his face that Mate's heart was melting.

Although she started out talking to both of us, it was only a matter of time before it was a two person conversation and I drifted off into the crowd looking for someone of my own.

The dance floor was packed with sweaty bodies inter-twined. The Michael Stanley Band was playing, putting the finishing touches on their *Stagepass* album. Mate was in heaven, touching and holding her once again.

"God, I can't believe how much you guys have changed. You look so much more, I don't know, grown up."

"I think just going away to college has cleaned us up. New friends, new experiences..."

He held her close. He wanted to say something witty, but was scared he'd screw up. He hoped the song would never end.

"How I miss you guys," she said. That surprised him.

"How I miss you," she said. That surprised him more.

She stepped up on her toes and gave him a long wet kiss on the cheek. That surprised him into ecstasy.

At that moment, with Jonah Koslen singing "Nothing's Gonna Change My Mind" in the background, Beth and Mate fell back in love with each other.

They caught up with me at the back bar. She kissed him one more time and said, "O.K. I'll be at your place Sunday at ten. See you then." She turned towards me and said, "See you Sunday for the Browns game, Greg," and then turned around to catch up with her friends and her ride back home.

Mate turned towards me and was beaming.

"Get that shit eating grin off your face," I said.

He wrapped his arm around me and with a big shit eating grin said, "You know, when you're the best piece of ass in the world it's hard for a girl to forget you."

"Fuck you!"

"Oh, it looks like we're back in business boys and girls," he said as we ordered a round of shots to celebrate.

It was the night before we went back to school. We had

hung around the Majowski house all day, drinking beer and watching the bowl games on T.V. Lots to eat, people coming and going all day. It was time for Beth to leave, and for us to catch our rides back to our schools. The holidays were over. Mate was very apprehensive. Was this a holiday fling or were things back on between them? She said her good-byes, and he walked her up the street to her car.

It was a snowy, chilly, romantic winter night. A clear night with stars dotting the sky.

"Well, where do we go from here?" she said.

"I don't know," he gave the usual male response.

"I've been so happy since we became a part of each others' lives again," she said.

"Me too."

Moments of silence. She thought of so many things. She thought of classes starting at the hospital the next morning and the upcoming semester, her hardest by far. She thought about the girls at school who revolved their precious few free moments around some boy at a far away college, and how she thought that was so high schoolish. She thought about how much fun this Christmas had been, how much she loved him, and loved being with him. She also thought about the differences in their lives at school, and their plans and goals for the future.

He thought about the Orange Bowl and how it started in fifteen minutes, and if we got our asses on the road, he could watch the second half with the fellows in his frat house. He thought about all the girls at school whose company he enjoyed, and what he would have to give up to keep his relationship with Beth. He thought about how in the long run, there was no doubt, she was the one.

"Listen," she said, as he started planting soft kisses on her neck. "I don't want us to fade away out of each others' lives again. But let's be practical, we'll be over a hundred miles apart."

"We can see each other on weekends."

"That's just it. We can't. So much of my school time is on the weekends. I have a lab almost every Saturday, and Sunday is really my only time to get caught up on my reading and studying. Plus I have to get my hours in on my floor sometime."

Her school really did sound like the real deal to him. In a perfect world she would let him go back to college and do whatever he wanted, and she would be patiently waiting for him when he came home for the summer. That would never happen, he thought. But then she surprised him.

"Listen, why don't we just live separate lives while you're at school. I mean, I don't want you to miss out on any of that college life stuff by not dating anyone. We know how we feel about each other. If you want to date someone else at school that's O.K. Just promise me when you come home for the summer I'm the only one. Promise?"

He paused for a moment to fathom what she had said. Is she serious? Did she really say that? He grabbed her and laid a big one on her, and hugged and held her tight before she could change her mind. They promised to write each other and to talk on the phone Sunday nights. She finally pulled herself away, and got into her car.

We sat in the back seat of Old Mate's car as he and Gus drove us back to our respective campuses, and Mate told me about his talk with Beth and about their arrangement for the rest of the school year.

"You lucky fucker," I told him with more than a touch of jealousy. Not only did he have the best girlfriend I knew, he also got the old Carte Blanch card for his life away at school.

What Beth didn't realize at the time was that her idea of seeing other people, and his idea of seeing other people, were two completely different things.

Jack Benny used to say on the *Tonight Show* when he talked comedy with Johnny Carson that the whole trick to it was timing. According to both of them, you had to have good timing to be a successful comedian. Well, if good timing is the key to good comedy, then bad timing was the key to Mate and Beth's relationship the second time around, just as it was during their first relationship.

There is a cliché that is becoming increasingly popular with

T.V. commentators when a professional football team doesn't play very well. The announcers often say that the players aren't all "on the same page." That term seems to apply really well to Mate and Beth during their attempts at having a relationship. In fact, for two people who were so in love with each other at various times, being at different stages in life, on different pages, really brought an end to their relationship more than once.

You have to remember that Beth was a year older than us, and always seemed to be making the next step in life when we were still firmly entrenched in the last one. Nowhere was this more of a problem for their relationship than when Beth was finishing nursing school, and Mate was still at Wesleyan.

Their lifestyles at their respective schools were so different. Beth entered the nursing program at Charity Hospital, which borders downtown and a slum masquerading as public housing. Her three years of nursing school were hard, demanding, and very structured. Her schoolwork consisted of clinical classes, labs, working in the hospital, and lectures. School took up her day from the moment she woke up, until when she closed her last book around midnight. Her studies also took up much of her free time on the weekends.

Life in the student nurses' dormitory was very structured, and rules very strict. There was a ten o'clock curfew during the week and midnight on the weekends. No T.V. was allowed after eleven and you had to be buzzed in and out of the building. If you got caught with a guy in your room, you got expelled. Her three years of nursing school were no picnic, and it was something Beth couldn't wait to get over. It was a seven day a week endeavor. Things were real serious at Charity Hospital's nursing school, and everyone was expected to take it seriously.

Mate, on the other hand, when they started their relationship again, was in the middle of his freshman year at what at that time was one of the premier liberal arts party schools in the Midwest. And, twenty-five miles down the road, his best buddy from high school was at the granddaddy of big time party schools. We were both at that stage where we were totally in love with college life, and thought it was going to last forever.

We were the new kids at our respective universities, realizing that the academic side of things really wasn't that hard. Mate loved it even more than I did. He lived in a coed dorm that never seemed to have the lights off. His school was one of those where most guys joined a frat, so he joined one that could only be described as a nontraditional fraternity. The place was out of hand. You can't forget that we came out of a Catholic high school with a thousand guys and one attractive typing teacher to look at every day for four years. We both came a little unwound.

You can't forget what time it was either. When we were off to school we were in that window of time between the sexual revolution of the late Sixties and Reagan Conservatism of the early Eighties. College dorms were coed, and had twenty-four hour visitation. The drinking age was eighteen, and keg parties were a way of life. States were decriminalizing pot, and the sweetleaf was always in the air in my dorm and I'm sure in Mate's, too. AIDS was still a thing of the future, and the worst thing you got around our schools was the crabs. We were still riding high on the coattails of Sixties liberalism.

No one I knew at that time was riding the coattails more than my buddy Mate. Now, I was no angel at that time myself. I have four years of report cards that document this, but Mate surpassed me. I tried to keep up, but gave up after a gallant effort. He was the right person in the right spot with the right people at the right time. And no one had a harder time understanding this than the woman back home he loved.

Mate wanted to do everything and miss out on nothing. He would always say it was part of his 'liberal arts education.' At my school all the complete derelicts who took eight years to graduate were liberal arts majors. At Mate's school, everyone was one.

The first time that winter that Beth planned to visit Mate, he had planned on being on his best behavior. This was after his French toast talk with his friend Blair, and he had been partying pretty hard since he had come back to school after Christmas break. He was enjoying himself tremendously, but he missed

Beth and was excited for her visit. She was just going to come down for a Sunday. She did a double in the hospital on Saturday, getting off after midnight. She woke up at seven, and made her way down I-71 to Mate's school, arriving around nine.

Her plan was to have a typical college day with him. Now, what she envisioned as a typical college day and what Mate usually did were two different things, but he had planned the day with her best interests in mind. Mate was going to take her to breakfast in his dorm, show her the campus, and even planned to study together in the library for a while. She was going to leave after dinner, so she got back to her place in plenty of time to get ready for Monday morning.

Mate had planned to take it easy Saturday night and hang around his room, and even clean it up a little. He didn't want to be tempted by the parties at the frats or the action downtown in the bars. He wanted to be bright eyed and bushy tailed for Beth the next morning.

The way it was planned, and the way it turned out, were two different things. A friend from the football team stopped by with a twelve pack to see what he was doing. Another couple of guys stopped by with a new baggy filled with that killer weed. Mate figured a little of this and a little of that wouldn't hurt him. Some girls from upstairs heard his stereo and came down to see what was going on. The next thing you knew his room was filled with a dozen kids and it was almost three in the morning. His room was trashed and he was trashed. After everyone finally left, he figured he would put his head down just for a minute before he was going to start to clean up. He was soon sound asleep.

The next thing he heard was a familiar voice as Beth tried to wake him up, "Mate, Mate, would you please wake up?"

"Huh, Huh," he replied, focusing his eyes. He saw Beth, then his room, and he had one of those time out of mind moments. What is she doing here? Oh my God, she's here to see me!!!

"I don't know what's a bigger mess, you or your room," She said in a slightly serious voice.

Mate didn't know what to do. They both looked around the

room. Empty beer cans everywhere, along with a spent bottle of Jose Cuervo. Overflowing ash trays and records spread out, many out of their jackets. A bong was sitting on his dresser.

Mate knew she wasn't happy. He hadn't been there to meet her on the front steps. His room was trashed. He was still slightly buzzed. He had to figure some sort of damage control.

But when their eyes focused on each other, he didn't have to worry. They had gone over a month without seeing each other, and the magic was still there. She leaned down to kiss him, he pulled her down next to him kicking the door closed at the same time. It took only one look to get their bodies inter-twined with each other.

When they came up for air, the rest of the day went as planned, except for one constant theme. Planned or unplanned, everywhere they went they encountered girls who said hi to Mate in what Beth perceived as an overly friendly style.

It started after they finally climbed out of the sack, but before they went downstairs to the cafeteria, when one of the girls from upstairs came down to claim some albums. She showed up in just a T-shirt and underwear.

"I just thought I'd get these back before they disappeared," she said, as she grabbed several and put them back in their jackets.

Mate introduced her to Beth. "You're a lucky girl. All the girls in this dorm think he's a sweetie," she said as she went out the door. Mate just smiled at Beth; she didn't smile back.

When they got to the cafeteria for a late breakfast, it seemed every girl in line said hi to him. The only table they could find was with some of the girls from the night before, who were busy trying to piece together who went home with whom. Mate introduced Beth around, they all said hi and smiled, then got back to their conversations.

The same thing happened when they got to the library. Every girl who walked past his table seemed to say hi or throw him a smile, and Beth was not real thrilled about it.

"They're just friends," he said. And most of them were. But she was starting to realize his idea of dating other people while they were separated, and her idea, might be two different things.

That spring Hags and I were driving home to spend Easter Sunday with our families when he asked me, "How's your plans for next year coming? Did you get that house you want for sure?"

"I think so. I got just a couple of more things to iron out."

"Do you still need one more guy?"

"Yeah. Know anyone?"

"Yeah. Me."

"You?" I said very surprised. Why would he want to live with us?

"Yeah. Me. I would really like to spend more time around some normal people. If I don't get out of that football dorm I'm going to go crazy." He went on to explain how he had no privacy, and there were just too many distractions being around the same guys all day and all night. He just couldn't get any studying done. "Most of those guys don't give a shit about school work because each one thinks they're a lock for the pros. I know I got a good shot at the pros, but if I don't graduate my parents will kill me."

When I returned for my second year at The Ohio State University, and our first year at the great house on North Campus, my roommates were three washed-up, former mediocre high school jocks and everyone's pre season first team All-American linebacker. The big man on a very big campus. Tom kept his mailbox and took most of his phone calls at the football dorm, but he lived with us for the next three years, including the two quarters after his rookie year with the 49ers when he came back to finish his degree.

It worked out for the reasons he wanted it to. He fit in with us real well, and kept his football mentality and ego over in the practice facility.

He really loved our monthly trips up to party with Mate and his friends at Wesleyan. On our campus, or anywhere in Columbus for that matter, Tom couldn't go anywhere without people asking for his autograph, or some drunk trying to be his buddy. Up at Mate's school, although it was only a half hour away, he loved to chase the girls because there was a challenge to it. You couldn't believe the girls he had stashed away around OSU. North Campus, South Campus, over in the Towers, at almost every sorority. Every girl knew who he was, and many of them wanted to do the big man on campus (and sometimes, when the stars were aligned right, his roommate). At Wesleyan it was a challenge. Most of those girls didn't have a clue of who he was. Shit, they thought soccer and lacrosse were actual college sports, let alone knowing Tom was the real deal.

The one time at a party when he was totally honest with one of Mate's female school friends, it backfired. When she asked him if he played any sports at his school he said, "I'm the captain of the football team at Ohio State."

She replied without hesitation, "No you're not. You're just another of Majowski's lying beer drinking buddies from back home."

If it wasn't bad enough when he lived in the dorm, Beth really hated it when Mate moved into his frat house his sophomore year.

Mate's frat house was one of those you only found at schools where almost all the guys joined a fraternity. It was what we used to call a non fraternity man's fraternity. Although they belonged to a national, and they were situated on a big circle surrounded by some pretty serious houses at a college with a rich fraternity tradition, the guys in Mate's house just didn't give a shit.

Down at OSU I lived on a great floor in the Towers my freshman year. It was a fun crowd and most of the guys didn't pledge a house, and those who did that was their thing, but I think they always remained tighter with the guys from their frosh floor than 'the brothers' at their houses. I didn't need that frat bullshit. Hell, I had played football at an all boys high school, and if that didn't give you the old ties that bind, I don't know what did. During my sophomore year, most of my crowd found houses up near north campus, and that area became our home base. We hung out at some great bars like the Northberg, the Out-r-Inn, the Varsity Club; had houses filled with girls on our block; and everyone was always throwing some kind of party. The place we lived in had a big old porch that stretched the width of the house and down one side. It was the place on Saturday mornings in the fall, and almost every afternoon in the spring.

We had friends then at what seemed like every campus in Ohio, and partied at one time or another with each of them. But nothing was like what Mate and the boys had going at Wesleyan.

Those guys were out of hand. We used to call their place 'Woodstock,' like what's going on at Woodstock this weekend? He lived for three years in a series of rooms in the basement of the house that emptied into their dining room/dance floor, that emptied into the backyard and their basketball court. In his room was always a fridge full of beer, a bag or two of dope, a great record/tape collection, and a giant stack of sports and porno magazines. A guy could entertain himself for weeks there if he chose to do so.

Made up of mostly washed up high school jocks and guys with the brains but not the ambition or grades for the Ivy League, the guys in his frat just didn't give a shit. All Mate's crowd wanted to do was get good enough grades not to flunk out, get fucked up as much as possible, squeeze in a little b-ball and touch football, and have as much sex with as many girls as they could. They were simple young men, not pretending to be anything but what they were.

Mate's boys did not take any of that real fraternity shit seriously. They hated their national, and ignored them as much as possible. They fired one of their cooks, took turns cooking on the weekends, and threw the extra money into the beer fund. Instead of chasing some stuck up sorority girls to hang around their house, Mate and the boys actively recruited any and every good looking or hard partying girl who wasn't in a sorority, or didn't give a shit about what the other sorority girls thought, to hang out at their place. There was a PBR button on their Coke machine, draft flowing constantly behind the bar, dope plants growing under infrared lights in the upstairs dormers, and rock and roll being blasted constantly.

Mate's house had the most unique group of guys in it. His

being one of those so-called national colleges, he had room-mates from all over the country. He had one short friend from Michigan they called Horse, who had a dick down to his knees and who loved to shake it around. He had another friend named Dickie who was obsessed by the 'big three,' catching a buzz, sex and basketball. Another group of guys lived in the attic, called it the opium den, and you could always find a good game of bonging for buffaloes in session. Mate was real tight with Solly, a big dude from Jersey. Mate and he would split a case of Little Kings and then listen to the first three Southside Johnny albums in a row, singing every word together at the top of their voices. He had another roommate from Texas. They would split fifths of I.W. Harper and Two Fingers tequila, and then go riding back to Luckenback, Texas with Waylon, Willie and the boys. There was a contingent of Cleveland boys, and every Friday afternoon they would drink POC's and listen to Mate's tape of the old Friday afternoon ritual on 'MMS, with Kid Leo washing up and punching out and then "Born to Run," "Friday on My Mind," and "Cleveland Rocks." Then when they were nicely buzzed, they would "Strike up the Band."

Of course, Beth hated it there. She just couldn't stand everyone having so much fun while she had to work her ass off. Too many drunks and druggies. Too many irresponsible people. Too many free spirited women who did what the fuck they wanted to do, when they wanted to do it. Mate's theory was deep down she was pissed off because of her own decision to go to a super hard, super strict, all girls Catholic nursing school twenty minutes from her parents, while other people were hundreds of miles away, having a good time and not feeling guilty about it.

Mate and his crowd would try almost anything, with the rationalization of it being part of our 'liberal arts education.' I'm sure Henry David Thoreau and Ralph Waldo Emerson never considered skinny dipping, happy hour and casual sex in any of their philosophical essays, but if they would've spent some time with Mate and the boys, those topics would have surfaced somewhere in some long ago book.

Beth and Mate had made the agreement that they both

could see other people when he was away at college. Of course, that had a different meaning for each of them. For Beth, it usually meant a movie and then some beers and a pizza with an old friend from high school or someone she met at the hospital, before being back in her hospital dorm room by the midnight curfew. She would go back to her room and stay up writing Mate letters about how she missed him, and how she couldn't wait until the next school break when they were both away from the pressures of their school work and could spend time with each other.

For Mate, it was a completely different story. Away from home and out of an all boys high school, he found himself a happy volunteer in the end of the sexual revolution. He would later say nothing but the truth, "I just couldn't help myself."

Before I go any further, let's have a few hundred words about sex. Sex is a natural biological function, not to mention how it could also mess with your head during times of un-planned abstinence. I would find out years later when on the threshold of middle age, there is nothing better than a passion-ate night of sex with someone you are deeply in love with, and who feels the same way about you. But let's be realistic, how much did you know about that stuff when you were in college? Almost as much as you knew about almost everything else, jackshit. Think back on your life and remember the times you confused sex with love. Think about the poor fools who didn't figure out the difference until they had two kids in a dead end marriage.

Those of us who went off to college, girls as well as guys, all had a chance to go through what we used to call our "sleazy stage." Even my sisters went through it when they went off to school. Going off to college gave you the unique circumstances to do all the bad things you ever wanted to do, enjoy most of them, and get them out of your system before you had to venture out into the real world. Anybody who didn't take advantage of that freedom while away at college fucked up. And many people who didn't go away to college, didn't go through their own sleaze period until it was too late or embar-rassing, as thirty year old divorcees with two kids leaving happy hours with a different one night stand each week, or unfaithful husbands dropping a hundred bucks a week at tittie bars.

The added bonus for those of us who were derelicts away at college was, after you graduated, you found out that all the bad things you did when you were away didn't count. That's right. If you don't believe me, ask anyone who did it. They will tell you when it was all said and done, it just didn't matter. Honest.

The straw that probably broke the camel's back occurred at the end of Mate's sophomore year. Beth hadn't been down to visit him since the fall, and she hadn't seen him since he came home for Easter. She thought a surprise visit on a Thursday night would be just what the doctor ordered to spruce up their relationship, and tie both of them over until he came home for the summer. She, however, did not realize that it was *Apocalypse Now* night at Mate's fraternity.

Beth finished a Thursday afternoon lab at the hospital and felt stressed and fatigued. She did not want to go back to her dorm and listen to her roommates bitch about how hard their classes were. She didn't want to drive home for the night and face her parents just to get a free meal. She was thinking of Mate and missing him. He had told her the previous Sunday on the phone how he had a tough week coming up, with a major test scheduled for Friday. She pictured him at the library at his school, looking over his notes and studying hard that night for the big test. Why don't I drive down there and surprise him? Maybe take him out for a pizza as a study break? It would be just like normal college kids do. It won't be a weekend night, and his school won't be in the middle of some big party.

Mate's poli sci prof had to go to Washington on some big secret mission and pushed their test back to Monday (like it really mattered). Mate took advantage of the situation to indulge in some heavy duty partying, and really throw himself into *Apocalypse Now* Night. Mate and the boys decided that it should be all fun and games, instead of the usual hazing of their frat's new pledges. The night before they had taken all the pledges to see *Apocalypse Now* at the local movie house. The next night they gathered all the pledges up, and told them that one of the actives had been kidnapped and that they were to go find him. As the pledges scavenged the campus looking for the kidnapped active, they encountered many scenarios that alluded to the movie seen the night before. It sounds pretty childish, but Mate and the boys put more effort into it than they usually did into their studies.

While Beth was driving down from Cleveland worrying about poor Mate studying for his big test, and thinking how happy and surprised he was going to be to see her, Mate and the boys spent the afternoon getting ready. The first thing they worked on, of course, was their buzz. Beers, bongs, and for the more adventurous, a few other things got them in the right frame of mind. Then they all got dressed in military fatigues, complete with a variety of complex play guns and ammunition bought and/or lifted from the local Fisher's Big Wheel. Faces darkened, they put several patrols across the campus that the pledges encountered in search of the kidnapped active. At each spot the pledges were told they had just missed the captive, but had to do something before they journeyed on.

At one dorm room the twenty-five pledges smoked a bag of dope, and they killed a keg of beer at another. At each designation the Doors "The End" played over and over again, and porno films were projected on the walls. While on their journey they 'surfed' through the snow, down the side of a hill. In one of the study rooms in the old library down on campus, they met hostile fire while running through, and had to put on a gun battle for the seventy or so serious students who were there studying for Friday tests. When everyone got back to Mate's frat, the actives had turned off all the lights and hung Christmas lights across the front of the house. They had a huge bonfire on the front lawn that exploded into flames when the pledges finally made it back, eerily resembling the final river scene from the movie. Actives were screaming at each other, *Who's in charge here?* And the response was, *I thought you were!* "The End" blasted so loud half the campus could hear it.

It was just a night of good clean fraternity fun for Mate and his friends. Everything happened according to plan except the surprise visit by Beth. When she walked in on Mate and his roommates in full army fatigues, faces shoe polished, buzzed into the comfortably numb zone, Mate was so surprised. Beth didn't know what the hell was going on, but she just assumed like most college kids Mate and his friends would be studying on a school night. Mate told her quickly about his test being postponed, the new frat tradition she was about to observe, and how happy he was to see her again. She immediately knew that he had quite a buzz packed on, and was more than slightly confused about the fact that all this was happening on a Thursday during a normal school week. It lent credence to her hunch that there was more and more partying going on, and less and less studying for Mate and his roommates and friends.

Beth got to observe most of the night's festivities first hand. When she got up early the next morning to make it back for her first class, she saw the trashed frat house with the remnants of the previous night's carnage, and saw all the girls getting out of the house in the early morning, going back to their own rooms to get ready for the day. She said to herself, *I am never coming down here ever again.* She would make just two more visits, including one more surprise trip the following fall.

The next turning point of their relationship came when we were going on spring break.

You have to look again at the different stages Mate and Beth's lives were at. Beth was finishing up her last year of three very structured years of nursing school, with labs, practicals, and intense intern hours. There was no messing around. Beth couldn't wait to finish school, start her career and get on with her life.

Meanwhile, Mate and I were in the middle of our second of four fun filled years of beer, parties, girls, spring break trips, and, yes, a class or two. We were still thinking that college was going to last forever. We had no clue or cares about careers, and life after college seemed very distant.

It was definitely yet another chasm in Mate and Beth's relationship. Mate, of course, saw no problem and laughed off any concerns. Beth, of course, saw it as an another sign of Mate being immature and caused her to doubt his future, starting to believe the notions planted in her head by her...Wait a minute, I'm getting ahead of myself. I remember Mate calling me ...

"I'm in trouble."

"What for?"

"Beth wants me to skip spring break so I can stay home and go to Mary Kay Gallagher's wedding. You aren't going, are you?"

I had already gotten the riot act read to me by Colleen, with whom I was having a bit of a back home romance of my own, but I stuck to my guns. "Miss a spring break after the time we had last year? No fucking way," I said.

"That's what I'm going to say, too. These girls are just too damn serious at times. You know they could both use a spring break, to lighten 'em both up. Of course, without us!" And we both laughed.

So "the girls" stayed home, went to Mary Kay Gallagher's wedding without their "steadies," and felt miserable because they had to "apologize" for us not being there. We heard all about it for a long time after, and we should have viewed that as a sign. But we were just too young and immature to realize such wise adult-like wisdom.

We went on spring break and had a blast. Our traveling entourage was half guys from Mate's house, and half guys from mine. We stayed at a place called the King's Crown Motor Inn in Lauderdale, and had ten fabulous days of sun, beaches, girls, beers, parties, and other such merriment.

Looking back on the situation from a distance of many years, I am so glad I didn't waste a spring break with a great group of friends, many unseen now for years, to go to what turned out to be the first of several marriages of a bitching insecure woman who tried to act grown up way before her time.

College was the best time of our lives, and spring break was the best time in college. This was when Lauderdale was still the spring break mecca, when the drinking age in Florida was still eighteen, and they let you do almost anything as long as nothing got broken and nobody got hurt.

We had three or four rooms for twenty or so guys and ours,

of course, was party central. The bathtubs were always filled with beers, girls coming and going, music blasting, only minutes of sleep at a time.

Everywhere we went that vacation we saw kids we knew from Cleveland. Some of them knew Beth and the girls, and word filtered back that we were seen intoxicated in the company of some fun-loving girls in the middle of the afternoon in some bar. That did not sit well back home. Oh well, we said at the time. Too fucking bad!!

The summer after our sophomore years at college, and after Beth's last year of nursing school, Mate and Beth's relationship was once again at the crossroads.

Beth was happy to be done with school and in the work force, getting paid for the things she had been doing for nothing while in school. She got an apartment with Colleen over in the eastern part of Lakewood, in the nice area up near the lake. They were both working full time and started their real life, including making new friends.

We came back from college pretty much unchanged from the year before. Mate's dad once again got us well paying jobs down in the mills, and we spent every day of the summer looking forward to the day we went back to school and our country club slamhead lives.

Mate and Beth had a constant running conflict that summer that never was resolved. Beth did not want another two years of being separated from Mate. And, she'd be damned if she was ever going to spend any more weekends, especially two years of weekends, visiting him in that 'god damn zoo fraternity house.' She did not think highly of the life of those who went away to college.

Mate had no desire to do anything but go back to college and live the good life. Beth tried and tried to get him to think about transferring to Baldwin Wallace or Cleveland State, so he could live at home and be near her. "Think of the money you could save," she would say. "We could save some money for the future."

He would just shake his head no. "I love it at school. I'm

getting the education I want and I'm having a damn good time, too."

Too damn good of a time if you asked Beth. Although they fought over this, they were constantly together over the summer and I could never imagine them living without each other.

At that point in time, I don't think Mate realized or appreciated how much Beth loved him. She just glowed when she was around him. She was always gently touching him, even when it was just a finger tip upon his knee when we would go see the Indians together.

It was the last summer for us together with the crowd we had been hanging with for several years. Except for Mate and Beth's running argument, it was a fun summer of Indians games, Parties in the Park, street festivals and trips to Cedar Point. Many times it was Mate and Beth and me and Colleen, and I just saw it as a carefree summer during the most carefree time in my life. I had no idea that when we both headed south again for school, how much our lives would change in such a short time.

When we went back to school that year, two typical carefree college juniors with nothing on our minds but two more years of the good life, Beth entered the real world. She worked rotating shifts at Charity Hospital, bought a Firebird, and moved out. Many of her girlfriends and classmates were either married or planning weddings. Some had already started families. Beth, in some respects, was just passing time until that moment came in her life.

She was quite confused about Mate. Oh, how she loved him, but did he love her as much? She was upset that he would not stay home for school. Several of her friends dated guys from local colleges, and she would have loved to have a relationship like that. And why did he have to turn into such a derelict down there at school? Boy, did she hate his whole college scene. She hated all the openness to drugs and sex. She hated all the girls she considered sleazy, who traded boyfriends weekly. She hated the fact that no one down there seemed to take school seriously, and that their school work seemed to always take the backseat to partying, drinking, and having a good time.

She was not pleased with Mate's plans for the future. Everyone said he would make such a great sales person, with his sense of humor and his happy disposition and personality. But he had his heart set on being a high school teacher and coach. And, as her mom would often remind her, what kind of life will they have together if he did become a teacher? At that time the starting pay for teachers wasn't much over ten grand, and colleges across the country were reporting all time lows of education majors, with the low pay being the main reason. Many young men were going to Wall Street or law school or for MBAs, but not many were going into education. Teaching at that time was considered a dying profession.

It only took her a couple of weeks to get tired of the same old social scene. Mate was back at school, and going out with the girls two or three nights a week got old fast. She occasionally was asked out but by no one special. She almost blew it off when one Friday she was asked by some old nursing school classmates, who she hadn't seen since the spring, to get together down at Fagan's for a night of beers and catching up.

In the four months that they hadn't been together, there was so much to talk about, who was working where and who was seeing whom, and the night was quite fun. Some time over the course of the evening, the table of nurses merged with the table of young lawyers next to them, and one of them switched seats with a buddy, turned towards Beth, smiled and said, "Hi, my name is Steven O'Brien."

She was immediately struck by him. Tall, handsome, dark wavy hair with a touch of a receding hair line. He was casually, but expensively dressed in the preppy outfit of the day: Oxford shirt, khakis, and top siders. Big smile, intense eyes.

In the small talk that followed, she found out all about him. He was not quite thirty, a lawyer, and lived in his own condo in Westlake.

At the end of the evening when the bar closed, she paused slightly before she accepted his invitation of dinner and a movie the next night. She thought it would be better than sitting at home or going out with the girls two nights in a row, and she didn't think long about her friend over one hundred miles away.

What she found the next night was that Steven was everything that Mate wasn't. He picked her up in his new Cutlass, and when she answered the door he greeted her with a single red rose. He took her to Heck's Cafe down in Ohio City for dinner, at that time one of the city's hippest restaurants (probably still is). He took her out to Westgate for a movie, and then stopped at one of the new yuppie watering holes on Detroit near the Rocky River. He dressed like a young man right out of GQ, told her about all the important cases his law firm was working on, and asked her to spend a day sometime the next week out on the lake on his family's sail boat. He blew Beth away.

She had just spent her typical summer dating Mate. A typical summer date consisted of picking her up in his dad's beater '67 Chevy Impala (after the Woody finally died on us), waiting in the driveway for her so he didn't have to face her mom. They would then go to the Stadium to sit in the bleachers, watching the Tribe usually get their butts beat by the Yankees or Red Sox or anyone else in the American League. While on their 'date' they would bump into more than a few of his buddies (present company included), and we would all sit together paying, as Mate use to say, a cheap cover charge to drink warm over-priced beer while the worst team in baseball played in the background. I don't care what you say, they were good times.

We would then all head for some cheap bar, the Tam in Lakewood or Baron's or Tommy's in Parma. Then Beth and Mate would end the night having sex in his backseat, after munching out at the Red Chimney or The Big Egg. It differed greatly from what she started to do with Steven.

Beth found herself in unfamiliar territory, with strong feelings for two different guys. At the beginning she didn't really worry about it, enjoying the fact that she had a regular social life, and someone handsome and dashing to take her around town.

Beth's parents, of course, especially her mom, loved Steven.

Again, he was everything Mate wasn't, and especially a lawyer. Beth's mom made it her mission that her daughter forget about her boyfriend away at college, and get closer and closer to this new beau.

Steven played his cards right. It was obvious to many from the beginning that his feelings for Beth were strong, yet he was patient and played the role of the perfect gentleman. He always took Beth to the nicest places, and always listened to her tell about her patients on her floor at work and all the loose gossip from around the hospital. When he finally met her parents, he over-charmed them, something her mom thoroughly enjoyed. He did not pressure Beth into a sexual relationship. She told him right from the start about her boyfriend at college, and Steven patiently waited for the right moment when he hoped she would be ready to melt into his arms.

When that moment came, it was a complete surprise to Steven, coming when it was least expected. They had gone out to a movie and dinner on a Friday, and the night had ended on a bad note when Beth told him that she was going to drive down the next morning to see Mate. "I haven't seen him since August," she said. "And," with a slight smile and a kiss on the cheek, "I really have to see him to sort out all these mixed feelings I have."

As she drove down that Saturday morning to see Mate she tried to separate all of her feelings and look at both relationships. She loved being with Steven, and he opened up a whole new world for her. She liked the normalcy of it, and she felt for the first time like an adult. She also loved being with Mate, and still anxiously awaited each of his letters, and often fell asleep at night wishing he was in bed with her and they were making love. What was she going to do?

Imagine Steven's surprise that afternoon when he was sitting around bumming that Beth had gone off to see Mate, and probably to spend the night with him. He got up to answer the knock on the door and it was Beth. She was upset, and her eyes were red from crying for 120 miles. She jumped into his arms and said, "Please just hold me."

It was late that afternoon in the bedroom of a young west

side lawyer that Beth made love to the second man in her life.

"And so this is it?" She said, trying to look him in the eyes, and that just made her angry, so she looked around at the surroundings, and that just pissed her off even more.

"I don't know what else I can say. I've told you my side of the story over and over. I don't know why you're being so impatient."

"Impatient...it has nothing to do with me being impatient. It has something to do with you."

"With me? You're the one who is changing...you're the one trying to act like some big grown up."

"Damn it Mate, we are grown ups. Can't you see? I'm done with nursing school. It's time to think about life in the real world. You can't go on living in this fantasy world you've created for yourself. Look at yourself. You've regressed as a person. The long hair and the earring. Jesus Christ! You really do look like a pirate."

Mate sat there taking it all in. He had nothing new or more to say. He had said over and over again what his position was. He had almost two more years of school left, and he was going to enjoy them. He loved and cared for her, but it just wasn't the right time to make any big plans. Shit, he said to himself, he didn't know how he was going to get through Environmental Chemistry, let alone make plans for life after college. How could she be so fucking serious?

"So this other guy... is he a better man than me?" He said looking dead into her eyes.

She stared back at him for a silent long moment then looked away, tears coming out of her eyes.

"I don't know if he is a better man than you but he's a better person. HE'S FUCKING NORMAL!!! He wears underwear and socks and goes to work every day and church on Sundays, and I never have to apologize for him. He cares for me and he tells me he wants to..."

"Wants to what?"

She couldn't just come out and say it. She stuttered...turned away and then just blurted it out, "He tells me he wants to marry me."

Mate was floored. There it was, his worst fucking nightmare out in the open. He was so afraid of what was going to come next.

"And what did you say to him?"

She again turned away. Long silence and more than a little tension in the air.

"WHAT DID YOU SAY TO HIM?"

"I said I would think about it."

Mate was stunned. He sat down and stared off into nowhere. He tried hard to gather his thoughts. "Let me understand this...You're really thinking about marrying him? I mean like..." and he just couldn't talk anymore.

Just then, the door to his room burst open with Gris, Burk and Toby dressed for basketball, looking for more players.

"Hey Mate, c'mon and go down to the gym with us for some hoops. We got a court reserved for one o'clock and we need a couple more guys." The intruders didn't gauge the intensity of the conversation they had interrupted.

Mate came out of the ozone and back into reality. "What? Basketball?" He said in a disorientated manner. He looked towards her, and then towards them and said, "Yeah, sure, give me a couple of minutes and I'll meet you down there." They rushed out of the room, and they were left alone again.

"You know that's your problem. As far as you are concerned there will always be another game to play... there will always be friends to hang out with. You know Mate, sooner or later it will all come crashing down on you. You know what song I listen to over and over whenever I think of you? 'Beautiful Loser.' You know why? Because you haven't realized that you just can't have it all. You think you can be down here for two more years doing whatever the hell you want to do, while I wait for you back home. And when you finally graduate, what the hell am I going to get? A burned out college grad who only wants to be a teacher and a damn coach. It will be worse than it is now. You'll never make any money, and you'll still be playing all your goddamn games!!! You know what the starting pay is for a high school teacher? Eleven thousand dollars. Eleven thousand fucking dollars!"

Mate had heard enough, just too much at one time to handle. The girl of his dreams had just told him she was thinking about marrying someone else; that he was a loser; that he wasn't going to amount to much; and attacked his chosen profession.

Mate was speechless for the second time in his life.

She looked at him again. "I want somebody to share my dreams with. Somebody has come along with the same dreams as I have. I want a family, a house, and somebody that can support them. I have dreams Mate. If I wait around for you, I'll be an old woman by the time you get your act together. And face the fact Mate, that if you keep on your goal to become a teacher, you're barely even going to make enough to support yourself, let alone a family."

Mate just sat there, lost in the confusion. How can she be so serious? Why all this concern about the future? Jesus Christ, he said to himself, there are still two years of college left. How could she do this to me?

"I thought that we had a game plan."

"You have a game plan...I have dreams. Everything to you has always had some kind of game plan. Well, I'm getting out of the game, Honey, and into the real world."

Silence. The voices stopped crescendoing and returned to a civilized tone. Mate sat in a chair put his head down, staring at the floor between his legs. He then looked up and with his eyes watering said, "You know I love you."

"Oh, Mate, don't start that stuff with me."

"But you know I do."

"IF YOU REALLY LOVED ME, YOU WOULD BE BACK HOME WITH ME, INSTEAD OF DOWN HERE SCREWING EVERY BIMBO IN THIS WHOLE FUCKING SCHOOL!!!"

"Beth, since we ..."

"DON'T GIVE ME THAT 'BLOW JOBS DON'T COUNT' BULLSHIT AGAIN. IT'S JUST NOT FUNNY ANYMORE," she screamed, pointing at him with an angry finger, then turning and looking away.

He sat there like a young boy who had just been yelled at

by his mother for getting caught with his fingers in the cookie jar. Shit, she was the one who once said it would be all right to see other people while he was away and she was back home.

"Beth," he said. No response and she didn't turn around. "Beth, would you please look at me...Please?"

She finally turned around, tears running down her cheeks.

"Are you telling me that you're going to forget all that has happened between us in the past? Nothing between us matters anymore?"

She replied with a silent stare as she wiped her cheeks with the back of her hand.

"What about that collage on the wall over there that you sent me? You wrote the lyrics to "God Only Knows" on it. When you gave it to me you said that I was it. Doesn't that matter anymore?"

"That was in the past. People change."

"For Christ sake, it was only last year. How much can things change in a year?"

"The thing that has changed is you. Listen Mate, this is getting redundant. Our lives have just taken different directions. I'm going one way and you're going another. Do you read me?"

"I read the fact that you've been reading too many of those women's magazines. Where the hell did you learn how to talk like that? 'Taking different directions'? What kind of shit is that?"

Right then she made up her mind to leave. She knew it was a bad idea to come down to talk to him. God knows why she did it. She went over to the couch, picked up her purse, and headed for the door. He swiveled in his chair, and his eyes followed her across the room.

He didn't know what to say. Looking back on it now from a distance of many years, at that time he did not realize that this really was the end. He looked up at her and said, "Just do me a favor. If you go off and marry this guy...If you go off and leave me out of your life and things don't happen the way you have them planned, don't ever come back to me and tell me about it. If you go off and do something stupid and it doesn't work out or you turn out unhappy or this guy turns into a dick or whatever...I don't want to know about it."

She opened up the door, turned around and looked at him. She gave off the impression she didn't hear his last comments, panned her eyes around the room, looked him in the eyes one last time, gave her head a disgusted shake, and walked out of the room. All without saying another word. Mate sat there trying not to consider that maybe this time she really did mean business.

When Mate came home that year for Christmas he didn't see or hear from her at all. She never answered the phone, or returned his call when he left a message with her mom or dad. Finally, her mother ripped into him, and came right out and told him never to call their house again.

"But can't I just talk to her once? Please?"

"You had your chance," she replied. "You wanted to go off to be a big playboy at school. And you want to grow up and be a teacher and live in poverty the rest of your life. You never once thought ever of my daughter's well being."

"That's not right, I've always thought of her. All the time. In fact, ever since I first met her, I haven't been able to get her off my mind."

"The only time you ever think of her is when you want someone to take out, get drunk, and go to bed with. That's when you think of her. Well, you blew your chance, and now there is someone else to take her out, and he's a real gentleman. We don't need your Southside of Cleveland crap over here anymore. Don't ever call this house again."

Before he could say another word, she slammed the receiver down.

The engagement announcement was in the *Plain Dealer* the day after Christmas, and mentioned in Mary, Mary's column the next. Mate had a beer or tequila in his hand every moment, from the time he saw the announcement to the time he went back to school. It was bad enough that it was the first Christmas in three years without her, but seeing that announcement in the paper really sent him on a bender. Things he had not planned on happened, and happened too quickly. It was hoped amongst family and friends that the change of environment back to school would do the boy good.

Some time that winter Mate and his crowd came down to our place for a night of bar hopping on High Street. Before we headed out, we sat around drinking beer, listening to tunes and telling stories.

It was an uncomfortable night for me because I had just received an invitation to Beth's wedding in the mail. I had spent the previous Christmas and summer breaks involved once again with Colleen, and she was in the wedding and I was expected to be there. Colleen had called several times that week to tell me that Beth's mom was bitching because I hadn't mailed in my response. I had such mixed feelings about it, and wasn't sure what I was going to do. I left the invite, response card and return envelope on my dresser that week as I tried to decide.

The morning after Mate and the boys visited I was awoken early from a very sound sleep by a call from Colleen, telling me to make sure I put my response in the mail that day. As tired as I was, I couldn't fall back asleep. I decided to get dressed and walked down to the Franklin Ice Cream store, to get a cup of coffee and the morning paper. I figured I'd drop the response in the mail box down on the corner, but suddenly I couldn't find the envelope. The invite and the response card were still on my dresser where they had been all week, but the envelope was nowhere to be found. I looked on the floor to see if it had fallen there, then through all the drawers, but I still couldn't find it.

Then something else hit me and I said to myself, *you dumb ass!* I remembered that before we went out in the cold night and hit the bars, Mate went in my room to borrow a sweatshirt. He had to have seen the invite! *You dumb ass, how could you do that to him?*

Then I got more frustrated because I still couldn't find the return envelope. Oh well, the hell with it, I said, relieved I had reason to delay my decision about going to the wedding.

It was three weeks before the wedding and Beth was at the point every bride gets before big weddings, wishing that it was just over with and that they were on their honeymoon cruise ship down in the Bahamas. She had a zillion things to do that afternoon, but not before she checked the mail for responses. Although it was less than a month to go, there were many people they had not yet heard from. She started to go through the half dozen returns that came that day, checking each one against the master list she and her mom kept.

When she got to the fourth one she did not find a response card, but instead a piece of paper ripped out of a college notebook. Written in an old familiar hand writing were the words to the song "Company" by Rickie Lee Jones...

I'll remember you too clearly but I'll survive another day
Conversations to share when there's no one there
I'll imagine what you'd say
I'll see you in another life now, baby,
I'll see you in my dreams
But when I reach across the galaxy
I'll miss your company
So now you're going off to live your life
you say we'll meet each other now and then
But we'll never be the same and I know
I'll never have this chance again
No, not like you
Company, I'll be looking for your company
Look and listen through the years
Someday you may hear me still crying for your company

Also in the envelope was a picture of her, Mate and I taken the summer before in the right field bleachers at the old Stadium on a sunny summer afternoon. Mate was wearing a Death Before Disco T-shirt and was looking into the camera and laughing. Beth is in the middle looking at him with nothing but love and adoration on her face. I'm sitting next to her leaning into them as if we are all sharing a laugh. A great spontaneous picture of real friends.

She filled suddenly with emotion and her eyes started to water. Before she got carried away, she grabbed hold of herself. *Those days are behind me,* she said to herself. She got up and went into her old bedroom, stuffing the letter and the picture in one of the many boxes packed to go to the new house in Rocky River.

I borrowed a car from a friend, a big old ugly yellow late sixties model AMC Rambler, a great road car, and headed north for the big wedding. I figured it would give me a chance to get my mom to do some of my laundry, mooch some money from my dad, and to have a good time with Colleen (i.e., get laid). I left Columbus on Friday afternoon, figured to spend Friday night with Mate and the boys in Delaware, and then leave Saturday for Cleveland.

I pulled into Mate's fraternity house parking lot, entered by the side door, and walked down the steps to his room. I had done that perhaps a dozen times on Friday nights over the last two years, and this was the first time I didn't hear the noise of the never ending party. No loud Friday type music, just Van Morrison singing about his "Tupelo Honey." I strolled into his room and was greeted by concerned faces.

"Boy, are we glad to see you," Tex said as he stood to greet me.

"We've never seen him like this before," added Solly, the big Jersey guy.

"C'mon, we'll take you to where we think he is."

We all climbed into the Rambler and they filled me in on Mate's behavior in the weeks leading up to the big wedding. He had been drinking heavily, taking up the habit of shots of tequila in the afternoon. During an early spring thaw he had passed up basketball and golf to kill afternoons in joints downtown. He had become uncharacteristically moody and introverted, on the edge of things instead of in the middle.

All of the times I had visited Mate and the boys in Delaware we had gone to places downtown. Great college bars, good townie joints and, of course, the Jug. This time they took me outside town, near some railroad tracks and empty grain silos, near a strip of bars that made up the town's skid row. These are the types of establishments that are patronized in the early evening by drunk old men with rotted teeth who don't shave, and don't have anyone at home to cook them dinner so they drink it; and college juniors who want to drink alone because their back home girlfriend is getting married the next day.

We found him in the second joint we looked in, a place called Rader's. There are a thousand places like Rader's in every small town in the Midwest. Cigarette smoke hanging near the pressed sheet metal ceiling. Not enough light even during the brightest of afternoons. Sad country songs about drinking and/or lost love on the juke box. Rader's had some Jerry Jeff Walker. A little Johnny Cash and Patsy Cline. A lot of Waylon and Willie. And, of course, George Jones and Merle Haggard.

He sat alone at the bar away from the door with a half filled Budweiser and a shot of Cuervo in front of him. There were also a fresh lemon wedge and about a half dozen used ones on a napkin, and a pile of singles and some loose change.

When we were just about upon him, he sensed our presence and looked up, startled and surprised to see us. He saw me and broke out in a slight smile.

"Wayne, let me buy these guys a round," he said, as he got off his stool to reach into his pockets for more money. He turned to me saying, "Stopped by on the way to the big wedding, eh?"

"I'm checking it out along with a few other things," I replied, trying to act casual about it.

I saw on his face the raw emotion that was at hand. It was as intense of an emotion that he had on his face before a big high school football game, but not the same type. He looked hurt, he looked depressed, he looked like a jake on a bender, he looked like shit.

For an hour or so we did nothing but drink Buds, do shots of Cuervo, play the juke box, get up to piss, and talked about things like friends back home and the upcoming Indians season. We talked about the Old Man who just got his first college coaching job, and we talked about our upcoming spring break trip. We beat around the bush talking about this and that and then he grew quiet for a moment. I think he realized again that the reason I was in town was to go home for the wedding, and he grew quite pensive.

I knew all along for him to talk about it, to get it off his chest, I'd have to get him good and drunk. He paused, stared out into space for a moment and said, "You know, I just can't believe she's getting married tomorrow...I just can't believe it." For the next hour, as the rest of the boys played one of those old fashioned baseball games that projected on the ceiling and the wall, I just listened and he just talked, and I heard for the first time many of the things I've told you in this story so far.

He talked about how he missed being around her. "Around her it's like I just don't care about anyone else. She makes me feel happy. It's like I never have any worries." He told about how she never approved of his lifestyle at college, and how it turned him into a 'drunk, dope-smoking male slut.' "I tried to tell her it's just a temporary thing, that one day I'll graduate and move back home and it will be over with. One day it will be like she wants it." He told me about how much her mother despised him, and how she was the one who kept tight reigns on her, not letting her go off to college, and emphasizing the good Catholic Girl bullshit to her daughter (get married and start having kids by twenty-three or there is something wrong with you). How it was her mother who never really approved of him. Maybe it was because his family didn't have any bucks, or a big prominent name. Mate kind of thought it was because "she doesn't want her daughter to marry a guy who 'only' wants to be a teacher, and not bring home the big bucks like a doctor or lawyer would." Mate added, "she wanted her daughter to have a guy that could give her the big fancy house and the new car every year." She was going to make sure her daughter moved upward.

I never knew that he had this animosity towards her mother. I had met both of her parents and they had treated me nicely. Her mother did seem a little stuck up, but at that time in my life, lots of women appeared stuck up to me. Mate was always nice to her mom, but he really got along with her dad great. They seemed a lot alike.

He told me how they made one of those "while you're away at college you can see other people, and so can I" deals and he had stuck to it. When he was home on breaks, she was the only girl he ever saw. He said she had no right to get upset about the girls he saw at school, she could have done the same if she wanted to.

I told him she had too much class to whore around like we did, and as far as I knew, she was marrying the only other guy she had ever gone out with. I said that you had to admit that on paper he was a pretty impressive guy, and it might be something she just couldn't pass up.

He just replied, "Yeah, you're probably right," and stared off into space for a moment before ordering another round.

He just couldn't understand how anyone our age, especially her, could make a lifelong decision like marriage. I responded that some people mature earlier than others, especially girls compared to boys. All he said was, "There's that maturity bullshit again."

Sitting in that joint he told me about the first time they had ever made love. How they had beaten around the bush (no pun intended), going for months doing everything but "it."

"You guys always talked about how lousy and scary it was the first time...in the back of a car at the movies or on the floor in somebody's basement under some blacklights trying to get a rubber on....When we finally got around to doing it...it was great...it was always great. She was always the perfect fit. I've liked it with other girls, but nothing compares being with her. She's my perfect fit."

We had our first ever semi-serious, don't forget we were more than semi-plowed, talk about the future, and that someday this college slamhead life will be over with, just as the high school football life had suddenly once ended.

"And what scares me is not so much that it will end one day, but the fact that when it does, and we all end up back home, she'll be with someone else and not me."

Tex then came up to us and said, "C'mon fellas, let's go down to the Jug and see what's happenin'. Some of the boys said they'd be down there around ten, and it's past that already."

Everyone agreed that it was a good idea so we ordered one more shot for the road and we headed out the door. I was the last one out, and I turned around to double check to see if we had everyone. As the cold wind blew a bit of snow through the open

bar room door, I glanced around Rader's, illuminated by the old
Rock Ola juke box in the corner playing the last of the songs
Mate had picked. As I turned to go into the night, I heard Kris
Kristofferson singing sadly...

I don't know the answer to the easy way
she opened every door in my mind
dreaming was as easy as believing
it was never going to end
Loving her was easier than anything I'll ever do again.

Friday nights were his usual nights to work at the Jug, but
he had switched with someone because he had a hunch I might
stop by, and he wanted to work Saturday to keep his mind off
the wedding.

We walked into the place and it was hopping, and Mate's
spirits immediately rose. He really loved the place and he knew
almost everybody there, both the college crowd and the townies.
Those guys had it made working there. Shit, they even got to
drink all the drafts they wanted while on duty, as long as they
could keep from falling down.

We stayed there the rest of the night circulating through the
place. It was big, with a long room with booths on both sides, a
bar that sat about a dozen, and a back room for the overflow on
Friday and Saturday nights. Mate just kept moving, never
staying with one group too long. He seemed to enjoy himself
partying with the people he usually spent Friday nights waiting
on. The place was filled with comments like, "Hey, Mate, let me
buy ya a short one," and, "Mate my boy, what's the scam," and,
"Mate, come and share a pitcher with us." He never had a beer
out of his hand, and managed to always keep a slight smile on
his face.

I spent a good part of the evening hanging out at the bar
with a girl named Jane, a lunch and dinner waitress who never
seemed to make it home after her shift ended. She was the type
of girl you often find waiting on tables or bartending. She
looked anywhere from twenty to thirty (depending on what
time of the day you saw her), divorced with a kid, but still

showed she had a lot of spirit. She asked me what had been bothering Mate the last several weeks, and I told her an abridged version of high school jock goes off to college only to be dumped by his back home girlfriend for a rich, big time lawyer. She immediately showed a great deal of empathy on her face, and although she kept talking to me for a good deal of the rest of the evening, she never let Mate get out of her field of vision.

When it was time to go back to Mate's house, he ended up back into our conversation at the bar. He stood between Jane and I, she slid an arm around him and whispered something into his ear. He started walking out the door with her, telling us over his shoulder that he'd meet us back at the house.

"I just feel like shit and unless I'm pretty boozed up, I can't stop thinking about her," he said as she hugged his face into her chest. They were in the front seat of her car, parked next to the Rambler in the lot outside Mate's house. It was a big Chevy Impala with a large front seat, which allowed her to sit in the driver's seat while he lay with his head in her lap, and his feet sticking out of the passenger window.

She became very motherly as she kept hugging him into her breasts, as he went on to tell her pretty much what he told me earlier in the evening. She had been through a sloppy marriage and a sloppier divorce, and knew what it was like to be let down by the person you thought would be the one.

They lay there for hours, holding and hugging, and telling each other that they each knew how the other one felt.

Just before daybreak, he came into the room as I was rolling around on the couch trying to get some sleep. Instead of going to sleep himself, he went behind the bar, grabbed a beer out of the refrigerator, popped a tape into the tape deck, and plopped down into a big easy chair. As I tried to fall back asleep, I heard bits and pieces of the tape, and caught glimpses of him sitting in the dark, drinking beer and staring off into the darkness.

The tape that he listened to was labeled "Crying in My Beer," and was nothing but sad rock and roll and country ballads. The first tune was the studio version of "Rosewood

Bitters."

After a couple of listenings of the tape, Mate got up and went to bed and tried to fall asleep. But every time he was about to drift off, every time he was almost within dreamland, he would wake up scared and frightened and wide awake, with a hopeless feeling of aloneness shrouding his body. It would be a good six months before he would get more than a couple of hours of sleep in a night, and although it would gradually get better, he would never sleep a complete night ever again.

Years later Mate and I shared the house in Lakewood and I was seeing Lori. She would stay with me a couple nights a week. Once she woke me in the middle of the night.

"Sh...honey, wake up. Can you hear him?"

"Hear who?" I mumbled.

"Mate always gets up at least once every night...sometimes he even gets up and plays a record. Why does he do it? Can't he ever fall asleep?"

I tried to explain to her how psychologists say that most of us have twenty or more dreams a night and that in Mate's repertory of dreams there is one that pops into his head almost every night that wakes him up, no matter how deep he is sleeping.

"How do you know that? Do you know what it's about?" She asked, forcing me more and more out of my own dreams.

"I know about it because I was there the first night it happened....the first time he couldn't fall asleep," I paused, trying to find the right words. "Let's just say Mate has had almost all of his boyhood dreams come true except really one....and he dreams about that one almost every night."

"What was it? Did he lose a big game?"

"No, nothing like that," I said with a smile because for a second I thought of them together on a picnic, laughing a long time ago. "Let's just say that a long time ago a girl sorta dumped on him...."

"And he's never gotten over it?"

"No, he got over it. It's just that something inside of him won't ever let him forget about it."

As I rolled over to fall back asleep, I heard her say, "So that's why he never seems to take any girl serious..."

I woke the next morning and immediately kicked over the coffee table, tumbling cans and bottles to the floor and covering the table top with a sticky layer of stale beer.

One thing I really miss from those days is how pliant my body was. I took a dump, grabbed a shower, and felt like a new man. I wish I could do that today. I left as he was still trying to sleep in the loft in his bedroom.

One of the guys from the night before, one of Mate's frat brothers named Ry, needed a ride to Cleveland to meet his dad who was there on business. He was a big jolly blonde kid from Buffalo. I was glad to have him along for the companionship.

We stopped at a drive-thru beverage store to get provisions, two cases of Little Kings and assorted munchies, for the long trip to Cleveland.

I had always hit it off well with friends of high school friends at other colleges, and Ry was no exception. The two hour trip up the highway, sipping beers, telling lies, trading jokes and stories was something that happened often in those days. A couple of enjoyable hours with a new friend I'd probably never see again.

Ry filled me in on Mate's behavior, and how it was no secret that his spirits were low. I told him some things that he didn't know, and he told me some things I didn't know.

"I don't think she was ever really comfortable down here," he said pulling on a greenie. "She always seemed intimidated by how fast we live, and how hard we party. And she was never comfortable with the fact that Mate knows so many girls down here. Not so much girls he has something going with, just girls who are his friends."

I told him that when he was home on break she was the only girl he ever went out with, and when he was away at school they agreed that he could see whomever he wanted to see, and she could go out with whomever she wanted.

"Yeah, I had sorta the same agreement with my high school girlfriend. I came to OWU and she went to Cortland State, and ended up fucking half the ATO house there and giving me the crabs at Christmas."

"You know," he added, "neither one of them probably ever thought that she would catch him red-handed."

"What do you mean?"

"You probably don't know....I was coming back from my girl's place one Saturday morning last fall and Beth's car was parked in the lot and she was sitting behind the wheel. I thought it was a little unusual so I went over to say hi and see if everything was all right. When I got close enough to see her face, I stopped. I knew something was wrong. She was staring off into space with tears rolling down her face and she was shaking, holding onto the wheel. It was just so fucking weird."

"What happened next?"

"I came through the door and down the steps to Mate's room to tell him she was there. Just as I reached the bottom, Mate came tumbling out of his room, squeezing into a pair of jeans and throwing a sweatshirt on. He ran up the steps and I peered into his room and saw Sweet Jane Fryerson brushing her hair, wearing only Mate's old Franciscan football uniform. I guess you could kinda figure out what happened."

So that's one of the things Colleen had been alluding to, I said to myself.

"I think she took off before he got to her car, because he was back in the house soon, in the kitchen, making up two plates of food."

Despite the fact she was marrying someone besides my buddy, I finally decided to go home for the wedding. I was psyched to see Colleen and reestablish our on again fling/ romance of Christmas break and of the summer before. I rationalized the situation to the point that I was going to go to the reception, but not to the ceremony. I figured no matter how strange the circumstances were, I'd still have a good time, and get to see Colleen. Wedding receptions always meant lots of food, lots of booze, lots of dancing and joking with old and new friends. I figured it would be hard to have a bad time when there was an open bar.

Colleen was in the wedding party, but I told her earlier in the week that I would meet her at the reception, probably after dinner. I didn't want to go through the scenario over what fork to use and forgetting to use my napkin in front of a table of strangers. I brought Ry home to my house before I dropped him off. He gave me a bit of a buffer between me and my parents. I was just such a slamhead at the time, living in such a different world. I just didn't want to be alone with my own family.

I took some dirty laundry downstairs, and left Ry in the living room with my not so little sisters while I took a shower. I put on a fresh set of clothes, said good-bye, and whisked Ry out of the house before too much of our buzz wore off.

It was around four o'clock, Ry had to meet his dad at six, and I had to be at the wedding around seven. I decided to show him some of the sights between my house and downtown.

We ended up stopping at Baron's over in the old part of Parma, where I'd hoped Old Mate and Uncle Gus would be, and they were. Baron's was a great place with cheap whiskey and cold draft beer. Shots, beers, much laughter, big band music on the jukebox, a ball game on the television.Gus and Old Mate were with their usual band of cronies, drinking, smoking stinking cigars, and telling lies and stories of their exploits during the games, women and wars of their youth.

"Look who's here, Joe College and Joe Schmoe College," said Gus as they all laughed and we sat and enjoyed their company, as always, immensely.

As we started to get on our way, we got the old man's opinion on the wedding. "I think she's making a mistake but, of course, I'm prejudiced about the situation. Although, for Junior's sake, and I know he won't agree with me on this, it might be the best thing that happened to him."

"Why?"

"We love her to death, but to be honest with you, she is the most dangerous type of woman known to man."

"Dangerous? Beth?"

"Yep. She's a woman with a hidden agenda and those are the most deadly kind."

We drove downtown and I showed Ry the Stadium, the whole time having him tell me how much Mate talked about sitting in the bleachers to watch the Browns and Indians play. Ry was impressed when he finally saw it, saying how huge and stately the place looked. I finally dropped him off on Public Square in front of the hotel, and drove up Euclid towards Cedar Hill.

To this day, I still get lost whenever I drive through the older eastern suburbs, especially around Shaker Heights. Big beautiful houses, winding tree lined streets, unfamiliar landmarks. It took me over an hour to find the place, but when I did, oh, what a place.

I pulled into a long winding driveway that divided two fairways. Even though it was still late in the winter, the place had that special feeling that a well-kept golf course gives off at the end of the day.

There were trees, pillars, a stately verandah, and a black dude in a funny uniform to park my car. I did not see any other Ramblers in the parking lot. I walked into a scene out of *The Great Gatsby*, a humongous ballroom with chandeliers and oak paneling from the floor to the high ceiling. I walked in on the balcony level and entered the ballroom on a winding staircase.

I was immediately intimidated as I looked around and everyone seemed a little bit older than me, and dressed to the hilt with lots of flashy jewelry and tailored clothes. I had on my favorite corduroy sport coat, a pair of dress Levis, hush puppies, and an old school shirt and tie. As I walked down the staircase, I felt everyone looking at me out of the corner of their eyes. I immediately went to the bar to have a cocktail to calm my nerves.

The bar was located off the ballroom, and was filled with a few people who decided to drink their dinners. It was a smaller version of the bigger room, except no chandeliers, but just as plush, with framed pictures of some old farts wearing knickers on the walls. "Chas Worthington, Club Champ '29," and all the boys.

"How about a draft?"

"No draft sir," the stately bartender said. He looked a little like my Uncle Roy if he'd ever dry out and get a hair cut.

"How about a Bud?"

"No Bud, sir, only Heineken, St. Pauli Girl or Beck's."

Boy was I impressed. I asked for two St. Pauli Girls ("one

for my date"), and chugged one down quickly as soon as I got out of the bartender's sight.

As I stepped out of the bar and back into the main room, I looked down the main table hoping to find Colleen and catch her attention to let her know I was there. When I finally saw her, I stopped, stunned. She looked great, in some sort of low cut gown, and hair fluttered and falling onto her shoulders.

And she had that look in her eyes. That look she gave me the summer before when we left everybody at the Agora and snuck off for a little romance over on Edgewater Beach. It was her, "Honey, do you mind if I get on top look." Big, round, deep blue eyes and an expression that either was a real mean smile or a weak attempt at a frown. The only problem was that she wasn't giving her look to me across the ballroom. She was giving it to the guy sitting next to her in the wedding party.

He was pushing thirty. *(Remember, I was a young man of twenty at the time. I'm still a young man, but that's another story).* My first impression was that the guy was an asshole. Bullshit disco haircut maneuvered in a way to cover his large (and getting larger) bald spot. Fancy watch and cuff links. Stupid little mustache. A short, little Italian guy.

As I approached, Colleen seemed startled to see me. I immediately knew she was buying every line the guy was selling.

"Oh, hi.....how are you?" She said awkwardly, struggling to take her eyes off the Italian Stallion.

"This is my partner in the wedding, Sandy. He's a lawyer where Steven works." He reached out his hand giving me an overly strong handshake to prove he was tough, and gave off the impression that he enjoyed looking down at me from the elevated platform the wedding party was on.

Just like that they went back to what they were doing, he talking about himself, and she just staring at him and lapping up his bullshit like a puppy. In the ten or so stunned seconds I stood there, I heard about his Trans Am, his three rich uncles, and his buddies downtown that always take care of him.

I didn't know what to do so I headed back to the bar. I borrowed a car and drove a hundred and twenty miles to hear,

"This is Sandy, he's a lawyer?" Things weren't going the way I planned, but little did I know they were about to get worse. I went to the bar, ordered another St. Pauli's, and looked for a familiar face.

I stepped into the john and noticed the groom standing in front of a mirror fixing his hair. I thought I'd do my business before introducing myself. As I stood at the urinal, Sandy the douche bag lawyer came in and started joking with the groom. As I approached a nearby sink, Sandy pulled out a vial and spread four lines of coke on the porcelain sink ("I got this from some guy in probate"). They both laughed very arrogant laughs. They did some quick toots and kept laughing, and then Sandy the Italian Stallion made two comments that really burned me. First he said, "I know I could get her," and followed it with, "the kid dressed like a bum, I have to worry about?"

I washed my hands unnoticed and headed back towards the bar. Boy, was I pissed! I didn't know what to do.

Making my way back towards the bar, I finally found a familiar face, the father of the bride. He was by himself, all dressed up in his tux, getting a beer. I went to congratulate him and he was just beaming. You could tell he was very impressed with the surroundings.

"Congratulations," I said, as he turned towards me with a sincere smile on his face.

"Hey, how the hell are you?" We stood there and shot the shit about the big event. He asked how things were at school and about my parents. Just as I was about to walk away, a concerned look came over his face.

"Too bad about Mate. He used to be such a fine boy."

I was stunned again. Too bad about Mate? I was about to say that I had just seen him, and beside the fact that his favorite girl was getting married to someone else, that he was fine.

"I hear he smokes dope, he's drinking a lot, and he's thinking about not playing football. Hell, the last time I saw him he had hair halfway to his ass and a goddamn earring."

I was too startled to speak. Sure, Mate smoked a little hooch, but what about his new son-in-law just doing lines in the john?

"And he's going to become a teacher. That's what's the matter with schools today. People like that becoming models for our kids. Bullshit."

Now I was really pissed. He obviously didn't know that I had decided to go into teaching also. I knew I had to get the fuck out of there before I did something stupid.

I tried my best to keep my composure and said to him, "Mr. O'Connell, I think someone is telling you the wrong scoop on The Mate. He's not a drug fiend and he found other things to do besides play football, and I think someday he is going to make a great teacher. And I don't care how great you think your son-in-law is, with his family money and prominent name. I think your daughter fucked up because there aren't many better than The Mate." At the time I didn't really mean all of it, I didn't know Beth's husband at all. I was just angry, and I guess I just wanted to take it out on someone else. I didn't know then what I know now.

I turned and headed up the stairs to the doors on the balcony. I stopped at the top of the stairs and turned around and took one last look at Colleen and Sandy the dueche bag lawyer, and I said aloud to no one in particular, "Fuck you and your cokehead lawyer." The last thing I saw was the bride's mother sitting by herself at the end of the main table. She had her nose up in the air as she sat, smoking a cigarette and looking over her big event. It didn't take me long to figure out who was saying those nasty things about my buddy. Through the whirl of her cigarette smoke she gave me one of those 'you really don't belong here anyway' looks, and I reacted by popping her the finger before turning and heading out the door.

I left without ever seeing the bride. I went out to the parking lot, found the Rambler and headed back towards home. I arrived at seven thirty, left at eight, and it was the worst half hour of my life.

When Mate went back to school that fall, the fact that it was going to be his last year hung over him like an ominous cloud. The world was changing and he couldn't stop it. Too much of his old crowd was gone. Horse, Blair, Lee, Annie, Van Husen,

Monroe, April, Susie Q., the list went on and on, had graduated and were out in the real world. He was still in fantasy land but for the first time he felt the end was near. Just like when the high school football days ended, so was this college slamhead experience.

The university had a large freshmen class and they seemed to Mate a bit young. For the first time in three years he wasn't the social chairman of his fraternity, relinquishing the position to a younger man. He wasn't going to bother with the task of getting the kegs anymore, just drinking them.

However, he was king down at the Jug. Through the time honored seniority system, he was given the title of head waiter. Along with it went many responsibilities and privileges. He got to pick his own nights to work, and nobody was hired without his approval. He got to bartend with the regulars, and drink bottles of Bud instead of drafts. He got a twenty five cent raise, and now made a half buck more than anyone else. He decided who got to go around the corner on breaks, and what shots and beers to drink over at Butsy's. He decided where they went before their shift started and what they drank and who would pay, usually himself. There were still times however, when he missed the old Jug crowd, when he was just a follower.

There was no secret he had a chip on his shoulder and an arrow through his heart thanks to Beth. He still couldn't believe she got married. *How could she do that to me?* It especially got him at those times when he knew the end of the road of college was near and being out in the real world, especially without her, really scared him.

But it was still college, it still beat working for a living, and it was a beautiful fall filled with hoops, touch football, pretty girls, cookouts, and the absolute minimum of school work. Life wasn't so bad. Some changes, yes, but it was still life in a bubble.

One thing that started to happen that Mate didn't expect, that helped make life bearable, was that he started to receive weekly letters from a girl from Connecticut who was a classmate. But she wasn't in Connecticut, and she wasn't on campus, she was in New Mexico on an art internship. Her name was Leslie and he had known her since they were freshmen. Finally, right before he went home for Thanksgiving, she showed up.

"God, it's so good to see you," he said as they took off their coats and sat in the booth.

"It's good to see you," she answered. Awkward silence. Even though they had been tight for three years, this was the first time they were both unattached. A little bit of sexual tension was in the air.

"I didn't think I'd see you until January."

"I know, but I had an opportunity to come back through Ohio on my way back home. I figured I would stop off and see how everyone was doing, and to make sure I had a place to live for next quarter." She also figured to look him up, but she didn't tell him that. "So, how's it going for you? Your first letter sounded kind of down, but your second one sounded a lot better."

"Yeah. Things started out slow, strange, too many of the old crowd gone. A lot of new faces. But, hell, it hasn't been bad. It still beats working for a living."

"How's your love life?"

"Well..."

"How's your sex life?"

"Typical OWU situation...sex life is O.K., but my love life stinks!"

They both burst into laughter, then followed by a short silence as they looked each other in the eye.

"Are you over Beth yet?"

"I, you know, it hasn't been easy...," then he quickly changed the subject. "I really enjoyed your letters."

She responded with a slight smile.

"I was really impressed with the fact that over all those thousands of miles between here and wherever the hell you were that you thought of me. Well anyway, the last couple of weeks have been better. When we first came back, everyone knew I had a big chip on my shoulder...but the one thing I'm trying to keep clear in my mind is that next year at this time we'll all be out in the real world, and I might as well enjoy myself as much as I can." He paused again, "You know, your letters really did help. The first one was a surprise, and I really looked forward to every one after that."

"Well, I was really worried about you. I knew what kind of shape this thing with Beth left you in when we left school last spring and well..." and now she paused. "I was kind of frustrated because for the first time since I had met you, neither of us was involved with anyone and I was over two thousand miles away."

"Really? That's what you were thinking?" He said and a slight smile came to his face. She smiled back. They kind of let it go at that, and then talked of old friends and plans for the holidays.

"Mate, do you think that if we would have done this years ago things might have been different between us?"

"No, it's best that we never did. It's kind of nice now, isn't it?" He said as he readjusted his body so he could use her breast as a pillow.

"I can't believe I'm spending the night with you in this stupid fraternity house after all this time. You know, Scott thought we were doing this all the time. He was always very jealous over you. He couldn't handle the fact that we were such good friends and nothing more. I guess until now."

"That's what's the matter with guys like him. They think women are only for one thing and that's to go to bed with them. And you know what the ironic thing is?"

"What?"

"Guys like that spend too much time chasing only one thing, whereas, if they spent the time getting to know a girl and treat her like a person, the opportunity for sex increases greatly."

"Yeah, is that so?"

"Well, look at us."

"I guess you're right."

"What's he doing anyway? Are you guys completely finished also?"

"I think so. He wrote and called me when I was in New Mexico. I kept telling him that he didn't mean anything special to me anymore. I'm sure he'll try to get in touch with me when

I get back home. I hope I'm not a sucker for his charm anymore. I've really tried to get over that, and I think I have."

"What's he doing?"

"Well, my dad got him a couple of interviews in the city, and I think he's working down on Wall Street someplace."

"I was always worried about you and him."

"Oh yeah?" She said, as she rolled and propped her head up on an elbow.

"I always thought that you were going to end up marrying him. He would ask you and you would say yes, and I always thought that you were a lot better than him. I've always thought that you are one of those girls who are too cool to marry the first guy that asks you. And you are definitely too cool to marry him."

There was a silence, then she aimed her mouth towards his and wrapped both her arms around his neck, and they proceeded to once again...

Mate returned home for Thanksgiving and his spirits had definitely lifted because of Leslie. I went back to Ohio State (we still had school right up to Christmas) and Mate stayed home and worked full time down at the mill (he was off until New Year's). When I returned a couple of days before Christmas, Mate had just spent a weekend in Connecticut visiting Leslie and he was glowing once again, looking as if he had finally gotten over Beth and had returned to his old self.

We went through our usual Christmas Eve routine, bar hopping and late minute shopping downtown. As we bopped in and out of the May Company and Higbee's and Halle's, and the Elegant Hog and Lincoln Inn and Fagan's, he told me all about her parents' "shack" in Connecticut, seeing a Broadway play and a Ranger's game, and having wild sex on the floor in a suite at the Waldorf Astoria.

I remember that Christmas as the last Christmas we had as kids. Although we were nearly twenty two years old, we were all still in college, I remember everybody's parents were still alive, and it was before many of our friends and families got fragmented across the country. We did a lot of the things we had done since high school for really the last time. What a great Christmas it was, and it was even greater because Mate was back to being his old self.

The end to Mate's relationship with Leslie would be swift and sudden and he would never really know why, although years later, quite through coincidence, I would find out the reason.

It was about a month into the winter quarter at school and Mate was enjoying life to the fullest. He had been smart enough to get his student teaching out of the way, and had nothing but gut classes scheduled for his last two quarters. His days were filled with a class or two in the morning, basketball at the gym at noon, followed by a late lunch at the Jug with a friend or two. He would usually see Leslie twice a week, once during the week and usually on Friday night. They had their own friends and neither wanted too structured of a relationship. Everything appeared to be fine.

Fridays were Mate's favorite days that winter. He had a two o'clock speech class, and afterward would meet a group of friends at a bar right across from the campus called Butsy's. The place would just jump on Fridays, as the students would start working on their weekend long buzz. Mate and a couple of guys from his frat would take over a spot halfway down the bar, where they could see who was coming through the door and still be in the direct route girls had to take to get to the washroom. Leslie would usually stroll in about four with some friends from the art department and would eventually end up on the stool next to him. They would stay at Butsy's until it was time for Mate to go over to the Jug to work. She'd walk him over, kiss him good-bye, and promise to be back by midnight.

Mate would use that God given talent that he had and just keep going. He would head to the coffee machine for a couple of cups of caffeine and was ready to go. He would take the front right section and serve pitchers, pizzas and hot roast beef sandwiches until closing time. Leslie would usually show up around midnight, all freshened up, and sit at the end of the bar and joke around with the regulars until Mate finished up his shift.

Geno, the king of the kitchen, would make Mate an un-cooked double cheese, mushroom, pepperoni and anchovy pizza. Mate would punch out, grabbing the pizza and a couple of eight packs of Little Kings. He and Leslie would walk back to her apartment. The nights were cold and clear, and the snow on the ground would sparkle in the moonlight.

They would pop the pizza in the oven when they got to her place, and Mate would grab a shower to get the smell of the bar off his body. More than once he would talk Leslie into joining him in the shower. Then they would lie in her bed, drinking Little Kings, eating pizza, making love, and watching old movies on television. They would often be up until dawn, and then fall asleep wrapped up in each other until early in the afternoon. Mate would later tell me those Fridays were the happiest times he had his last year in college.

Mate never volunteered much information on how the relationship suddenly ended. I thought everything was going fine until I called him in February to finalize the plans we had for spring break that year.

"How's Leslie?" I asked innocently.

"Fuck her!"

"What?" I asked very surprised.

"Fuck her!"

"What happened?"

The line was silent for a moment and then he said, "You know, I don't really know. Two weeks ago I did something I promised myself I would never do at Wesleyan, spend two nights in a row with the same girl. I just never wanted to think I was having a big heavy duty relationship like some of the people around here. Well anyway, I spent both Friday and Saturday with her, I talked to her the following Tuesday, and I haven't seen her since. She calls me on the phone and tells me she can't go to the Jimmy Buffett concert and she hangs up. I'm out jogging the other day and I run past her place and I see her old boyfriend's car parked in her driveway. I see her roommate down on campus and she tells me that Leslie's a big fuck up and one day she is going to regret what she's doing. I just can't figure it out."

He went on about how shitty he felt.

Here we go again, I said to myself. Not again. I especially didn't want to go on another spring break with him like the one last year, when he was a walking drunk zombie lamenting Beth's marriage. I wanted the old Mate on vacation, the one from our freshmen and sophomore years who was the life of the party.

That March I got a ride up to Delaware from Tom Haggerty. I was going to party a night in Delaware, Mate and the boys were going to finish some tests in the morning, and we were going to leave the next afternoon for Fort Lauderdale. I got dropped off at Mate's house and walked down the steps to his room and saw a note on his door:

> *Greg,*
> *Stow your gear and meet me at Rader's. If you can't*
> *get a ride, here's a map.*
> *Mate*

Not again. I remembered the year before finding him at Rader's, the night before Beth's wedding, and I anticipated the same scene. Drunk at the bar, filled with too many shots of Jose Cuervo. I just wasn't going to put up with it. As I followed the map through town and over to its eastern ridge, I mentally formed my game plan. I was going to walk in and just start yelling at him. Tell him how I was sick and tired of all his love problems, and how everyone was sick and tired of hearing his broken hearted bad luck stories. We all had own problems, and everyone was sick and tired of hearing his.

I was all psyched when I saw Rader's neon sign appear down the street. I wasn't going to sugar coat it; I was going to give it to him straight. Imagine the surprise I received when I opened the door and the first thing I heard was his jolly laugh filling the room. This time he wasn't sitting at the bar strung out on tequila, but he was the center of about five guys surrounding the control panel of the baseball game that projected onto the wall.

"You just missed my grand slam," he shouted at me as he quickly shook my hand and showed great happiness on his face. "Two fucking outs, and an 0 and 2 count, and I put it over the left field fence," he said.

"Lucky fucker," Solly said. Everyone looked buzzed, everyone looked happy.

"Hey, I thought you guys had a final tomorrow." I said and they all looked at each other and laughed.

"Well?"

"Well," Tex responded, "the woman who teaches the class gives the same test every year and well..." and he walked over to a stack of books on the bar and pulled out a blue book. "And, well, since she gives the same test every year, we just thought we would make things a little easier for ourselves and fill in our test booklets tonight instead of tomorrow." And sure enough, his test book was dated the next day, and all the pages were filled with rough drafts of the essay questions and neatly written final drafts.

Mate added, "The hard part is to fill the two hours up during the exam period that you are supposed to be taking the test. I think this year I'm going to write a few letters to the Forum in Penthouse about last weekend," and they all broke into a hearty laugh.

I was amazed and happy that Mate seemed himself. He immediately went to the bar and said to the barkeep, "Wayne, food and drink for my men and horses."

"But Mate, you know no food after eight."

"Then make it shots and beers for my men and horses," and a round was bought and toasted.

Later that evening when we were doing our damnedest to get to know a couple of sorority girls down at the Jug, I asked Mate if he was all over his latest tragic romance.

"Fuck, yeah!" He said, and then he paused and said quite seriously (considering the buzz we had on), "I give you my word that I will never, ever take another woman seriously in my life."

And, as far as I know, he never did.

Years later, we were down in Florida on spring break again, but this time as high school teachers, not as college students. We were staying in Sarasota with a friend of Mate's from OWU who teaches down there. Everyone else went to get in a round of golf before hitting the beach except for me. I wanted to go down to the beach early and get a good hard run in before we started to party again. I needed to blow some of the booze from the night before out of my system.

I was running south along Siesta Key beach towards the wall at the south tip that separates the public beach from some private homes. Down and back is about four miles from where I left my blanket, and I planned to run about three and a half of it and then walk the rest as a cool down.

The beach was still relatively empty and about a half mile into my run I saw a woman about my age playing in the surf with a young girl who looked about three. As I passed the woman, I saw her staring at me as if she knew me, and her face followed me as I jogged past her. She looked faintly familiar to me, and I assumed it must have been someone from the bar the night before, or possibly someone from back home down in Florida on a holiday.

I ran up to the wall and back, and stopped running and started to walk around the spot I had seen the woman. I started to get my breathing back and was about to dive into the surf when the woman walked up behind me with the child in tow.

"Hi, Greg," she said with a very sexy smile. "Do you remember me?"

She looked vaguely familiar but I couldn't place her. Great smile, a good tan and a fine set of breasts. Boy, they looked familiar.

"You do look familiar, yet I can't place a name."

"Leslie. I went to OWU with Mate."

"God, Leslie, I'm sorry. Boy, you look great."

She smiled, and we stood on the beach making small talk for about ten minutes. Her daughter, whose name I was told was Melissa, started to complain and tug at her mother's arm, saying she had to go to the bathroom.

Leslie gave off the impression that she wanted to continue the conversation.

"Want to come up to my place for a morning beer? Melissa needs to go to the ladies' room."

I said sure, and we walked up to one of the condos that seem to be taking over the south portion of the Key.

"I can't believe he is down here with you," she said when we finally got around to talking about Mate. Somehow, I knew that was the first thing she wanted to ask me, but she was hoping I would bring him up first.

"Yeah, he's out hitting a round of golf with the guys we're staying with and should be down here on the beach in a while."

She got up, got a couple of more beers out of the refrigerator, and came back and sat down in the chair right next to me. She opened the beers, handed one to me, looked me in the eyes, paused, and then asked, "I would be lieing if I told you I never think about him." Long pause. "Probably a week doesn't go by when I don't think about him."

I sat there, racing through my mind, trying to remember what I knew about her. As with Beth, Mate never talked much about her. I did remember that Mate and she were real good friends before they became involved. And, of course, I remembered how their relationship suddenly ended and that Mate had told me later that she had gotten married. That day in her condo I knew that her marriage had ended because she definitely gave off the impression that she was single.

"Does he ever talk about me?" She asked.

"To be honest with you, no. He never talks too much about college or girls he has gone out with."

She turned her head and looked down, obviously embarrassed, especially after her comment about him.

"But, to be honest with you, that's just the way he is about certain things. He hardly ever talks about personal things like that. He just keeps stuff locked up inside himself."

She got up and looked out the window into the blue surf. She turned around and said, "I just can't believe he's here. You don't know how many times I have thought of him and thought about calling or writing him. It's just that, you know, our relationship just ended so suddenly, and so shitty...I was such a dumb, blind girl at the time. You know, at the time he was right about a lot of things. I was just too self-centered to hear him."

"About what?"

"Oh, a lot of things," and then she quickly changed the subject. "Whatever happened to the girl from high school, you know, the girl *that ripped his heart out?"*

I filled her in on what had gone on in all our lives. Then I asked her again, "What was Mate right about?"

She paused and got up. "Excuse me for a moment, I have to check on Melissa. Do you want to sit on the patio?"

She met me on the balcony a couple of minutes later. "She's all wrapped up in the new toys her grandmother has bought her; she should be good for a while," she said as she opened and then closed the sliding screen door that led onto the patio. We were about ten stories up, with a beautiful view of the beach and the water below. I looked down and saw Mate and the boys had arrived and had set up around my towel and chair. The beach was filling up. She brought with her a couple more beers.

"I had met Mate my first year at school, in the spring at a fraternity party," she said as I settled into the chair and listened. "We were both freshmen and I had an immediate crush on him. He was so funny and honest and such a gentleman. He had this way of making you feel that he was really listening to you. That night at the party we spent the whole time together and I remember we got really drunk. When he walked me back to my dorm, I kept expecting him to make the moves on me. I was trying to decide whether to say yes or no. I think I was leaning towards yes. But when we got to my door, he leaned over, kissed me on the cheek, and said, 'thank you for your company, it was a real pleasure.' And that was it. No excuses to try to get into my room, no grabbing at my breasts. It was thank you, a kiss, and good night. Let me tell you, that didn't happen often at that time in my life." She laughed for a moment and then continued.

"Well, the next time I saw him it was just about the same thing, and by then I was getting kind of frustrated. When I asked him why, he told me about this girl back home he had just started seeing again and how much he was in love with her. The way he talked about her, it sounded like she was some kind of queen."

"We got involved my senior year. I came back from an art internship in New Mexico and felt a little out of place because I had been away for a while. I had hung around with an older crowd and most of them had graduated. Mate's girlfriend Beth had dumped him and gotten married, and we were both kind of lonely, and one thing led to another, and we finally went to bed together. For a while, I was really

happy..."

She paused and I quietly asked again, "What was he right about?"

"I'll get to that. Don't you want to know why it ended? Did he ever tell you?"

"No, he never told me. All I remember him telling me was that it was over and that after the thing with you, and the thing with Beth, he was never going to take another girl seriously."

"Has he ever?"

"Not that I know of."

"Wow," she said quietly to herself. She stared blankly off into space.

"Well, tell me, how did it end? What did he tell you?"

"Uh, what?"

"I said, tell me how it ended. What was it he told you?"

"Well, God, I remember it so clearly. But first, you've got to promise that you will never tell Mate what I tell you. There are a couple of things he doesn't know about. Even though it's been years, I don't want him to know. O.K.?"

"O.K."

"It was Christmas break during our senior year, and I was back home in Connecticut working at Macy's at the mall and missing Mate a lot. I also saw my old boyfriend a couple of times but my heart was with Mate. He had graduated from Wesleyan the year before and lived in Darien, a couple of towns over. Well, anyway, the weekend before Christmas, Mate came out, we got a hotel room in the city, and had a great time. My dad got us tickets to a show and a hockey game and we saw all the department store displays. We sipped champagne in bed, made passionate love, the whole bit. On Sunday, we went to my parents' Christmas party and my folks, and everyone else for that matter, was so impressed with him."

"After Mate left, I couldn't wait until break was over. I wanted to get back to Ohio and see him...but I also saw my old boyfriend, Scott, a couple of times and even went to bed with him once. Scott and I went out on and off for a couple of years at school. He never really treated me that well, but I was young and was happy to have a handsome young man to go to formals and parties, and to go to bed with."

"Well, anyway, I got back to school after the New Year and I was back with Mate and everything was fine, and then," another long pause. She looked directly into my eyes. "You've got to promise me that you'll never tell him this. You really have got to promise me."

"O.K., I promise."

"I missed my period. I kept waiting for it and it just never came. I went to the school health center and I got the news. Seven weeks pregnant. I was stunned. I didn't know what to do."

"Was it Mate's?"

"That was the bad part. I didn't know. I traced it back and it pointed to the week over Christmas break when I was with both Mate and Scott. I had been using a diaphragm...the weekend with Mate we did it so often. Shit, we did it in the car after I picked him up at the airport. I couldn't remember if I used it all the time. And the night with Scott I didn't expect anything to happen, so I didn't..." and her voice cracked slightly and she showed a bit of a tear in her eye.

I got up, got a couple of more beers and came back, giving her time to regroup.

"Well, anyway, I didn't know what to do. I find for the first time, what did Mate call it?..True love, and then I go and do something stupid to screw things up."

"What did you tell Mate?"

"Well, ironically, as I came out of Edgar Hall, that's where the health center was, he comes waltzing down the street on his way to the Jug for lunch. He asks me to join him, and he tells me he's got something to tell me. 'He's got something to tell me?' I said to myself. We walk into the place and sit down in a booth. It's crowded so instead of waiting for a waitress he goes up to the bar to order for us. I noticed that he was so happy, laughing with all the regulars. He came back to the booth and he was just beaming. Before I could say anything, he just started talking..." she paused again. "I can't believe I'm telling you all this, I don't think I've told anyone all of this..."

But she wanted to and I let her.

"Well, anyway, he sits down with a pitcher of beer, pours two glasses and says to me, 'I wanted to thank you for bringing me out of the funk that Beth had put me in since last year. One thing she used to harp on me about was that I always said too little too late, so, I just wanted to tell you I really enjoy the time I spend with you, and I'm really glad that you're my friend and lover.' He then went on about *what a great time he had in New York, how he was really excited that spring break was coming up, followed by spring quarter. It was going to be nothing but good times until the end of the school year.*

I broke into a cold sweat, and didn't know what to say. All I did know was that it wasn't the right time to tell him about my little problem. I asked him what the future held for him and me, and he took a gulp of beer and told me, 'Let's not get too serious about the future right now. What do we have to worry about? We're seniors in our last two quarters at one of the biggest party schools in the state. Pretty soon we're going to go out and get real jobs, and we might as well kick back and enjoy things while we still have time to do it. There's just too many good times in the months ahead. Time is short.'

I asked him if he had interviewed for any jobs and he said, 'I'll get something up in Cleveland. Not too many English teachers coach, and I'll coach anything. That makes me real marketable. I'll rent a house with some buddies from high school, we'll get Brown's season tickets, you'll come and visit'...and he went on and on."

"So you never told him?"

"No, I just couldn't. I panicked. I wasn't sure who the father was, plus I knew I just wasn't ready for motherhood. I knew I'd probably get an abortion, and you know I couldn't tell Mate that. He wasn't religious at all, but he was just too Catholic. Does that make sense?"

"So what did you do?"

"I did stupid things. I panicked and I needed someone to cry on. So I couldn't tell Mate, and I called Scott and broke down on the phone and told him that he was the one responsible. I just ignored Mate. Scott came out that weekend, and he took me into Columbus and I had an abortion." *Her voiced slowed and trailed off. How many women go through life thinking about what would have come of an abortion of long ago?*

"What did you do then?"

"Scott sort of just moved in with me. Things happened too fast. He hadn't found a career type job since he had graduated the year before, so he just stuck around. Both our families had bucks, so money was no big deal. And he had never treated me better than at that time. I know he had heard that I was seeing Mate and it probably wised him up a little bit."

"And what about Mate?"

"Oh, poor Mate. Like I said, things just moved too fast and I just ignored him. I'm sure after he saw Scott around, he figured out what happened. I never went into the Jug or near his frat house again. I tried to rationalize everything to myself. I knew Mate had his heart set on teaching and living in Cleveland, and I was an Eastern girl, you know, it was bad enough I had to go to school in Ohio. I told myself I would never live there. Near the end of the school year, I saw him a couple of times. We attempted to have a conversation once, but it was rough. Neither of us could say anything."

"You still haven't told me what he was right about."

"When school ended and I came home, I panicked again and thought the best thing to do was to settle down and marry Scott. My dad got him a job as a salesman at his company, and I started working there as a kind of Girl Friday for my brother, who also worked there. Scott and I got married the following fall. About a month before the wedding, I got a letter from Mate in the mail..." she paused again. Sad emotion showed on her face. "He wrote that he heard I was getting married, and he told me I was too cool of a girl to marry the first guy that asked me. He also said that I was selling myself short, not pursuing a job as an artist, and that I was a very talented person and getting married is something that you can do anytime. And now I'm a divorced woman, with a child, down in Sarasota, Florida, trying to piece my life together, and trying to start painting again, and blurting my life story to a stranger..." and she got up and went to the bathroom. I could hear her crying, and the sniffling and the blowing of her nose.

When she came out I pointed to where we would be sitting on the beach and asked her to join us. She said that when she could get a break from her motherhood duties that she would make it down. I thanked her for the beers, kissed her on the cheek, warm and red from the tears, and headed down to Mate and the boys on the beach. I didn't say anything about her; I wanted Mate to be surprised.

I never saw her again. She never showed up on the beach. I stopped at her condo the next day, and the woman across the hall told me she had left to go back to her home in Connecticut earlier that morning.

I never said anything to him about her until we were back on the plane heading north. We were still pounding beers, making our vacations last to the final moment before we were home. I told him *about seeing her that morning I was jogging, and filled him in on going back to her condo and talking to her on the balcony. I left out what I had promised not to tell. When I had finished, he grew quiet and then said, "Probably better off that way."*

"How's that?"

"When it was all said and done, and we were back home for good from school, I pretty much came to peace about all that."

"What do you mean by that?"

"I guess in the long run she was a lot more like him than me, even though we were such good friends. They were both a couple of reckless rich kids. It's so easy to be reckless when you're rich. Daddy pays your tuition. Daddy pays for your apartment. Daddy pays for your car. They were both reckless rich kids and I got caught in the crossfire."

We both sat there silently for a while nursing our beers, both of us thinking about all the rich assholes we had encountered at school. I glanced over to him and I saw a smile forming across his face.

"Lots of rich assholes at school," he stated.

"Yeah," I agreed.

"You know what though," he said as our eyes met. "We drank their beer and did their women."

"That we did my friend, that we did," I replied.

Part Three
Sometime in the Early Eighties
Adulthood

So you're a little bit older and a lot less bolder
than you used to be
So you used to shake 'em down
But now you stop and think of your dignity
So now sweet sixteen turned thirty-one
You get to feelin' weary when the work days done
Well all you got to do is get up and into your kicks
If you're in a fix
Come Back Baby
Cause Rock and Roll never forgets
    from "Rock and Roll Never Forgets" by Bob
    Seger and the Silver Bullet Band

Those first four or five years out of college just flew by. For many of our college friends it was a hard adjustment, from the country club life of a college campus, to the responsibilities of the real world. For Mate and me, for the most part, it was another period of good times and irresponsibilities, although it didn't match up to college, nothing we thought ever would. We all got our first jobs and our first weekly paychecks. We were still relatively young, durable, and optimistic that things were going to turn out great for everyone. Mate and I were teaching, and consequently, we got to enjoy our summers along with having time off at Christmas, and we still had time to go on

135

spring break each year. Those first few years out of college were a lot of fun.

After going through trying times with Beth and later with Leslie, the last thing Mate had on his mind was finding Ms. Right. He figured it was time to get ahead in teaching and coaching, work on his Masters at Cleveland State, and spend his paychecks. He had found true love once, or one and a half times, and he wasn't going to pursue it for a very long time. I was still just along for the ride. I had three or four attempts at having a relationship at Ohio State that always seemed to end with some teary-eyed girl upset with me because I liked hanging out with my friends drinking, playing sports, and listening to records more than going to the library or some sorority function with her. Deep down I always believed someone would sooner or later come along and capture my heart.

Our social life became a cycle of the seasons. In the fall we were serious young teachers and football coaches who hit the bars on Saturday nights and made Sundays the best day of the week. If the Browns were home, we'd make a day out of it. Mate's parents always assumed that our crowd would take over their tickets eventually up in the upper deck in right field. However, they weren't giving them up. They were still partying pretty strong, so we had to get our own. And, being broke most of the time, made the fact that the bleachers were the cheapest ticket an easy sell. It had nothing to do with the fact that you could still smoke dope out there, or smuggle in almost any kind of beverage. That had nothing to do with it. Honest.

In the winter we took grad classes at Cleveland State, and I coached basketball at the middle school. Spring would start in March with St. Patrick's Day and Opening Day for the Indians in April, and we would spend our springs counting the days until summer vacation.

Summer would come and we would once again be the undisciplined party animals we were in college. We were the envy of all of our friends as we got the summers off and saw our paychecks still come every two weeks in the mail. We'd work basketball camps our district put on, or work at camps put on by friends who coached at other schools. We played softball, went to the beach out at Headlands, and went out almost every night. We'd hit the Lakewood bars, the Parma bars, the Lee Road bars, went to the Flats, and even went with Old Mate and Gus to the AMPOL Club.

On Sundays, we continued something that we started in high school and watched the Tribe play. On almost any given summer Sunday afternoon you would find twenty or so of our friends spread out in the right field bleachers, still paying a cover charge to drink over-priced warm beer and to watch the worst team in baseball.

It was one of those Sundays early enough to watch all of batting practice, during our first summer home from school for good, that I found myself with Mate. We found ourselves there all alone in right field, as we watched Andre Thornton crank one after another out of the park, because Mate said he had something important to tell me.

"I just want to tell you something," he said. "I've been putting a lot of thought into some of my actions over the last year or two pertaining to my love life or, to be more precise, the disaster of my love life. I realize that I have been extremely self-centered at times, and looking for sympathy from too many people. I just want you to know that I'm over and done with that stuff now. I realize that things could always be worse, I've led the life of a prince, and I should be grateful for all the good things that have happened to me. I am never going to feel sorry for myself again."

Wow, I said to myself. What a brutally honest statement.

He continued. "The next time I start feeling sorry for myself, all I want you to do is look at me and remind me about Uncle Gus."

Oh, I said to myself, Gus must have talked to him. "Gus give you a little heart to heart, huh?"

"No, that's not it. Didn't I ever tell you about Gus?"

"No."

"Well, anytime you ever feel sorry for yourself, just think of Gus."

"Why? What ever happened to him?"

"Everything, man. Everything. First, did you know he really isn't, by blood anyway, my uncle? He was a friend of my Dad's whose parents both died during the end of the Depression. Gus was in the third grade and orphaned. I forget what his mom died of, but his dad had cancer and spent six months dying right in front of Gus. His mom had already been dead, and it was just Gus and his dad, and Gus took care of him. Feeding him, changing his sheets, even wiping his ass. He was just a kid and he watched his dad die, then he had nobody. The rest of his family was still in Poland and he had nowhere to go, so my dad brought him home after the funeral. Isn't that wild? If he hadn't been my dad's friend, and if my dad hadn't skipped school to go to Gus's dad's funeral, who knows what would have happened. My dad literally asked Gus if he was hungry and brought him home for dinner that night, and he never left."

"God. That sounds pretty tough."

"That ain't half of it. Gus fell in love with a girl of questionable morals before he went off to the war. I guess she was the neighborhood tramp, but Gus got her on the straight road. She cleaned up her act. Gus was in love, and she promised him her unending loyalty. Gus went with the Army to Europe, and she ended up fucking every old man in the neighborhood while he was gone. When he came back she was living with some old dude down off Denison and had already had a kid with the guy. Gus was crushed."

Oh, I said to myself, that's why the two of them were so tight.

"And then Gus just poured his heart into his job and baseball. He and my dad were still relatively young men when they came back from the war and they played baseball, not softball, for some pretty high-powered teams. Well, one day at work, Gus was looking one way and out of nowhere from the opposite direction a big crane came down landing on him. Knocked the shit out of him! Broke his shoulder and a bunch of ribs, gave him a massive concussion, and pretty much ended baseball for him."

That wasn't the end of it.

"So Gus is laid up for almost a year, most of it in the

hospital. The good thing is he meets Mary, his wife, at the hospital where she was a nurse."

"I didn't know Gus was married."

"Yeah, he was once. Do you remember twenty years ago, we must have been only a couple of years old, when an oil tanker truck came down Granger Road and didn't stop, causing a big fire and an accident that killed a bunch of people? Well, three of those people killed were Mary, and Mary and Gus's two kids. That was the saddest night of my life. My parents rushing to the hospital. My dad and Gus up all night drinking whiskey and crying. The funeral with the three coffins. It was the worst. It's really the first thing I ever remember."

A long pause and we both stared out into space. I was in shock. I had no idea. I mean, Gus, to me, was one of the happiest, most content people I knew. "Man, that's a lot of shit to go down for one person, you know."

"I do know, and that's why all this stuff that I was feeling sorry for is so ridiculous. If that's the way it is, then that's the way it is. My problems with a couple of busted relationships are nothing compared to the stuff that some people have gone through. People like Gus."

I later confirmed all this with Mate's mom. "For the most part, that's the way it happened," she said. And you know, that's why Gus loves you guys so much."

"Why's that?"

"Those two children killed in that wreck were both boys. Gus's boys. His pride and joy. Gus was going to raise them to be champions, and you guys just have naturally taken their place. And he really does. He loves both of you more than you'd ever know. He's always been so proud of both of you. You mean so much to him."

During those first years out of school I don't think Mate and Beth ever crossed paths. However, I had several encounters with her.

The first was during the summer after our first year of teaching at D'Poo's in the Flats. I was meeting a girl I was teaching with for some mid-summer cocktails. I was leaning against the bar waiting for her to show up and bullshitting with Tommy Rockwell, a guy that Mate and I first met in high school who was at the time coaching at Westlake. We were discussing the upcoming high school football season, and I kept glancing at the front of the bar to see if my date had walked in. Suddenly, the front filled with the noise of the laughing and screaming of thirty drunk nurses, who were rolling into the bar on what appeared to be a mobile bachelorette party. Rockwell and I watched from across the room and the sight of thirty attractive and drunk girls made us forget who was playing who the first weekend of the season.

Just when I turned away from the girls to say something to Tommy, I heard a laugh above the noise of the crowd that I hadn't heard in three years. It had to be Beth. My eyes searched the crowd until I found her, her arms around another girl, whispering in her ear, and then they both broke up in laughter.

I think she sensed that someone was staring at her. She walked up to the other end of the bar, ordered two pitchers of beer, and then made her way back to the front corner where her friends had congregated, all the while glancing around the crowd. As she put down the pitchers, she looked up and saw me across the bar room, and a big smile covered her face.

"God, it's great to see you," she said as she wrapped her arms around me and gave me a long, wet kiss.

"And it's great to see you," I said, obviously enjoying the moment.

"Are you going to be here for a while? Let me get the troops settled down and I'll be back in a couple of minutes," she said as she disappeared into the crowd.

"Who the hell is that?" Rockwell said, obviously impressed.

"Oh, an old friend from high school. She used to be Mate's girlfriend a long time ago."

"Jeez, what happened for him to give up on her? What a nice piece of work!"

"A lot of bad timing, and then she met someone else."

"I don't know, man. I've only seen her once and she's impressed me."

She reappeared several minutes later, carrying a small tray

with two Buds and two shots of tequila on it.

"What about a short one for old times sake?" She said with that great smile she had always had.

We each grabbed a shot, toasted to 'old friends,' and then stared at each other awkwardly. After several moments of silence, we broke into a burst of laughter.

"How are you guys? What are you doing? Where are you living?" She asked one question after another, seeming sincere and concerned about our well beings.

As we talked and talked and rambled on, the unexpected happened. Over the course of about an hour, and more than our quota of tequila, we got ourselves totally shitfaced. My date showed up and saw I was busy talking to an old friend, so she hung out at the bar with Rockwell. Beth and I ended up in a booth along the wall, and talked about old friends and families and just kept pounding them.

The last time I saw her, or was supposed to see her, was at her wedding. So pristine in her gown, so serious looking. The girl I was drinking with seemed like a different person. She reminded me of herself of years ago, back before what Mate called her "taking life too serious" stage.

Sprinkled in and around our conversation were several comments about marriage. Not about her marriage, she said, but about marriage in general.

"I really don't know if marriage is what it's cracked up to be," she said. "Sometimes I really like it and at other times I don't. I mean, I have a lot to be grateful for, a hard-working husband with a great salary and a beautiful house in Rocky River, but sometimes I find it kind of boring."

After a couple more shots she brought up marriage again. "You know, I don't think you or Mate (it was the first time she brought up his name) could handle being married. You guys couldn't handle having your wings clipped."

Then after a few more shots she said, "If you or Mate ever think about getting married, I'm going to talk you out of it. For you guys, it would just suck. Too much structure."

After about an hour one of her girlfriends came and got her, and the bachelorette party headed back out into the street, onto the bus, and down the road to the next bar.

Over the next several days, I tried to analyze what Beth had said in that bar that night, but I couldn't come up with any concrete opinions. Even though we were sharing a house in Lakewood at the time, I never mentioned to Mate that I saw Beth. She then drifted out of my mind until the next time I saw her.

I hadn't seen her in over three years, yet I saw Beth once again a month later at the same bar. It was the morning of the first Browns home game that year and we had decided to meet there before the game. I drove down alone because I had to go to my parents house for dinner after the game. I was standing in the same spot, nursing a beer and staring at the door waiting for a familiar face to waltz in, when I saw Beth walk in with her husband. Even though I had only seen him once, I knew it was him. Blown dry hair trying very hard to cover a bald spot or two. Expensive flannel shirt with a more expensive sweater wrapped around his shoulders. She saw me when she first entered the place and whispered to her husband that she would be right back. She came over and gave me a much more sisterly kiss than she did the last time I saw her.

"What do you do, live here?"

"I was just about to ask you the same thing," I said and we both burst into laughter.

"C'mon, let me buy you and your husband a short one, or at least a beer or a bloody mary."

"No, no, I can't. How about a coke or something like that?"

Right away I knew. "You're pregnant, aren't you?"

A smile covered her face. "Just found out on Tuesday. God, I feel great about it." She rambled on about when it was due, what names they were thinking about, and even the color of the new wallpaper she ordered for the baby's bedroom.

She drank her coke, made some more small talk, gave me a kiss on the cheek, and made her way back to her husband and their crowd.

At the time I wrote these off as encounters with an old friend who was just trying to make her marriage work. If nothing else ever happened, I would have forgotten that first meeting in the bar and just remembered Beth from the second, when she was glowing and how happy she was to be pregnant.

The third encounter with Beth was an indirect one that happened later that year over Christmas break. It had been a hectic fall, teaching and coaching football and then middle school basketball, and by the time Christmas break came I was overdue for some hard core partying. I needed a couple of nights out, and an opportunity to meet a new lady or two.

I bumped into a girl I knew from OSU while Christmas shopping, and she was with a friend named Lori. Lori had a great smile, so I got her number from my friend and asked her out for a movie.

We seemed to hit it off well and in the course of small talk on the way to the show, she mentioned that she worked for the law firm run by Beth's husband's family.

When I mentioned that I was good friends with Beth and asked her what her husband was like, Lori gave me a real cold stare and changed the subject. I made a note to pursue the topic later in the evening.

After the movie, a pizza, and a couple of beers that loosened both of our tongues, I brought up the topic of Beth's husband again.

"You gave me a real icy stare when I mentioned Beth and her husband before. Is it because you don't want to talk about work? If not, that's all right."

"No, it's not that. Well, it's just that...," and she stumbled over her thoughts, paused for a second, and then continued. "It's just that, you promise not to tell anyone? I mean this is personal stuff."

Before he got married Beth's husband was a bit of a spoiled rich kid, working at his family's firm throughout high school, college, and law school. During that time he was always hitting on the legal secretaries, many times unsuccessfully, but sometimes successfully. He had gotten himself in trouble occasionally. Lori remembered a DWI, but his old man was always able to bale him out.

"It wasn't because he was a bad person, because at times he

really could be a good guy. It's just that he never let you forget that he was the boss's kid, and you just knew he never had to worry about money or anything else like that."

She went on to tell me that eventually his father called him into his office, after he had been out of law school for a couple of years, and told his son it was time to settle down, cut down on the partying, and find someone to marry if he wanted to move into the hierarchy of the law firm like his brothers and cousins. That was when Beth entered his life.

"Everyone thought that she was the best thing that ever happened to him. Here was a good, family-oriented girl who seemed to worship him. We heard she had just had a falling out with her boyfriend who was away at college, something about him being on drugs or something. Steven seemed to really settle down. The next thing you knew, they were planning a wedding."

It was what had happened after they got married that caused Lori to give me the icy stare earlier in the evening. Lori told me that for the first couple of years Steven and Beth were married, everything seemed to be fine. Beth's husband had settled down and became the happily married man. It was when his father pushed him up and made him the youngest full partner in the law firm that things started to unravel slightly.

"He got this new position with power over other people's jobs and more responsibility and he just hasn't been able to handle it." She went on to tell me power had gone to his head, and caused him to revert back to some old behaviors.

"First, I know he's started to do a lot of coke, because he's hanging around with some other lawyers at work who live for the stuff. I know on Friday afternoons and on nights they work late, they're doing it in his office. You can just tell. Maybe the pressure is getting to him. All I know is if his old man finds out, the shit will hit the fan."

Then she paused and asked, "How well do you know Beth?"

I told her that we were pretty tight at one time, but since she has gotten married I had only seen her twice.

"Well, with all this power and maybe the coke, I don't

know, he started to flirt around with the secretaries at work again. And, well, rumors have it he has something going with one of them. I mean, he's always asking her to work late, and she makes no secret about what is going on between the two of them. I think it just stinks. What a rat. And now his wife's pregnant. Do you mind if we talk about something else?"

We did, but not before I filed our conversation somewhere back in my brain to think about at a later date.

By January, Beth was excited about being a mom. She was going to keep working at the hospital until she was about six weeks away, and she was spending a lot of time getting her house ready for the new addition to the family.

It was a Thursday afternoon and Beth and her mom were trying to hang the curtains they had bought for the baby's room. They were both on chairs trying to balance a curtain rod when Beth suddenly felt a very sharp pain, stretching across her stomach and into her abdomen. She blacked out, and tumbled off the chair and onto the floor.

At the time of Beth's accident, Mate and I were living together in Lakewood. I remember that it was a Thursday night and I was the only one home. Mate was up at the Tam-o-Shanter watching a hockey game and drinking beers with the girls who lived next door. I was sitting on the couch grading some papers when the phone rang.

"Greg, is Mate there?" I heard Beth say, her voice sounding very hoarse, like she had been crying.

"No, Beth, he isn't. He's up at the Tam. Can I leave him a message?"

There was a long pause and she said, "No, that's all right. I just wanted to talk to him," and she hung up without saying good-bye.

I was perplexed. Why did she call? What did she want to talk to him about? Why did she sound so lousy?

I never saw Mate that night. I fell asleep on the couch grading reports. The next day was very hectic at school and our paths didn't cross. He went out scouting for the varsity that night and I went to their game, so we didn't catch up to each other until sometime around midnight with all the other coaches at the bar. I got him caught up on our game, then he pulled me aside and out of the blue asked me, "Have you heard from Beth lately?"

Before I could respond he continued, "Because the last several days I've had the worst dreams about her. I keep having this dream where she's in trouble. She's like down in a hole, and she's screaming for help, and I just can't get her. Isn't that weird?"

I started to try to talk again and tell him about last night's phone call, but be kept going, "It was just real fucking weird. Let's not talk about it. It's too depressing, and I haven't let her get me depressed for a long time. Hey, need another beer?" Before I was able to speak, he was up at the bar buying another round.

I wanted to do some investigating into the matter before I said anything to Mate. A couple of days later I got the low down from Lori.

When Beth felt the sharp pain through her middle, she probably lost the baby then, not when she hit the floor like she has always taken the blame for. Her mother first panicked and then called the ambulance.

The miscarriage was messy. By the time they got her to the hospital, her clothes were soaked with blood. Beth had become hysterical when she realized what had happened.

By the late afternoon it was all over and Beth lay in bed staring off into space, trying to deal with the fact that the thing inside her wasn't there anymore, that it was the puddle of goo she saw in the ambulance and on the table in the emergency room. What hurt just as bad was the fact that she was alone. *Where the hell is he?* She would say over and over to herself. *Doesn't he know how much I hurt? Where is he?*

Beth's husband had left Cleveland early that day to go down to Columbus to take care of several matters for clients with the state attorney general's office. He also needed to have some records looked up at the State House, so he brought along his favorite secretary. His plan was for both of them to work the morning separately, then meet for lunch and do some work together.

His law firm couldn't track him down, and it wasn't until a very long lunch was over with that he bothered to call in.

By the time he traveled back up I-71, got his secretary home, and made his way to the hospital, it was very late.

When he finally did appear in the doorway to Beth's room, Beth was relieved. She needed someone to share the pain and hurt, she needed someone to hold her. That's when Beth first saw the real side of the guy she at one time thought was Mr. Perfect.

"What the hell were you doing on top of a chair? What are you, fucking nuts? Look what you have done!" She just froze. She couldn't believe what she was hearing.

"How can you jeopardize the safety of my child? What the hell were you thinking about?" He went on and on, blaming everything on her.

She was shocked. The worst thing that had ever happened to her, and she got no support and all the blame. She had never felt worse in her life.

After her husband was done yelling at her and blaming Beth for what had happened, he stormed out of the room and disappeared down the hallway, looking for Beth's mom to share the blame. It was sometime soon after, that Beth made the call looking for Mate. I think she just needed someone to support her and talk to, and he was the person who came to mind.

Steven would later come back all apologetic and sorry for the things he said, laden with hundreds of dollars worth of flowers and gifts. But she had already seen something she had never seen before, a side of him she didn't like, and things would never be the same between them.

Beth's husband always had everything handed to him throughout his life, and he couldn't handle it when anything didn't go along as planned. He breezed through Ignatius, Georgetown, and Law School at Case, with his old man footing the bills. He got by on money, charm, and good looks. He had found a real prize in Beth; he was moving up in the firm; and the new house was great. But Beth's miscarriage wasn't in the plans and it couldn't have been his fault, because bad things didn't happen to him. So he blamed her and didn't give her support when she needed it the most. That fucking son of a bitch.

The only positive thing out of this whole ordeal was that Beth quit looking at him through rose-colored glasses, and started to realize that maybe she might have made a mistake or two in her young life.

For some unexplainable reason, I never told Mate that Beth called that night, especially when I put all the pieces together. It was just too emotional of a thing. When he found out through the grapevine that she had had a miscarriage, he showed genuine concern for her.

"I think she was close to having everything she ever really wanted and she must be greatly disappointed," he said.

It was a cold, wet September Thursday evening during the first year we taught together. The Indians, thirty games out of first place, were playing the Twins at the Stadium. Mate was looking for someone to go to the game with. I said I had to run over to my parents' house for dinner. A little white lie to get out of being one of seven hundred people in a stadium that sat close to eighty thousand for a meaningless game during another awful season.

Mate was desperate to find someone, so after practice he ran over to one of our elementary schools looking for Fred the janitor. Mate always had a list of people who would go to see the Tribe play anytime, and Fred was on that list.

Mate was disappointed that Fred had left, but surprised the building wasn't locked up. Sitting in the office were two of the best looking kids you could imagine. A dark haired Hispanic girl of about twelve, and what looked like her slightly younger brother.

The only other person in the building was the office secretary, who was in a state of panic.

"Mr. Majowski, I don't know what to do. These two students are stranded here. Their mother is stuck at work, and I should have been home an hour ago."

She filled Mate in on the situation. The two children were

Carmen (aka Connie) and Carman (aka Manny) Lopez. It was their first day in the school district. Their mother had her first day at a new job, and thought she'd be done in time to pick them up by four. She called in a panic that because of an emergency, she wouldn't get there until six at the earliest. We would later find out that the emergency was that the mom was stranded at her place of employment because her car had been repossessed.

Mate saw the obvious solution to the problem. He asked the secretary for the number of the mother at work. He explained to the woman that he'd be glad to take her children home, if he could borrow them for a couple of hours. The woman was still unsure how she was going to get home herself, let alone get her children home from school. He'd drive them home, but not before a couple of stops.

He walked over to the kids, bent down and said to them, "Hi, my name is Mr. Majowski. Do you guys like baseball?"

"Baseball," the girl responded. "Mommy never lets us watch baseball."

"Well, tonight I don't think she has a choice."

Mate first took them to his parents' house for dinner. The girl did all the talking in the car while the young boy sat quietly staring out the window and doing whatever his sister said.

The kids loosened up a little bit when they arrived at the Majowski household to grab something to eat. They walked in on one of Old Mate's and Uncle Gus' spontaneous dueling accordion concerts. Mate's mom dug out assorted Indians and Browns clothing to keep the two kids warm at the Stadium. Mate tracked me down and explained the situation with the two kids, and how there was a need for two adults. So I spent another cold September night with seven hundred or so other diehard fans, in that huge ball park freezing my ass off, watching our beloved Indians lose another one.

It was an eventful night, however, because little did we know the roles those two scared kids would later play in our lives.

Connie and Manny had a great time at the game. It was a night of many firsts for them. Their first major league ball game. Their first Indians game. Their first trip to Cleveland Stadium.

Their first night at the Majowski household. Their first night of unlimited hot dogs and cokes. Their first night of Stadium Mustard. When we ended up finally driving them home, Mate didn't have the heart to take back all the Indians and Browns stuff the kids were wearing. They looked so damn cute, he figured what the hell.

After some snooping around the next several days, Mate found out about Connie and Manny's background. The mother, Anna, had moved out to River Boro to escape the poverty of Cleveland's near west side and get the kids in a decent school system. Although Connie was a year ahead of Manny in school and acted much older than him, they were actually twins. They lived in the new public housing built in the north end of town. Their mom got a job working as an orderly at the new hospital. Every two weeks she would work from three to eleven, which wasn't very conducive to having two young kids, but it was the first real job she ever had that had hospitalization. For the first time since she had given birth, she was off the welfare roll. How long it was going to last, no one knew.

Anna wasn't that much older than Mate and I. She was on her last gasp of hope. A product of Cleveland's poor Hispanic west side, she never knew her father and grew up in a house that housed four generations of her family. She grew up a beautiful young woman, just like her daughter would, and caught the eyes of many male members of the Cleveland Hispanic community.

At a party at the Latino Community Center not much past her sixteenth birthday, she met Julio Martinez. Yes, the Julio Martinez who spent three wasted years of an otherwise good career, playing second base for the Indians. Anna was immediately charmed by the handsome professional athlete, who was treated like a young prince in the Hispanic community. Tall, muscular, flashy smile, gold chains around his neck, Julio was a charmer. He was also married at the time, but his wife and children spent the baseball season at their year round home in the Dominican Republic. Julio loved the freedom of the baseball season in America, and he didn't want his family responsibilities to get in the way.

With no father or older brother to look out for her, and a mother who would probably have done the same thing, Anna became Julio's young lover.

He would meet up with her after long road trips and they would make love upstairs at her house while her mother was at work and her younger brothers and sisters played in the streets. Or they would meet at the apartment he shared with several other ball players in Westlake.

Anna was young, naive and stupid as she spent the summer in love with a twenty-five year old married man. When he left at the end of the baseball season to go back to his family in the Dominican Republic, he left behind empty promises and a pregnant and scared teenager. That winter Anna would give birth to beautiful twins and the Indians would trade Julio Martinez to the Dodgers in the National League. He would never again set foot in Cleveland.

After that first night, Connie and Manny became our unofficial little brother and sister. Starting that winter they became our tag alongs, which included being managers and ball boy and girl of whatever team we would be coaching, and we would drive them home whenever they needed a ride. Mate's parents just loved them and had them over for dinner all the time. Looking back on it now, I find it hard to even remember a time when they weren't a part of our lives.

After reading this story so far and knowing that both of us majored in secondary education in college, you probably assumed that we would both end up teaching at Franciscan. It didn't turn out that way. They had the opportunity to hire both of us and they didn't, and it worked out for the better. Teachers have it bad enough at times, but the Catholic schools really treat their teachers like shit. Low wages, lousy benefits, poor administration. It's no secret that Franciscan isn't the school that it used to be, and it has something to do with what's wrong with Catholic education and the way Franciscans do things, which has nothing to do with this story, so I won't elaborate on it anymore.

I got a job while still in college at River Boro and the

following summer Mate got in. We thought it was so great that we both got into the same system.

Mate and I both coached football, I did middle school basketball and track in the spring, and he did girls softball. He got involved in basketball really by accident.

In his second year at River Boro, Mate was finishing up junior varsity football in the late fall and was looking forward to his winter time duty, weight room monitor, when Stan Sapara had a heart attack that laid him up for the winter. Stan had coached ninth grade basketball for what seemed like forever, and when they needed someone to take his place in a hurry Mate volunteered.

Mate had never played basketball in high school or college on any varsity team, but he did play a lot of basketball. When you had gone to an all boys high school and lived in a frat house in college with its own court in the backyard, you got to play a lot of hoops. And Mate was a good hoopster. To make up for his lack of any real size or jumping ability, Mate knew his way around a court. He played tough on D; could pick, roll and hit the open jumper; and knew it was a team game.

After playing and coaching only football, Mate was first surprised at the simplicity of basketball. Instead of having fifty kids on a team spread out over the field at practice, he had twelve kids inside a gym. There were no broken shoulder pads and missing spikes. Kids couldn't easily fake an injury to dog practice. It didn't rain in the gym, plus if he wanted to, Mate could throw himself into a drill or scrimmage, which he really liked.

Mate's first team was a good group of kids. What Mate lacked on b-ball X's and O's, his team made up with hustle and defense. Mate had those kids playing like tigers, never letting up and they finished a surprising 12-3, the best ninth grade record that anybody could remember.

Stan decided to give up coaching and the ninth grade team was Mate's. His next two teams only lost one and two games respectively, and both won league championships. They didn't play much differently than his first one, but every year Mate knew a little more hoops, and picked up little tricks. Plus, and this is a big one, the talent kept getting better and better.

At the same time Mate was also promoted to varsity line coach on the football staff, and that was his first priority. Everybody, including Mate himself, just assumed that if he ever became a head coach, it would probably be in football. That's what he played in high school and in college, and everyone just assumed that.

The guy who was the varsity basketball coach had decided to retire from coaching because he wanted to watch his sons play. He lived outside the district and his kids played at Brecksville. Everyone just assumed that the JV coach, Tom Wilson, would get the varsity job. A good coach, but also an asshole. He was real arrogant, thought his shit didn't stink, and started acting as if he had the job before it was given to him.

At the same time the superintendent of the district, Dr. Kaniecki, was also retiring. What a great guy, our district still misses him today. Wilson had always rubbed Kaniecki the wrong way, and Kaniecki didn't want Wilson to get the head basketball job.

Kaniecki had five kids go through our system, had seen almost everyone coach one of his kids, and he always liked Mate. Mate had coached his daughter in softball, and she just raved about him. Mate had coached his youngest son in basketball, and Kaniecki was always impressed with the fact he didn't give him any special treatment, keeping the kid on the bench for the most part. The next year on the j.v.'s, Wilson always made a point to play the kid whenever he knew his old man was at a game, a facade that Kaniecki saw right through. Kaniecki was a rarity in public schools, an administrator who didn't expect special treatment for his children. Most administrators and school board members think it's a fringe benefit that comes with the position.

Our school system has the policy that if someone teaching in the district applies for a coaching position, he or she gets first dibs on the job. As far as we knew, Wilson was the only person who applied for the basketball job.

One day Mate got a note in his mailbox from Dr. Kaniecki to stop in and see him during his free period. He was rather scared. "What do you think the old man wants to see me about?" He asked me as we crossed in the hall. He hadn't been in his office since he was hired, although he had interacted with him several times. Kaniecki was another rarity among administrators, he never snooped around, and he liked to come to the teachers lounge to socialize and to tell a joke or two. He also liked to stop for a beer or two on Fridays after school or after a game, and so did Mate.

"Mate, I'm going to be honest with you. Do you ever want to be a head coach? Run your own program?"

"Well, to tell you the truth, I still think I'm years away. I mean, football is just such a complicated game. I've asked Shorty if I could coach maybe defensive backs next year, just to learn the position."

"Mate, I'm not talking football, I'm talking basketball."

Mate sat there, stunned for a moment. Basketball? It had never entered his mind. He loved doing it, but he still considered himself such a novice.

"You know that the basketball job is open, and Wilson is the only guy who has applied for it inside the district. If the football job ever came open, and I don't see that happening for years, we would have four, maybe five guys inside the district applying for it, including you. I don't think you'd get it. Not that you're not a good candidate, but the other guys would be just a little more experienced, longer in the system." He paused. "But I sense that one day you want to be a head coach. I would hate it if the system ever lost you, and that is one reason I want you to apply for the basketball job. The school board will choose whomever I recommend, and just between you and me, I think you would be the best candidate."

Mate was stunned. He had never thought about the job and just assumed that it was Wilson's for the asking.

"Another reason I want you to have the job is because I think you need it. You still have too much of the college kid in you, and this will settle you down. I have no doubts that you will be a great coach. Don't even let the thought enter your mind. Get those kids playing defense like you've had your ninth grade teams play, and you'll be in every ball game. Here's the application. If you're interested, get it back to me tomorrow."

The day that Mate got the basketball job was another one of those days I'll never forget. When word was out that he was seriously in the running, a lot of people started rooting for him. He became the student body's obvious choice, and that of most of the faculty. But that didn't make him the obvious choice overall, especially with Wilson having more experience. And, you have to remember, it was a decision being made by school administrators and a school board, two groups of people who have long histories of not regularly making the right decisions.

But, as promised in one of his last moves before retiring, (little did we know he had another coaching move up his sleeve), Dr. Kaniecki convinced the school board to choose Mate. Kaniecki broke the news to Wilson first, face-to-face in the privacy of his office. Again, a sign of class on Kaniecki's part because most administrators would have just put a 'fill in the blanks' form letter in Wilson's mail box.

Back then we were both still coaching spring sports, and Mate was summoned to the main office as everyone was going out to practice. It had been a suspenseful two weeks since his meeting with Kaniecki, and the more he thought about it, the more he wanted the job. He didn't think he was really going to get it, especially since he never played the game on the high school or college level. He had confidence in himself as a coach, but he just wasn't sure he was going to be the first pick for the job.

The day he was officially offered the job was a rare one at school. It was probably the only day that spring that none of our teams had a game or meet, and everyone was trying to practice at one time. When this happens every team overlaps onto each other. Softballs land on the running track, distant runners cut across outfields, whistles from the sprinters distract tennis players.

Mate got the job and everyone thought it was a great choice, except, of course, Tom Wilson. Wilson pouted about it for a while and then resigned his JV position, which was fine with Mate. Mate had always gotten along with Wilson, but he also couldn't stand him. Whenever Mate asked him for advice, Wilson would give it to him as if he was talking down to him.

Wilson never showed much class about getting passed over. He would constantly moan about it and often would say negative things about Mate's coaching ability behind his back. He later would get back into coaching, taking over the girls team, but he never let it go unknown that he still coveted Mate's job.

When Mate went into the board office and Wilson was seen pulling out of the teacher's parking lot, the word spread through the practice fields that the job was Mate's. When Mate appeared jogging across the football field towards the softball diamond, he had a smile on his face and you knew that it was true. Before he went over to his JV softball team patiently waiting for him on the bench, he sprinted over to where I was working with the high jumpers.

"Guess what?" He said, trying to contain his emotions.

"What?"

"I got it."

"What?" I replied, playing dumb and holding back a smile.

"The basketball job. I got the basketball job."

I still tried to play dumb. "I didn't know it was open." I couldn't keep a straight face and shook his hand and gave him a big hug. Within minutes he was surrounded by kids and coaches from every team, shaking his hand and congratulationing him.

It had been one of those warm early spring days when you didn't feel like teaching, and the kids bitched and moaned all day about how hot it was. The quarter had just ended the week before, and that meant most of the teachers had spent the weekend before doing grades. Spring break was still two weeks away. It was a Thursday that should have been a Friday, and it seemed like the whole school had spent the day going through the motions. I decided on the spur of the moment that Mate getting the head coaching job would be a good excuse for a coaches/faculty get together.

A couple of the guys who had gone to Franciscan with us

had bought one of the bars in the old part of Parma, renamed it the Traveling Circus Tavern, and in a shrewd marketing ploy signed Mate and I up as official juke box consultants. Mate thought it was because he had the best record collection of anyone we knew, but I knew it was because we'd each be good for fifty bucks of business a week. It soon became the hang out for our faculty and coaching staff. As coaches came over to congratulate Mate, I started to whisper in their ears about that evening. Word spread and I ended practice early and called as many people as possible who I thought might show up. By the time Mate and I rolled into the joint that night, we had a contingent of thirty or so.

Mate was genuinely surprised and appreciative of everyone's good wishes and enjoyed being the center of attention for the evening. The night was pretty spirited and everyone was happy for Mate and happy to have a good time. No one was concerned about school the next day, and it felt good to be out and enjoying each other's company.

Time flew and things were still going strong when at eleven Mate announced he had to leave. "I want to go over and tell my parents before they hear it from someone else. They're really going to be excited." After one more round of hugs and handshakes, Mate disappeared out the door, heading over to the south side and the old neighborhood.

Being a Thursday, Mate knew his mom would be over at the church helping with bingo. He figured he'd catch his dad at home or at one of the neighborhood joints, and then they would wait up to tell his mom when she came home around midnight.

He pulled into the driveway and saw the light on in the front room so he knew his father was home, probably sitting in his easy chair watching the news on television. Mate was so excited he had trouble putting the key into the lock of the back door.

"Dad! Dad! Guess what!" He yelled through the house as he made his way through the kitchen to the front room. He heard no reply.

"Dad, Dad," he repeated, but was cut short by the sight of his father laying face down across the middle of the living room floor. Mate immediately knew what had happened, as he reached for his father's neck to see if there was a pulse. All he found was cold clammy skin.

"Dad, Dad," he whispered. "Dad, Dad I got the basketball job," he said, as he reached down and hugged his father's body to his own as tears rolled down his face.

Chester "Old Mate" Majowski was honored with a wake and funeral befitting a man who was a veteran of two wars, twenty-five years down in the mills, an active member of his church and several veteran and nationality groups, and a loving and respected husband, father, uncle, cousin and neighbor. As contradiction will often have it at such times, the three day period between his death and his burial at Holy Cross was filled with much warmth and laughter. With many of Mate's uncles and guys from his dad's neighborhood and work together at one time, both the booze and the stories were flowing. Before and after the hours at the funeral home, and at the funeral itself, the Majowski house was constantly filled with people, with the bar always open and the kitchen table constantly filled with food.

Mate held up well, and seemed to enjoy the warmth and love of his relatives and friends. He enjoyed hearing for the umpteenth time all the stories, true and untrue, involving his father.

He really only lost his composure twice, and both happened at the funeral mass when everyone else did too. After communion, when there is a moment of silence and then a song or prayer for reflection, from the choir loft high above the rear of St. Barbara's Church, the fat lady started the first line of "Waltzing Matilda." As her voice filled the church with the ballad about the young soldier and his lost love that Mate's father first heard around a fire camped on a beach in the South Pacific forty years earlier, there was not a dry eye in the house. After the service was over and as Mate, Uncle Gus, and few of his cronies carried Old Mate's flag-covered coffin out of the church, the same fat woman led the congregation in "The Battle Hymn of the Republic." The same eyes filled with more tears.

For me there are two other moments from that weekend I

still remember. The first was how hard Connie and Manny took Old Mate's death. At that time, Connie was in the high school with us as a ninth grader, and Manny was in the eighth grade. By that time they had become regulars with us. We took them to Tribe, Cavs, and Browns games. They showed up to chow down at Mate's parents' house at least twice a week. In appreciation, Manny took over the lawn mowing duties there. Connie helped clean and would often baby-sit for Mate's sister Barb, whose kids were still quite small at that time. Being around us, and hanging around the Majowski household, was the most stability their lives had ever had, and they loved it. Because they were such good kids and so likeable, they blended right in.

That weekend they did all the family things and were at the funeral home the whole time, stayed every night at the Majowski house until everyone left. They helped clean up and get the place ready to do the same thing the next day.

The other thing I remember is from the second night of the wake. The funeral home was packed, you wouldn't believe how many of the kids from school showed up, and out of the corner of my eye I thought I saw Beth come in the front door. I immediately went over to greet her, but as I fought my way through the crowd, she disappeared. For a moment I thought I was imagining it, and then I got into a conversation with an old friend and didn't think about it until much later.

To get on with his life, Mate literally buried himself in the basketball program. He continued to coach the varsity line on the football team, and the time he was putting in was phenomenal. He really attacked the basketball job. He went to clinics, worked camps during the summer, and had the gym open as much as possible. He was twenty-six when he got the job, single with no real responsibilities, and had the time and energy to put into the program.

Becoming head basketball coach also put some direction into Mate's life. He cut down on his partying and the amount of time he had to goof off, which caused himself to inject some self-discipline into his life and lifestyle.

It also caused him to keep up with his policy of not taking

any particular woman too seriously. He knew, that at least for the time being, he didn't have the time to pursue a full blown relationship. We knew way too many coaches who either were divorced, or caught all kinds of heat at home for the time they spent on coaching. He knew neither of those situations was for him.

That June before he would officially retire, Dr. Kaniecki would make another coaching decision that would take a lot of people by surprise, none more than myself.

The school year ended and we had gotten into our summer routine. Mate was still upset about the death of his father, and to a lesser extent so was I. We were sharing a house in Lakewood and both of us were finishing our masters at Cleveland State. One day I came home and there was a message from Mrs. Wilcox, Dr. Kaniecki's secretary, asking if I could stop by at my convenience the next morning. Right away I got scared. Did I do something wrong before school ended? Why would he want to see me the last week that he was superintendent?

When I sat down across from him the next day, the floor of his office covered with packing boxes, he immediately put me at ease. But after five minutes of small talk, he still had me confused as to why I was there.

"Did Mate tell you about the conversation we had before he became basketball coach?"

"Yes, in part he did."

"Well, I'm about to have almost the same conversation with you." He went on and explained the situation to me.

Our current head football coach had decided to give his position up. That was a surprise. We had struggled for the four years we had coached with him, a lot of it because of a big deficiency in talent. We just didn't have the kids. Our school system at that time was at the end of a cycle, with too many of the better athletes in the community going to Catholic schools.

"Who do you think should be the next coach?"

I then went over each of the assistants (excluding Mate and myself), pointing out the good points of each. Most had been on the staff for many more years than either of us, and all of them were more qualified.

"I have talked to each of those gentlemen over the course of the last two days, and they agreed completely with each other on three things. Whoever got the job would have to sink themselves into it completely, year round, probably for several years before we would see any results on the varsity level. They all agreed that it would be great if the new coach was already in the building, and that we wouldn't have to start out with a stranger over the summer. They all agreed that none of them wants the head job, and that the best candidate is you."

I had found most of it hard to believe, especially the last item. But, as I was later to find out, it was true. The other coaches, the ones I had thought would all die for the head coaching job, weren't in the position to put in the time or to deal with the aggravation. Most were in their mid to late thirties with young children, and they wanted to spend time doing things like coaching their sons' little league teams. All said they would like to hang on as assistants, but no one wanted the time-consuming job of head coach.

The same things went through my head that went through Mate's when he thought about taking the basketball job. It was going to take a couple of years before things might noticeably improve, but, if we could keep the kids in the district, help was on the way. We had some potential studs coming up. We knew that from coaching at the middle school and on the lower levels at the high school.

The last thing he told me was similar to what he had told Mate several months earlier. "Don't doubt your ability to coach. You're going to learn a lot on the job, but you already know a lot now. And being head coach will be good for you. You still have a bit of the college kid inside you, and the responsibilities as a head coach will keep you out of trouble."

And so, within a matter of a few months, both Mate's and my life changed direction when we became the head football coach and the head basketball coach at the same high school.

Mate and I had already decided that I was going to be his assistant for basketball, so it was decided that he would be line coach and defensive coordinator for football. We both worked

161

our asses off during the summer, not really knowing what to expect.

Becoming the head coaches of the two most popular sports in our school really called for a lifestyle adjustment for both of us. Much of our free time disappeared, we just had so much to do. One day that summer we got a letter from the Old Man, who was then on the staff at Wisconsin. Across the top of the letter embossed in bright red was BADGER FOOTBALL.

Dear Gentlemen,

I just thought I would drop you a line to congratulate you on the positions you have recently been appointed to. I can honestly say that I am very proud of both of you, and know that both of you will do a fine job.

There are several thoughts that I want to share with you. I hope that you both realize the responsibility that both of your positions require. In the short time since we have been together at Franciscan there have been big changes in kids and the role that a coach plays is more important in a young man's life. Don't ever forget how many of your players don't live with both their biological parents. Don't ever forget how many of your players have family histories of drug and alcohol problems. Don't ever forget that most of your players haven't had the opportunities and the support that you had growing up.

Don't you ever forget that they need you more than you ever needed us.

The other thought I want to share with you is also about responsibility, specifically the responsibility of responsibility. You have both willingly taken the reigns of the two most important positions in your school. You will be the most visible representatives of your school district. No one in your district can tell you who the English department chairman is, or who is the junior high

*assistant principal. But you can be damn sure
everyone knows who the varsity football and
basketball coaches are. Don't ever jeopardize your
team or your position.*
    Good Luck and God Bless,
    Coach P.

Since we were now head coaches we both thought about moving closer to school. We had been living in Lakewood in this big old double on Clifton that we really liked, but it was a little too far from school and we both needed more room.

I knew both of us thought about going our own way and finding our own places. Maybe it was time, we thought. But summer was soon to turn into football season, and we hadn't decided what to do. It was Mate's mom who made the decision for us.

"I got something to tell you boys and I don't want you to say no," she said as she was making us a late summer supper. Mate had been spending the summer trying to get her to sell the house and move into a smaller place, maybe in a safer neighborhood. She didn't want to live in the big old house by herself, and keeping up with the maintenance was something she had no desire to do. She came up with the solution, and would not let us change her mind.

"I'm moving in with your Uncle Gus," she said. "His house is as big as this, and he hasn't used that second floor of his in years."

Mate was bummed that his family house would soon belong to another family, but he knew it would be best if his Mom was living with his uncle across the street.

"That would be great Mom. You should get a decent price for the house. This part of the neighborhood is still pretty good."

"Why should I sell it?"

"What are you going to do, give it away?"

"Yes. To you two."

We argued that you just don't give people houses, but she didn't want to hear about it. "Listen, Gus and I thought about maybe both of us moving out to Parma or Strongsville some place. But if you really look at it, this is the only neighborhood we have ever lived in. We're too old to move and we're too old to live alone. So we'll live together. We've been like brother and sister for years anyway. And you guys are too busy to look for a new place to live, and probably too poor to buy your own houses yet. It is almost the perfect situation."

It was that August at the beginning of the football season that we moved from Lakewood to the big house on Redmond Avenue. I looked at it as a great temporary situation for me. I never expected to live there for more than a couple of years, and I thought it would give me the opportunity to save some money so I could one day buy myself a house of my own.

Not only did we get the house, we got the best cook in town doing our grocery shopping and, several times a week, cooking a batch of food for us. That first year in the Cleveland house we each gained ten pounds. When we came home from a hard day of teaching and coaching, there was always a roast or a batch of stuffed cabbage in the fridge. With Mate's mom in charge of the kitchen, Uncle Gus stocking the beer refrigerator, and Connie and Manny in charge of maintenance, we lived the life of kings on Redmond Avenue.

We were so lucky to have the kids we had in place when we first took over our teams. They were not talented, there were no physical specimens, but they had great attitudes and they were sick of losing. All they wanted was to play sports for their school and occasionally win some games.

They also knew the score on something that was an important factor in us taking the head coaching positions, their little brothers. Because they knew, just like we knew, that if we could make it through the first few seasons help was on its way, because coming up through the school system were several excellent classes of athletes. Mate and I knew about them from coaching at the middle school, and we knew if we could get things in place, by the time they reached the varsity level, things would be looking good.

I will always love that first group of kids. They did nothing but play their hearts out night after night. During football season we won only three games, but we played tough every week. The three that we won came out of our last four, and the one we lost we blew a fourth quarter lead. We closed the season upsetting Valley Forge, and knocking them out of a tie for first place.

During basketball we went 8-12, losing our first seven games, and then winning five out of our last six. We even won our first sectional game, before getting clobbered by a loaded Collinwood team.

While we were struggling with the varsity teams, Mate and I talked some of the old timers in the district to come out of coaching retirement to coach the middle school, ninth grade and junior varsity teams. These guys were great coaches who recognized the potential of the younger kids, and really worked on developing their skills. That first year we won or came in second in our league in ninth grade football and basketball, as well as JV football and basketball. We also got some of the district's graduates going to college locally and living at home to coach in the youth leagues. We doubled the amount of kids involved, as well as the number of volunteers, and the benefits of that are still felt in the school district today.

We knew if we kept all the kids involved playing sports, by our third season we could have as much raw physical talent on our teams as anyone in the area. We had some real athletes coming up, and we knew they could lead us to some fantastic things.

To show the talent we had coming up, the varsity basketball team finished winning five out of six against some pretty good competition. Before our first tournament game, I organized some of the kids on our ninth grade team, along with Manny, who was still in eighth grade, to be a scout team for our varsity. We were playing Parma in our first game, and I worked with the scouts to run their open post offense and the half court trap press they used. We spent the last forty-five minutes of practice all week playing against the varsity. Remember, these were just eighth and ninth graders, but they played the varsity tough every night. One night they couldn't stop Manny, and he was just a skinny little thing. And this was back before Richie Simmons had his growth spurt, and we played him as a wing and he hung tough, crashing the boards and running the floor. By the end of the week, some of the varsity kids started to get pretty confident about beating Parma, because "they can't be any better than these guys." And we did beat Parma 53-46.

When that first basketball season ended Mate and I took a good look back on both football and basketball, talked about our potential, and where we were going. Both of us felt in our hearts, that great things could happen one day.

Connie and Manny really grew into good kids, and it was great having them around. My little sisters were off in college somewhere, and Mate had never had any younger siblings, so they filled that role in both of our lives.

Their lives, when they were younger down on Clark Avenue had been a circus, and hanging around with all sorts of people just seemed natural for them. Mate's mom and dad just loved them, and always included them whenever they could in any family activity. When we lived in Lakewood we hired them to clean our house, spending hunks of Saturdays and Sundays with us. They always tagged along to go to Indians games, and they knew if they wanted a ride anywhere, or to go see a certain movie, that they could always talk Mate or me into it.

We became the absentee older brother/father figure they never had, and got them involved in things like little league and summer basketball camps.

We weren't really that much older than they, and as they got older, they became more and more like our peers than our little brother and sister.

When they got to high school, they started spending more time with their friends, and less with us, but that was O.K. Now that we were all in the same building and we saw each other constantly, we saw enough of each other.

Connie entered high school a determined young lady. Not wanting to make the same mistakes as her mother, she buried herself in her school work and activities. She played sports, never missed the honor roll, and was always around the building involved in everything from student council to school plays.

She was a cold woman to the fellas. When she got to the ninth grade, she really started to become a real looker. All the older guys in school noticed her when the freshmen arrived, but she put everyone in their place. No one could get close to her, and if she became friends with a guy or even went out with one, it was always on her terms.

She got a reputation early of being a bitch, but she was mislabeled. She just didn't put up with any role playing or any BS from any of the guys. Actually, as she got older, she became one of those girls at school who would accumulate just as many guy friends as girl friends. But she was always giving off the vibes that all she wanted was friendship, and no boy could figure her out.

She really did turn into a young beauty. The summer between her ninth and tenth grade I went almost two months without seeing her, and when she showed up at our place one Saturday to get caught up on the cleaning, she had breasts. Mate and I were sitting around reading the paper and deciding whether to catch the Tribe or head off to some street festival someplace, when she came in and started to do her usual routine like putting away albums and doing the dishes. We both noticed her growth spurt at the same time, and when she was out of ear shot, we both turned to each other and said, "Where the hell did she get those?"

Connie and Manny had such a mix of nationalities, Puerto Rican, Dominican, Caribbean Indian of some sort, and Connie got the best of all of them. She peaked out around five foot seven, black curly hair that fell down to her shoulders, skin that gave off what seemed like a permanent tan. She had an athletic body, the above mentioned breasts, and a great set of legs. She went from a skinny little bony junior high girl to a very attractive young lady in a matter of just a couple of school years. By the time she was a junior, all the boys ogled her, but they all respected her hands off policy.

Manny, on the other hand, remained a skinny kid all through middle and high school. By the time he was a junior, he was over six foot, but he weighed less than a hundred and fifty pounds. However, being a bean pole did not hamper him athletically. While in high school, he would never develop the confidence socially or academically that his sister did, but he fell in love with sports and excelled at each one he became involved in. He would be all conference in football, basketball and baseball his senior year, and also accumulate state recognition. As a wide receiver for three years, he would catch everything we threw to him. We still have some place a highlight video of all of his impossible catches. He would be the leading scorer on the basketball team his junior and senior years, and to this day I have not seen a smoother high school infielder.

We were the best thing that ever happened to Manny. I'm not saying that to slight Connie in any way, but she was just such a determined young lady that even if she didn't stumble into our lives she still would have been successful. But Manny, I don't know...

Several things were evident about Manny from the beginning. The first was that his English needed great improvement. He didn't speak or understand English very well, and that caused him to be misdiagnosed in school. He had been in and out of many schools as his Mom moved her family from relative to relative when they were younger. He was always living in households where Spanish was spoken, and he never developed the English language skills he needed to be successful at school.

That first summer when Manny became our full time tag along we started working hard on having him learn all the important words needed to survive in America in the late twentieth century. His vocabulary greatly increased as he spent time with us. Jump shot. Double play. "Look at the rack on that one." Beer Man. "Hey bar keep, food and drink for my men and horses." Hot Dog with extra Stadium Mustard. Slaw Dog. Go Tribe. Hooters. "Send the pie through the garden, hold the fish."

By the time he entered the seventh grade the next fall, he was a new man. Not only had his English improved, but after spending the summer around us, plus Old Mate and Uncle Gus, his confidence around his own peer group greatly improved. It also helped that for the first time ever he was going to the same school two years in a row. And, for the first time ever, he became involved in team sports and would discover the true passion of his life. After just a couple of days of middle school football practice, it was obvious that someday he was going to be something special. Without ever playing before, he was the leading scorer on the seventh grade basketball team. He got bumped up to the eighth grade team at the end of the season and led them to a conference tournament championship.

By the time he entered high school he blended in quite well. He knew all the older kids in sports because of us, and many of them looked out for him and involved him in things. He got a lot of respect for what he could do in athletics, and he had a sister who was one of the best looking girls in the school. He had come a long way in a short time from his life on Clark Avenue.

As she got older, Connie developed one annoying trait that drove me nuts. She became a part time smart ass. She was never happy with any of the women I dated, and she let me know it. She always had a comment about each one, and whenever I did end a relationship she'd let me know how happy she was about it and how the girl was not good enough for me. Everyone was either a bitch, a bimbo, or a ditz. She would always point out, whether real or imagined, fat thighs or droopy breasts or funny ears or a large nose.

When we started living in the big house on Redmond Avenue, she got in this habit of always showing up at our house on the mornings whenever I would have someone staying over. How she knew this, I didn't know. If the girl would be hanging around for breakfast or small talk, Connie would go about her chores as if the girl wasn't there, or as if the she was in the way and it was a hassle.

One time I accused her of sabotaging my relationships. "Why don't you ever do that to Mate's women?" I asked her.

"Do what?" She responded innocently.

"You know what. You can't fool me."

"It isn't my fault that your choice of overnight companions feels uncomfortable around younger people. Obviously a character flaw on their part."

One thing was evident for Mate and I from the start as head coaches, that there never was enough money to do things the way you wanted to. We increased the amount of kids in football, and game attendance went up drastically for football and basketball, but we always seemed to need something we couldn't pay for. We really wanted to upgrade many things, from uniforms to locker rooms to equipment. Sometime during our first season, I'm not sure when, we started to receive unsolicited help anonymously for both of our teams. We started to call it our 'guardian angel.' We had no idea who it was. We just assumed it was one of the parents of one of our wealthier kids, or possibly a business man from town who wanted to do something for the athletes. It always came at the right moment; and always seemed to be something special.

When we played down state at Upper Arlington, someone paid for a chartered bus so we could travel in style, instead of on a school bus. When we wanted to get team sweaters for our basketball team a due bill for three hundred dollars arrived from a local store. When we played Akron Butchel in football, three one hundred dollar bills appeared in my mail box at school to stop at McDonald's on the way home.

It was Connie who came up with the term 'guardian angel.' Mate, Manny, Connie and I went for pizza the night we went to order the team sweaters with the due bill. Mate and I were both teasing each other because we both thought the other one knew who it was.

"C'mon, tell me," he said.

"No, you tell me."

"I can't tell you something I don't know."

After ten minutes of this, Connie finally got tired of listening to it and said, "I think you both should start acting your age and just be thankful for what you got."

She said it so seriously and adult like that we both did shut up, and turned to her with great looks of surprise on our faces. Manny was surprised too. All three of us waited for what she had to say next.

Greg Cielec

"You should be grateful that our football and basketball teams both have a guardian angel to look out for us. What does it matter who it is, as long as we benefit from their actions."

She was right. Mate and I we both continued to believe that the other one knew who it was, we were both very grateful to whoever was our guardian angel.

As I went along writing this story, Connie would read it over and give me a suggestion or a word of encouragement. It was at this point in my first manuscript that she walked out onto the front porch, looked at me with the most angry eyes, and threw at me all two hundred pages of what I thought was going to be the greatest American book since Tom Sawyer.

"You pathetic, fat old man."

"What are you talking about?"

"I just got to the point where you talk about your first years as head coaches."

"Yeah, so?"

She stared at me for a long moment. "Aren't you forgetting some things?"

"Like what?"

"Like what? All of the sudden it sounds like our lives all got real serious. Don't you remember anything? It sounds like you both turned into Father Flanagan."

"Well, ..."

"Well, what about all the stuff Manny and I were sworn to secrecy about? All the things we couldn't tell any of our friends at school."

"Like what?"

"Like what? What about the time we walked in on Mate and Jennifer Martin screwing on the middle of the living room floor in the middle of the afternoon? What about the time you called us in sick for school, then called yourselves in, and we all went to the Indians' Opener?"

She kept on going. "Yeah, you did a lot of growing up. How about the summer you taught Manny to drive so you guys could have your own personal designated driver?"

"I thought that was a pretty mature and responsible idea."

171

"Greg, he was fourteen years old. He was in the eighth grade. And how many times did you guys sneak us into the Agora or the Euclid Tavern to see concerts? You wrote about going to college I.D. Night at the Agora when you were juniors in high school, you guys took us to see Southside Johnny there and I don't even think we were fifteen yet. Remember, you bribed the bouncers to let us in?"

She went on and on and you could tell that she was dead serious. "And what about our sixteenth birthday? How bad do you think it killed us that we couldn't tell any of our friends that I spent the night of our sixteenth birthday on the stage at the Euclid Tavern having Mr. Stress's Blues Band sing me "Sweet Little Sixteen." Don't you remember?"

I finally stopped her. "Connie, you're taking this way too seriously. How do you remember all of this stuff?"

She paused and then sat down. She had gotten pretty worked up. She chilled out for a moment and then looked up at me and said, "You know how you talked about the good times you guys had in high school with your friends, and Mate's parents, and Uncle Gus and everybody? What do you think it was like for us to be around you guys? It was the best. We lived for those moments. You have no idea what it meant to us to be a part of..." and her voice trailed off and she looked away so I couldn't see that she was crying. "I'm just saying, don't forget about all the fun and happy things. That's all, just don't forget all the fun we had."

Part Four
1986/87 School Year
The Best Year of Our Lives

*I have learned that the countless paths one traverses
in one's life are all equal. Oppressors and oppressed
meet at the end, and the only thing that prevails is
that life was altogether too short for both.*
    Don Jaun quoted by Castanada

*When the hard winds of change blow through your
life, they blow away a lot of structures you thought
permanent, exposing what you thought was trivial,
buried and forgotten...the small things are lasting
things.*
    John MacDonald in The Lonely Silver Rain

Two women played important roles that summer, causing
the biggest rift between Mate and I ever.

We first knew of Jennifer Martin when she was a pretty fair
athlete at another school in our conference. She was a big busty
girl who played volleyball, basketball, and threw the shot and
discus. She handled herself well as a high school jock, especially
since she was carrying about twenty-five pounds of useless
baby fat on her frame. She didn't really bloom in the looks
department until she went off to school. Wow!!! Did she change.
She got into weight training and aerobics and just went crazy,

turning herself into a physical piece of work, and even got her hoops game together enough to walk on and make the varsity team at the University of Toledo. She turned into a big, athletic, sexy young woman full of confidence.

Mate met her at a bar in Lakewood the week school let out. Jennifer had just graduated from UT with a degree in elementary education, but was going to go back in the fall as a graduate assistant in the women's basketball program.

At the time Mate was on the prowl for his usual summer squeeze. This lucky young lady had to meet two important criteria. Number One: She had to like the big three; beer, baseball, and sex; not in any particular order. Number Two: She had to realize and accept that the relationship was going to end the first weekend of the high school football season when there was, of course, no time for frivolous things like a girlfriend. He wasn't like a lot of coaches who needed a wife or girlfriend at every game, waiting for him outside the locker room after a win or a loss. You're supposed to leave that shit behind in high school, where Mate had.

It was love (or lust really) at first sight. They made a good pair, she was a great tag along, plus Mate loved the fact that she was going back to school in the fall. "Ain't that great," he told me, "no big break up scene. No accidentally bumping into her around town or seeing her at a Browns game." He was so proud of himself and his new summer girlfriend.

Mate and Jennifer out in the right field bleachers on Sunday afternoons. Mate and Jennifer closing the Harbor Inn on Friday nights. Mate and Jennifer keeping me up all night at our place several times a week.

I thought it was just another of his summer romances and didn't notice that anything was amiss until we took our basketball team down to Columbus for Ohio State's team camp. Whether it's for a basketball camp, a Buckeye game, or the state wrestling tournament, going to Columbus as coaches is almost as much fun as going as students when we were in college. You do your coaching gig during the day and at night you go with all the other coaches over to the Varsity Club and get hammered. You get a bunch of coaches together pounding beers and they gossip more than the women at the beauty parlor on a Saturday morning. By the middle of the summer, most of the teachers/coaches are in prime drinking condition and the nights are long and fun.

After the first day of camp, and with the kids safely in the hands of the camp staff, it was time to go to The Varsity Club. Except Mate was out cold!!! He said he was exhausted from spending the weekend with Jennifer up at Kelly's Island, and that he'd be his same old self the next night.

But the next night came and went and he couldn't answer the bell. That had never happened before, and let me tell you he was catching a lot of shit for it. People were asking, "Where's Mate? Where's Mate?" Most of our Columbus crowd remembered Mate from the state basketball tournament of several years earlier when he stood up on a chair in the middle of the back room, shook a can of Bud, and then snorted the whole thing up his nose, just to shut up some young coaches just out of college who thought they were cool shooting beers and getting sloppy about it. With most of the beer up his nose, and the rest sprayed on his face, he threw the empty into one of the youngsters laps and said, "Come back when you can do that, asshole."

While we were cleaning up to go out Wednesday night, his first night out, I glanced up and saw Mate stepping out of the shower and noticed the map of North America embroidered into his back with sucker bites.

"What the hell is that?" I said with mock concern.

"What?"

"Those marks on your back. Did Jennifer do that to you?"

He turned and glanced over his shoulder into the mirror. He turned towards me and said with a smile, "That ain't nothing," and pointed to the one leading up to his genitalia.

I have been around guys in shower rooms showing off their girlfriends' sucker bites since I was in grade school, but I have never seen anything like this. They were everywhere. I mean everywhere. Every nook and cranny. Every patch of skin had something on it. And the coloring was phenomenal, dominated by the colors of the rainbow with a slight neon tint.

"You know when this summer is all said and done, we're going to have to have a little talk about her. What an athlete!" He said with an illegal smile.

I didn't have to wait until the end of the summer to hear about her. That night was a great night at the VC. We ended up in a group of about twenty, including a few females. Some old friends from my OSU days, a couple of guys who coached in the Columbus area who went to OWU with Mate, some guys we coached against up in Cleveland.

One thing led to another, everyone was buying beverages for everyone else, and the story telling was outstanding. I don't remember what lead up to it, but I got Mate to show everyone the topographical map of Argentina that was in the middle of his left ass cheek.

"Ooh! Ooh!" People exclaimed as he got up on a chair and dropped his drawers quickly to show off the hickey on his bare bottom. He let everyone stare at it for several seconds for affect, and then quickly pulled up his pants.

"Show the Altoona Islands," I said, and he rolled up his sleeve and showed the bruises leading up his upper arm onto his shoulder.

"Now Idaho," I continued, and he lowered his shirt to show the mark that started above his right nipple and ended at the bottom of his neck.

The crowd was rolling. Mate was really hamming it up with some bumps and grinds.

"And, for the grand finale for today's geography lesson, North America!" And Mate turned around, and pulled up his shirt. He did a slight body builder flex that showed off the muscles in his back. He then removed his shirt completely, showing off the giant hickey on his back that resembled, of all things, a map of North America.

We had accumulated quite a crowd by then and everyone was just dying with laughter. The comments that followed were brutal, but nobody was laughing harder than Mate.

"Mate, you're not doing it with undomesticated animals again, are you?"

"Mate, when did you get into tattoos?"

"Did you do that with a vacuum cleaner with a clitoris?"

That night when we went back to our dorm room and as we lay in the dark in our small twin beds trying to cope with the summer heat, Mate elaborated about his summer with Jennifer.

"Now, you know, I like sex as much as the next person. I mean, I'll be the first to admit that there might be a bit of rif raf on my resume, but there also is some talent. But nothing beats this summer with Jennifer. On the all time list she checks in there behind you know who, but the thing is she is wearing me out. If we go out, there is always one in the car after I pick her up. I mean, Jesus Christ, how old do you get before you stop having sex in a car? If we go to the movies, her hand is always on the big fella. You'd be surprised at all the places we've done it down by the Stadium. I never thought I'd ever say this, but the girl is wearing me out."

By the time double sessions were going to be coming around, he was going to be dragging his ass through practice like an old hound dog.

I'll always have a soft spot for Jennifer because she was my first experience at what everyone today calls 'phone sex.' When we came home from OSU after our team camp, she went up to work a couple of weeks of girls camps at UT. She and Mate went almost two weeks without seeing each other. Mate was gone somewhere, and I went down to the Flats with a couple of buddies on their vacations for some afternoon cocktails. I got home around dinner time and fell asleep on the glider on the front porch. I was awakened by the phone, and I answered it half asleep.

"Mate," I heard Jennifer say.

"Urg, Org, Dung," I responded, suffering from cotton mouth and hot pipes. I guess she thought I was Mate because she continued on.

"I miss you so much. I miss you so much and all I can think about is licking every inch of your body."

"Mmmm," I said, slowly becoming conscious.

"I just want you to know that everyone is downstairs eating dinner, and I'm up in my dorm room with nothing on except the AC and my vibrator." Then she really got going. It is really hard to put into words the sounds I heard next. They were a combination of a lot of things. A good size dog with her tail caught in the door...Tom Waits on one of his early albums...

In between these bursts of sounds, in a low husky come-fuck-me voice, she went on and described all the things she was doing to herself with her vibrator. She touched it everywhere, and stuck it in every possible orifice. "I'm now running it along the crack of my ass wishing it was your tongue."

I knew she was close to the end when she started to pray. "Oh God...Oh God...OH GOD...OH GOD!!! She said in a voice that crescendoed to a scream. Then, without saying a word, I heard her breathe heavy for five or six seconds and hang up.

When Mate came home from where ever the hell he was and I told him what happened, he just smiled. "What did I tell you, a real blue chipper."

The other woman that played an important role in our lives that summer was Maggie Williams. If Jennifer was Mate's summer squeeze, then Maggie was mine. I ran into her at a teacher's workshop at the end of the school year, then a couple of weeks later at a happy hour. She was about our age and teaching in an east side school district.

I knew we knew Maggie from sometime/somewhere else. I knew it was from the first year or two out of college, but I wasn't sure from where. It just didn't seem important, we knew so many girls like Maggie back then.

The short time we were together that summer was fun. Both being teachers, we spent a couple leisurely days doing the art museum, a concert at Blossom, and a day on the beach at Cedar Point. When we became physically involved things were good. She had a slight touch of full bodiness about her, which I like, and she enjoyed sex and all the neat things two people could do with each other.

Over the course of the summer, even though we lived together, Mate and I saw very little of each other. I'd be off someplace working a basketball camp, he'd be working a football camp or vice versa. He'd be out east visiting friends from his Wesleyan days, I'd be down in Cincinnati with some OSU buddies. And when we were both around, he was spending a lot of time with Jennifer.

It was when we were both around, that things were getting a bit stressed between us because of Jennifer. She got in the habit of hanging around our house in the morning or late at night with just a T-shirt and panties on. We had girlfriends in the past do this, but none with the body, youth, and raw sexuality that Jennifer possessed. When she was hanging around with her (what seemed like always) hard nipples protruding out through her shirt, and her tanned hall of fame legs stretching out from her perfect butt, you could not concentrate. It got to the point where I would leave the house; I just couldn't handle it. She was one of those women who fully clothed could give every guy in the room a woody, let alone when she was close to naked.

I was kind of pissed at Mate for that, but I couldn't figure out why he was kind of pissed at me.

Mate knew Maggie from whenever I originally knew her, but it wasn't until half way through the summer that he realized that we were an item. It seemed to bother him for no apparent reason, and I thought maybe it might just be the time for us to go our separate ways. Maybe, finally, find my own place to live. We were approaching one of those birthdays that ended in a zero and sooner or later you stop living with your buddies. We were pushing the envelope on middle age, and maybe it was just time.

Maggie was not around our place a lot anyway. She definitely preferred her place to ours. The older ones were like that. Our house always had people coming and going. Connie and Manny still took the place over with friends, spontaneously to go through our record collection and sit around and eat pizza. For Jennifer, the college like atmosphere was what she was used to, but Maggie had outgrown it years earlier.

Her place was one of those stately old colonials in Lakewood, off Clifton near the lake. It was clean and comfortable, with hardwood floors and lots of women things like matching throw pillows and a canapé bed. Her place reflected her, a classy professional woman.

We had gone to a movie, out to eat, and then to her place to make gentle love. We were snuggled up when we finally started the conversation we knew we had to have soon. What were we going to do when the summer ended? And, as far as I was concerned, was it going to end the next morning with the start of football practice? She being a teacher, I knew she had been through a few of these summer flings. I really liked her, and thought this one might last for awhile.

I had told her about Mate's criteria for a summer girlfriend, and so when she said, "Am I supposed to disappear after tonight?" I was not prepared for what she said next.

"You know, that's why I cut it off with him. I wanted a little bit more than that."

"What? When?"

"You know...six or seven summers ago when we were all taking summer classes at Cleveland State."

"You guys dated?"

"Well, as you probably remember, I don't think any of us really dated back then. We did have a thing for awhile..."

I let go of her, rolled over on my back and stared at the ceiling.

"What's the matter?" She said.

"Nothing. Just stretching, that's all."

She rambled on about her fling with Mate without giving too many details, I could only imagine, and I kept staring at the ceiling.

Oh my God, I said to myself. I've been doing one of his. That's why he was pissed at me!

Believe it or not, that had never happened. At least, as far as I knew, it had never happened. Guys are usually very territorial with their women, and I knew that we were. Going back to high school Mary Ann Sladky was one of mine, and Kathy Miller was his. Beth was one of his, Colleen was one of mine. In college, Mary Jo Collins was one of mine, Shelly Gordon was his. The list went on and on.

And not just with girls we were involved with or had a fling with. This also pertained to an unwritten criteria that usually referred back to who discovered or first saw someone.

Mrs. Jankowski, the fiftyish secretary at school with the great wit, was mine. Krissy, the sleazy janitor, was one of his.

Megan, the cute blond at the video store, was mine. The tall red head at the grocery store deli department was his. We never knowingly crossed lines.

I lay on the edge of the bed still staring at the ceiling, and she rolled over and cuddled up along my side. I closed my eyes and pretended that I dozed off. I kept pretending even as she started to kiss the side of my neck and started to stroke me. Her skin felt cold and clammy, instead of soft and warm. I was non responsive to all of her actions. Visions of her in bed with Mate giving him a hummer clouded my mind. Finally, she gave up and fell asleep.

When I left her place early the next morning, I knew it was over between the two of us. I snuck out of her place unnoticed at the crack of dawn, and got back to our place to ride with Mate to practice. He was already up, sitting at the kitchen table drinking a coffee and reading the paper.

"Five minutes and I'll be ready to go," I said.

Mate was becoming, in our old age, one of those coaches who couldn't wait for summer practices to start. I, on the other hand, still equated the start of football with the end of summer and that still depressed me.

On our way to school, he rambled on about what we were going to do in practice while I read the sports page and tried to wake up at the same time. I was the head coach, but he was the defensive coordinator, and the first day of practice was always conditioning and defense, so he ran things. When we got near the school he changed the subject.

"Let's talk about women for a minute," he said. "Let's talk about Jennifer Martin and Maggie Williams."

Uh-oh, I said to myself. This is it. I'll have to find another place to live.

He admitted that he felt the tension between us over the summer, but felt with some changes and the start of the school year things could get back to normal. He told me it was over between him and Jennifer. "I told her yesterday. She took it O.K. We'll have one more go at it this weekend and then she's back to school for good anyway. I'd never make it through doubles if it kept going like it did."

We had gotten to school and he drove around back and pulled into one of the empty spaces by the locker room doors. He parked the car, turned off the ignition, turned in his seat and faced me.

"And about this Maggie Williams thing," he said. "Just tell me one thing."

"What?"

A slight smile crossed his face. "How did I taste?" And before I could react, he bopped out of the car and went and greeted a group of the kids who were waiting to get in the building.

Dave Van Husen was among the generic, preppy Eastern types that inhabited the top two floors of Mate's college frat house. A personable guy, Dave had the reputation of being an electronics whiz and television junkie.

It was Dave who climbed the phone poles on the residential street behind fraternity hill and illegally wired Mate's house for cable. He took care of the house d.j. system, and he would be up all hours of the night, strung out on black beauties and cheap beer, watching sitcom reruns even before there was a thing called Nick at Nite.

Although Dave was several years ahead of Mate, they became good friends. Dave took care of the house's sound system and Mate was in charge of the tunes. They both shared a love for the current frat rock of the time, songs such as "Rosalita" by Bruce Springsteen; "The Smoke From a Distant Fire" by the Sanford Townsend Band; "Strike Up the Band" by MSB; and the late Seventies country rock bands like The Outlaws, Marshall Tucker and Pure Prairie League.

Mate always remembered a conversation he had with Dave. It was the spring after Dave had graduated and he came back to party for a weekend. Dave spent the fall and winter trying to break into the ground floor of cable T.V. that he saw booming wide open in the Eighties.

Over afternoon beers in The Jug, Dave told Mate about the two job offers he was considering. "There are these people out in California who are going to have a cable network with nothing but rock and roll on all day and night. Concert clips, promo stuff. Some of that Don Kirschner Rock Concert stuff. It's going to be a cool thing and they're going to call it MTV, Music Television."

Mate listened intently.

"Then there's these dudes up in Connecticut who are putting together another cable network that's going to be nothing but sports twenty-four hours a day. Everything. Big stuff, little stuff. Not pro wrestling, but things like minor league baseball, Canadian football, college basketball, all the fucking time. Plus interviews, update shows. They're even thinking about having six and eleven o'clock news shows with nothing but sports."

"What are they going to call that one?"

"ESPN, the Entertainment Sports Programming Network."

Mate sat there amazed and looked at the world of the future being a happy place with a twenty-four hour sports TV network.

"So I think I'm going to try to latch on with the guys in Connecticut. They seem a bit more stable. Too many west coast types with that MTV crowd."

Dave Van Husen jumped onto the ESPN bandwagon before there was a bandwagon, and grew with the network and became one of its behind the scenes early heroes.

When Dave showed up that summer and said that he was in town on business and wanted to treat us to a night on the town on the company expense account, I thought nothing of it. When he came out to school the next day and spent forty-five minutes checking out our gym, I got a bit suspicious, but still did not have a clue of what he had planned.

We stopped at one of the joints by the airport when we were driving him back for his flight, and over some cold Buds he started to tell us what he had in mind.

"You know, we're looking to do more live stuff. We want to get some of the packaged shows we have eliminated."

We sat and listened expecting to hear more gossip about his work mates. Mate was obsessed with knowing about Gayle Gardner.

"I want you guys to help me with one of my projects."

We stared at each other, wondering what could we possibly do to help him.

"You guys feel you're going to be pretty good in hoops next year. You got everyone coming back."

"Yeah, so?"Said Mate.

"The week after Christmas you play Washington D.C. Industrial Tech as part of their road trip that goes out to Chicago and back."

"How'd you know?"

"We did a feature on them for Sports Center this year and I saw your name on next year's schedule. What do you think," he paused to look at our expressions, "what do you think if we use your game against them as the first one of a series of live high school sports events we want to try to televise?"

It didn't register with me right away, but it did with Mate. "You mean a live ESPN telecast of one of our games from our gym?"

"Yes. At least six cameras, one of our college crews doing the game, the whole bit."

Maybe it was me, but I didn't get it right away. But I did see the wheels turning in each of their heads.

Jamie McGowan was always a good athlete. When he was in grade school he excelled in every gym activity, and was a standout in little league and flag football. On those teams Jamie was often coached by his idol, his father, James Sr.

James McGowan, Sr. was like many of the little league dads who everyone seemed to look up to, handsome in a rugged and jock way. He had the pretty young wife, the new split-level on a cul-de-sac in a new development, and a young son whose athletic prowess people talked about even though he was only in the fifth grade.

James Sr. held one of those investment broker jobs that always had him involved in one big deal or another. It was such a shock to his neighbors and admirers in the community when they awoke one morning to find his picture on the front page of the *Plain Dealer* for involvement in a money laundering and investment scheme. Also involved were factions of Cleveland's Italian, Irish and Jewish mobs, as well as three banks, several brokerage houses, and a politician or two. James Sr. was named as the front man and deal maker for the guys who had the real money. He became one of the fall guys, in an operation that also included money made from prostitution and drugs.

Gone from Jamie's life was the facade of the "perfect" family. Lawyers' fees took away the new house, and a plea bargain for a reduced sentence took away Jamie's dad. Because drug money was involved, he would be sent away for a minimum of eight years.

Jamie's mom moved the family from Bay Village to River Boro to escape the gossiping behind her back and the aura of being a criminal's family. Anyone they met just assumed they were another fatherless family. Jamie and his younger brother Timmy would tell their new friends that their parents were separated, and their father lived in another city.

Jamie entered the seventh grade in a new school with slightly tougher kids than the preps he knew in Bay Village. He played on school sponsored sports teams for the first time without his father on the sidelines as his coach and mentor. His mom went from a stay-at-home housewife to a single working mom. The structure around Jamie became less firm, and he became a confused boy. He was both mad at and sorry for his father, and couldn't stand the monthly trips to see him in prison fatigues that left him crying on the long trip home.

Jamie did what many confused seventh graders would do. He started to rebel. In a matter of one school year he became what you would call a bad kid. He ran with the wrong crowd, started smoking and drinking, and started lying to his mom.

He hung in sports on his own natural ability until he made it to high school, where his lifestyle caught up with him. Mate and I ran the football and basketball programs with the least amount of structure and rules as were needed to be successful. We understood that our athletes weren't angels, especially away from school where we had little control over them. But when a kid like Jamie kept getting into trouble the way he did, he only got so many chances. During the ninth grade alone he got busted twice for smoking on campus, drinking at a dance, calling a female teacher a fucking bitch, and blowing off his school work to the point that he was ineligible for sports by the end of the year.

Mate and I tried to intercede; we did everything we could. Not only was he a good athlete, but we thought deep down he was a good kid with lots of potential. But when you have rules and policies that seventy other football players and thirty basketball players follow, you sometimes lose one. When it was a kid like Jamie whom you basically liked, not to mention the fact that he hit like a ton and had a sweet jump shot, it hurt. We wrote him off completely, and never thought we would get him back.

He approached us in the spring of his junior year. Mate and I were sitting in the coaches' office shooting the breeze after practice, trying to decide where to go for dinner.

"Can I talk to you guys a moment?" He said as he stuck his head in the door.

"Jamie, come on in." He entered and stood before us.

Silence. Mate and I waited for him to say something. He stumbled for words.

"Listen. I know for the last several years I have been a big disappointment. Especially to myself. And I know I have let you down before...I want to come back. What would I have to do to come back?"

Mate and I were surprised, not so much at what Jamie said, but how he said it. We heard a sincere cry for help in his voice. We told him that he was welcome back, but one problem and he was gone. We told him to catch up with us later in the week and we'd draw up some sort of guidelines.

"You know, he could fill a couple of spots if he came back. Think he can do it?" Mate asked after Jamie left.

"Well, let's try to make sure that he does."

We got him a job working at a landscaping company run by one of our boosters. That way he would be working for some-one we knew, with kids he knew, and everyone could keep an eye on him.

As far as football goes, he had to be in the weight room

three times each week, benching at least two twenty by the time doubles started.

As far as basketball, he had to make every open gym over the course of the summer, and go with our team to the team camp that we were going to attend at OSU. We expected him to play as much as possible.

Jamie had the best summer. He was with our linemen opening up the weight room every Monday, Wednesday, and Friday morning. He'd go hard through his workout. He didn't miss a day of work, and the work was good for him. At night he became a gym rat, not only coming to our open gyms, but traveling someplace every night looking for somewhere to play.

By the time football practice started in August, he looked like a different kid. The sun had tanned him, he had lost ten pounds of fat and added fifteen pounds of muscle. He didn't stink from cigarettes anymore. His hair was no longer oily and greasy, and his complexion had cleared up. He was no longer an inconsiderate, selfish kid, but a polite and respectful one.

The coaches all crossed their fingers and hoped it would keep up through the school year.

From the *Sun Newspapers* football preview...
...Everyone's pick to win their first conference championship in twenty-nine years and make their first state playoff appearance are the River Boro Warriors. Lead by running back Chuckie Jones, two way tackle Richie Simmons, receiver Manny Lopez and the city's best defense, the Warriors have ten starters back on both sides of the ball from last year's 7-3 team. The Boro's talented senior class has high aspirations this year.

"We will accept nothing short of a conference championship and a state playoff appearance," states Tri Captain Simmons. "And that goes for basketball as well as football. We expect this year to be the best year of our lives."

What a change from the time not long ago when

> the Warriors were the doormat of their league. Coach
> Greg Stanley's three year record as Head Coach
> stands at 18-12.

It was late in the football season when I did something I said I was never going to do. I lost it in front of them after a win. A win we definitely should have lost. A win where we had played as badly as we have played in two or three seasons. We were fucking lucky and I was pissed.

I told everyone to sit down and shut up. When it was quiet, deathly quiet, I started in on them.

"You guys think we can play for and win the league championship next Friday playing like this? Do you think that we can compete in the state playoffs playing like this?"

"We have taken several big steps backwards. Some people saw it coming. We've been on top of the world the whole season. We're so used to reading about ourselves in the paper. Well I'll tell you what we are tonight fellas. We're just pretty damn lucky is what we are. Because we must be pretty damn lucky not to have lost."

"We thought we could screw around in school all week. We thought we could take it easy in practice all week."

"I thought we'd never get to the point where I wouldn't enjoy a victory. Tonight this is it," and with that I exited the room. I heard the captains tell everyone not to move, and heard them start in on their teammates.

I went out into one of the deserted hallways. I sat on the floor and my mind was filled with great self-doubt.

Here we go. Disaster waiting to happen. We're going to get our asses cleaned next week. All that championship talk is going to turn out to be bullshit. You called a shitty game, etc., etc., etc.

I think anyone in any job occasionally has great doubts of self worth and self esteem. Mine had never been stronger than at that moment. I just knew our great season was going to fall apart during this last week. Good-bye league championship. Good-bye city ranking. Good-bye state playoffs. All those things I thought were eminent were all going to fall away.

I looked up and saw the junior high coaches down the hall walking towards me. They had been out scouting Garfield, and the last thing I needed was for them to tell me how good they looked! Shit, I said to myself, wait until you see how good they'll look next week.

Hos looked down at me and with a big grin on his face and said, "Congratulations!"

"You wouldn't be saying congratulations if you saw how we played."

"I didn't mean congratulations about winning tonight's game. I mean congratulations on winning the first football league championship in thirty years. Garfield lost."

I looked up. "Don't shit me. How could Garfield lose?"

"Easy. Brooklyn came out to play and knocked Nessersmith out of the game in the first quarter, and Harris blew his knee out in the second. They played two sophomores in their place and couldn't get the ball in the end zone."

"Plus, Brooklyn played the game of their lives. All those kids we knicked up when we played them were back and healthy."

A thousand thoughts were running through my mind. Earlier in the season, there was a Friday night when it stormed and rained like crazy. There were a bunch of upsets, the weather being the great equalizer. Garfield had tied Maple, while we squeaked out a 14-6 win over Strongsville.

The light suddenly went off in my head and I said to myself, "holy shit, even if we lose next week, we're still conference champs."

"Did you tell the kids yet about Garfield losing?"

"No, we figured you'd want to tell them."

As I walked back into the locker room, everyone was silent except the captains who were busy berating their teammates.

I walked up to them, back to the spot I stood and berated them myself minutes before, and quietly said, "Rich, Chuck, please sit for a second." The calm, quiet tone of my voice surprised them.

In the same tone of voice I turned to the team and said, "Guys, can I have your attention again."

They all sat down where they were, and looked at me. They had just come as close to losing a game as they did all year. They had played the worst game they had played all year, I had just bitched them out pretty bad, and their captains had laid into them as well. It was not a happy locker room.

I was an explosion of emotion waiting to happen. We had won the conference championship that night, yet I was feeling bad, because I probably ruined the moment for them. I forgot what it was like to struggle, when any win was worth celebrating. Jesus Christ, they were just kids.

When I got their attention again, the room was silent and all eyes were on me. I paused for an uncharacteristically long time. I knew what I was going to say, but I couldn't get my emotions under control to say it.

I started talking twice, both times my voice broke and I tried to start over again. No luck the third time.

I looked around at each of them, trying to do what the Old Man used to do, look everyone in the eyes all at the same time. I was looking for help, then I caught Mate's face in the back of the room. He was looking at me with a 'what the fuck is wrong with you?' look. I looked at him dead in the eyes and then he got it. He looked at me and then silently worded with his lips, "Garfield lost, didn't they." I read his lips and nodded my head, and he immediately knew the situation.

"Tell them," he screamed, puncturing the silence in the room.

"Tell us what?" Rich Simmons said from the front.

I regained my composure, every eye again on me. I spoke each word slow and strong, so everyone in the room heard them. "Gentlemen, sometimes life takes great twists and turns. I'd like to be the first to congratulate the first championship team for River Boro in thirty years. Garfield lost to Brooklyn tonight, we have clinched at least a tie for the conference championship."

The place went crazy, and we went around and hugged and congratulated each player.

The celebration was short lived, as the captains got up on the bench and got the team's attention. Rich again spoke. "Let us not forget that we started this season with a lot of goals, and winning the conference is only one of them. We haven't beaten Garfield in the three years I've been here, and I don't want to share a conference title with them. The dream does not end tonight, it is just getting started."

It was a hard week of preparation. Although it was nice to clinch the conference, we had set higher goals. Except for our putrid performance of the preceding Friday, we had been playing really well. We were overdue to play a shitty game, and, although we didn't want to admit it, many of us, coaches and players, were looking ahead to the Garfield game. It showed on Friday night, and it showed in the films.

We had finished our pregame and were back in the locker room. The players were taking their last pees, and the coaches were going over the final details. We gathered everyone in the middle of the locker room, and it was time for me to say a few words. I'm not one of those coaches who gives the big pep talk every Friday night, but every so often I do. And that night was one of those nights.

I faced the kids and started. "Every one of you is something that you weren't last week, or ever before, for that matter. You are champions. The first championship football team we have had in over thirty years. It took a lot of work to be champions, a lot of sweat and blood, a lot of it from guys who aren't here any more, the guys who had laid the ground work the last four years. But there is one thing we haven't talked about yet, and that's the responsibilities of being champions. Being a champion from now on for us is not going to be a one time thing. It's an all the time thing. Champions play and act like champions every game. They act like champions every day. They don't brag or play dirty, they don't dance in the end zone or taunt the other team. Champions do it with style and confidence and class."

"Now tonight we play a team who for the last three years has beaten us. But they haven't done it like champions. They haven't accepted the responsibilities of being champions. They fight and bite and whine and cry and mouth off, and just leave a big stink on the other side of the field. We're not going to be like that."

"Tonight, we are going to go out and play the best game of the year. And we are going to do it with the class and style of true champions. Then we are going to come in here and celebrate amongst ourselves afterward, and then we are going to be one of those teams, one of those championship teams, that's going to sit around all weekend waiting to hear who we play next week. Are you guys ready?"

And, yes they were, as we went out and played awesome, beating Garfield 42-7 on the night when we won the first out right football conference championship for our school in thirty seasons.

After the game there was hooping and hollering, but it was over quickly, as the kids realized that for the first time ever our season was not ending after ten games. The state playoffs lurked around the corner, and we knew that if we played like we did that night, there was a good chance that we could be playing for not just one, but three more weeks.

At that time it took three more games to win the state, with eight teams in each division making the playoffs. The system was the computer system that is still used today, with teams getting points based on the strength of schedule of the schools that you beat. Being the only undefeated team in our region, and having beaten a couple of teams with good records, we rolled along with computer points the whole year. We were safely in first place and expected the call from the state on Sunday night to tell us when, where, and who we played next.

We had the kids come in on Saturday to watch the video and do some loosening up. We were living on the high that the championship and the state playoffs gave us.

Over beers and cheeseburgers that afternoon, the coaches talked over our chances and we were all surprisingly quite confident. We had beaten some good teams, several better than some of the teams we were going to see in the playoffs. It was the consensus of the coaches that the only team that could stop us was ourselves, and we swore amongst us, that we were not going to let that happen.

The only down moment was something that bothered Mate and I. "I still feel bad about bitching them out the night we clinched the championship," I told him. "I was just upset about how we played. But it took away from the moment, it could've been a great moment."

"I know," said Mate. "That could've been one of those moments that the kids would've never forgotten. But look at it this way. You only get so many of those, and maybe ours is still to come. We really could make some noise in the playoffs."

A blurb from the scholastic page of the *Plain Dealer* from that Sunday...

...After their thrashing of always powerful Garfield Friday night, many area high school grid fans point to River Boro as Greater Cleveland's best chance for a state title. Coach Greg Stanley's Warriors have rolled all season, showing great striking power on offense and the area's stingiest defense. Running back Chuckie Jones is the area's best back, and under-sized tackle Rich Simmons leads offensive and defensive lines that have dominated the line of scrimmage in each of their games.

From the front page of *The Cleveland Plain Dealer* that Monday...

Recruiting Scandal Hits High Schools
State mandates three schools to forfeit all wins
Has repercussions for state playoffs

Columbus—The Ohio High School Athletic Association on Sunday announced the findings of a month long investigation into the use of illegal players by several Greater Cleveland High Schools. Garfield High, Central High, and Taft High were all found to have illegally recruited players who lived out of their districts on their teams. All three teams were forced to forfeit their games. The games played amongst themselves will each count as a tie. Each team will officially end the season with identical 0-8-2 records.

Ironically, the team hurt the most by these sanctions is Valley Conference Champions River Boro, who beat all three handily during the season. However, since each of the punished teams were forced to forfeit their own victories, this caused River Boro's computer playoff points to dip enough for them to drop from first to fifth in their region, and not let them qualify for the state football playoffs which begin Friday.

When informed of this last night at a closed team meeting, players and coaches of River Boro left their school with horror and utter shock on their faces and issued "No Comment" statements as they left their building.

It would have been the Warriors first appearance ever in the state playoffs. They finished the season with a 10-0 mark, and were one of the favorites to capture a state championship crown.

Basketball season for me didn't really start until the night of our football banquet. We were all in a funk, greatly disappointed that we were denied the opportunity to play in the state football playoffs. Although everyone got on with their lives, it left a subtle anger in all of us.

I moped around as badly as anyone. The kids took it better than I did. Most of them either played basketball or wrestled, and practice started the Monday after the last regular season football game, so they buried themselves in their next sport.

Mate was very disappointed also, but it wasn't the worst thing that ever happened to him. For me, in my sheltered life until that point, I could not even think of anything that happened to me that was worse than not getting in those fucking football playoffs. I just knew in my heart that we could have gone all the way. Mate knew that too, but in emotional moments this ranked behind living with Beth's marriage and his father's death. Also, as he reminded me several times, Uncle Gus and all the hardship in his life, and how he had endured and never lets it show.

But I was still a self-centered human being, and even the kids knew I wasn't the same. To make matters worse, our football banquet wasn't until the Sunday before Thanksgiving, a good three weeks after the season was over. It was scheduled that way to follow the state playoffs, which everyone assumed we would be in. If it had been up to me, I would have had it right away, especially with the way this season had ended.

The banquet was the usual affair at the local VFW, with chicken and roast beef and the usual speeches by the usual people. The parents all sat there proud, snapping pictures of their sons receiving their letters and trophies. As the night wore on, I caught myself getting sentimental, knowing that this was the last time all of these kids would be together as a team, and wondering if we would ever coach a team this good again. After the last set of awards were presented, I got up to say a few final words. Suddenly the things I had scribbled on the paper in front of me weren't good enough, and in front of hundreds of people I was lost for words. Once again the kids saved me. Before I started to try to speak, the captains were standing behind me asking me if they could say something. Richie Simmons stood at the podium and spoke to the crowd.

"Ladies and gentlemen, before this night ends the team has one more thing to do. Most of us have been in this football program since sixth grade, and for all of us it has been the highlight of our school years. All the stupid things that our coaches have told us over the years have come true. 'If you work hard, you can do great things.' 'Champions are made, not born.' 'The best friends you will ever have will be the guys you played football with.' 'There is nothing better than being exhausted in victory with your teammates.' Every kid who played high school football this year heard all of these things from their coaches, and for all of us they all came true."

"However, many of the things our coaches told us, especially our head coach and our defensive coordinator, didn't come from Vince Lombardi or Paul Brown. They always seemed to come from Coach Majowski's late father or his Uncle Gus. When the coaches would tell us stuff like 'always shake the hands of the refs after the game,' we would ask why and they would say, 'because Uncle Gus said so.' Boy, were we surprised when we found out there really is an Uncle Gus." Everyone who knew him quickly glanced at him sitting at one of the back tables, puffing on his ever-present cigar.

Rich continued, "Well anyway, one of the things the team has talked about since our last game was that we needed one more moment to remember as a team. Now we had all assumed that our season was going to end a little differently than it did, but there is nothing we can do about that now. So what could we do? Looking back at summer practices, when it was hot and sweaty and no one wanted to be there, one of the things the coaches always said that came from Coach Mate's dad or his Uncle Gus, one of the two, is 'you had to work hard to be a football hero.' There is 'nothing better than being a football hero.' And then they would start singing the chorus to some stupid song that went 'You got to be a football hero.' For some reason, listening to our two coaches sing the chorus to some song that they learned from their dad and uncle, on a hot and dusty practice field, is one of those stupid insignificant moments that I will always remember. 'You got to be a football hero.'"

"When the team got together without the coaches the last several weeks, and we were talking about all the good times and things that we will miss, we tried to come up with something that we thought would be a good way to finish our season tonight, for us seniors as we finish our football careers here at River Boro. And someone said, 'I wonder if there really is a song about being a football hero?' With the help of Mrs. McKee down in the library, we found out there really is."

At that moment all the players got up and stood behind the varsity coaches sitting at the dais at the front of the room. The seniors stood in front, and many of them put their hands on our shoulders. After they were all in place, Richie continued.

"With our first ever undefeated team and first school football championship in thirty years, our coaches made everyone on this team a football hero. So this is for them, especially for our head coach Greg Stanley, and we hope this brings him out of his funk, because we need him to win the state basketball championship. They can't keep us out of that tournament." Richie paused again, but he wasn't finished.

"Ladies and gentlemen, for the last time together, the Championship River Boro Fighting Warriors Varsity Football Team." He came and stood behind Mate and me with a hand on each of our shoulders. There was a moment of silence when everyone, especially us, wondered what was coming next.

Then one of the kids in back counted softly, "One...Two...Three...Four..." and all at once sixty voices joined together...

> *You gotta be a football hero*
> *To get along with the beautiful girls.*
> *You gotta be a touchdown getter, you bet*
> *If you wanna get a baby to pet.*
> *The fact that you are rich or handsome*
> *Won't get you anything in curls;*
> *You gotta be a football hero*
> *To get along with the beautiful girls.*
> *In spite of all a million dollars can do*
> *A tackle or two will mean more to you*
> *If you can make the winning touchdown*
> *You'll never have to buy them pearls;*
> *You gotta be a football hero*
> *To get along with the beautiful girls.*

When they had finished there was nothing I could say. It was a great finish to a great but incomplete season. I stood up and said, "There's no way I can top that. Thanks for coming," and turned around and hugged each and every one of them.

From the Plain Dealer's *basketball preview...*
...Opponents of the River Boro Warriors had enough to worry about with all five starters coming back from last year's 16-6 squad. But the pain of not being in the state football playoffs has thrown further motivation into the hearts of an already determined team.

"There isn't going to be any stupid computer to keep us out of the basketball tournament," says senior point guard Tim Williams.

"We all still feel the pain of the football fiasco," states Head Coach (and football defensive coordinator) Mate Majowski. "You got to remember ten of our twelve varsity players also played football. But we're trying to use it as a positive, telling the kids the best is yet to come."

Returning for the Warriors besides Williams are 6'2" post player Richie Simmons; 6'5" post player Tom Bandmoor; 6'1" wing Chuckie Jones; and smooth 6' shooting guard Manny Lopez.

An early season highlight for the Warriors will be a Christmas break visit from Washington D.C. Industrial Tech, USA Today's *preseason pick as the nation's top boys prep squad. "I've just seen one of their games from last year on video tape," states Majowski. "They are loaded. They have at least three guys that are bonifide NBA candidates and they go seven or eight deep with serious major college recruits. We'll have our hands full. They haven't lost a game in almost three seasons."*

Tom Haggerty's elbow was a mess that season and after the 49ers had clinched their division in early December, they put him on the DL so he would be healthy for the playoffs. Using the excuse that he wanted his own doctor at the Cleveland Clinic to look at it, Tom was able to come home and spend the week after Christmas with his family and friends. This was something he had not been able to do since high school. During his OSU years, he'd always be off at a bowl game. During his pro years, he was always out on the west coast with the 49ers.

Tom checked in with us and told us he was psyched for our game that Friday on national TV. He said he was staying around an extra day for it.

Mate and I were really surprised when he showed up at school the next day to watch practice. Of course, the kids were

Greg Cielec

just in awe when he walked in.

I was bullshitting with some of the them as they shot free throws when he snuck up behind my back. I saw all the kids' eyes widen as they stopped what they were doing. Just as I was going to turn my head, he picked me up and I heard his laugh. It was good to see my old college friend again.

I knew some of the kids thought we were bullshitting them when at times we would mention we knew Tom. "Yeah, sure. You guys know one of the starting linebackers on the best team in football."

Tom watched practice from the sidelines, and Mate asked him if he'd say something to the kids at the end of practice. He seemed more than happy to.

It was our regular end of practice meeting with the kids sitting on the floor in a half circle around Mate, as he would go over the practice and tomorrow's agenda.

"One special thing today. We have with us one of our old friends who we played sports against in high school. You guys know who he is, Tom Haggerty."

Tom walked to the spot where Mate was standing and the kids were starstuck, six three and two hundred forty pounds of chiseled frame. He had long, curly hair, a diamond earring, and a tattoo of the Tasmanian devil on his forearm. Every kid noticed the Super Bowl ring gleaming on his finger.

"Gentlemen, Coach Majowski asked me to say a few words to you. You know, I loved playing high school sports. Basketball wasn't my game, football was. But whatever sport it is, there is nothing like having a big high school game like you guys are going to have this Friday. I'll be honest with you, I'm slightly jealous."

"But you know fellas, the game I remember most from high school is not one we won, but one we lost. In my four years of high school football my team lost only one game. One lousy game, and it still haunts me today." He glanced quickly at Mate and me. All the kids' eyes were glued to him.

"We just didn't take care of business that Friday night long ago. We were playing a team that had never beaten us before, and did not have nearly the amount of talent we did. Man-to-

199

man we were ten times better, but they were the better team. Just like you can be the better team this Friday."

"You know, there are several things that I remember about that loss that I will never forget. They had this center on their team that just never quit. I outweighed him by sixty pounds, yet he never backed off. All game he kept coming after me. He was like a summer mosquito that never went away."

"And then they had this tight end. Another small, short, white kid. They're driving for the winning touchdown. It's fourth and goal and they run him on a little back side drag off a play action fake to the other side. I read it the whole way, and timed my hit so I was going to lay him out just as he touched the ball. I mean, I creamed him. Broke his ribs I hit him so hard. But you know what that son of a bitch did? He held onto the ball in what turned out to be the winning touchdown. I thought the dude was dead and he holds on to the ball for the winning touchdown."

He paused for a moment and a slight grin crossed his face. "And losing the game wasn't the only bad thing that happened. We had this cheerleader who was hot. I mean hot," and he paused and formed a sizable bust line with his hands and the kids all laughed. They knew what he meant by hot. "Everyone on our team was kind of afraid of her because she was just too cool. Not only was she a fox, she was funny and sociable and everyone had a crush on her, yet everyone was afraid to ask her out. After the game we all walked off the field to the locker room, and I see our cheerleaders standing there in a huddle. She's standing with her back to us and all I wanted was for her to turn around and give me a smile. I was hurting so bad because we lost. All I wanted was a smile."

"The next thing I knew, that little center from the other team, the one who had given me so much trouble, walks up to her, taps her on the shoulder, and turns her around. He picks her up and lays the greatest kiss on her I have ever seen."

"Then after about fifteen seconds of sucking her face he just kind of drops her, picks up his helmet and runs whooping it up into the tunnel with his teammates."

"That could be you guys this Friday, beating the number

one team in the country, and then having a good time when it's over."

The kids thought that was it, but hoped for a little bit more. They got it.

"Oh, one last thing. Those two guys from that other team, the center who just hassled me all night and kissed the girl and the tight end who hung onto the ball after I broke his ribs are"...long pause..."those were your two coaches, standing right over there."

All at once, the kids turned towards us, catching Mate and I off guard and slightly embarrassed. But, as I glanced at the kids, they all had subtle looks of respect on their faces as they looked at us from a brand new angle. They knew by the way Tom had told the story, and the looks on our faces, that most of it was true.

Although he was our captain, a three year, two-way starter, and the stud on an undefeated team, Richie Simmons came out of the football season unnoticed. At least unnoticed as far as the people who mattered to him, the college football coaches of the Big Ten. He had always had his heart on playing Big Ten football.

Richie really only cared about two things, sports and his saxophone. When he wasn't at football or basketball practice, you usually found him in one of the rehearsal rooms in the music wing. The combination of being one of the school's main jocks, and being first chair in the school's orchestra, made him the most popular kid in the school.

Even the Mid American Conference was ignoring him, and that really aggravated us. Mate and I called every college coach we knew. We kept hearing the same things, 'too small to be a big time lineman.' We said play him at linebacker. We said take our word. They asked why we didn't play him at linebacker. We said our team needed him on the line.

That's how it went from the end of the football season until the holidays. No one would take a chance on Richie Simmons. Mate and I had been in coaching long enough to know Richie had it. Fuck the scouts and fuck his too-slow 5.1 forty. We knew he was still growing, going from under six foot his junior year, 6'1" the next summer, and over 6'3" by basketball season. We knew he was athletic enough to jam a basketball in tenth grade, and that he had a heart that pushed him beyond his physical limits.

"Come on down for the big game and you can check him out in person," I told the Old Man on the phone. He was then on George Perles's staff at Michigan State, coaching the defensive line and recruiting the Cleveland area.

"We've seen him on film and he just doesn't show enough to take a flier on him. Listen, you guys love this kid as much as you say, I'll catch your game when I'm in town. By the way, how's your buddy handling this week?"

I filled him in on the events of the week, the beginning of what was becoming a media circus, and the quality of Friday night's opponents. He just laughed.

"What the hell did you guys get yourselves into? And on national TV on top of it. What are you guys, crazy?"

I told him why I thought we had a chance, how the kids would be ready, and all the things planned for the rest of the week. I told him that we had the kids convinced that it was their chance to do the impossible, their moment of glory. That sometimes things like pride running deep in your soul make a difference.

The other end of the line was quiet for a moment, then came a soft reply, "You know, maybe you're right."

The fact that we were playing the number one team in the country on national TV was reason enough to get a lot of local attention that week. But literally, except for the Browns/Jets game the next day, there was not another sports story of note. We got time on all the six and eleven o'clock news shows. All three channels sent mini cams to cover the game. There were no other high school games scheduled until the next week when everyone was back in school. The Cavs were off until Sunday, and Cleveland State and Ohio State each didn't have a game until sometime the next week. All of the big high school wrestling and hockey holiday tournaments had been the weekend before.

Everyone from our community was going to be at the game, as well as a lot of other local coaches, players and basketball junkies, because they all wanted to check out Washington D.C. Industrial Tech and what they were going to do to us.

The night before the game was going to become one of our usual Thursday night pizza and video nights. The kids were sitting around the team room waiting for the coaches. As with everything so far that week, Mate had everything planned perfectly.

He had the VCR set up, and the kids didn't notice the speakers he had planted for special effect. He knew the kids enjoyed watching video of this week's special opponents. Mate wanted one of the kids to turn the tape on spontaneously, to surprise the kids with what was really on it.

Sure enough Manny got up, impatient for the coaches, thinking the tape was another one of their jam feasts from an earlier game. The room was immediately silenced and all eyes glued to the screen. They saw themselves on the screen, not as teenagers, but as fifth and sixth grade all stars from the first year we did the Saturday morning youth league. With Todd Rungren singing "The Dream Goes on Forever," the kids watched a video slide show that covered them, their families, friends, and coaches, from the time we first met them when they were in elementary school, up to the present.

The slides included great pictures of smiling kids; pictures of our first varsity basketball team, the guys with very little talent but a lot of heart; pictures and newspaper clippings about our recent successes and championships; lots of fun pictures from practices, dances, and pep rallies; and news clips from the *Plain Dealer* and *USA Today* about this Friday's game. The tape ended with quotes from Mate's that had been our team mottos all week...YOU ONLY GET SO MANY CHANCES TO DO THE IMPOSSIBLE, DON'T BLOW THIS ONE, and IT'S GOING TO BE THE BEST NIGHT OF OUR LIVES.

The next day at the pep rally, with the gym covered from the floor to the ceiling with posters and banners, with the student body in an absolute frenzy, we played the tape again. As it played, all the people in the video not part of our student body, parents, former players, etc., filtered into the gym. When the lights were turned back on, and the players took their eyes off the big screens we had projected the video on, the first thing they saw were their moms, dads and former teammates home from college for Christmas, and there was much spontaneous hugging and kissing, with more than a few misty eyes in the crowd.

The fighting Warriors were now ready to take on the nation's number one rated high school basketball team.

We stood in the corridor between the locker room and the gym along the cafeteria, and the noise from the gym was so loud for a moment we stopped and wondered what was going on. When we turned the corner and looked into the gym, the people opposite the doorway saw us in our uniforms, and the place really went crazy. The screaming got so loud I almost lost it. I looked over at Mate and the hair on the back of his neck was standing up; emotion filled his face.

Our players were instructed to stand next to the production guy from ESPN, who had a head set on. He was going to tell each of our kids when to run out onto the court. I remember our players just standing there and hearing the ESPN guy yelling into his head set, "I can't hear you...I CAN'T HEAR YOU!"

The place was totally out of control. Finally he just started sending our guys out across the floor...no one could here the PA announcer...and the noise that seemed to be as loud as it could possibly be, increased with each player's name.

This is the first great scene on the tape of the ESPN broadcast. They introduced our opponents first, and the tape shows a head shot of each of them and an on-screen graphic of their size and statistics.

As soon as their last starter is announced, the noise level on the tape greatly increases. They cut to a crowd scene of our cheering section, and every single fan in the stands is on their feet and screaming.

Then the tape cuts to the corner of the gym next to the stage where we would be entering. You hear a bit of our public address announcer before he is drowned out by the crowd, "And now ladies and gentlemen, the Pride of Cleveland, the River Boro Warriors..."

The tape zooms in on Manny, the first of our kids to be introduced. Because the camera was on him, the tape does not show all the kids running from the bleachers onto the floor to form a human tunnel leading from the gym corner all the way to our bench.

It was at this point that the noise in the gym just got too loud. On the ESPN video you can't really hear the PA announcer or the ESPN guys, but it just doesn't matter because the picture on the screen tells the whole story. ESPN had a hand held camera on the floor, and the tape stays with a ground level shot of our starters coming through all their schoolmates, getting high five after high five from many of them. When they finally get to Mate you can see him coming through the same human tunnel, followed by me and the rest of the team, as the kids are chanting, "Mate, Mate, Mate..."

The gym was packed to the rafters. TV cameras were everywhere. The best fucking team in the country was on the other bench. Flash bulbs were going off like bottle rockets.

We huddled our team in front of our bench and Mate tried to talk but the players started screaming, "We can't hear you, Coach. We can't hear you..."

Mate paused and looked around and then the team looked around and we took it all in...The people in the stands were going berserk...the noise was deafening...the gym was on fire...we were ready to do it like it's televised.

Mate circled the team as close as they could to him and said above the noise, screaming so each kid could hear, even though they were less than a foot away, "Let's just fucking do it fellas, let's just fucking do it!!!"

Both teams went out for the jump ball and we noticed the crowd was getting to our opponents. They stood out there waiting for the noise to die and it just didn't. The crowd never let up. They won the jump, ran a play for a lay up, and when Reggie Robinson went up for the dunk, Rich Simmons went with him. Even though he was called for the foul, Rich sent the ball halfway down Robinson's throat. The crowd loved it. Robinson was rattled, and he only made one of the free throws. We came down and walked the ball inside, then kicked it back to the wing for a jumper from fifteen.

During this whole opening sequence, the crowd never stopped. On the bench our ears were ringing. No one could hear the person sitting next to him in the whole building.

Over beers later that evening the engineer for ESPN would tell us how loud it really was. "I've been everywhere. I've done football at LSU, college hoops in every gym in the East. Never have all the dials gone past ten at one time, ever. Your gym was so loud it couldn't even register on our equipment. It was the closest we have ever had to blowing it off the boards."

Playing great defense, coming down and controlling our offense, we did what no team had ever done or would ever do against Washington D.C. School of Industrial Arts. We jumped out to a 17-4 lead. Their kids had yet to adjust to the noise in the gym, and we had yet to make a mistake.

When they finally called a time out, you would have thought the game was over. But there was a reason they were so good, a reason that they had won every game for the last two seasons, as well as the *USA Today* poll. When they came back out, they were a different team. They slowed it up, because we were converting too many of their transition mistakes into points. They took better shots and cut down on their turnovers. They tightened their defense, and the next thing you knew they were back in the game.

The noise never let up. Our fans stood on their feet the whole half, and every time they made a run to get even with us, the crowd would pick it up a notch. They tied it for the first time with two minutes left in the half, and we needed to do something to get the momentum back before we headed to the locker room. Manny had the ball at half court, threw it out to the wing and faked his backside pick. He caught their guy anticipating, was able to cut to the basket cleanly, and got the give-and-go pass while moving toward the basket. He went up strong, yet hung onto the ball for what at first looked like for too long. Robinson came over on backside help and was ready to slap the shot away, when Manny's move caught him by surprise, and he ended up hitting more hand than ball for the foul. Anticipating the foul, Manny tossed the ball straight up instead of off the backboard, the ball hung in the air as the ref blew the foul, and then it came back down through the hoop. Nothing but net for the basket and a chance for a three point play!

Manny made the free throw. They pushed the ball up court and set up a back side ally oope pass and caught us sleeping, but they missed the wide open dunk. The ball went flying off the rim and we got the rebound on the run up court, and Williams hit a fifteen foot jumper from the wing at the buzzer to take us in the half up five and with the momentum.

At the half, the noise from the gym never ceased. The crowd was pounding on the bleachers to the beat of the songs the spirit band was playing. We coaches went into our office while the kids rested by their lockers. Mate was ecstatic.

"Do you believe it? What a rush!!!" He went on to describe our great plays of the half. We were so excited. We came out of our office, and we could tell the kids weren't going to rest on their first half laurels.

We made some adjustments and went over our game plan again. The door opened and a ref gave us the three minutes to get back on the floor. Once again the noise from the gym blew us away.

Mate looked at the troops before we went back out on the floor. "Remember, if this is going to be the greatest night of not only our lives but for everyone in that gym, the greatest night in the history of our school, we have to play one more half better than the one we just played. Don't you ever forget, every so often you've got to do the impossible. And gentlemen, we are sixteen minutes away from doing something no one has ever been able to do, and on top of it, do it on national TV."

The moment that the game turned back in our favor for good happened at the beginning of the fourth quarter. They had once again scraped back to within a bucket, and we called a time out simply to get our kids off the court after we had let them go on a 12-2 run. A couple of fast break dunks had pushed the momentum over to them and, for a moment, took the crowd out of the game.

You could say that it was planned. It was one of those 'if this, this, and this happen, then we'll do it' things. Rich and his friends in the band had rehearsed the song for several weeks. Mate came up with the idea of doing it during the game, and Dave Van Husen knew it would be great for a time out late in the game that didn't have a commercial break.

This is one of the incidents from the game that just jumps out at you on the ESPN tape. The tape shows an on screen graphic detailing their 12-2 run, and how many of their baskets were dunks. You hear the noise level of the crowd, constantly loud until this moment, greatly diminish. Mate stands up, a look of great frustration on his face, and signals to Manny to call time out.

The tape shows an overhead shot of both teams going to their benches, their team giving each other high fives, ours with our heads down.

The tape doesn't show what was said or done in our huddle. After a few moments allowing our guys to sit down, towel themselves off and get a drink, I glanced at Mate to see if he wanted to discuss anything before we talked to the kids. I noticed he was trying to fight back a smile, and I knew he had something up his sleeve.

He walked into the huddle and turned his head towards Richie Simmons and said, "Richie, it's time to get this crowd and this team back into the game."

"Anything you say, Coach," he said and stood up, split the huddle, and headed over to the stage where both our spirit band and student section were.

While this is going on, the tape shows a head shot of the ESPN announcers discussing their run. While they are talking, suddenly in the background, you hear the crowd going bonkers.

Dave Van Husen was manning the dials and switches in the ESPN truck parked out in the parking lot, and he did a great job all night, especially at this moment. The next cut on the tape, with the announcers still being heard discussing the game, is a shot of the horn section of the spirit band jumping off the stage and running to set up shop in front of our student section. All of them are wearing Hawaiian shirts, one of them is carrying a saxophone that he hands to Richie as he meets them halfway across the floor.

Then you hear one of the announcers say, "It's important for the Warriors to get the crowd back in the game, and it looks like that's what they're trying to do right now."

The ESPN tape switches to another shot of all the horns in front of the crowd. You can see Richie adjusting the reed on his sax as one of the trumpet players can be seen counting down, "a one, a two, a one, two, three, four!"

Then you hear the opening blast of the great Bruce Springsteen/Clarence Clemons saxophone boogie number "Paradise by the C."

For years "Paradise by the C" was always the number the E Street Band opened the second half or the first encore of their shows with. If you have a copy of the 1985 Bruce Springsteen live box set, it is the first song on side two. If you have a bootleg tape of the '78 Cleveland Agora show, it is the first song after the intermission. Mate had turned the kids in our spirit band onto it earlier that basketball season, when they had asked him for some new rowdy tunes to play at the games.

The original Bruce and the E Street Band version, which we saw performed live at least a dozen times, did the same thing each time, it got everyone up on their feet dancing and screaming and clapping as loud as they could. It was Clarence 'the Big Man' Clemons wailing away on his horn, up against Danny Federeci's Hammond organ, while 'Mighty Max' Weinberg pounded the beat.

The River Boro High Spirit Band version had three saxes, three trumpets, and two trombones blasting away the Clarence Clemons part, while assorted bass drums and snares pounded away the beat. Although not as professionally done, but with just as much heart and soul, it had the same effect. It got everyone in the gym on their feet screaming and clapping for their team. And, whatever their coaches were telling their team on their bench, they didn't hear it. Because all of their players were watching our spirit band and our cheerleaders across the floor, blasting out the tune and dancing and screaming while getting the crowd into a frenzy.

For many of the kids at school, it was their favorite moment of the game and of the ESPN broadcast. The tape switches back and forth among some great crowd scenes, kids dancing in the aisles, some close ups of some of the more animated fans, the cheerleaders dancing in synch with each other on the floor, and the spirit band blasting away on their horns, especially Richie in his sweat soaked uniform. As one of the kids would say Monday morning in one of my classes, "At that moment, every high school kid in the country watching that game wished that they went to our school."

When it was time to get back to the bench for some last second instructions, Richie brought the brass section, all of the cheerleaders, and the first five rows of the student section back with him to the huddle. We all surrounded Mate as pandemonium enveloped us. Everyone stuck a hand into the huddle on top of Mate's, and he screamed above the noise, "Let's go out and put this one away. Defense, one, two, three!!!"

"Defense!!!" Everyone screamed as we broke the huddle, only to hear the referee's whistle blowing us a technical for too many people on the floor.

"You got to keep your fans under control," he screamed at Mate and I and, of course, it just energized the crowd even more.

Their token white stud, Danny Meredith, went to the line to shoot the T's. He would finish his high school career shooting 82%. At Duke for four years, he would go on and shoot 89%. Later in the pros, he would have three seasons of shooting over 90%, leading the league two of those years, and coming in second behind Mark Price in the other. But all I know is on that night in our gym with our fans screaming their heads off, he missed both technicals. He would then try to in bound the ball to one of their wings, only to have it intercepted by Jamie McGowan, who would then hit Manny on a three quarter court pass for a lay up. The crowd went crazy, and we were up by four.

After that it was all over with. There was nothing they could do. The crowd had blown them away, and we were smelling blood. We came out and ran off another ten unanswered points, and it was never close again.

They called time out for no apparent reason with :06 left on the clock and us up 66-57. We were later told by their coaches that they called time out to remind their players that it is just as important to lose with class, as it is to win with it. It's not that they had bad kids, in fact they had a great group of kids, it was just that they had not lost in over two years, and their coaches wanted to make sure they handled it correctly, especially on national television.

We got everyone in our huddle and each of us, coaches, players and managers, just stood there taking it all in. The spirit band was blasting away at something, but the noise in the gym was so loud we couldn't hear them. The crowd was on its feet screaming and clapping. The gym was completely packed and not a soul had left. There were security cops in front of the student section trying to keep the kids off the floor.

Finally, Mate got everyone's attention. Even though we were all in a tight huddle, we could barely hear him. He looked each of us in the eyes and screamed, "How does it feel?"

All the kids went crazy, looking around and taking it all in. "Just remember fellas, we always win with class," was the last thing he told them.

Even if I hadn't watched the ending of the game and what followed hundreds of times since it happened, the images of what happened would be something I'd never forget.

The ESPN video really does the moment justice. The tape shows the last seconds of the game with Williams under our basket slamming the ball hard off the floor and having it bounce to the ceiling. The kids off the bench running onto the floor and mobbing him. The kids out of the stands running onto the floor mobbing the team. The players on their team standing in disbelief and staring silently at what was going on.

Then it shows Mate and I going over to shake their coaches'

hands. What the tape doesn't tell you is what Coach Fraser said to us. "That was as fine of a coaching job as anyone has done on us. Great job fellas." And believe me when I tell you, that meant something from someone who is a living legend. The John Fucking Wooden of high school basketball.

ESPN kept the camera on Mate after we shook hands, and he turns towards the camera to look out at the total chaos going on in the middle of the floor, with our team being mobbed by their classmates coming out of the stands. Then he is mobbed by a group of girls from his first period class, big busty girls who go to the vo ed in the afternoon for cosmetology classes. They kiss and hug him, and even leave some lipstick marks on his face that you can see on the tape.

He then scans the crowd behind our bench, probably trying to find his mom and Uncle Gus, and makes eye contact with someone far up in the stands. You can tell he is greatly surprised. It is a woman wiping away the tears she is trying to keep from running down her face. She smiles at him because she knows this moment is really special, and she is just happy to be another face in the crowd.

The ESPN tape, however, doesn't show Beth up in the stands. The camera stays on Mate. You see his eyes scanning the crowd and that something really special catches his eyes. He looks dumbfounded for a moment, then breaks into a very sincere smile, shruggs his shoulders slightly, and wipes a tear from his own cheek. He stands completely still for another moment, before that moment is interrupted by him being tackled by the guys on the basketball team.

By the time we got to the locker room, a mob scene had developed. Mini cams from Channels 3, 5, and 8 were all at the game, and all three were busy interviewing our players in the hallway. Both Mate and I got stuck talking to reporters before we even got in the door. By the time I made it into the team room, it was filled with what seemed like every basketball or football player we had ever coached, most home from college for the holidays, congratulating their younger former teammates on a job well done.

Win or lose, Mate and I both always had a moment alone

with the team in the locker room after every game, football or basketball. The Old Man always did, so we always did. By the time we got all of our guys together in the team room, and all of the guests and reporters and TV people out in the hallway, we all had enough time for the magic of the victory to sink in. There had been a lot of big ones with this group of kids, but nothing like this one.

"Fellas, I just want to tell you one thing," Mate said, still with a bit of the dumbfounded look on his face, "Enjoy this one. We have had our share of victories over the years, many with you guys and many with the guys before you, but this one is special." He stumbled for a second, what would the Old Man say next? "You don't ever forget a night like this, especially when something comes along later, something you don't think you can accomplish. Just remember what we did tonight. Don't forget that we still have a date with destiny in March down in Columbus, but for now, let's enjoy this one." The kids whooped it up one more time, as we retreated to the coach's office to let them enjoy the win amongst themselves.

In the coaches' office was quite a crowd, including the Old Man, Tom Haggerty, Dr. Kaniecki, the Postman, and Dave Van Husen. Mate surveyed the room and then nonchalantly said as he shut the door behind us, "Just another day at the office, fellas."

A moment later there was a knock on the door and Jamie McGowan stuck his head in. "Coach, remember, I got to make the call by ten." We both glanced at the clock on the wall that said a quarter till.

"Do you want us to leave?" I said.

He paused for a moment. "No. You guys might as well stay, as long as you keep quiet. Sometimes the connection isn't that good."

Everyone in the room quickly glanced at Mate and I as we signaled for them to be quiet. We shut the door as Jamie dialed the number he read off a wrinkled piece of scrap paper.

"Hello. May I please speak to inmate James McGowan, Sr., number 01-14?"

A long pause.

"Well, what did you think Dad, did we play great or what?" And for the first time since a little league game during the summer between fifth and sixth grade, Jamie McGowan was able to talk over one of his games with his dad, because one of the places that ESPN brought the game to was the minimum security wing of the Mansfield Reformatory.

It didn't take long for everyone in the room to catch on to what was happening, and we all tried our hardest to listen in and act like we weren't at the same time. All we heard was Jamie's end of the conversation, but we all had no trouble following it.

"Yeah, I know they had some great players...We worked on that all week...I think both of those guys will make the NBA...it was so loud half the time we couldn't hear the coaches in the huddle...yeah, Mom was there and Timmy and Grandpa and Grandma...I should not have taken that shot, I just got lucky...I just made him work for every shot they took...Is it time already? Oh well...the only thing that could've made it better is if you were here in person but I guess on TV wasn't so bad...and I love you too Daddy, and miss you as much as always...It was great to talk to you...Yeah, just like old times...Bye, see you a week from Sunday."

When Jamie left the coach's office to rejoin his teammates, there was not a dry eye in the room.

Richie Simmons, as was his custom after all football and basketball games, was the last one out of the shower. He'd wait until almost everyone was finished. Then he would take the old lawn chair we had in the coach's office and a Playmate full of cans of icy cold Dr. Pepper, and sit in the corner of the shower room with several shower heads raining down on him. He had played an awesome game, leading everyone with twenty-nine rebounds and controlling the boards against a couple of studs.

Afterward, he sat contentedly on the bench in front of his locker, his teammates high from the victory and anticipation of the dance.

The big win had helped dissipate the hurt inside him caused by hearing about all the guys whose asses he had kicked all fall signing with Division I schools.

He didn't notice when we approached him, or the Old Man sitting next to him on the bench. He first looked up, smiled at us, then turned and looked at the man sitting next to him.

The Old Man smiled, put his arm around Rich and said, "Son, that was quite a performance you had tonight. Showed a lot of heart. So much heart I was wondering if you would like to come and play football at Michigan State with us."

His face lit up. He looked at us then at the Old Man.

"I figure the way you played tonight, I wanted to be the first to ask you."

The kids were finally out of their uniforms and into their party clothes, as they gathered in the locker room near the door so they could all walk into the dance together.

"O.K., you guys ready?" Richie asked.

"Wait a minute. One more thing," they turned toward us. "You got to tell us one more time the story."

"What story?"

"You know, the story. The story Haggerty told to us this week. You know, the story about Coach Mate kissing the girl."

I thought it was weird that they wanted to again hear another one of our stories before entering the cafeteria to the best dance of the year.

I told the story again and Mate just listened. He smiled when I got to the part where he kisses Beth and her feet leave the ground. I finished the story, and watched the kids hesitate one more time.

Richie was, as always, their leader. He turned to his teammates and said, "O.K., everyone ready?"

They all nodded.

"And remember, everyone together and no one pussy out," then, noticing Connie standing in the room, Richie said, "Sorry Connie, nothing personal."

She just blushed and acknowledged his apology with a smile.

I figured that the kids had something up their sleeves, but had no idea what it was, as they walked into the gym for the

Hawaiian Beach Party Dance.

The Hawaiian Beach Party Dance was another of our ideas that we brought with us from things we did in college, without the garbage cans filled with Hairy Buffalo. It had become very popular with the kids, and was always held after a basketball game over Christmas break. It was just a natural tie in with the greatest night of our lives theme for the evening.

We got a local construction company to loan us a truck full of sand, and the kids from shop class had made a huge sand box to use as a dance floor. The kids all wore Hawaiian shirts, swim suits, sandals and sunglasses. Mate and I got some of our old buddies to be the band, and beach music played all night.

It had turned into a pretty popular night with the kids and teachers. Mate and I picked up the post dance bar bill for any teacher who chaperoned, and most of the cool people would get into it.

The kids had it planned so well. They entered from the locker room corner of the lunch room, filled with kids dancing in a rainbow of colors. The band lowered their volume when the team entered the room, but kept punching out a steady beat. The voice of one of their classmates filled the room.

"Ladies and Gentlemen...Can I have your attention. Now entering the dance hall from the northwest corner are the men of the hour...the Gentlemen who have just brought this fine academic institution its biggest athletic victory in the history of the school...the men of the hour...The River Boro Fighting Warrior basketball team!!!"

The kids walked single file through the crowd, big grins on their faces, waving and completely enjoying the genuine warm greeting they were receiving from their classmates.

And then, as if on cue, it happened. They all went off in different directions. Each walking very determined through the crowd, looking for someone. Then one by one, they found what they were looking for. It hit me. I knew what was going on.

Mate and I stood there staring, then looked at each other and smiled as we realized what was happening. As we looked around the cafeteria we saw everyone on the basketball team, from the seniors down to the managers, all picking out a girl (or, in the case of the girl managers, a guy), throwing their arms around them, and giving each one a kiss they would never forget.

Everyone in the gym was aghast as they darted their eyes around, seeing who was kissing whom. As far as I could tell, no one was turning down the affection.

We were in the corner of the room, staying out of the way, letting the kids have their moment.

It happened so fast. Someone tapped me on the shoulder, and I instinctively turned around. Someone had her arms around me, and her lips upon mine, giving me the most sensuous kiss I have ever felt. Sparks flew from her to me and back again.

I felt a large and excited pair of breasts across my chest. Imagine the shock that I felt when I finally opened my eyes, after enjoying the moment a moment too long, and realized I was being attacked by Connie.

My senses immediately came back to me, I grabbed her by the hand, and dragged her out in the hallway where no one would see us.

"What the hell are you trying to do, get me fired?"

"No. Just trying to get your attention," she said, as she tried to smother me again.

I let her linger for a moment on my lips again, a beautiful moment that I let last too long.

I grabbed her by the shoulders and pushed her away. "Listen, Connie, you, I mean we, can't do this. Teachers get fired for this type of thing."

"Too fucking bad," she said, as she tried to power me again, and for a slight moment I let her.

She stopped, stepped back, looked me in the eyes and said, "I just want you to know where I, I mean we, stand. I know we can't do anything now. I just wanted you to know how I feel."

She turned and walked back into the dance. I stood there for a moment, back against the wall, and said to myself, 'so this is the way it's supposed to feel.' I felt more than a little flutter in my heart.

As if the game wasn't enough, and if being with the kids at the dance wasn't enough, we were completely surprised and thrilled by the reception we received when we finally got to the bar.

We left the dance around eleven, and when we got to the joint the parking lot was packed. They always did a good Friday night business, plus it had become the place for our crowd to go after our games. But neither of us expected to see all the familiar faces that were jammed in there that night.

As we stepped through the front door I heard someone say, "They're here!" and everyone turned toward us and applauded. Comments were yelled out like, "Great job fellas," and, "Way to go." We saw so many old and familiar faces that we both started circling the room, celebrities for a moment, shaking hands, kissing girls, and getting patted on the back. Everyone seemed to be wearing something in River Boro blue and gold.

I got the shock of my life when I looked across the room and saw my parents with my sister Amy and some of her Kent State friends. When I went over to greet them, I saw a look on their faces I don't think I'd seen for years. They were just beaming, showing the world that they were proud of me without actually saying it. I couldn't believe it. After an awkward moment of silence Amy finally said, "Go ahead, Mom. Tell him." We all looked at her.

"When we got home after the game there were ten messages on the machine. From everywhere! Your Aunt Eva in Hawaii. Your Uncle Gene in Denver. Your Uncle Sam and Aunt Emma down in Florida. Everyone! They all watched the game and called us to tell you congratulations."

"They told me to come down here and tell you, and I said why don't you tell him yourselves. And so they did!"

Just then the room got quiet as highlights of the game came on Channel 5, and the voice of the late, great Nev Chandler, filled the room...

"On the eve of tomorrow's big Browns-Jets playoff game there was another big game in town tonight as Cleveland's own River Boro High upset the nation's number one high school basketball team, Washington D.C. Industrial Tech, 66-59." The screen then cut to video from the game, starting with some great crowd shots. "In front of a packed, enthusiastic, standing-room-only crowd, as well as millions watching on ESPN, the Warriors jumped out to a fourteen point lead only to lose it by half..." They cut to several of the key plays of the first half, including a three pointer by Manny and several dunks by their studs. "But the turning point came in the second half after the Warriors were assessed a technical foul for having too many people on the floor. Industrial Tech's All American Donnie Merideth went to the line, only to miss both technical shots. The Boro then stole the inbounds pass for a quick lay up, and then it was nothing but Warriors the rest of the way out." They showed a shot of the ref giving Mate the 'T', Merideth missing the first one, and the crowd going crazy.

Mate's face then filled the screen. "This victory really belongs to our school. We've been down pretty much since the end of the football season, and we told our student body that if they gave us all they've got, we'd give them all we've got, we'd have a shot at 'em. This really is a great win for us. I can't think of a bigger one."

Then the screen filled with the face of Chuckie Jones. "Our coaches have reminded us over and over again that playing this game tonight was a rare opportunity to do the impossible. They had great players," he said. "We have a great team."

The face of Richie Simmons popped on next, with his name and game stats across the bottom of the screen. "Not enough can be said about how our coaches prepared us for this game. We have great coaches, they made us believe..." and then his voice faded with everyone in the bar hooting and hollering about what he had said about Mate and I.

The last shot showed Nev standing in the doorway of our locker room. His hair and clothes were slightly amiss, as he got caught up in the celebration. As he wrapped up his story, you could see in the background several members of the team and two coaches playing air guitar and jamming to Van Halen's "Why Can't This be Love."

"And in what is the upset of the year in high school

219

basketball, our own River Boro Warriors up-end the nation's number one team, Washington Industrial Tech 66-59, handing them their first loss in almost three seasons."

The Tavern again burst into applause. I started to make my rounds again, and in every direction was another familiar face. My family. Mate's family. Dozens of former players home from college for the holidays. A couple of tables of boosters and parents. Hags and some of our crowd from OSU. Coaches from some of the other schools in the area. Some of the ESPN crowd. A couple of the sportswriters. It was awesome.

"Man, you wouldn't believe what it was like in here during the game," Tom the bartender told Mate and I as he leaned over and gave us a couple of cold ones. "You would've thought it was already tomorrow's Browns game. The place was almost as crowded as it is now, and everyone was going crazy. And what about that shit you guys pulled with Simmons and the spirit band and getting that technical. Just fucking outstanding. That kid wanted no part of making those shots. The crowd took him completely out of the game."

Mate turned to me and said, "I never thought it would work, let alone get a chance to use it."

We went back to making our rounds. We crossed paths again when we ended up at the juke box together, throwing dollar bills in and punching in the tunes. We heard a familiar voice behind us.

"Boy, I wonder who's in charge of the juke box around here. All it plays is Springsteen, Southside Johnny, McGuffey Lane, Marshall Tucker, and Michael Stanley."

I turned around and said sincerely, "Hi Beth. God, it's good to see you." She gave me a big hug and a sloppy peck on the cheek.

Mate acted like he was still looking for some more songs on the juke box, even though we had no more credits. Finally he turned around and made eye contact with her for the second time that night, the second time in God knows how many years. "Hi Beth," he said with a slightly confusing smile on his face. No immediate body contact. They kept looking into each other's eyes. More than enough tension in the air. Sexual or nervous, I couldn't quite tell. I decided to break the ice.

"What brings you here? You haven't been in this part of town in years."

"Gus invited me. I saw him at the game."

All three of us looked at him, standing in the corner surrounded by a bunch of college kids. Gus had a beer in one hand and was waving his cigar in the air in other, obviously telling the young lads once again how he and Georgie Patton kicked the Kraut's asses all across Northern Italy. All three of us broke into laughter.

When I turned back and looked their eyes were zoned into each other, and I headed back to the bar as the opening piano chords of "Romeo's Tune" danced out of the juke box. I turned to look at them once more, words were still not being said, and I heard Steven Forbert sing...

> *Meet me in the middle of the night*
> *Let me hear you say everything's all right*
> *Let me smell the moon in your perfume*

She finally broke the silence. "It was a great game. Are yours always this exciting?"

"No. We don't always beat the best team in the country on national TV every night."

"You have some good players on our...I mean, your team."

"We're not bad, but still, they had some thoroughbreds."

"It's nice to see you guys," she said.

"It's nice to see you," he replied. "We've missed your company."

They both had no immediate thing to say, but they each couldn't stop staring into the other's eyes...

The next thing I remember is that it was closing time, and I was one of the last to leave. I had lost track of Mate and Beth, and I thought about how good it would be to finish the night cuddled up next to someone special. Maggie Williams had been there earlier with a few of her girlfriends. I hadn't seen her since the summer, but I avoided her, and had no real desire to be with her. Something was bouncing around inside me. All the excitement of everything that had happened had finally taken its toll and I felt exhausted. Then it hit me as I walked out alone into the cold to my car, thinking about how great Connie's body and lips had felt for that brief moment when she had given me that kiss.

What a fucking day, I said to myself, as I made my way home.

When I did get home I did not get much sleep for three reasons. Reason #1: I was still too pumped up from the events of the evening, the big win, seeing so many friends in the stands, my confusing moment with Carmen, and the great time at the bar. I was exhausted, but my heart was racing. Reason #2: In less than ten hours was the kickoff for the Browns vs. the Jets playoff game, to this day still my favorite Browns game of all time. Reason #3: Our house was rocking, because Mate and Beth, for the first time in far too many years, were upstairs doing the nasty.

As soon as I stepped into the house, the scent of sex was everywhere. There is no other way to describe it, the whole place smelled from pussy.

I tiptoed into the living room, but they had already retired to the boudoir. Shoes and socks were scattered across the floor. The pillows were thrown off the couch. Two opened beers, with less than a sip gone from each, were on the coffee table. The second side of the first Karla Bonhoff album was just finishing on the turntable.

Wide awake I watched for the first time, but surely not the last, the ESPN tape of our game. So many things on it blew me away. I tried to get a couple hours of sleep, but that was impossible. My heart was still beating from the events of the evening, and even if I was dead tired, there was no way I'd be able to fall asleep with the noises coming out of the other bedroom. I heard both of them crying, I heard both of them laughing, I heard both of them scream in passion. The bed board was smashing against the wall, the bed springs maxing out. But I wasn't upset they were keeping me up. I had one of those feelings like something wrong in the world had been fixed, and the sounds of them doing the nasty was a sound that had been absent for too long from our lives.

It was Carmen's idea to have everyone at our house for breakfast before the game, and I told her it was fine as long as she and Manny got there early to clean up and cook. When I got up, the two of them were crashed on the couch in our living room. They had stayed up all night at a friend's house watching the ESPN tape and gossiping about the dance, and came straight to our house instead of heading home. They were easy to wake up because neither of them were able to sleep either, because the noises from the other bedroom had continued, and still continued into the morning.

They both washed their faces, and Manny and I started getting the food ready as Carmen straightened up the living room. Manny looked at me quizzically and asked, "Man, what's that smell?"

I very dead panned replied, "We had fish for dinner the other day." He didn't get it.

All of a sudden the bed board once again started to hammer against the wall upstairs. The three of us pretended to ignore it, until we just couldn't, and we all broke up in laughter. As Carmen was putting the vacuum back in the closet in the kitchen, her eyes caught mine behind her brother's back. I gave her a dirty look, pretending I was upset over her little stunt at the dance. She just smiled and threw me a kiss. I turned away; I didn't want her to know how confused I was on the matter.

It was just then that Beth appeared, dressed to go home. She was glowing, she was a happy woman. "What's going on here?" She asked, noticing the kids and I getting a feast ready.

"We're having everyone over before the Browns game today," Manny said with enthusiasm. I don't think anyone loved our get togethers more than him.

"We got about twenty of us going to the game today. Are you going?" Carmen asked.

"No," she replied.

"Do you have to work?"

"No," she replied again.

"Oh, Beth, go to the game with us. I know we must have an extra ticket," Carmen said with a degree of familiarity, as if she already knew Beth.

"Do you guys know each other?" I asked, surprised at the blank and confused looks on their faces. They quickly glanced at each other. After an awkward moment of silence, Beth changed the subject.

"I'd love to go if you have an extra ticket," she said, and plans were suddenly made for her to meet us at the game. Connie went and got one of the tickets from the cabinet where we kept them, and walked Beth to the front door.

Before I had a chance to find out what the looks between Beth and Connie were about, our house started to fill up with guests. Uncle Gus brought a roaster full of kielbasi and sauerkraut into the kitchen. He took the smelly cigar out of his mouth, exaggerated a couple of deep breaths, then smiled at me and said, "One of you guys get lucky last night?" I just smiled and rolled my eyes towards his nephew, who had just rolled himself out of bed and was greeting people in the living room.

The crowd at our house that morning was on an emotional high. Most had not come down from our basketball game the night before, and all were pumped for the Browns/Jets game. Manny had made a big batch of home fries with onions smothered in cheese. I was making omelets. Connie made three huge stacks of blueberry pancakes. Mate's sister, Barb, brought a big tray of angel wings and potato pancakes. The cocktails were flowing, and it wasn't even nine yet.

It was a good crowd. A hunk of Uncle Gus's crew, now referred to as "the Dinosaurs," were present. A dozen of our friends from section 60 and 61 were there. I let the kids invite a couple of friends, so Richie Simmons and Jamie McGowan were there. Even some of the ESPN crew stopped by, as well as some of the people from the bar the night before.

It was nine o'clock in the morning before a Browns playoff game and the house was packed with new and old friends. The smell of food was in the air. Beers were flowing, laughter was abundant. On the turntable was that old scratched record highlighting the 64 championship season, with the Browns fight song being played over and over. As John Steinbeck once said, 'the world was again turning in greased grooves.'

By the time the Cleveland Browns had returned to the playoffs under Coach Marty Schottenheiemer and Quarterback Bernie Kosar, we had settled into the lower bleachers in sections 60 and 61, the first few rows of seats slightly towards right field in the bleachers. We loved it there. We knew everyone in our section, were so close to the field it was like being at a high school or college game, and were right in the middle of things, from the start, in all the Dawg Pound hysteria that exploded at the time. We were constantly on television, both nationally and locally, and if we had friends come visit from another part of the stadium, it was easy to squeeze them in.

Those were great times. To watch that team be put together, starting with Clay Matthews and Ozzie Newsome who were left over from the Brian Sipe era, to the great defensive backs (Hanford Dixon, Frank Minniefield and Felix Wright), and, of course, the maneuvering to get Bernie Kosar.

I had never seen the Stadium more psyched for a game than for that 1987 playoff game against the Jets. It was a perfect Saturday afternoon in January for football. Clear, sunny skies with the temperature in the thirties. By the time we got everyone organized and out of our house at ten, still a good two hours to kick off, downtown was hopping. We parked over in the Flats in the long parking lot that stretched from the Stadium over along the tracks to Fagan's. People of all ages, races and economic backgrounds, were partying hard. A half hour before game time, the Stadium was packed. Everyone in the crowd had their game faces on that day.

Until late in the fourth quarter things were looking bleak. The Browns were down three, but finally got something going. They had the ball on the Jets three, and it looked like they were going to punch one in for the score. But then on a quick slant to Webster Slaughter, Kosar tried to force a pass between two cover guys and got picked off in the end zone.

The Jets got the ball back on the twenty and got a drive going, but the Browns eventually forced them to punt, and got the ball back on their own 17 with 4:31 to play.

On the previous drive, Kosar had thrown his first interception since November. And, in his terrific career going back to Youngstown Boardman High School and then the University of Miami before coming to the Browns, he had never, ever, thrown interceptions on two consecutive plays. Let alone in a championship game. But that's what he did. On first down, Bernie tried to hit Herman Fontenot and was picked off again. The Jets took over on their own 25, and on first down Freman McNeil swept right end and went the distance to take the Jets up 20-10 with just a little over four minutes left.

The crowd sat silently. Things had happened too fast, and no one expected things to turn out the way they were going. Many in the crowd remembered six years earlier and Brian Sipe and Red Right 88 (*).

One minute we were on the two going in for the lead, the next thing we knew we were down ten with four minutes left.

But at that moment, the crowd in the bleachers around us seemed to decide together that defeat was not going to be accepted that afternoon. I remember the Browns return team huddling then running on the field towards us, and the whole bleachers standing as one to greet them. I remember John Big Dawg Thompson running the length of the bleachers, with his dog bone raised above his head, and everyone in the front row giving him a high five. I remember the Bleacher Creatures, facing the crowd from their seats in the first row, screaming for the crowd to get on their feet and to stay there.

People were streaming out to their cars from other parts of the Stadium, but out in the Dawg Pound we had refused to believe that the game was over.

After the kick, the Browns started their drive on their own 32. After a couple of stupid penalties and an incomplete pass, they found themselves facing a second and 24 from their own 18. Bernie tried to get half of it on an under route, only to throw a pass no one could catch. Third and 24. But wait!!! In what

* In the coldest game in Browns history on what appeared to be the winning drive, Brian Sipe threw an interception into the end zone with :49 seconds left in a 1981 playoff game against the Oakland Raiders. The play was called Red Right 88, and the Browns lost 14-12. The wind chill was 30 degrees below, and when we walked silently stunned out of the Stadium, our hearts were as cold as the wind .

226

would turn out to be the pivotal play of the game, defensive end Mark Gastineau, who had the tools to be the best but only was very good on his best days, would hit Kosar late and was given a personal foul. Instead of third and 24 from our own 18, it was first and ten from the 33. Kosar got to work hitting short passes to four different receivers, and Kevin Mack punched it in from the one to pull the Browns to 20-17 with two minutes left in the game.

The crowd around us was going crazy, and chants of DEFENSE, DEFENSE filled the huge stadium. You could see people filtering back to their seats.

The Jets played it safe, running the ball three times. The Browns used their last time out to stop the clock on third down, and by the time the Jets punted, it was under a minute left.

The Browns got the ball back on their own 33 and got a big break on first down when a Jets defender interfered with Brian Brennan. That pushed the Browns to the Jets 42, first and ten with zero time outs left.

The Browns were headed towards the closed end of the Stadium, so we were watching the game from behind their offense. Even when the action was at the far end of the Stadium, it was still a good seat, especially if you were a coach, because you always had someone to key on and it was a good angle to watch a play open up.

On the next play, another big play on an afternoon of big plays, Kosar hit Slaughter for 37 yards before he was tackled out of bounds in front of the Indians dugout at the five yard line. The whole Stadium went crazy as Slaughter was mobbed by his teammates.

I then had the biggest feeling of impending doom and disaster I have ever felt. From where we were sitting, not only did I have a perfect shot of Web-star catching the ball and being tackled, but I also had a perfect shot of the referee marking Web-star tackled in bounds instead of out of bounds, meaning the game clock would start as soon as the ball was marked. I started screaming at the top of my lungs, "Set up the offense! Set up the offense!!" Everyone around me looked at me strangely; they were too busy celebrating Slaughter's catch. Oh my God, time's going to run out before they realize he wasn't out of bounds. We're going to lose!! We're going to lose!!

There was one other person in the Stadium who realized that the ball was marked in bounds, and that was Bernie Kosar. He ran over to where everyone was celebrating, literally grabbed the offensive line and dragged them over the hash, where the ref was just finishing placing the ball. Kosar took the snap, tried to hit Slaughter in the end zone, but it fell incomplete. But, most importantly, it stopped the clock, allowing the Browns to kick the field goal on the last play of regulation to send the game into overtime.

From the end of regulation to the start of overtime, the crowd never sat down, and more and more people came back into the Stadium from their cars.

The Browns lost the toss and kicked off to start O.T., but the 'D' stuffed 'em and the Browns started their first drive on their own 26. Kosar would hit five out of six passes to drive the Browns down to the Jets 5, where the field goal team trotted on the field for a 23 yard chip shot. Everybody in the stands was celebrating, giving high fives and hugging each other.

The snap. The hold. The kick. NO GOOD!!! Mark Mosely, one of the most reliable kickers of his era, wide right.

Uh-oh. I said to myself. Here it comes again. We had our chance and blew it. Another Cleveland sports tragedy about to happen. Come from ten points down with four minutes left to send it into O.T., only to miss a field goal to win it. I should have known. *Why do I take this shit so seriously?* I said to myself, as the Jets took over possession of the ball on what I was sure was to be the winning drive.

But it wasn't. The Browns and Jets would trade punts back and forth several times before the Browns got the ball back with a little over two minutes left in the first overtime on their own 31. They would run ten plays, five of them tough yard rushes by Kevin Mack, as they drove down inside the Jets ten where Mosley did not make the same mistake, kicking a 27 yarder for the win.

To this day, many years later, I get a lump in my throat remembering what it was like out in those bleachers at the old

Stadium at the end of that game. It was one of those moments when nothing else mattered. It didn't matter if you were black or white or rich or poor or young or old or a city kid or from the suburbs. Everyone was a Browns fan and hugged, kissed and congratulated everyone else, as if we all had a part in it.

I remember so much about the rest of the night because for the first time in a long time, the three of us went out. We sent all the kids home, and then went bar hopping in the Flats. People were partying in the streets, every place was jumping. Everywhere we went we were treated like kings because so many people had seen our game Friday night. We even hit Steve's Lunch for slaw dogs before we headed home. It seemed like old times with me driving and Mate and Beth going at it in the back seat.

The next week flew by even though we were back in school. The kids were all local celebrities, sharing the spotlight, of course, with the Browns. Since we had played more than the usual amount of games over the holidays, we did not have one that week. That gave us a nice space of time to enjoy the after glow of our big TV win.

ESPN did a nice recap of our game that they showed several times that week on Sports Center. It opened with Chris Berman saying, "The Browns-Jets game wasn't the only big game this past weekend in Cleveland..." and it went into the highlights including many crowd scenes, Rich and the horns playing in front of the stands, and the crowd running on the floor at the end of the game. It closed with a short commentary by Dick Vitale about the joys and excitement of high school basketball, and how high school coaches are "the real heroes in America, teaching five to six classes a day and then staying late for practice, out scouting, not getting home until midnight on game nights." Thanks Dick.

We got cards and letters from family, friends and alumni across the country who had watched the game on T.V. My parents were dumbfounded at first . They must have gotten a dozen more calls from long distance relatives. This was, finally, the end of their bitterness about my being "only a teacher." All the pub that our football team, and then the hoops team, had garnished had finally caused them to rethink my chosen profession. I was finally O.K. I may not have been making the big bucks, but being a local celebrity of sorts and the attention it brought them, as well as me, was something they really enjoyed. I wasn't in the financial world of my cousin George the dentist or cousin Norman the CPA, but neither of them had ever done a root canal or balanced a ledger on national television or on the front page of the *Plain Dealer*.

I tried to avoid Connie as much as possible. I was scared shitless that someone had seen us in the hallway at the dance Friday night. I had never felt like that before, but I also had no one to talk about it with. Mate would have probably thought it was incest, or that I had molested his kid sister.

I was sitting at my desk grading some tests Thursday afternoon during my free period when she found me. I didn't want to talk to her, and I didn't want to be alone with her.

"Aren't you supposed to be in choir?" I said.

"Relax, I have a pass. Besides, we have something to talk about."

Here it is, I said to myself. I didn't know what to say, and then imagine my surprise when it wasn't us who she wanted to talk about.

"He hasn't called her all week. Nothing. Zippo."

"Who hasn't called who? What are you talking about?"

"Mate hasn't called Beth all week. He hasn't talked to her since after the game last Saturday."

"Hey, that reminds me, did you two already know each other? You seemed awfully chummy Saturday."

She stood silent for a second, looking down as if she was trying to figure out what she was going to say. She did not answer my question, but instead said, "I asked her to go with us again Sunday for the Denver game." She paused for a second, then looked up at me for the first time. I immediately looked down at the papers on my desk and she said, "Why hasn't he called her? I never saw him so happy. Why hasn't he called her?"

"Connie, there is not enough time left in this day to discuss their relationship and why he hasn't called her."

"Do you think he will? Do you think they'll get back together?"

We had managed to avoid real eye contact with each other. I thought about what she asked me, as I was pretended to be reading one of the papers on the desk.

"I don't know what's going to come of it, but I do know he's not going to do anything about it this very moment. There's just too much stuff going on, especially if we go to states and the Browns go to the Super Bowl."

"Yeah, you're probably right."

"Yes, I'm probably right and, yes, you have to go back to class."

She turned and started walking towards the door. I looked up and watched her walk away and said, "Tell her to hang in there. Her time will come." I got almost all of that out of my mouth before she turned around and looked me dead in the eyes. The world stopped. I felt the magnetic pull pushing us towards each other, and the energy we were both using to keep us apart. We stared at each other, then the bell rang to end the period and to bring us both back into reality. She turned and walked out the door and got lost amongst the kids rushing through the halls on their way to their next class.

Beth called and asked if I'd meet her for a beer. She wanted to talk but she couldn't get started, so I took the initiative.

"What happened? I mean, most of us thought you had it made. The house in Rocky River, hanging with all those high rollers, the ski condo at Holiday Valley. You were definitely playing in another league. Didn't you have everything you always wanted?"

She paused for a moment. "Sometimes things change what you want. Sometimes you realize what you are chasing after is what someone else wants, or what you were led to believe you want. "

I gave her a confused look. I wasn't sure what she was talking about.

"Listen. When I had it made, or thought I had it made, you

231

know what I missed? I missed real people and real laughter. I never again want to spend time at a social function or vacation with a bunch of tight ass lawyers talking about their shit. I never want to spend my free time with people I don't like because I have to. I made a promise to myself that from now on I'm going to lead the life I want to lead, and hang out with the people I want to be with."

She paused for a second.

"I fucked up. I became someone I wasn't, and in the process lost the people I love the most. I'm never going to let that happen again."

"I remember seeing you that one time before a Browns game when you told me you were pregnant. You were glowing, you looked so happy."

She didn't smile. "Do you remember a little time after that, me calling for Mate on the phone? He wasn't there, but you answered the phone."

"Yes, I do. I remember that you sounded like shit."

She then went on and told me about her bloody miscarriage. "And believe me, that wasn't the worst thing that happened." I didn't ask her to tell me anything more. She didn't need to, I saw the pain on her face and heard it in her voice.

She asked me if she was making a mistake.

"I don't want to see you get burned, and I don't want to see you waste your time. Not that I think you guys getting back together again is a bad idea, it's just that he's such a stubborn person, and he's carrying a lot of scar tissue from you. I think it would be very hard for him to swallow his pride, and whatever else he'd have to do, to get involved with you again. He's built himself his own little world and I just don't see him changing for anyone, including you. Especially for the next few months. Since we beat Industrial Tech, everyone thinks we're going to win the state. It ain't that simple."

She looked at me with a touch of disappointment showing in her face.

"He's got that stupid pride of his. There are some things he'll never forget. The way he looks at things, and the way you look at things, are different. You used to look at us as so immature and reckless and out of control when we were away at college, but in the long run who made the reckless and stupid decisions? Sure we were hard partyers and we went through a pretty promiscuous stage, but so did everyone else we knew. And I'm sure you heard him say that we were just having a good time. Was there anything wrong with that? No. And we got it all out of our system, and got on with our lives, and didn't do anything really stupid like get involved in a fucked up marriage. I'm sorry if this seems brutal to you, but I'm just telling you the facts."

"But what about last weekend?"

I didn't know what to say.

She sat there quiet for several minutes, nursing her beer. Thousands of thoughts were flying through her head. "Well, whether we become an item again or not, whether we ever do what we did together the other night again, you guys are to a certain extent stuck with me. You're the best friends I ever had, and I really need friends now."

I didn't know about Mate, but to be honest, it was good to have her amongst my friends again.

Sunday, lower bleachers, Cleveland Municipal Stadium. Fourth quarter, game tied 13-13. Browns ball on the Broncos 48, third and six. Brian Brennan runs a little shake and bake route and the safety comes up and bites on it, thinking the Browns are going for the first down. Kosar pump fakes and then throws over the coverage, and Brennan catches it in stride and runs untouched for the touchdown. The place goes crazy!!!

Everyone around us was yelling "Super Bowl." Mate and I, as lifetime Cleveland sports fans, weren't one hundred percent sure. But when Denver muffed the kickoff and ended up starting their possession on their own two yard line, and we looked up and with less than five minutes left in the game, we were finally convinced the Browns were headed to Pasadena and the Super Bowl. The Broncos hadn't crossed midfield since the first half, and the Browns defense had been getting stronger as the game went on.

As the Broncos huddled in the end zone of the closed end

of the Stadium, they looked a hundred miles away from us. It was then that we had our moment. Hard even now, years later, to explain how we felt, I am still now filled with emotion recalling it. We had twenty or so of us jammed in our fifteen seats, with Connie and Beth sitting directly behind us. Mate and I hugged each other and screamed into each others' ears, "We're going to the Super Bowl!!! We're going to the fucking Super Bowl!!!" He turned around wrapped his arms around Beth and buried himself into her, disappearing into the hood of her parka. At the same moment I was swept away and grabbed Connie and did the same thing. The hell with everyone else, I didn't give a shit. The Browns were going to the fucking Super Bowl and that's all that mattered.

On third down at the other end of the field, John Elway went back to throw from his own end zone, and Chip Banks came flying in on a blitz and just missed him. Elway somehow scrambled out of the pocket and gained eleven yards and a first down.

We started to talk about our plans for going to the Super Bowl in Pasadena. "We'll have to get our game with Cuyahoga Heights rescheduled for later in the month," Mate said, his eyes dancing with excitement. "Dennis Kushlak is the coach over there and he'll be cool about it."

Out of the corner of my eye I saw Elway hit two quick slants, and Denver had the ball near midfield as the two minute warning sounded.

"I'll call my buddy McGinnis in LA and we'll stay at his place," I said.

"How are we going to get tickets to the game?" Beth asked.

"If we don't get them on our own, I'm sure Tom Haggerty can get them for us," I replied.

How often I have thought of those few moments, Beth hugging Mate, Connie hanging over me, everyone in the Stadium going crazy. The Browns were going to the Super Bowl, we were both with the women we loved, and it was all happening in our favorite spot in the whole world. Looking back, I should have known it was just too fucking perfect to last.

Three plays later and with less than a minute to play,

Greg Cielec

Elway, John fucking horse face son-of-a-bitch Elway, had the Broncos on the fourteen yard line. As everyone in the bleachers started to chant DEFENSE, DEFENSE, Mate and I just stood there in disbelief. Where the hell did they come from? On first down he threw an incompletion. On second down it looked like he was sacked twice, before he again scrambled out of the pocket down to the five. And on third down, third fucking down on the five, he hit Mark Jackson for the touchdown at a spot ten feet from our seats. Shitfuck.

We were stunned. It happened too fast. Our perfect moment had come and gone, and would never ever return. We should have realized that it 's never over until it's over. Mate and I sat there in shock. Even though everyone was up and screaming to get ready for overtime, and even though the Browns won the toss and would receive the opening kick in overtime, we knew, deep down inside us we just knew, that it was too good to be true.

We both sat there stunned and oblivious to everything and everyone around us, especially the two girls sitting behind us, until, and for a good fifteen minutes after, Rich Karlis kicked the game winning field goal five minutes into overtime. Eighty thousand Browns fans walked away stunned once again in silence as they emptied the mammoth Stadium.

I was across the bar, leaning against the wall, too shocked to say anything to anyone. The place was packed, but strangely quiet.

I told myself I wasn't going to take it that seriously anymore. I told myself I wasn't going to get so emotionally involved.

It was de ja vu all over again. I told myself after Red Right 88 seven years earlier that I would never again let them disappoint me. And here I was, crushed once again.

If I felt that way, imagine how Mate felt. He sat at the bar, still completely oblivious to what was going on around him. Beer in front of him, head down; shock, surprise and defeat in his eyes.

I still see everything that happened just as it did that day.

235

I saw Mate sitting at the bar, and Beth start to approach him from his right. It looked like she was going to gently slide up next to him and put her arm around him to comfort him.

He did not see her or sense that she was near. He had to get out. There were too many people around him, and he wanted to be alone. He heard someone behind him start the old, 'but they had a good year, we'll get them next time' bullshit. Fuck the next time, we wanted the god damn Super Bowl.

When things started closing in on him, he got up to go outside. He got up out of his bar stool without seeing Beth, even though he knocked her over as he tried to get through the crowd. It could have been anyone, but it was her.

I lost him in my sight line as he disappeared into the crowd. I saw her land on her ass on the floor and disappear beneath the crowd. I finally saw her reappear as someone helped her up. I saw her look for Mate in the crowd. She saw him near the front door and took off after him, fighting as strongly through the crowd as he had a moment earlier.

I was a step or two behind her out the door.

She caught up to him walking up the bottom of the Lakeside hill under the bridge.

"Hey," she said, but he didn't hear and continued walking.

"Hey," she said louder, but again no response.

Finally she caught up with him, grabbed his shoulder and said it again slightly louder, "HEY."

He turned around and looked at her without saying a thing, giving her one of those 'time out of mind' looks.

"Hey, you didn't have to do that," she said, unaware that he did not know what he had done.

"Do what?"

"Knock me over."

"Knock you over? Where? What the hell are you talking about?"

"All I'm saying is you didn't have to do that."

He kept staring at her, still totally unaware of what she was talking about.

"Yeah, well, you didn't have to go and marry some asshole, did ya?"

That stopped her dead in her tracks. You could see her emotions shrivel up, and the hurt not just on her face but in her whole body.

"You didn't have to say that."

"Well, you didn't have to do that," He responded. A deadly moment of silence. She was too hurt to say anything, and he was still in an emotional fog and saying things without thinking first.

"Why are you here? Why did you start to come around?"

"I needed you guys. Especially you."

"Isn't it a little too late?"

"I thought..."

"You thought you'd come and open up some old wounds and make me feel shitty all over again, huh?"

"You said last Friday that that's all behind us now, that we were just kids."

"Well, that was last Friday and this is today."

"You know we can't change the past," she said.

"You're telling me about changing the past. When you had everyone feeling sorry for you when your marriage went bad, did you ever think about how I felt and how much I hurt? How do you think it feels when every time I've finally gotten you off my mind, I bump into one of your old friends some place and they tell me how big of an asshole you married. At least you could've married a good guy and saved me that part of the grief."

She stood there, too stunned to say anything.

"I don't want to think about it anymore. It's over between us, it was over years ago. Do me a favor, if we see each other anywhere again, no matter how badly we get the urge to tear our clothes off and go at it, let's just wave to each other and go our own way. O.K.?"

She did not respond. She stood there staring at him, too emotionally wrecked to say anything.

He turned and looked at several groups of bystanders who had stopped and were observing what was going on. He gave them one of those 'don't you dare fuck with me' looks, and they all started walking again and got on their way. He turned and started walking again up the hill. She stood there in shock, in the middle of the street, for what seemed like an hour but was just a moment. Finally a car honked for her to move, she realized where she was, and she turned around and walked the other way, in the direction where her car was parked.

According to what little I saw, what the police records say, and what Glenda Johnson would remember, this is what happened next...

Mate, emotionally drained and mentally in a fog, left Old River Road and walked up the foot of Lakeside beneath the Main Avenue Bridge, back towards Walter Johnson's parking lot that used to be at the corner of Lakeside and West Ninth.

He was a mess. So many thoughts were going through his head. He said what had to be said, something that had been trapped inside him for years, locked away with everything else he kept locked up. He realized that, despite the mirage of the last several weeks, he had closed the books on her forever. It was finally, once and for all, finished. *Why do I feel so shitty?*

She had been his first crush, his high school girlfriend, the girl who'd dumped him and broke his heart once, his college back home sweetie, the girl who'd dumped him and broke his heart a second time by marrying someone else, the girl who had ruined it for anyone else who tried to get close to him. She was his excuse for always ordering another round, the reason why he never slept through a complete night, and finally the woman who, for a brief moment, returned. And now, finally and abruptly, done with.

It was finally over and now what? *God, it was great to be with her again.*

I ran after and caught up to him. He sensed I was there, turned around and said, "Hey."

"Hey," I responded.

He immediately realized that I had heard and/or seen everything that went on between the two of them.

"What was I supposed to say? After all of these years she wants things back to square one. I'm sorry, that isn't how it works."

Then I said something that really surprised me. "Yeah, I know. We're just going to sit around till we're old men crying the blues about all the ones who slipped away. Then we'll just ignore or treat like shit the ones who come stumbling back. Is that it? Do I got it right? We'll just sit around and pound beers until we're old and gray and alone some place, all the while thinking about the ones who got away."

He looked at me with anger in his eyes. "She expects me to forget everything? She expects me not to remember how bad I felt? All those nights rolling around unable to fall asleep. She wants me to forget that she fucked up more than her life when she went off and married some asshole cokehead who hit her, cheated on her, and just treated her like shit? No way. Fuck her."

"Fuck you!" I shot back to him. I had said that to him thousands of times in a thousand different ways, but never until that moment had I really ever meant it.

I expected him to do something but he just stood there, dead in his tracks.

"Yeah, fuck you," I went on. "What are you going to do now? Mope around for another ten years? You think this has been easy for her? She ain't the first woman to go off and marry an asshole. She came back, finally, to you, didn't she? She is genuinely sorry, isn't she? Isn't that what you always wanted? What the hell could she otherwise possibly do?"

He looked at me and said, "Now why did you have to go and say that?" But the way he said it I knew that he knew that I was right.

"You think I should have been nicer to her, huh?"

"All I know is that it must have been pretty hard for her to come around the last several weeks. She doesn't have friends like us anymore. And her parents have pretty much disowned her since she got divorced. I think everything that's happened the last week or so has meant more to her than anyone else. Did she tell you she was sorry?"

Long pause. "Yeah."

"Did she mean it?"

"Yeah."

"Did you accept it?"

"Yeah."

"Then what else can she do? You can't change time. You can't turn back the past. And you know, things have been a hell of a lot better for us than it has been for her."

He paused again and turned completely towards me. He was speechless, I could tell things were going over in his mind like tumblers in an old clock. He thought it over, he thought it over, he thought it over.

Without saying anything, he started off in the direction that she had left to go to her car. Then he stopped, and jogged quickly back to me. He then did something he had never done before. He put his arms around me, gave me hug and even a slight peck on the cheek, and said, "Thanks for the advice. You're right, you know." He smiled, turned and ran down Old River Road, back towards where the love of his life was walking towards her car.

I stood there watching him jog down Lakeside under the Main Avenue Bridge, and for a moment thought things were still going to turn out all right.

Before he got to the bottom of the hill, he heard Glenda's scream.

Glenda had left her crowd at their tailgate party, the loss to the Broncos not leaving her in the mood to party. She had walked up the same hill as Mate, several minutes ahead of him. Her less than month old Mustang was her pride and joy, the first new car she had ever owned. When she came upon someone breaking into it, she acted instinctively. Instead of running to get help, she immediately hurled her one hundred twenty pound body onto the back of the thief, and started ripping the shit out of his face and upper body with her nails.

What she didn't take time to realize was that there were two of them. As she dug her nails deep into the neck and cheeks of the first one, the second one came out of nowhere, grabbed her by the hair, and yanked her off the back of his partner. She screamed, and that was the scream that Mate had heard.

The scream, the call for help, ignited the emotional adrenaline inside Mate's body. All he saw were two guys hitting a woman and he exploded. He sprinted towards them, ran up the back of a nearby car, leaped through the air, and tackled Glenda and her two assailants, sending them crashing onto the gravel parking lot. He separated them from Glenda, and with what she would later call "eyes possessed by the devil," kicked, punched, and literally knocked the shit out of both car thieves.

But as he finished with one and started to finish off the second, he didn't see the tire iron. The tool of the trade, what the papers and lawyers would later call "the weapon," lay on the ground next to the nearly unconscious first assailant. As Mate stood and pounded the second one against the body of Glenda's Mustang, the first one saw the tire iron through blurry and bloody eyes. Bringing together every ounce of strength left in his body, he grabbed the iron, got to his knees and then to his feet, and with the last surge of energy his body could muster he cracked Mate squarely across the bottom of the back of his head. Mate immediately collapsed, the assailants limped off into the night, and Glenda screamed and cried for help.

Being a nurse herself, Glenda Johnson knew the blow to Mate's head was serious.

Beth went almost twenty-four hours before realizing what had happened. She walked to her car, parked in the opposite direction, towards the Central Market area in a lot that is now part of the new baseball stadium. She, too, was in a state of emotional disaster. She didn't know what to do. She got into her car, pulled onto I-90 and just drove and drove. When she got to the Pennsylvania border, she turned around and headed back.

When she got to her apartment she knew one thing, she didn't want to talk to anyone. She unplugged the phone in her bedroom and shoved the one in the living room into the closet. She went back into her bedroom, buried her head in the pillows, and tried to cry herself to sleep.

She said to herself that, yes, it was finally over. Her sense of hope that had kept her going since that glob of blood and flesh had fallen out of her body years ago was gone. The optimism of the last several weeks had proven to be false, and finally they were out of each other's lives for good.

Beth was scheduled to start work the next day at three. She woke up later than usual, still wearing the clothes she wore to the game. After a full night's sleep, she still felt exhausted. Her eyes were red and swollen. She looked and felt like shit.

He had been her first true love, the guy she had lost her virginity to, the childish boy who had driven her crazy, the boy she thought of on her wedding night, the person she had always been in love with.

She moped around all day at home. She turned off the answering machine, and didn't even turn on the television or radio. She left the newspaper on the front porch and didn't open the mail. She was an emotional wreck from the roller coaster she had ridden the last several weeks. And now, before it had ever really gotten started again, it was over.

She got to work a few minutes early, hoping to get everything off her mind. When she checked in with the desk on her floor, everyone seemed afraid to talk to her, and seemed to avoid her. *Do I look that bad?* She said to herself, knowing her eyes and face showed a night of heavy crying.

She started to make her rounds, and at her third stop there was a note from the day nurse to check the patient's temperature. Beth woke the patient up, rolled her over, and stuck a thermometer in her mouth. While she was waiting for it to register, she glanced at the front page of the *Plain Dealer* that was on the patient's table. It was folded, banner side up. The headline, of course, was about the Browns emotional loss the day before. She started to read the lead article and when she got to the fold she flipped the paper over. It was then that she saw a school photo of Mate staring at her with the headline above it, POPULAR LOCAL COACH AND TEACHER INJURED IN POST GAME ASSAULT.

She stood there stunned as she read the article. Without taking the thermometer out of the patient's mouth, she turned around and went running down the hall to the stairwell. She took two steps at a time down to the second floor. She knocked a nurse and a doctor over as she slammed open the door to the intensive care unit. Then she went down the hall, looking into every room, until she found the one with Mate lying motionless in a bed.

Monday night Beth and I drove Mrs. Mate and Uncle Gus home. We stayed with them until Mate's sister Barb came over to spend the night.

At that time things were looking O.K. Mate's vital signs were stable, the back of his head too swollen and bruised to know anything conclusive. Uncle Gus and Mrs. Mate were old enough to have been through too many moments like this with too many loved ones. They were holding up well and promised to call if they needed anything.

Beth wanted me to run by her house with her, where she was going to grab a shower and a change of clothes before going back to the hospital. There was no trying to change her mind, she was going to stay with him.

When we got to her place I camped myself on the sofa in her living room while she did her thing. She came into the living room in an oversized robe before hitting the shower, holding to her chest what looked like a large photo album.

"I want to show you something," she said as she put it down on the coffee table in front of me. "Look through this while I'm in the shower."

I opened the big over-sized book and on the inside cover was an old picture of her, Mate and I taken at an Indians game in the right field bleachers in the Stadium, along with the lyrics to an old Rickie Lee Jones' song written out in Mate's hand writing. On the first page was an article from four years earlier from the *Cleveland Press* with the headline FORMER TEAM-MATES BECOME HEAD COACHES TOGETHER, above a picture of the two of us taken in front of our school on the day it was announced that I was the new football coach. I turned page after page and was dumbfounded to find every article, every box score, every picture that ever had to do with one of our teams neatly cut out, mounted, and organized. Halfway through I turned to the end and, sure enough, the last four pages were filled with articles about our big basketball win on national television a week earlier. In the back of the scrapbook was a brown business envelope stuffed with something. I took it and shook out the contents, and out fluttered several dozen receipts. What are these? I wondered. Then I took a closer look and saw from where and when they were. Rumito's Pizza $50. Kennat Sports Goods, thirty new sweaters $875. Lakefront Trailways, one deluxe coach on a Friday night $475. It hit me. Beth had been our guardian angel. She was the one who had been our anonymous benefactor over the last four years.

I looked up, and she was standing before me dressed and ready to go.

I did not know what to say.

"Yeah, it's been me. It's been kind of fun not getting caught. You guys almost found out a couple of times."

On the drive back to the hospital she filled me in. "The summer I left Steven for good and filed for divorce was the worst. The divorce split our crowd into several factions, and all they talked about was us. My family couldn't understand, and I had no one to talk to. Everyone I knew thought I had it made, and was making a big mistake. I needed a hobby. Then I saw that picture of you two in *The Press*, and you guys became it."

"And you found out when we needed something from Connie."

"Yes."

"How did you guys hook up? I still can't figure out how you guys know each other."

"Well, you know she is a very determined young lady," she said, looking directly at me for some kind of reaction. "A while ago she was cleaning your house, and she found the letters he saved that I had written him when he was away at school. She looked up my old phone number, told my mom that she was an old friend from nursing school, and found out where I was working. She just showed up one day. She started planning her bus trips back to her old neighborhood around stopping and seeing me. She'd come and sit with me during my breaks and talk." She paused again, as I could see her regrouping her emotions. "She was just such a breath of fresh air. It was just after I got divorced, and I needed a friend, and she started to show up. She really is a good kid. For all she's been through, she's quite the little grown up."

"What did you talk about?"

"Oh, the usual girl things. She kept me up-to-date on you guys and everything that went on in your school, and who you guys were dating. She loved to talk about Mate's parents and Uncle Gus and everyone. You guys will never know how much you meant and still mean to her brother and her."

"Have you ever come to see us play?"

"A couple of times. But it was hard. I wasn't ready yet to make face-to-face contact, which seems kind of stupid now with all that's gone on the last several weeks. Then I kinda got into my guardian angel role."

"But what about all the money? Over the last couple of years you must have spent a couple of grand on us."

A slight smirk came over her face. "What did Mate's dad use to say? 'It's only money.' That's one thing I learned when I married into a family that had a lot of it. It really is only money."

I dropped her off at the hospital. Before she got out of the car, she leaned across the seat and gave me a big hug. "Why does everything you guys do always have to be a big production? But, I'm finally realizing, a lot of people's lives would be pretty boring if everything wasn't that way." She got out, and walked through the night back into the hospital.

The next day at school was a little more normal. Everyone all day asked me if I had heard anything, and all I said was, "No change."

We had our first practice of the week and it went well, all things considered. I gave the team the latest medical update, all of them probably knew it anyway, and everyone had a slightly good feeling that things were going to work out. One of the T.V. stations sent a mini cam and interviewed some of the kids, and they handled that with class and composure. No one was panicking, everyone was praying and hoping for the best.

Connie, Manny and I left school after practice and stopped at our house on the way to the hospital. I wanted to grab a shower and a change of clothes in case I ended up staying at the hospital all night, and going to school the next day from there.

We had stopped and gotten Taco Bell on the way, and we were sitting around the table in the kitchen eating when the phone rang. I was just getting up to hit the shower so I grabbed it and said, "Hello."

It was Beth. "Who's there with you?"

"Connie and Manny. Why?"

She tried to speak but couldn't. I heard her voice break again and the sound of her holding back tears. "If you want to see him alive again, you better get down here as quick as you can. His brain is hemorrhaging everywhere, and the doctors don't think he's going to make it another hour."

Mate's mom, his sister Barb, and her husband Bob and their two kids, and Uncle Gus were there. So was Father Chester from their church, Beth, Connie, Manny and me. Several nurses and a young doctor were trying to make things as comfortable for Mate as possible, but it really didn't matter. Any feeling he had in his body was gone. The damage to the bottom of the back of his head had been too great, the nervous system in his body had started to shut down, and it was almost over. His body would occasionally jump and twitch, and there was nothing to do as it became harder and harder for him to breathe.

Beth sat in the chair next to his bed, where she had spent every moment since I had dropped her off the night before. We did not know what to do, glancing at Mate, at the machine with the lights and screens on it, and then at each other.

Suddenly Mate started to gasp. I saw his right hand open and grab Beth around her wrist, his body shook for a moment, and then it went limp and it was over.

Someone later asked me if that was the hardest part of the whole ordeal, watching the life go out of him. That wasn't the hardest part. The hardest part was going to tell the best group of sixteen and seventeen year olds you could ever meet that their coach and teacher had died.

Pete Posterman got his first job writing for the old Cleveland Press *back when Mate and I played football at Franciscan. He would*

Greg Cielec

later cover high school sports for several papers during the time when we coached together. We had, on more than one occasion and in more than one setting, shared a beverage or two with him. This was his article published the day after Mate's memorial service. It was chosen as one of the Best of the Year for Sportswriting by the Ohio Sportswriters Association in 1987.

A School Says Goodbye
by Peter Posterman

The gym was packed yesterday at River Boro High, but it wasn't for the River Boro/Avon Lake basketball game that was scheduled. Instead, it was for the memorial service for Head Basketball Coach "Mate" Majowski, who died this past Tuesday from a head wound he received Sunday after the Browns/ Broncos game breaking up an assault on a woman in a parking lot downtown.

Mate, as he was known to almost everyone who knew him, was a popular teacher and coach at the school. Along with his former high school football teammate and current River Boro Football Coach Greg Stanley, they revitalized River Boro's sports program into one of Greater Cleveland's best. Coaching both sports together, they finished this past football season undefeated and rated number one in this paper's Top Fifty poll. Last Friday their basketball team beat the top rated team in the country, Washington D.C. Vocational Tech, in the first ever nationally televised high school basketball game.

Mate was always one to spread the credit around. After the basketball win last week he said, "It's easy to coach when you have great kids like we do, and when you have fine coaches working with you."

He was a fun loving guy who was a throw back to the way coaches all ought to be like. In this age of high pressure win-at-all-costs-us-against-you coaching philosophies, he was not only successful, but also

247

made things fun for everyone around him and was popular with other coaches. He liked nothing more on a Friday after a game than to meet up with other coaches, have a beer or two, and share victories or commiserate a defeat.

For most of the young people at the memorial service, it was the first time many of them faced the death of someone they knew. And, as kids are apt to be, they let their emotions show, but you know that deep down they will make it through this tragedy. There have been a lot of tears in the River Boro hallways this week, as many of the students and athletes had one of those coming of age moments. All of them grew up a lot this week.

The memorial service was planned and put on entirely by the kids, and they did a beautiful job. Rich Simmons, the senior football/basketball player told humorous stories about the things Coach Mate did to motivate the football linemen, including taking them to pro wrestling the night before a big game. The school's choir sang several songs and hymns, including an emotional rendition of the Beatles' "In My Life," which was one of his favorites.

His high school buddy, coaching colleague, and best friend Greg Stanley spoke. "When we were your age, he used to tell me about when we got older, and out of college, how we were going to be teachers and coaches. 'It'll be great' he used to say, 'we'll have the best life.' He always reminded me about telling me that, and all the time about how lucky we were to be teachers and coaches. The guys we grew up with, they're mostly salesmen of some kind. Trailers, cars, building products. A couple of them are accountants, a few lawyers. They all have two things in common. The first thing is that they all hate their jobs. The second thing is that they have always been jealous of Coach Mate and I, because they know how much we like our jobs, and because we got to teach and coach all of you." Coach Stanley finished by saying, "He would want us to remember that life is too short for all of us, that we should get as much out of it as possible, and to enjoy it as much as we can."

Carmen Lopez, senior class president and unofficial adopted little sister of Coach Majowski, spoke next. Since a chance meeting on her and her brother Manny's first day in the River Boro school district six years ago, they have had a special relationship with Coach Majowski and his family. It was not easy for her to address her school mates on the loss of their teacher and coach and her special friend. "I know what he would say if he was able to say something to us right now. I know exactly what he would say. He'd say 'don't you guys forget about all your dreams and plans, and don't you guys ignore them while you're wasting your time crying about me.' He'd say 'enough of this, it's time to move on.' I know he would be really upset if anyone in this room would use his death to cast a cloud over any of our lives. He's some place looking down on us right now, and all he's remembering are all the good times. He's smiling and remembering Friday night football games and beach dances, and packed gyms for basketball games. He's remembering all the funny things that have happened in class, and pizza parties and proms and graduation ceremonies. He's remembering all the good times."

And then for the first time her voice showed emotion, and she paused for a moment. "If there is one thing he would want me to say right now, it would be that we all must keep moving forward. I know what he would tell me. He'd tell me to be strong and show everyone that life goes on. And that's what I'm going to do. I lost my best friend and my older brother, as well as my teacher and coach. But I'm not going to spend the rest of the school year crying about it." By this time tears were rolling down her cheeks in rivers, but she ignored them and kept going. "I'm going to *remember the good times and lock them away in my heart, and get on with my life because I know that's what he would want me to do."*

The young lady spoke with class and dignity, and it was noticeable that many of her school mates look up to her.

The students, on two huge bulletin boards in the school lobby, made a picture tribute to their fallen teacher and coach. Those of us who only know of someone as a coach sometimes don't realize that most times coaches are also teachers. Or more importantly, teachers who happen to coach. When I looked over all the photos that the kids at River Boro had pinned to the collage, I was surprised at how many of the pictures were from the classroom and other school settings, and so few were from games and practices. And, without exception, all of the pictures featured Mate in a variety of situations surrounded by a group of kids and they all had one thing in common, they were all laughing or smiling. I think of all the blame and hassles that teachers everywhere have to put up with, and I thought, looking at those pictures and the smiles on the faces of all those kids, that here was a guy who did something right.

The service ended with the choir leading the whole assembly in Todd Rundgren's "The Dream Goes on Forever."

So, as I was told along with the student body of River Boro, it is time to put the events of the last week behind me and get on with my life. Like a lot of other people, my friend Mate Majowski is no longer with us, but I know it was a pleasure that our paths had crossed. So long buddy, I'll always speak well of you when people ask.

We had graduation that June out at Blossom Music Center. What a great place it is for that type of thing, and it turned out to be a beautiful day weather wise. At least things finally happened on a big day like they were supposed to, the teachers joked to each other as we marched to our places on the big stage.

Carmen did a great job with her valedictorian speech. She opened it by joking, "The last time I spoke in front of this many people it ended up on Sports Center that night. Today I guess we will just have to settle for the six o'clock news." Yes, the mini cams were there. So much of these kids' lives, of all of our lives for that matter, had become an open book, and it just seemed appropriate that our graduation ceremony would be shared with all of Northeastern Ohio.

Carmen's speech was beautiful. She touched on all that had happened over the course of the school year and, at the only time she directly mentioned Mate, she said, "When he promised us we could have the greatest senior year ever, he wasn't lying." She told her classmates that because of what they had been through with a little hard work "the real world won't be all that hard to conquer." She said, "Our emotions this year have danced with the stars and swum with the lowest fishes in the sea. Sometimes on the same day, in the same minute. Anything can be possible for each of us standing up here today."

The ceremony was on a Saturday morning, and with my parents still living in Brecksville, we had our crowd over to their house. At one time, my parents would have been concerned about having such a 'diverse' (i.e., racially mixed) crowd over to their house, parked up and down the street on a Saturday afternoon. Not anymore. One positive thing that year's events had caused was my parents to finally rid themselves of their prejudices, to finally accept the life their oldest son had chosen.

It was the best time I ever remember having at my old house. Everyone was there. My parents and sisters. Mrs. Mate and Uncle Gus. Carmen and Manny's mom, and all of their relatives from Clark Avenue. Many of our student athletes and their families. Carmen made it her business to make sure to invite all those kids, and it was a surprising amount, who didn't have anyone come to graduation, or lived with a single parent or grandparent, who didn't have any plans after the commencement.

I played host as Carmen and her fellow graduates were the center of attention. The kitchen table overflowed with food and drink, and the crowd spilled into the front and back yards. I don't think the conservative yuppies on my parents' street had ever seen anything like it before. Many of them lived in that neighborhood so they never would have to. Latin and rock music playing; white, black and Hispanic teenagers everywhere; all sorts of cars looking like they were going to be left for junk up and down the street. But the kids were all dressed up, everyone behaved themselves, and there were lots of hugs and laughter. My parents were enjoying themselves tremendously because they had finally realized it just doesn't matter what the neighbors think.

Several times as I bopped through the crowd I overheard Carmen being complemented on her big day, and I heard her respond, "Yes, it is a big day for me." Each time I heard her say that it would cause me to turn and glance towards her, and I would catch her looking at me. We would make eye contact, she'd smile, then she would turn away from me and turn back towards the person she was talking to.

After everyone left, I stayed with Mrs. Mate and Gus and helped my parents clean up. By the time I dropped them off and got back to the house, I was exhausted. I loosened the tie, kicked off my shoes, and collapsed into the oversized easy chair in the living room.

I was awoken slightly by the sound of the back door slamming, and the sight of her in the doorway. She still had on the colorful summer dress that she wore that morning. Her hair was now let down and fell over her shoulders. She was barefoot, except for the ankle bracelet we had given her for her sixteenth birthday.

Without saying a word she came across the room and sat down sideways on my lap, throwing her legs over one side of the chair. She wrapped her arms around my shoulders, kissed me lightly on my cheek, and fell sound asleep. I soon joined her, and the last thing I noticed before I fell asleep, by the way she was laying across me, was that she didn't have on any underwear.

I awoke to the darkness of night. The house was only

illuminated by a light from the kitchen. Connie was resting on top of me as if she were a part of me. As I turned to glance at her face, her eyes opened. We stared at each other, then she quickly kissed me on the lips and said, "Let's go upstairs."

I gathered her up, and at the base of the stairs she said with a slight smile, "Go put on one of his tapes."

I walked over to the stereo and found one that said 'all time great make out tunes.' As we climbed the steps, Bob Welch was whispering about his "Sentimental Lady."

I remember entering my bedroom, and she and I locked in a kiss that I had wanted so badly since the last one last winter in the hallway at school. I remember unbuttoning the back of her dress, the dress falling to the floor, and us falling onto the bed.

Everything was long and slow and tender and passionate. Our hands gently explored each other, and I felt each touch upon my skin. When it came time to enter her, she whispered to me to be careful. She was tight, but quite wet, and I entered her with no problem. Before any rhythm started we held each other close as she wrapped her legs around me, and we both wrapped our arms around each other. Our bodies, at once together, opened up and we fell into each other. What did he once call it? The perfect fit? I never knew what he was talking about until that moment.

As we lay there afterwards, bodies twined, in and out of sleep, I heard Jonah Koslen and the original Michael Stanley Band up the stairwell from the stereo down in the living room.

> *I don't know the words to say*
> *And they come out so awkwardly*
> *But I have to speak my mind*
>
> *Wouldn't you like to stay tonight*
> *Waste a little time on me*
> *We can pretend that we're old friends*
> *Wouldn't be so hard to believe*
> *And wouldn't you like to waste little time on me*

Epilogue

Five Years Later
Ohio State High School Football Playoffs
Division III Championship Game
Paul Brown Stadium, Massillon, Ohio
River Boro vs. Central Northeast Hayes

There were no time outs left, and I had to call the next play with no time to think about it. Skups and Wilson were up in the booth and they were thinking the same thing I was thinking, this was it, and we couldn't count on having enough time to run another play after this one.

Third down on their 14. Down by four. Clock running, both teams out of time outs. My mind was unclear, nothing was jumping out at me. For a second, the line to the booth upstairs seemed to go blank, but in a cool calm voice I heard, "I have it. Pro right, mo right, 119 boot, tight end delay drag."

It sounded good to me. I made a mental note, that if it worked, to make sure Skups got the credit for calling it. I grabbed one of our messengers, gave him the play, and as he ran on the field I looked up at the clock. I knew it was going to be the last play of the game.

When we broke the huddle, the clock was at :19 and counting. We spread them out in a pro, they countered with a hard cover 2, with corners up on both of our receivers and two safeties back.

The key to the play for us was how they were going to react to the motion. We were in the middle of the field. When our left halfback went into motion to our right, it caused them to go into some type of rotation to that side. It was a good move on their part. They must have thought we were going to do one of two things, two things that we had done in similar situations all year. Either a quick pitch to our remaining running back, who would try to turn the corner behind all of the interference in front of him. Or a flood pass, where our quarterback rolled out to that side, and we would flood all their zones hoping someone would be open.

If it was the quick pitch they thought we were running, then it also meant we were going to try to run to plays. Half the distance on the quick pitch, then out of bounds to stop the clock.

They should have realized, however, that when Tim let the clock slip down inside :10, that it was going to be this play or never. He had that much confidence in it.

The key to the play was when we snapped the ball the way our quarterback, Timmy McGowan, opened and made it look like the quick pitch. The halfback did a great job, raising his hands acting as if he was going to catch the pitch. Our line fired out in great play action form, causing everyone on the field and in the stands to think it was a run to the right.

Timmy, again, was the key to the play. It had been one of our 'only if we really need it' plays for the two years he had been our quarterback. We ran it over and over again every week in practice, but hadn't used it in over a year in a game. The kids knew we were saving it, and saving it for now.

The key was Tim's ability to pause and hide the ball for a second, to make anyone keying on him think he really didn't have it, before he rolled out to the left side.

Smitty the right side guard pulled left while the rest of the line fired and disguised the play as a run. He noticed the contain end hanging on the line, and hooked him.

As Smitty made contact with him and wrapped his body so it was now between the end and where the quarterback was going to end up, he heard the kid say, "Oh, fuck!!!" And knew that he had done his part.

Ricky Michalsky, our tight end, did his part beautifully also. He took a hard outside release, coming out of his stance showing everyone that he was looking for someone to hit. One step, two steps, three steps to the outside, the whole time rotating his head looking for someone to block. As the strongside linebacker came on his pursuit route to make contact with him and then go through him to make the tackle, Ricky side stepped him as if he were playing a game of chicken, but really to start on his route across the field and with destiny.

Our weak side receiver, Howie Thomas, also did a fabulous job. Their rotation to our strong side left him man-to-man with the corner. He would shake and bake the guy, stepping irregularly, taking him into the end zone and across the middle of the field. The corner concentrated on Howie the whole time, but knew in his heart that the play was going away from them.

When we sent our back into motion, it caused the safety to that side to come up into the flat as an extra defender, and the other safety to cheat over and play center field. That is exactly how we would have played it.

It was the job of this centerfield safety to look for anything out of the ordinary, and he did spot Ricky cutting across the field, but it was too late. Howie had cleared the zone out, our play action fooled the defense, the line did an outstanding job, and Timmy had faked superbly. By the time he ended his fake and started his roll, it was a matter of throwing it or running it. If he ran it, would he get in? But being the bright (and not to brag, well coached) athlete he was, he knew if he threw it, and it wasn't for some reason caught, the clock would stop and there might be time for another play.

He didn't need to worry. He stopped his roll and planted, no one was within seven yards of him. Ricky Michalsky caught the ball on a full run at the three and ran untouched into the end zone. As he crossed the goal line the clock showed 0:00, our benches and fans poured onto the field, and I was mobbed on the sidelines. We had finally won our first State Championship.

The scene outside our locker room was unbelievable. Everyone was there. When Carmen finally found me her eyes where filled with tears as she hugged and kissed me, and knew that we finally did the one thing left undone. I found my mom and dad and Mrs. Mate and Uncle Gus in the mob also, and hugged and kissed each of them before I faced the press and talked to the team.

The question was bound to come up as I was surrounded by reporters and TV crews, and I'm glad it was my old friend Peter Posterman who asked it.

"Coach, does this make up for the state championships you didn't win five years ago, with a football team and a basketball team similar in talent to this one? And, have you thought yet today about our old friend Mate Majowski?"

"One thing I have learned about all those things that happened five years ago is that you can't change the past. One good thing about finally winning this thing is that our kids and our community have something new to wrap history around. Time won't be measured now from that school year of five years ago, but from today, when we won the State Football Championship."

I paused for a second.

"I thought of Mate once today. When Coach Skupski called down the last play from the press box, he sounded so calm and confident, his voice reminded me of Coach Majowski's. In fact, if I didn't know better, I would have thought it was him calling the play."

The questions got back to the game. The reporters started getting comments from the kids. Timmy and Ricky were surrounded by TV cameras and loving every minute of it.

Finally, when we had our moment with the team and I was holding the State Championship trophy in my hands I said, "For the rest of our lives, this will always belong to us. This will always be our moment. I hope you all go on in your lives and accomplish bigger and better things, but I hope this will always be special. I want you to share it with your families and your classmates and the community, they all deserve some of the credit." I paused for a moment to get my emotions in check. "Ten years ago, when we first started all of this, there was a group of players and coaches who had awful big dreams. Dreams they knew if they ever came true, they wouldn't be around to see it. But they knew that their dreams would go on forever. I hope that if one of those people is an older brother or a neighbor down the street that you share your celebration with them. Great job fellas, the coaches are real proud of each one of you."

When I finally got to the coach's office all the other coaches were waiting for me. We hugged and slapped each other on the back, and there was not a dry eye in the room. It had been a long time coming for this group of guys, and we were so glad to share it with each other.

Skupski then started to speak, "I can't believe you remembered to call that play. It had been so long since we ran it, and I don't think I would have remembered to call it."

"What are you talking about not calling it? You just did!"

"No, Greg. I didn't call the play. You did. We were so excited on the play before that, the bomb that Howie caught, that I stood up and kicked the cord out of the wall. There were no phones on that last play."

I stood stunned for a second. Everyone stared at me wondering what was wrong. I sat down, and a strange smile covered my face.

"That son of a bitch. He just couldn't stay away."

A few last words...

Now, years later as I sit on the front porch of this house that played such an important part of this story, I still think of him and all that happened, and when the world was still young to all of us.

I am often asked do I ever think of him.

I think of him in the fall with the first scent of autumn in the air, and the smell of mud on the cleats of the players running from station to station on the practice field. And when I give that speech that he used to give, holding a football in one hand and pointing to my heart with the other, "If you don't love this game and your teammates, than you better go find another sport..."

I think of him the first day of basketball practice when we've got eighty kids trying out for twenty spots, and I'm trying to run some of them off and I'm yelling, "Who has what it takes to make this team?"

I think of him at school when someone's little sister is about to graduate, and she has gone from a chubby little girl to being a real looker. I realize that maybe I'm the only person who has noticed, and I realize that he would have too.

I think of him when I throw in an old tape, label long gone, into the tape deck of my car, and "Rosalita" comes blasting out of the speakers and I'll think of a long ago concert, us dancing in the aisles.

At Christmas when Beth leaves her new friends in San Francisco to come home to Cleveland to spend a few days in the city she grew up in, she'll stay with us. We'll stay up long into the night, talking about old and new friends and adventures. We'll end up in the old chair, her on my lap, and we'll hug each other, listen to old songs, and think about an old friend.

Every Christmas we'll have a party at our place with all the kids, coaches and friends from that year. We'll drink some beers, put out a spread of food, kid each other about thicker waist lines and thinner hair cuts. And we'll watch the ESPN tape. I only watch it once a year, but each time I do, I still get the chills. I find it harder and harder to remember all we did over ten years ago. God, we were young and idealistic and, at times, pretty stupid.

But looking at it now from a distance of over a decade, I take it for what it was. A marvelous moment shared with people who deeply loved and cared for each other. It really was a magical night, during a special time, with special people.

And, as far as I'm concerned, it was just another of the special, magical and crazy times that I shared with my best friend Mate Majowski.

Appendix

I first got into writing some time in the late Eighties when I sent some letters to the *Plain Dealer* they turned into essays that were published on the Opinion Page. I then sent several record reviews to some regional magazines, and that really took off. I started to get disks and tapes in the mail to review and it has turned into a fun and slightly profitable hobby.

After school during the spring and often during the summer, you can find me on the front porch with my note pad in hand working on a project, good tunes playing in the background, maybe a cold one nearby. Often Uncle Gus or Mrs. Mate strolls across the street and sits and talks for awhile.

One day last summer Mrs. Mate walked across the street and came and sat quietly on the glider. I finished the paragraph that I was writing and looked up and greeted her with a smile. She smiled back at me, and I noticed she had a slightly more serious demeanor than usual.

"You enjoy your writing, don't you," she said with those eyes that still sparkle now deep into her late seventies.

"Yeah, I guess I do," I responded.

"I want you to write something for me," she said.

"Anything, Helen. You know I'd do anything for you," expecting a letter to a faraway relative or something for church.

Then she got up and did something I never saw her do before. She grabbed the front rail of the porch with both hands, and looked down both ends of the street. She turned and looked into every nook and cranny of the porch, and then turned and looked at me. "I want you to write about what happened. I want you to write about everything."

We looked at each other through several moments of silence, both knowing what she was talking about. "I want my grandchildren to know about what happened. Someday you'll want your children and your grandchildren to know. I want them to know about everything. Everybody will never forget the bad stuff, but I want them to know about everything else. There were so many good things that happened. I want them to know about all the good stuff."

I saw a tear starting to crawl down her cheek, and I got up and we hugged and I held her tight. "Barb's kids were so little when my husband died. He was such a good man and all they've got to remember him are some old pictures and a few stories that get told over and over again. I want them to know what he was like. And what happened to you guys, I would just hate..." as her voice trailed off and I kept hugging her.

I had planted in the back of my mind that I would start after basketball season. I talked it over with Carmen and Manny and they thought it was a great idea, and at Christmas time Beth was especially enthusiastic. "I have never even tried to tell my friends about all that happened. They see the pictures I have of you guys on my wall in my house but they've never heard me talk about you. They probably think that you're all dead. I would love that so much."

"Can I talk about everything?"

"You better," she replied without hesitation.

I thought it would be easy, but it didn't start out that way. Springtime came, I had my note pads and pens and even my Macintosh computer, and when it was time to put on paper all that was in my mind, all the stories I had told and heard over and over, I was stuck. I just couldn't get started.

Carmen noticed I was struggling, and she was the one who came to the rescue. Like many people today we listen to most of our music here at home on compact disk. We still have a wall of albums but they are, for the most part, just for show. At Christmas time someone might spin a few of them, and occasionally Manny will sit and listen to an old one. I was sitting on the porch staring off for I don't know how long, when I heard the scratching sound of an old album being played on the turntable, and then the opening chords to "When the Morning Comes" from Hall and Oates' *Abandoned Luncheonette* filtered through the windows out to the porch.

"Boy, I haven't heard this one in a long time," I said, as she came out to check on how I was doing.

"I know. I figured you might need some inspiration," she said as she handed me a beer and turned around and went back in the house. And, yes, it did inspire me, and I was able to jot down a page or two of notes about high school and college.

It was a couple of days later during another dry spell that I went in the house and started going through the albums and pulled out a couple of big stacks of them. Then, in no particular order, I started to listen to them one after another. Those albums are listed in the music appendix that is in the back of this book.

But music wasn't the only thing I needed for inspiration. There was still something else. Carmen and I have had for years a running conversation/ argument about food. Real food. Carmen on her way to being a woman of the Nineties neglected one important aspect of her education. How to cook real food. I'm part of the blame. She and her brother did spend a couple of nights a week through junior and senior high school eating dinner with a couple of young teachers/coaches in a variety of fast food/pizza/bar establishments. Connie didn't learn how to cook when she was a kid, but she knew about the burgers at the Jigsaw, the perogies at the Red Chimney, the fish fry at the Good Old Daze, and the pizza and wings at the Rascal House.

She decided that while I worked on "our book" that she was going to learn to cook. Her expertise up until that time was the ability to cook anything in a tortilla. Mostly simple stuff or things you can reheat out of a can. Scrambled eggs in a tortilla. Refried beans in a tortilla. Left over Kentucky Fried Chicken in a tortilla. I had always been after her to learn to cook the things that Mate's mom used to cook. Mrs. Mate still puts a spread out on holidays and for birthdays, but she had to surrender her day to day cooking to the arthritis in her arms and hands.

While I sat on the front porch writing away, Carmen and Mrs. Mate were back in the kitchen, putting together the best summer of eating I ever had. Those great smells once again filled the house, drifted through the front porch, and caused every passerby to make a comment. The smell of stuffed cabbage, potato pancakes, and homemade gravy and mashed potatoes filled Redmond Avenue once again last summer. Mrs. Mate took Carmen through every step of each dish, showing her the importance of kneading the perogi dough, and how to scrape the chicken fat off the top of soup, leaving just enough behind for flavor. She showed her the best way to shred cabbage for cabbage and noodles, and how to cook cabbage leaves just right for stuffed cabbage. Carmen learned how to use all those important 'secret ingredients,' like lard, bacon fat, and real butter.

While they were working away, Carmen made detailed notes on each ingredient and each step in each recipe. The aromas that came out of our kitchen last spring and summer, as well as the final products, gave me much inspiration and filled me with many of the memories in this story. The best of those recipes are included in the food appendix.

Music Appendix

Eat a Peach and *Live at the Fillmore* by The Allman Brothers Band. I remember sitting on the lawn behind Mate's frat house on a beautiful spring day. We had just played a game of hoops and we were sharing a blanket with a group of girls. A keg was tapped, everyone was laughing, and "Blue Skies" came on the stereo.

Any album by Artful Dodger. These guys from somewhere out east never hit it big nationally, but they were very popular in Cleveland. "Scream for You" is a great tune, and "A Girl) La La La" always still tugs at my heart whenever I hear it.

Closer to It by Brian Auger's Oblivion Express.
Person to Person by The Average White Band.
Pet Sounds by The Beach Boys. The album "God Only Knows" is on.
The Grand River Lullabye by Alex Bevan. A Great Cleveland album.
Agents of Fortune by Blue Oyster Cult.

Karla Bonhoff and *New World* by Karla Bonhoff. A couple of lost gems that were and still are great make out albums. Another find of Mate's. I think "If He's Ever Near" is as good as it gets. When Carmen went off to college for her freshman year Manny and I really missed her, and I think she missed us. I came home from practice one day and she left the most emotional message on my answering machine. I could tell that she had been crying, and all she said was, "Go get the new Karla Bonhoff album and listen to the last song on the first side." We both knew how much Mate loved Karla Bonhoff, so I knew it had to do with him. I went and bought it that night, and for the first time listened to "Goodbye My Friend," and I still listen to it when I think of him.

> *Oh we never know where life will take us*
> *We know it's just a ride on the wheel*
> *And we never know when death will shake us*
> *And we wonder how it will feel*
> *So Goodbye my friend*
> *I know I'll never see you again*
> *But the time together through all the years*
> *Will take away these tears*
> *It's O.K. now, goodbye my friend*

Ziggy Stardust and the Spiders from Mars by David Bowie. A great high school/college party album. Bowie and Mick Ronson at their absolute best.

Breathless. Jonah Koslen's first effort after he left MSB. A very solid album.

A1A, A White Sports Coat and Pink Crustacean, Havana Daydreamin, Living and Dying in 3/4 Time, Son of a Son of A Sailor, and *Changes in Latitude, Changes in Attitudes* by Jimmy Buffett. Jimmy Buffett is as popular as anyone on the planet right now, but these are his albums from the Seventies before anyone ever heard of a Parrothead.

Mate entered his dope phase and discovered Buffett about the same time, and spent a whole quarter at college doing afternoon bongs and listening and laughing to "God's Own Drunk" over and over again.

Slowhand by Eric Clapton. The Clapton album of our school years with some great songs that have been played on the radio too many times. I don't know how many proms and dances over the years I've chaperoned and have seen dance floors full of kids slow dancing to "Wonderful Tonight," just like we did many years ago.

Nightrider and *Fire on the Mountain* by The Charlie Daniels Band.

Machine Head by Deep Purple.

The Captain and Me by The Doobie Brothers. A great pre Michael MacDonald Doobie Brothers album, with the party dance standard "China Grove" and that great make out on the couch tune "South City Midnight Lady."

Jonathon Edwards. What a great tune "Shanty" is.

Fundamental Roll by Walter Egan. Contains the frat rock anthem "(When it's all said and done) I think I'd Rather have Fun."

The Euclid Beach Band. A local release that got some air play with the bubble gum tune "There's No Surf in Cleveland," but contained one hidden gem, a boogie woogie party tune with a great Rick Bell sax solo called "Don't You Know What You Mean to Me."

Fleetwood Mac and *Rumours* by Fleetwood Mac. I guess I'll always look at these two albums as one. What great stuff, one song after another. All those ballads about trying to fix or repair broken relationships always remind me of the girls that traveled through my life at that time.

The Visitor by Mick Fleetwood. After Fleetwood Mac had great commercial success in the mid Seventies, Mick Fleetwood, years before Paul Simon's Graceland, went to Africa and made this great native music album. This album contains one outstanding cry in my beer tunes, a great version of "You Weren't in Love." If you ever see this album at a used record store buy it, just to hear this tune. I don't think this album ever came out on CD.

Jack Rabbit Slim by Steve Forbert. Here's a guy that never lived up to his promise but what a great song "Romeo's Tune" still is.

Frampton Comes Alive by Peter Frampton. O.K., this album got played to death, but twenty years later it holds up pretty well. One of the classic rock stations here in Cleveland had Frampton on live a couple of years ago with just him and his guitar singing all of these tunes and they sounded great.

Moontan by Golden Earring. Too bad classic rock stations have destroyed "Radar Love" because this album is more than one song.

Mars Hotel by the Grateful Dead. I didn't take enough drugs and my dope smoking days didn't last long enough to become a Deadhead, but I always liked this album and loved to boogie to "U.S. Blues."

Any Seventies album by The J. Geils Band. An old friend of ours for the last fifteen years has sent out beautiful customized Christmas cards with embossed lettering and always a real traditional religious Nativity scene on the front. When you open it up he lists his three Christmas wishes and they are always the same...

Peace on Earth
A Cure for AIDS
And for Peter Wolf to get back together
with the J.Geils Band

Abandon Luncheonette by Hall and Oates. Another of Mate's first college friends was from Philly and he turned him on to this album. A great album from before they made it big with "She's Gone" and "When the Morning Comes."

Dreamboat Annie by Heart. One of those soundtracks of life albums. I wonder how many times from our school days this record was playing in the background?

You're Never Alone with a Schizophrenic by Ian Hunter. The album with the original version of "Cleveland Rocks."

James Gang's Greatest Hits. Another album everyone our age from Northern Ohio had in their record collection. What about Joe Walsh's guitar work on "Funk #49"? And on more than one cry in my beer tape was "Walk Away."

264

Waylon Jennings Greatest Hits.

The early albums leading up to *The Stranger* by Billy Joel. Mate's college crowd was a lot more Eastern than mine, and he got into Billy Joel before anyone else I knew, before even *The Stranger* hit it big. In his dorm his freshmen year he heard a lot of Billy Joel from his Long Island buddies, such as "She's Got a Way" and "Streetlife Serenade."

Don't Shoot Me, I'm only the Piano Player and *Good Bye Yellow Brick Road* by Elton John. In the seventies and early eighties Elton John got played to death on the radio, but "Crocodile Rock" was a great dance tune, and "Good-bye Yellow Brick Road" was always in the regular rotation when we were just sitting around partying.

Rickie Lee Jones. What a great album, highlighted by two boogie tunes that became hits, "Chuck E.s in Love" and "Danny's All Star Joint." And also has, of course, "Company." However, the one thing that tugs at my emotions on this album is a picture on the back cover of Rickie and her two brothers, taken when they were kids in 1963 in their hometown of Santa Monica. It's her and her two brothers but it could be Mate and his sister or me and my sisters. It's a picture that everyone's parents took at one time or another. Everyone has been there.

Live in Las Vegas by Tom Jones. More than once drunk on Old Dutch Beer, the good beer, we would crank this album and sing "Delilah" at the top of our lungs.

Kiss Alive by Kiss. Some dudes my freshmen year in the Towers covered every inch of wall space in their dorm room with tin foil with the Kiss logo painted on it. They would get pretty buzzed on Friday nights and put the Kiss make up on and go into the other dorms and raise hell.

Brasilia by John Klemmer. O.K., you're saying what the hell is this doing on this list back from our scuffling days? There was more sex going on while this album was playing than probably any other. All those romantic sax tunes, highlighted by "Tropical Snowflakes," which on more than one occasion in my sheltered life has caused a young lady to take her clothes off in my company. Scouts honor.

Special Light by The Lamont Cranston Band. Saw these guys at the old Columbus Agora and they boogy and woogied their place in our hearts.

Led Zeppelin IV. Yes, I had my first sexual experience in Molly Henderson's basement, drunk on Mad Dog 20/20, underneath a black light poster of Janis Joplin, trying to get (and then keep) a rubber on, while "Stairway to Heaven" was playing on the stereo.

Pussycats Can Go Far by Buzzy Linhart. Buzzy was a Cleveland/New York City folk artist of great and wasted talent that did have some great tunes especially "You Got to Have Friends," which reminds me always of the crowd we hung around with back in high school.

Waiting for Columbus by Little Feat. I still listen regularly to this album even today.

Sitting In by Loggins and Messina. Another soundtrack of life album. All their albums were good make out albums, and their concerts out at Blossom were always date nights.

Pronounced Lynyrd Skynyrd by Lynyrd Skynyrd. What a great first album. Probably the first taste of a genre we would love, country rock. Because of its hard edges it got played on 'MMS back even when we were still in high school. What about "Freebird?"

Uprising by Bob Marley. Everyone chipped in and bought Mate's dad a new accordion for Christmas, so Mate took his old one back to school with him. He'd play around with it, but got frustrated because he couldn't get as good as his dad or his uncle. The one tune he did do great was a very simple rendition of "Redemption Song," with him mouthing the words a little like Lou Reed.

Certified Live and *Let It Flow* by Dave Mason. *Certified Live* is one great tune after another, back from those post *Frampton Comes Alive* days when everyone had a double live album. If you get a chance, check it out again. And much of *Let It Flow* was Mate and Beth.

Band on the Run by Paul McCartney and Wings. A good album that made the transition from a high school record to a college one.

McGuffey Lane and *Aqua Dreams* by McGuffey Lane. For those of us who went to college in Central Ohio in the mid Seventies to early Eighties, these two albums will always have a special place in our hearts. Great country rock from the best band you never heard of. Mate always felt that those of us from Cleveland who went to school around Columbus brought with us the dreaded Cleveland curse that affected the Michael Stanley Band and the Indians for so many years, and put the whammy on these guys. These were and still are great albums. "Lady Autumn" always reminded Mate of Leslie, and once I saw it bring a tear to his eye.

Bat Out of Hell by Meatloaf. Where do you start with this one, only with the fact that we were there from the beginning when it was originally released on Cleveland International Records. For all the two zillion times I have heard it, (and I still hear it every time I chaperone a dance at school), "Paradise by the Dashboard Light" still gets me revved up all the way until the very end, when you hear his voice fading away. And I know more than once in his post college/early teaching days when a young lady would say to Mate, "Why can't we get closer? Why don't I ever feel that you love me as much as I love you?" He'd respond, "It's one of those two out of three situations." Someday go pull this one out of the closet, (or borrow your kid's copy), and look at all the great players who are on it. Stud after stud.

One More Song by Randy Meisner. A good album from the time we were first out of college with "Hearts on Fire."

American Fool by John Cougar Mellencamp. We had Springsteen, Seger and Michael Stanley through high school and college and John Mellencamp joined them soon afterward. He played Cleveland a lot in his early days and we saw him several times at the old Agora and you knew he was going to be a big thing. Mate liked him because after a long day of teaching and then yelling and screaming at practice, when he came home and hit the shower he thought he sounded "almost exactly" like him.

Eddie Money. His first album with "Two Tickets to Paradise."

Moondance by Van Morrison. Mate and I both took regular d.j.. shifts at our respected college house/fraternity's parties. We both preferred the late night after one a.m. shifts, when all the riff raff and lightweights were back in bed. This album was Mate's quarter to four closer, because you could just put on the first side and play it straight through, while you finally got up and danced with the girl you talked into hangin' out with you for most of the night. This was Mate and Leslie's album. I remember partying at his house in the big room in the basement, and stepping outside to catch some air. The sun was starting to come up, and I turned around and they were the only couple left on the dance floor. They were wrapped up in a blanket and each other, and they were swaying to the beat as Van Morrison sang his great lyrics in the background.

Stardust by Willie Nelson. In a very shrewd marketing ploy, whether it was planned as one or not, Willie did some stadium dates with the Grateful Dead during the late seventies, during the time this album dominated the country and pop charts. This exposed his music to a whole new crowd, including white slamhead college kids in the midwest. The *Stardust* album is filled with remakes of pre World War II standards superbly done, and when Mate brought it home it became a big hit at the Majowski household. It also became one of the great make out albums of all time. I remember a girl from Chilicothe, the fireplace in the house on North Campus, a chilly winter night, and this album on the turntable.

The Adventures of Panama Red by The New Riders of the Purple Sage. As our college point averages showed, we all liked to more than occasionally ride along with Panama Red.

The Outlaws and *Hurry Sundown* and The Outlaws. Two fucking great albums by "the guitar army" that really defined country rock. Both albums filled with great tunes like "Holiday," "Hurry Sundown," "Song in the Breeze," and "Stay With Me Tonight." On the night that Mate died, and when I finally stumbled home and I stayed up all night listening to a lot of these records, I remember I played "Green Grass and High Tides" more than once.

Wish You Were Here and *Dark Side of the Moon* by Pink Floyd. Two albums which preoccupied our (and everyone else's) dope smoking days.

Amnesia by Pousette Dart Band. Whatever happened to these guys, I don't have a clue. To this day I have never seen any of their stuff on CD. Another great country/folk/rock album and the title track is a classic.

John Prine and *Diamonds in the Rough* by John Prine. When Beth was gone for good and reality settled in when we came back from school, Mate really got into John Prine. When he couldn't keep asleep at night, he'd crawl out of bed and go downstairs and put one of these albums on. He would listen over and over again to great songs like "Illegal Smile," "Hello in There," "Sam Stone," "Angel from Montgomery" and "Souvenirs."

Bustin' Out by Pure Prairie League. How many girls now in high school or college are named Amy because of this album? Plus "Early Morning Riser" and "Falling In and Out of Love," another Mate and Beth tune.

Suzi Quatro Raw sex and rock and roll. Remember "48 Crash?" Remember Suzi on the back cover in black leather?

City to City by Gerry Rafferty. A cool album filled with more than just

"Baker Street."

Down to Earth by Rainbow. Probably don't remember this one, but had one great hard rocker that was big for a summer or two when we lived in Lakewood, "Since You've Been Gone." One of the tunes Mate would crank after closing the bars.

The Rasberries' Best Everyone our age from Cleveland loved the Rasberries. We had all the original albums, but it was this greatest hits record we brought out at parties. Great stuff. How talented was/is Eric Carmen? Mate swore that there was a dirty bridge vocal in "Go All the Way," and would sing it when he played this album with just the guys around. I loved the ballads, especially "Starting Over," "Don't Want to Say Good bye," and "I Can Remember." Again, one of those albums that fills me with voices and faces and long ago memories.

You Can Tuna a Piano, but You Can't Tuna Fish by REO Speedwagon. A great album before they had their moment in the sun with "Roll with the Changes" and "Time for Me to Fly."

Seconds of Pleasure by Rockpile. This was the party album the first year out of college when we shared the house out in Lakewood. Nick Lowe and Dave Edmunds have done a lot of good stuff over the years, but nothing as good as this album they did together. What a great couch dancing tune "You Ain't Nothin' But Fine, Fine Fine" is.

Sticky Fingers and *Exile on Main Street* by The Rolling Stones. The Stones albums of our era. Guitar driven blues rock with Ian Stewart's boogie piano and Bobby Key's sax. Great party tunes like "Brown Sugar," "Rip This Joint," "Tumbling Dice," and scraping the shit right off the shoes of "Sweet Virginia."

The Romantics. Someone in Mate's frat was from Detroit, and knew someone who knew someone's brother in this band. They booked them for a frat party right before this album was released, and I happened to be there. They ripped the place down. Everyone was dancing like crazy, and by the time they got to "What I Like About You," the dance floor was out of control with everyone jumping up and down and slamming into each other. You had to be there.

Heart Like a Wheel, *Prisoner in Disguise* and *Living in the USA* by Linda Ronstandt. Mate once made a make out tape with one whole side of ballads off these albums, and a few of them always ended up on any 'cry in my beer' tape. Mate was always fond of her version of Hank Sr.'s "I Can't Help if I'm Still in Love with You," and I always liked her version of Elvis Costello's "Alison."

Something/Anything and *Todd* by Todd Rungren. Todd made a great double album called *Something/Anything*, filled with a bunch of good tunes, only charged what it cost for a single album, and made a ton of new fans with it, like me! I then went back and got into his first album, and that's were I found "A Dream Goes on Forever."

The Best of Leon Russell.

Smoke from a Distant Fire by The Sanford Townsend Band. What a great lost party album this is. I went looking for it on CD last Christmas and none of the kids in the record store had ever heard of it. Too fucking bad. This album just jumps, with at least three all time great tunes.

Santana's Greatest Hits. You just knew the place was jumping when "Everybody's Everything" would blast out of the speakers.

Silk Degrees by Boz Scaggs. There's just a few of them. "We're Alone Now" off this one, "Sentimental Lady," "Ladies Choice," where if I hear just a piece, all my senses are filled with memories, the smell of long ago perfume, the whisper of a young voice, the touch of breasts across my chest...Connie says it's the romantic in me and that I better not change. I hope not.

Live Bullet and *Night Moves* by Bob Seger and the Silver Bullet Band. Live Bullet came out while we were still in high school, and was huge in the midwest but not a lot of other places. When we went off to college we met kids who didn't know Seger, especially a lot of the Eastern types with Mate at OWU. That all changed the next year with *Night Moves*. When it started to break for good between Beth and Mate, she sent him the lyrics to "Beautiful Loser" with the line about how you just can't have it all underlined.

The Main Event by Frank Sinatra. Connie has a favorite picture that is framed and sits on the top of her dresser. She took it in front of the fire place in the living room a long time ago. It is Mrs. Mate surrounded by her husband, her son, Uncle Gus, me and Manny. Old Mate and Uncle Gus are holding accordions. All of us look a little glazed. It was Mrs. Mate's birthday and we all have our arms around each other and we're all laughing. It was taken just as we finished singing and playing for her Frank Sinatra's version of Cole Porter's "Under My Skin."

I Don't Want to Go Home, This Time It's for Real and *Hearts of Stone* by Southside Johnny and the Asbury Jukes. Cleveland paid the Juke's bills for years, and we saw them everywhere from the Agora to Blossom. One year while I was at OSU they played the old Columbus Agora the night before the Michigan game. They came out for their first encore in bright red shirts with BEAT MICHIGAN across the front. Too cool.

Only the Lonely by J.D. Souther. I love this album, still listen to it.

The Wild, Innocent, and the E Street Shuffle, Born to Run, Darkness on the Edge of Town and *The River* by Bruce Springsteen and the E Street Band. Yes, in the history of rock and roll we were from the Springsteen generation, pre *Born in the USA* era. We saw him every time he played within one hundred miles of us back then, from the legendary Allen Theater show to sold out coliseums. Mate used to say that everything was there, music and poetry, with songs about true love and rejection and growing up and hope and despair. Party songs, lovers' ballads, personal anthems. *Born to Run* is the greatest rock and roll album, "Rosalita" the best frat rock tune.

I have seen hundreds of concerts in my life, and nothing has ever compared to the Springsteen concerts of the late seventies. Maybe the best fifteen concerts I have ever seen were those shows. It was always the moment you lived for when nothing else mattered, and for close to four hours you were experiencing something that all these years later I still can't put into words. I still put *Born to Run* on, sit down in the dark, and my breath is taken away when I hear the opening introduction to "Thunder Road."

My Cleveland Story

Friends and Legends, You Break It...You Bought It, Ladies Choice, Stagepass, *Cabin Fever* and *Heartland* by The Michael Stanley Band. In the late Nineties as I write this, Cleveland is considered one of America's Renaissance cities. A revitalized downtown, a new baseball stadium and two new basketball arenas, and, of course, the Rock and Roll Hall of Fame. Things were different back when we were in high school and college. The Cuyahoga River did catch fire once, the city did go in default, there always seem to be Cleveland jokes on television. But, you know what, and you probably do if you have read this book, we loved living here during that time. And one of the big reasons was the music scene. Music played an important part in the city just as it does today, but things were a little different. Cleveland really did have the best radio station in America then, the old WMMS compared to the current modern/alternative (which it is really neither) 'MMS of today. We had the best live rock club between the coasts, the old Agora on 24th Street behind CSU, that would have any and all new bands several nights a week as they criss crossed the country pushing their new releases. And we had a good local stable of bands and musicians, led by the Michael Stanley Band. Because of all of this, we had a knowledge of rock and roll that kids from other parts of the country didn't have. Clevelanders knew Robert Palmer ten years before MTV made him "Addicted to Love," back when he was "Sneaking Sally Through the Alley." Although the kids from Michigan also knew of Seger, and everyone on the east coast knew of Springsteen, and others might have known of Bob Marley or the Allman Brothers or Brian Auger, we knew of all of them, plus we knew about the Michael Stanley Band. That was before we realized he was cursed, because we had always thought there was never any doubt that it was just a matter of time because you just knew they were that good. If you asked anyone our age from Northern Ohio what the greatest live album of all time is they would probably say *Stagepass*. While the rest of the country went from *Frampton Comes Alive* to *Saturday Night Fever*, kids in Cleveland were listening to "Midwest Midnight," "Nothing's Gonna Change My Mind," and "One Good Reason." I remember just hanging around my house at OSU with my buddies with nothing exactly to do except get over served on quarts of Little King Boch Beer, jam along on lacrosse sticks and golf clubs, with everyone screaming the vocals cause everyone knew all the words. Mate and his roommates at Wesleyan made a tape and labeled it "Mellow MSB." It opened with "Ladies Choice," and was followed by songs such as "Waste a Little Time on Me," "Dancing in the Dark," and the acoustical version of "Let's Get the Show on the Road," with the great David Sanborn sax solo on it. "Ladies Choice" was such a great song because when you were with a girl you didn't know well yet, and it was late at night and the moment of truth, it really was a lady's choice. That tape, the big old couch they had, and an old afghan that Mrs. Mate had made, were the key ingredients in the beginnings of more than a few love affairs for those guys.

The Strays Cats. Good roots rock stuff that still sounds good today. I know he has had the balls to go off and do some pretty non mainstream stuff, but I always had Brian Seltzer pegged for super stardom. Maybe it ain't important to him.

Katie Lied, Aja and *Can't Buy a Thrill* by Steely Dan. You know you still hear a lot of Steeley Dan on the radio today and whenever I hear it I think of people who I thought at one time were too fuckin' cool and intellectual for me and how fucking wrong I was. Some of the preppy Eastern rich douche bags that Mate went to Wesleyan with...the spoiled dickheads on my floor freshman year from Bexley with their new cars...the older crowd that Beth married into. And all the time Steely Dan playing in the background trying to tell me different, but I didn't hear it back then.

Year of the Cat by Al Stewart. Another one everyone had. A great late night one more bong or beer before you went to bed album.

Bombs Away Dream Baby by John Stewart. If the second side of this album was as good as the first, people would still be listening to it.

Every Picture Tells a Story and *Gasoline Alley* by Rod Stewart. Over twenty years later and you still know almost every song on both of these albums.

Protect the Innocent by Rachel Sweet. Rachel was a sweet (no pun intended) young thing a couple of years behind us from Firestone High School in Akron. She put some great albums out on the old Stiff label, back when she was still a teenager. What a voice.

Breakfast in America by Supertramp.

Sweet Baby James by James Taylor. For my fifteenth birthday, Mate gave me a tape ("Happy Birthday to my good buddy Greg") with this, *Tapestry*, and *Bridge Over Troubled Water* on it, and I fell asleep listening to it every night my sophomore and junior years in high school.

The Temptations Anthology. There wasn't a frat house or a college dorm in America in the seventies that didn't have a copy or two of this. When no one would get up and dance, when all else failed, we always played the Temps.

George Thoroughgood. What a great surprise this one was. I think it started all this whole blues revival that's been trying to get started for the last fifteen years. One of the absolute highlights of our young single days was inviting George and his band out to the bleachers in right field after they played a Saturday night gig at Music Hall. They showed up and hung out and even bought more than their share of beer.

Contents Dislodged During Shipment by Tin Huey. A great alternative album before there was any such thing as alternative music. Much better than all that whiny 'my mom made me get a job' stuff the kids listen to today. You've got to check out this album by yet another great long ago unheard of Akron band, just to hear their cover of the Neil Diamond/Monkees tune "I'm a Believer" (no kidding).

Funky Kingston by Toots and the Maytals. A great party album from our college days. This brought raggae music to white suburban college punks, especially Toots's versions of "Louie Louie" and "Take Me Home, Country Roads."

John Barleycorn Must Die by Traffic. 3 a.m. Mate's old room in his frat house. A couple of lonely guys lamenting a few broken relationships.

My Cleveland Story

The Marshall Tucker Band, Running Like the Wind, Carolina Dreams, Where We all Belong and *Searchin' for a Rainbow* by The Marshall Tucker Band. We thought since we were from Cleveland we knew it all about music, but we found out a few things away at college, and one of them was country rock and the Marshall Tucker Band. At one time these guys were probably my favorite band. I can still listen to these albums over and over. One time for the Delaware County Fair Mate and his buddies at the Jug chipped in and bought a horse to race at the fair. They were arguing about what to call it, and then MTB came on the juke box and they named it "Can't You See."

Probably my favorite tune is a boogie woogie blues number "Walkin' and Talkin'" off *Searching for a Rainbow*, with a great lead guitar by Tommy Caldwell and a fiddle solo by Charlie Daniels.

Aqua Lung by Jethro Tull. Jethro Tull and Aqualung made three important contributions to Mate's liberal arts education.

1. A character in his favorite Dickens novel.
2. The name of one of his favorite albums.
3. The name of his favorite bong.

Concert for Voice, Piano, and 500 Screaming Assholes by John Valby. And, yes, without a doubt, we were assholes.

Small Change and *Heart of Saturday Night* by Young Tom Waits. It was one of those arguments that they had a lot that summer, about Mate transferring to a local college so he could be near Beth and they could have some semblance of a regular relationship. Of course, he wanted no part of it. "And we could save some money and see each other all the time," she said. "You're crazy," he responded. "I'll only be gone two more years. Plus..." he stumbled for another reason. "Plus, I could never replace the education I'm getting at Wesleyan." Both Beth and I burst into laughter together, each knowing that the stuff he was learning stretched the boundaries of any college." The only sign of any education you have received over the last two years is the fact that you can completely sing some Tom Waits tune about going to a strip joint," she said. And, of course, she was talking about "Pasties and a G String." Years later I came to appreciate Tom Waits' song writing ability, and I always think of Mate, and an old girlfriend or two, whenever I hear "San Diego Serenade."

Jerry Jeff Walker. One of Mate's frat bros was from Texas and he brought Jerry Jeff to our attention. Another great singer/songwriter/story teller. Jerry Jeff just couldn't get off that L.A. freeway at the same time Mate could not get Beth off his mind.

The Smoker You Drink, the Player You Get by Joe Walsh. Everyone, I mean everyone, from Ohio had this album back when we were in school. Listening to it today twenty-five years later it still holds up extremely well.

French Kiss by Bob Welch. Until the day he left this planet for good, Mate always got misty eyed whenever he heard "Sentimental Lady."

Whiz Kid by David Werner. A great lost album by a California answer to David Bowie during his glam rock period. Mate never made a make out tape or a cry in the beer tape without "A Sleepless Night" on it, with Return to Forever's Joe Ferrell's great sax solo. Last Christmas when I was working on this project, Beth was in town and staying with us like she does every Christmas. I was listening to this album and when it got to "Sleepless Night," the last song on it, she was stunned. The rest of it she knew was some old album from who knows when, but to hear a song she last heard making love to Mate a long time ago was one of those time out of mind moments.

The Great Fatsby by Leslie West. Another great album that I don't think ever came out on CD. Recorded after the demise of Mountain, West recorded this guitar driven album that features the best version ever of "Honky Tonk Woman." Yes, even better than the Stones or Tina Turner. Mate use to say it was one of those real blues meets real rock and roll moments.

Keep on Smilin' by Wet Willie.

Comes a Time by Neil Young. A great Neil Young album that has been lost in time. Great ballads with Nicolette Larsen singing background vocals. The last cut is Neil's version of Canadian folk singer Ian Tyson's great ballad "Four Strong Winds" which is reason enough to buy this album. The last couple of springs at college, when it was the last week and people were going back home and others were sticking around for graduation, and unkept plans were made one day soon to get everyone back together, when friends who had been together every day for three or four years were realizing that they would never be together again, this was a good album to play the last nights together drinking and telling stories about spring breaks and old girl friends.

Excitable Boy by Warren Zevon. What a great album with not a weak song on it.

Food Appendix

Perogies
5 cups flour
2 teaspoons baking powder
1 teaspoon salt
2 eggs
2 tablespoons vegetable oil
1 1/2 cups milk
Mix the dry ingredients and then add the eggs, shortening and milk. Mix well and knead the dough until it's elastic. Divide the dough into four equal parts, then roll each of these parts until they are 3/8 inch thick. Cut them into 2 1/2 inch circles. Place one heaping tablespoon of filling on each circle, then fold and seal each one.

Drop them in boiling water until they float to the top. Then you have two options. You can keep them in the boiling water for five more minutes. Or you can drop them in a frying pan, in either butter or bacon fat, and fry until a light brown.

These are best served with sautéed onions and sour cream.

My Cleveland Story

Perogi fillings
  Sweet Cabbage
one medium head of cabbage shredded
four ounces butter
one teaspoon salt
dash of black and white pepper

Put all ingredients in covered skillet. Cook on medium heat until cabbage is lightly brown, usually around 30 minutes. Cool before using.

  Sauerkraut
one medium onion chopped
four tablespoons of butter
one large can sauerkraut
salt and pepper to taste

Sauté onions and butter. Before adding sauerkraut, squeeze all the water/juice out of it. Add the kraut, salt and pepper and cook 15 minutes. Cool before using.

  Cheese
one pound dry cottage cheese
one tablespoon butter
one small onion
3/4 tablespoon sugar
one teaspoon salt
one egg

Sauté butter and onion. Then add balance of ingredients and mix well. Let cool before using.

  Potato
six medium potatoes
four ounces American or cheddar cheese
one tablespoon butter

Peel and then boil the potatoes until cooked. Put into mixing bowl with other ingredients and beat until smooth. Let cool before using.

Stuffed Cabbage
3/4 pound lean ground pork
3/4 pound lean ground beef
2 tablespoons salt
1/2 teaspoon black pepper
2 cloves crushed garlic
one large onion, chopped fine
one head of cabbage
2 eggs
3/4 pound cooked rice, washed well
2 cans tomato soup mix with one can water

Core cabbage and place in enough boiling water to cover it. With a knife in one hand and a fork in the other keep cutting off the leaves as they become wilted. Drain and trim the thick center vein out of each leaf.

Mix all the other ingredients together with the exception of the tomato soup and water. Place a heaping tablespoon of mixture on each cabbage leaf and roll, tucking in the edges. Place in a baking dish. Mix tomato soup and water together and then pour over rolls. Cover and bake at 350 degrees about 90 minutes until tender.

Cabbage and Noodles
one large head of cabbage, shredded
half pound of butter
one tablespoon salt
one teaspoon black pepper
one 16 ounce package of extra wide noodles cooked
    according to package's instructions
Melt butter in skillet then add cabbage and salt and pepper. Cook over medium heat until cabbage is medium brown, usually about 45 minutes. Stir every seven or eight minutes. Add cooked noodles and mix.

Roast Pork and Homemade Gravy
You can use a loin or rib roast. Ask the butcher to loosen the ribs. Rub the roast with salt, pepper, garlic salt, and onion salt. Place in open roasting pan with fat side up. Roast at 350 degrees, 35 to 40 minutes per pound, until the meat thermometer registers 185 degrees. Remove meat from pan. Drain off excessive fat and add 1 and 1/4 cups water.

Place pan on medium heat on top of stove. Bring to boil. Take a glass jar with a lid and fill with 1/4 cup water and two tablespoons flour. Shake until smooth and then slowly add to the boiling gravy in the roasting pan. Mix until thickened, about two minutes. Add sautéed onions or fresh mushrooms if you like.

Big Potato Dumplings
Boil 10-12 pounds of skinned potatoes in salted water. Drain and then mash them, adding milk and butter. Make sure they are not runny, then refrigerate over night. The next day break the potatoes up, working in Sapphire flour. Mold the potatoes into several big balls. Drop the big balls of potato into boiling water for 20 minutes with the lid on. Then remove and cut into bite size pieces and add to your favorite gravy.

Small Dumplings
2 cups flour
half teaspoon salt
three eggs
half cup milk
Mix all ingredients together. Dough will be thick and sticky. Place half the dough on a cutting board. With a knife cut into small pieces and drop them into boiling water. Repeat with balance of dough. When dumplings come to the surface of the water, cook for five more minutes. Drain and rinse

in cold water. Serve with your favorite gravy.

Big Pancakes
2 cups flour
2 teaspoons salt
2 eggs
one and three quarters cup milk
one stick butter
one 16 ounce carton of cottage cheese
Mix all ingredients except butter and cottage cheese in a bowl. Beat until smooth. Heat a skillet. Add a tablespoon of butter to the skillet. When the skillet is hot and the butter is melted add a ladle of the batter. Brown lightly on each side. Roll up with cottage cheese and serve with syrup. Makes six roll ups.

Beef Soup
2 pounds beef chuck— trim fat
3 cloves garlic—press or dice fine
2 medium onions chopped
3 stalks celery—cut into thin slices
3 large carrots—julienne
8-10 ounces of mixed vegetables, either fresh or frozen
2 to 3 heaping tablespoons soup base
Place beef in 5 or 6 quart pot. Cover with water and bring to boil skimming several times. Remove meat, cut into small pieces and return to boiling water. Add garlic, onions, and celery. Simmer until meat is tender. Add vegetables and beef stock. Cook until vegetables are tender.

Chicken Soup
one pound soup chicken
one zucchini
three carrots, sliced
2 medium onions
2 to 3 tablespoons chicken stock
four cups cooked rice, or one pound cooked noodles
Place chicken in four quart pot, cover with water, bring to boil skimming several times. Remove chicken and cut into small pieces, and return to pot adding vegetables and chicken stock. Bring to boil and then simmer until all is tender. Serve with noodles or rice.

Potato Pancakes
four large potatoes
one onion
two eggs, slightly beaten
two tablespoons of flour
3/4 teaspoon salt
dash of nutmeg and pepper

shortening, lard or bacon fat for frying
sour cream or apple sauce

Grate the potatoes and onions, then drain them. Combine in a bowl with eggs, flour, salt, nutmeg, and pepper. Mix by hand until consistent.

Heat oil in skillet, hot but not smoking. Put tablespoon of mixture in, flattening with a spatula. Fry 2-3 minutes each side until brown.

Serve with sour cream or apple sauce.

Potato Salad
Cook six pounds of potatoes until tender, 35-40 minutes. Peel, cube, and put in a pan. Cover the potatoes with Italian dressing and let sit overnight in refrigerator.

Then mix the dressing. Combine half cup of mayonnaise and half cup of slaw dressing. Add one chopped onion, half cup of chopped celery, and half cup of chopped carrots. Mix together and let that sit overnight in the refrigerator also.

The next day mix the dressing with the potatoes. Cover with a layer of sliced hard boiled eggs.

Real Mashed Potatoes
Boil five large potatoes until tender. Cut into cubes, and then mash with a hand masher or blender until of the right consistency. While mashing add a quarter cup of cream, butter, salt and pepper. The best ones are slightly lumpy.

Kielbasi and Sauerkraut
Buy the best kielbasi from a real butcher that you know, and make sure it is made of pork butts, fresh garlic, fresh pepper, and other fine seasonings.

Rinse and cook two pounds of kielbasi for an hour. Cut the kielbasi in serving size pieces, cook another half hour. In a frying pan, fry four diced slices of bacon, slowly add 2 tablespoon of flour. Add along with sauerkraut to the sausage and cook another five minutes.

Angel Wings
6 egg yolks
quarter teaspoon salt
half cup sweet cream
two cups all purpose flour

Beat first three ingredients. Add flour to make a soft dough. Knead a few minutes on a slightly floured board or pastry cloth. Roll dough one eighth inch thick. With a sharp knife, cut dough into 2" by 1 1/2" strips. Make a slit in the middle of strip and pull edge through slit. Fry in hot fat or shortening, till golden brown. Drain in a brown paper bag. Sprinkle with powdered sugar.

Nut and Poppyseed Rolls
two cakes yeast

half cup lukewarm water
six cups all purpose flour
one teaspoon salt
one cup dairy sour cream
one egg yolk
half cup butter
three tablespoons sugar
two tablespoons milk

Dissolve yeast in lukewarm water, set aside until bubbly. Mix together flour, salt and sugar. Cut in butter. Add yeast, eggs and sour cream; mix and knead until smooth. Cover and let rise while preparing fillings. Divide dough into five balls. Let rest ten minutes. Roll out to 1/8 inch thickness on a floured surface. Spread with filling. Roll up like a jelly roll and place on a greased baking sheet. Cover and let rise 30 minutes. Beat one egg, brush rolls with egg, pierce with a fork in several places. Bake at 350 degrees for 45 minutes.

Nut filling
one pound crushed walnuts
two cups sugar
three stiffly beaten egg whites
three tablespoons melted butter
quarter cup milk

Mix all ingredients until well moistened but not watery.

Poppyseed Filling
one pound poppyseed
three cups sugar
three tablespoons melted butter
three tablespoons lemon juice
3/4 cup milk

Mix all ingredients until well moistened. Add more milk if necessary.